When in Rome

When in Rome

A Novel

Sarah Adams

Dell
New York

2022 Dell Trade Paperback Edition

Copyright © 2022 by Sarah Adams

Published in the United States by Dell, an imprint of Random House, a division of Penguin Random House LLC, New York.

DELL is a registered trademark and the D colophon is a trademark of Penguin Random House LLC.

Library of Congress Cataloging-in-Publication Data
Names: Adams, Sarah, 1991– author.
Title: When in rome: a novel / Sarah Adams.
Description: Dell Trade Paperback Edition | New York: Dell Books, 2022.
Identifiers: LCCN 2022010987 (print) | LCCN 2022010988 (ebook) |
ISBN 9780593500781 (trade paperback) | ISBN 9780593500798 (ebook)
Subjects: LCGFT: Novels.
Classification: LCC PS3601.D3947 W48 2022 (print) |
LCC PS3601.D3947 (ebook) | DDC 813/.6—dc23
LC record available at https://lccn.loc.gov/2022010987
LC ebook record available at https://lccn.loc.gov/2022010988

Printed in the United States of America on acid-free paper

randomhousebooks.com

2 4 6 8 9 7 5 3 1

Book design by Sara Bereta

To my grandma Betty.
I wish you could have read this one, because you would
have loved Mabel. I miss you and your smile and your
Santa Claus sweater.

"I was born with an enormous need for affection,
and a terrible need to give it."

—Audrey Hepburn

When in Rome

Amelia

This is okay, right? I'm okay?

I take a deep breath and wrap my fingers a little tighter around the steering wheel.

"Yes, Amelia, you're okay. You're fantastic actually. You're just like Audrey Hepburn, taking your life into your own hands, annnnnd . . . you're talking to yourself . . . so maybe not completely okay, but given the circumstances, semiokay," I say, squinting at the dark road outside my windshield. "Yes. Semiokay is good."

Except, it's completely dark, and my car is making this noise that sounds like loose coins tumbling around a dryer drum. I'm not a car whiz, but I'm thinking that's not a good sound for it to be making. My favorite little Toyota Corolla, the car that has been with me since I was in high school, the car I was sitting in when I first heard my song on the radio at age eighteen, the car that I drove to Phantom Records and signed my recording deal ten years ago is reaching its expiration date. It can't die, it still has the smell of my old volleyball kneepads ingrained in the fabric.

No, not today, Satan.

I rub the dashboard like there might be a hidden genie inside waiting to pop out and grant me three wishes. Instead of wishes, I'm granted the loss of cell service. The music I'm streaming cuts off, and my Google Maps is no longer registering the little arrow that's supposed to lead me out of this middle-of-nowhere-serial-killer-backwoods road.

Yikes, this feels like the start of a horror film. I think I'm the girl in the movie people yell "you're an idiot!" at, while popcorn crumbs leak from their greedy smiles. Oh geez, was this a mistake? I'm afraid I left my sanity back home in Nashville along with my iron gate and Fort Knox security system. And Will, my fabulous security guard who posts up outside my house and stops people from sneaking onto my property.

Earlier tonight, my manager, Susan, and her assistant, Claire, downloaded me with information about my upcoming, jam-packed schedule for the next three weeks before we leave on a nine-month world tour. The problem is, I just finished my last day of a grueling three-month tour rehearsal. Almost every day of the last three months has been dedicated to learning the concert choreography, stage blocking, solidifying the set list, rigorous exercise, and rehearsing the songs, all while smiling and pretending that inside I didn't feel like a rotting compost pile.

I sat silent as Susan talked and talked, her long, slender, perfectly manicured finger scrolling endlessly across an iPad screen full of schedule notes. Schedule notes I should feel excited to hear. Honored to have! But somewhere in the middle of it, I . . . shut down. Her voice took on the Charlie Brown *wah, wah, wah* tone and all I could hear was my own heart thumping in my ears. Loud and painful. I went absolutely numb. And what scared me the most was that Susan didn't even seem to notice.

It makes me wonder if I'm too good at hiding. My days go like this: I smile this way at this person and nod. *Yes, thank you.* I smile that way at that person and nod. *Yes, of course I can do that.* Susan gives me a script perfectly crafted by my PR team and I memorize it. *My favorite color is blue, much the same as the Givenchy gown I'll be wearing to the Grammys. Why yes, I do owe much of my success to my loving and devoted mom. A day doesn't go by that I don't feel incredibly blessed to have this career and my amazing fans.*

Polite, polite, polite.

A hot splotch of tears falls onto my thigh and I realize I'm crying. I don't think I'm supposed to be crying thinking of those things. I'm a two-time Grammy winner and I have a signed contract for ninety million dollars with the top record label in the business, so I shouldn't be crying. I don't deserve to be crying. And I definitely shouldn't be in my old car in the middle of the night driving frantically away from everything. The list of people I'll be letting down runs through my mind like a scroll, and I can barely withstand the guilt. I've *never* not shown up for an interview before. I hate disappointing people or acting as if my time is more valuable than theirs. At the start of my career I vowed I would never get a big head. It's important to me to be as accommodating as possible—even if it hurts.

But something about Susan's parting words tonight wrecked me. "Rae,"—because she prefers to call me by my stage name rather than my real name, which is Amelia—"you're looking tired. Get some extra sleep tonight so you won't be puffy in the behind-the-scenes photos of the *Vogue* interview tomorrow. Although . . . the exhausted look is trending again . . ." She looked thoughtfully up at the ceiling and I half expected God himself to beam down an answer to her concerning the bags under my eyes. "Yeah, forget I said anything! It'll stir sympathy from your fans and bring a little more buzz."

She turned and left—her assistant, Claire, pausing only briefly to toss me one last hesitant glance over her shoulder. She opened her mouth like she was going to say something, and I found myself desperately hoping she would. *See me, please.*

"Good night," she finally said and then left.

I sat in the ringing silence for so long wondering how I let my-self get here. And how do I crawl out of this shell I've accidentally created? This hollowed-out feeling started to find me a few years ago, and I'd hoped it was because I was sick of the L.A. lifestyle and needed a change. I packed up and moved to Nashville, Tennessee, where I could still be around the music business scene, but not quite as high-profile living. It didn't work. The hollowness fol-lowed me.

Some people turn to family for questions like that, some turn to friends, and some turn to Magic 8 Balls. But I turn to the one per-son who never lets me down: Audrey Hepburn. Tonight, I closed my eyes and skipped my finger over my collection of Audrey DVD cases (yes, I still own a DVD player) while playing a game of eenie-meenie-miney-mo until I landed on *Roman Holiday*. It felt cataclys-mic. In the movie, Audrey plays the part of Princess Ann, who was feeling much like I have been—alone and overwhelmed—and she escapes into the night to explore Rome. (Well, more like meanders into the night since she's loopy on a sleeping sedative, but that's neither here nor there.)

And suddenly, that was it. The answer I'd been looking for. I needed to get away from that house, from Susan, from my respon-sibilities, from absolutely everything, and escape to Rome. Except, Italy is way too far to travel when I head out on tour in three weeks, so I settled for the nearest Rome that Google Maps could give me. *Rome, Kentucky.* Exactly two hours away from my house with a lovely little bed-and-breakfast in the heart of its town ac-cording to Google. Perfect place to get my shit together and over-come a breakdown.

So I went to my three-car garage, passed the other two expen-sive vehicles I own, and pulled the tarp off the sweet, old car I've kept tucked away for the past ten years. I started her up, and I drove off in search of Rome.

And now I'm on a creepy back road and I think some of the emotional numbness is wearing off because I'm beginning to see how ridiculous this idea is. Somewhere in heaven Audrey is looking down with her halo and shaking her head at me. I glance at my phone's glowing screen. The words *no service* are pasted where the signal bars usually live, and I swear those words are somehow blinking at me. Taunting me. *You made a bad choice. Now you get to be the next story on* Dateline.

I swallow and tell myself that I will be totally fine. No problem. Everything is good. "Dry your tears and kick this gloomy attitude in the pants, Amelia!" I say out loud to myself because who else does a girl talk to when she's alone in the car in the middle of a mental breakdown?

I only need my car to keep moving for another ten minutes until I emerge out of this scary-as-shit back road and arrive at the little town B and B. Then, I will happily allow my car the dignified death she deserves—where there are streetlights, and hopefully not Hillbilly-Joe-Serial-Killer waiting to dump my body in a ditch somewhere.

But, oh, would you look at that? My car has taken on a new sputtering sound and is jolting . . . literally *jolting* like this is the early 2000s and I installed hydraulics. All I need are purple lights under my car and I'm set to time travel!

"No no no," I plead with my car. *"Don't do this to me now!"*

But she does.

My car comes to a stuttering, highly undignified halt on the side of the pitch-black road. I frantically try to start the engine again, but it's not having it. A series of clicking noises is all it makes. My hands are still tightly clamped on the steering wheel and I stare out into the unmoving night as realization settles over me. I tried to make it on my own without Susan's help for *one* adventure and I failed on the first night, two hours in. If that isn't the most pathetic thing you've ever heard, I don't know what is. Sure, I can sing on a stage in front of thousands, but I can't do something as simple as drive myself one state over.

Since there is nothing I can do but sit in my car and wait until morning when the sun is up and I can clearly see if anyone is holding a bloody chainsaw in my direction or not, I lay my head back against the seat and close my eyes. I let defeat take me. Tomorrow morning, I'll find a way to call Susan. I'll have her send a car and I'll force myself out of this melancholy mood.

Knock knock knock.

I scream and jump in my seat, bumping the top of my head on the ceiling. I look out the window, and oh shit, there's someone standing outside my car! This is it. This is the moment I will get murdered, and after the true story of my death airs on *E Hollywood News,* all I will be remembered for is my grisly cornfield demise.

"Everything all right? Do you need help?" comes the muffled voice of the man outside my car. He beams a flashlight through my window, temporarily blinding me.

I hold my hands up to shield my eyes from the light, and also obstruct his view so he doesn't recognize me. "No, thank you!" I yell through my closed window, my heart beating wildly against my ribs. "I'm fine! I-I don't need any help!" Definitely not from a strange man in the middle of the night.

"You sure?" he says, finally realizing he was piercing my eyes with his flashlight and turning it away from my face. He has a nice-sounding voice, I'll give him that. Sort of rumbly and tender at the same time.

"I'm sure!" I say in a cheery tone, because everything around me might be falling apart but at least I still know how to muster up pleasantness. "Got everything under control!" I make the okay sign with my hand for added measure.

"Looks like your car broke down."

I can't admit to that! I would basically be telling him that I'm a sitting duck. *My phone's out of service, too! Would you like for me to step out so you can abduct me or would it be more fun for you to break the window yourself? Choose your own adventure!*

"Nope. Just . . . taking a break for a minute." I smile tensely, keeping most of my face turned away, hoping he won't realize a performing artist worth millions is sitting in this beat-up Corolla.

"Your engine is smoking." He shines the flashlight on the dense cloud of smoke billowing out from under the hood of my car. That can't be good.

"*Oh* . . . yeah," I say as casually as possible. "It does that sometimes."

"Your car engine often smokes?"

"Mm-hmm."

"I can't hear you."

"Mm-hmm," I say louder and perkier than before.

"Right." He's clearly not buying my story. "Look, I think you need to get out. It's not safe to stay in a smoking vehicle."

Ha! He'd like that, wouldn't he? Well, there is no way in hell I'm getting out of this car. Even if he has a nice-sounding voice.

"No, thanks."

"I'm not going to murder you if that's what you're thinking."

I gasp and look out at the darkly silhouetted man. "Why would you say that? Now I really think you're going to murder me."

"Thought so," he says, sounding irritated. "What do I need to do to prove I'm not a murderer?"

My forehead creases as I think about it. "Nothing. There's no way you can prove it."

He grunts softly and walks to the front of my car, standing in front of the lights. I can see him now, and *wow*. Hillbilly Joe sure looks a lot like Wilderness Ken. He's wearing jeans and a plain white T-shirt. His sandy blond hair is cropped shorter on the sides but has a bit of play on the top. A scruffy short beard covers his strong jaw, and let me tell you, it pairs nicely with the wide shoulders, lean body, and biceps that jump enticingly when he knocks on the hood of my car. The entire effect is . . . rugged in a way that makes me wish my air-conditioning was working.

"Can you pop the hood so I can make sure nothing is on fire?"

Uh-uh. Sorry, but no. Sexy or not, there's no way I'm opening that hood. What if he . . . well, honestly, I know nothing about cars and have no idea what he could do to make this situation worse, but I'm sure he can do something.

"Thanks, but I don't need your help! I'll wait until morning and call a tow truck," I yell loud enough for him to hear me.

He crosses his arms. "How are you going to call a tow truck? We don't get cell service out here."

Well, shoot. He's got me there.

"Don't worry about it. I'll figure it out. You can go back to wherever you came from now." Probably a nearby bush where he'll be waiting to pounce on me the second I'm out of my safe vehicle. And yes, I realize I'm being a little over-the-top paranoid, but when you're used to stalkers trying to climb the gated fence outside your house, pose as a plumber to get past your security guard, and/or send you locks of their hair asking you to place it under your pillow at night, you tend to develop a sense of paranoia toward strangers. Which is why I should have NEVER left my house alone. I need to accept the fact that I'm not just *me* anymore and never will be again.

Wilderness Ken doesn't walk away. He returns to my window and leans down again, one hand firmly planted above my door, showing me just how ample his wingspan is. "A smoking engine is not good. You need to get out. I promise I'm not going to hurt you, but you will be hurt if this car goes up in flames. I promise I'm a trustworthy person."

"That's what all the murderers say . . . before they murder someone."

"Met a lot of murderers in your time?"

One point for Wilderness Ken.

I smile and try to sound as kind as possible. "Sorry but . . . can you just go away? Really, I don't mean to be rude, but . . . you're sort of making me nervous."

"If I go away, will you get out?"

I laugh a stunted laugh. "Definitely not now! Where did you come from anyway?"

The man nods toward the other side of my car and doesn't sound at all impressed when he says, "You're in my front yard."

Oh.

I turn, and sure enough, I'm pulled over in a front yard. *His* front yard apparently. I can't help but smile at the cute house. Small. White. Black shutters. Two lights beside the front door, and a hanging swing on the front porch. Large expansive land around it. It looks homey.

"I think I already know the answer," he says, "but do you want to come in and call someone? I have a landline."

I laugh so loud at his suggestion that he winces. Oh dear, that was rude. I clear my throat. "Sorry. No. Thank you . . . But no," I say it solemnly this time.

"Fine. Suit yourself. If you need anything and decide I'm not a killer, I'll just be in there." He gestures toward the house and rises to his full height again. I watch as he crosses his long front yard and his shadow disappears into the house.

After he shuts his front door, I sigh with relief and sink into my seat, trying not to worry about the smoke still streaming from my car's engine, or how freaking hot it is in here, or that I'm hungry, or that I really need to pee, or how disappointed Susan will be with me once she realizes I'm not showing up to that interview in the morning.

I'm not okay. Everything is definitely *not* okay.

Chapter 2

Noah

She's still out there. It's been twenty minutes, and she's yet to so much as crack her door. And, yes, I am watching her creepily from my window acting like the psychopath she thinks I am. I'm not, for the record—though I'm not sure my opinion really counts in this situation. I am a little worried she's gonna die tonight, however. It's 80 degrees outside and she's not allowing any ventilation through her car. That woman is going to smother herself out there.

Whatever, not my problem.

I let the blinds snap closed and pace away from the window.

And then I pace right back and open them again.

Dammit, get out of the car, woman.

I look at the clock. 11:30 P.M. I shoot up a prayer to anyone listening above that Mabel won't be too pissed at me when I call and wake her up. After dialing her number, I have to wait six rings before her scratchy forty-years-of-smoking-but-recently-quit voice answers. "Who is it?"

"Mabel, it's Noah."

She grunts a little. "What do you want, son? I was already dozing in my chair for the night, and you know I have insomnia so this better be good."

I smile. "Believe me, Mabel, I wouldn't be disturbing your beauty sleep unless it was an emergency."

She acts tough but her heart is mush for me. Mabel and my grandma were best friends—more like sisters really. And since my grandma was the one who raised me and my sisters, Mabel always treated us like family, too. Lord knows we act related. We look different, Mabel is Black and I'm white, but we both share the same general dislike for people being up in our business. (And yet she's always more than happy to be all up in mine.)

"Emergency? Noah, don't string me along. Your house on fire, son?" She's called me "son" since I was in diapers and continues to despite the fact that I'm thirty-two years old. I don't mind. It's comforting.

"No, ma'am. I need you to speak to a woman for me."

She coughs with disbelief. "A woman? Honey, it's good to hear you're looking again, but just 'cause you're lonely in the middle of the night doesn't mean I have a list of ladies on speed dial ready to—"

"No," I say firmly before she continues with what I'm sure would be a string of words I never want to hear exit her mouth. "The woman is in my front yard."

I hear the squeak of a chair and imagine Mabel snapping her EZ Boy recliner shut, sitting bolt upright. "Noah, tell me now, are you drunk? It's fine if you are, I'm not the judgy type, you know this. I've said many of my best prayers to the Good Lord after a night with Jack Daniel's, but I need for you to call James or one of your sisters when you're drunk, not—"

She'll go on and on if I don't stop her. "Mabel, a woman's car broke down in my front yard and the engine is smoking but she's scared to get out because she thinks I'm going to hurt her. I need for you to act as my character reference so she'll get her ass out of there." I would call one of my sisters but they would definitely say something off-color about how long it's been since I've slept with anyone and then ask the woman what her relationship status is. Definitely not calling them. Definitely don't care what that woman's relationship status is.

"Oh, well, baby, why didn't you say so! Get out there and let me talk to the poor girl!" I hear a twinkle of excitement in Mabel's voice that I don't appreciate or want to encourage. This whole town has been on my back lately to give dating another try, but I'm not interested. I wish they'd leave me alone about it and let me live in peace, but that's not their style. And now that I think about it, I'm not so certain Mabel won't say something similar to what my sisters would say.

I peek through the blinds again and see the woman fanning herself aggressively with her hand. I swear, if I have to call a paramedic and spend the whole night in the hospital losing sleep with this strange woman because she gave herself heatstroke out there, I'll never open my front door again. I'm *one more woman wrecking my life* away from boarding up all my windows and turning into a hermit that yells profanities at Christmas carolers.

"Don't get any ideas, Mabel. This isn't a romantic thing. I just don't want her to die in the heat out there."

"Mm-hmm. Is she pretty?"

I pinch the bridge of my nose and shut my eyes against the annoyance building up my spine. "It's pitch-black outside. How would I know that?"

"Oh, please. I asked you a question. I expect an answer."

I groan. "Yes." So damn pretty. I only got a brief look at her with my flashlight, but what I saw had me doing a double take. She had dark hair piled in a bun on her head, a pretty smile, thick lashes, and sharp blue eyes. The odd thing is, I feel like I've met her even though I've never seen her car in town before. It must have been one of those weird instances of déjà vu.

"Well then," she says with a pleased sigh. "Take me out to our fair beauty."

"Mabel . . ." I use a warning tone as I open the front door and step outside. The summer heat immediately threatens to strangle me, and I wonder how the woman has survived this long in her car with the windows rolled up and no air-conditioning.

"Oh, hush! It's not every day a woman is dropped into your lap like this, so zip your lips and hand the phone over." This is what I get for living in Rome, Kentucky, most of my life. My neighbors still treat me like the boy who ran through town in his Superman underwear.

Leaving the front door cracked so the phone cord doesn't get pinched, I walk through the yard toward the little white car. It's too dark out here to see her features without shining the flashlight at her again, but I do see the silhouette of her face turn my way. And then she immediately throws her seat back. She's trying to trick me into believing she's not in there. I refuse to smile at the ridiculousness of it.

When I knock on the window, she screeches. *Jumpy.*

"Hey . . ." *You? Woman? Lady currently killing the grass in my yard?*

"Uh . . . Here. This is a friend of mine on the phone. She's going to act as my character reference so you can feel safe to get out of your car."

The lady pulls the lever on her seat and the whole thing comes flying up. She yelps and I have to bite the inside of my cheeks. Her big eyes peer up at me through the glass, and unfortunately, there's not enough light to figure out how I know her, but now I'm convinced I do.

She frowns. "How do you have cell service right now?"

"I don't." I raise the phone up so she can see it.

Her eyes drop to it and she laughs. "What is that?!"

You'd think I was holding a rare species of animal by the way she's gaping and laughing. "It's generally called a telephone."

"Yes, but . . ." She pauses to let out another delighted laugh and the sound curls around me like a cool breeze. "Did you steal it from the museum of 1950s history? Now the mannequin with the blue gingham print dress and matching headband won't receive her husband's call saying he'll be late for dinner! Oh my gosh, that cord has to be fifty feet long!"

I narrow my eyes. "Are you going to roll down your window or not, Smart Mouth?"

Her eyebrows lift. "Did you just call me . . . *Smart Mouth?*"

"Yes." And I won't apologize for it. I'm not trying to make friends with her or make her feel cozy—besides she insulted my phone. I love my phone. It's a good phone.

Oddly, her face splits into a full, gorgeous smile and she laughs. It makes my stomach tighten, and my heart thump angrily. I tell them both to shut up and behave. I will not be moved by another woman passing through my town. I'm going to help her tonight because (1) it's the right thing to do; (2) so she doesn't die in my front yard; and (3) so I can get her the hell on her way again.

"Well, okay, then." She cracks the window only about two inches so I can slip the phone in. Our fingers brush in the exchange and my whole body reacts to it because apparently it wasn't listening to the threatening speech I gave it a minute ago. The woman whips the phone into the car and zips her window back up before I can slide a pitchfork in and impale her.

She eyes the phone warily before raising it to her ear. "Hello?"

Immediately I can tell that Mabel takes over because the woman's eyes grow twice their size and she listens with rapt attention. Five minutes later, beads of sweat are rolling down the back of my neck as I lean with folded arms against the hood of her car, waiting for Smart Mouth to finish laughing her ass off with Mabel.

"He didn't!" she says practically howling and now I know it's time to take the phone back. I go to her door, knocking against her window. "Time's up. Are you getting out or not?"

She holds up a finger to me and finishes with Mabel. "Uh-huh . . . uh-huh . . . yeah. Okay, it was great talking with you, too!"

I have to back up when, surprise, surprise, the woman opens the car door and steps out, handing me back my phone. At her full height, she comes to my chin, but her messy brunette bun stands to about the top of my head. I don't want to admit it, but she's cute—classy. She's wearing a navy-and-white-striped T-shirt tucked into white, old-timey-looking shorts. They're the kind that climb high on her petite waist, hug the soft curve of her hips, and cut off high on her thighs. She belongs on a sailboat in a black-and-white photo—not from around here, that's for damn sure. She'll be gone in the blink of an eye, so there's no use letting myself admire her looks.

She turns her face up to me, but her gaze bounces nervously back and forth between me and my house. "Your friend, Mrs. Mabel, gave you a glowing recommendation, *Noah Walker.*" She says my name with a greedy emphasis, gloating that she knows my name but I don't know hers.

"Super, I'm so relieved." My tone is the Sahara Desert. I cross my arms. "And you are?"

Whatever ease she was starting to feel vanishes, and she takes one large step away, anxious to crawl right back into that death trap. "Why do you need to know my name?"

"Mostly so I can know who to charge for my grass seed bill." I don't mean for it to come off as friendly or jokey, but she seems to take it that way.

She smiles and relaxes again. I'm not so sure I want her to feel relaxed. In fact, I have a strong urge to tell her not to get comfy at all.

"Tell you what," she says with a sparkling smile of camaraderie that I don't return. "I'll leave some cash on the counter for you in the morning." In the gaping silence that follows her statement, I lift an eyebrow and she finally hears what she's just said. "Oh! *No.* I didn't mean—I don't think you're a . . . not a prostitute." She winces. "Not to say you can't be a prostitute if you—"

I hold up a hand. "I'll stop you there."

"Thank goodness," she whispers, dropping her gaze while running her fingers over her temples. *Who the hell is this woman?* Why is she driving through my backwoods town in the middle of the night? She's jumpy. She's a nervous chatterbox, and she gives off the impression of a woman on the run.

"You can stay in my guest room tonight, if you want. There's a lock on the bedroom door so you can feel safe while you sleep . . . Unless there's someone you can call tonight who will be able to come get you?"

"No," she says quickly. I can't read the look on her face. It's guarded and defiant at the same time, and dammit, I wish there was more light out here. There's something my brain is trying to put together about her but I can't quite make it out.

"I . . ." She hesitates, like she's looking for the right words. "I was actually headed to stay at a bed-and-breakfast near here for some time away from work. So . . . as strange as it is, I think I will take you up on the use of your guest room tonight and then tomorrow I can call to have my car towed somewhere to get it fixed?" Why does she phrase it like a question? As if she's waiting for me to confirm that's a good idea.

"Sure," I say with a shrug that conveys I don't care what her plans are as long as they don't include me doing anything else for her.

She nods once. "Okay, then. Yep . . . let's . . . see your house, Noah Walker."

A few minutes later, after helping her get a bag out of her trunk and carrying it up to my front door, I step inside my house and hold the door open for her to walk through. When she passes me, her soft, sweet smell slips under my nose. It's so opposite of my *me*-scented home it scrambles my brain for a second. It takes a big eraser and smudges over my usual *I'm happy being alone* thoughts and doodles in obnoxious little hearts.

She hesitates with her back to me, taking in my living room. It's not much, but at least I know it's not garbage, either. My sisters helped me furnish the house after I renovated it, saying I needed a Traditional Farmhouse decor style, whatever the hell that means. All I know is now I have some rustic, wooden-looking shit that cost me a lot of money and a big white comfy couch that I rarely use because I prefer the leather chair in my room. It's homey, though. I'm glad they convinced me to do it and didn't let me keep living like a miserable bachelor when I moved back here.

My eyes trail from my couch to the little wisps of dark hair clinging to beads of sweat at the back of her neck. And then as if she can feel my gaze on her, she turns sharply. Her eyes collide with mine, and my stomach drops off a cliff. It makes sense now why she wouldn't tell me her name. Why she didn't want to get out of her car. Why she looks like she's been standing on pins and needles this whole time. I know exactly who Smart Mouth is, and any prayers Mabel is currently sending up to heaven are going to waste because I will absolutely *not* be letting myself form any attachments to this woman.

"You're Rae Rose."

Chapter 3

Amelia

"No, I'm not!" I say quickly—panicky—with darting eyes that make me look like a squirrel trying to protect a precious acorn secret. I want to stuff that secret into my cheeks and run.

He doesn't flinch. "Yes. You are."

"Nope." I give a serious shake of my head. "I don't even—who is that singer, anyway?" I don't quite make eye contact with him. I'm not a coward—I'm just not particularly courageous.

"Never said she was a singer."

I scrunch my nose. Looks like Wilderness Ken has me cornered.

"Okay. You're right. It's me," I say, letting my hands rise and then fall back to my sides. I refrain from tacking on a dejected and angsty, *Now what do you want?* But I can't say that because Rae Rose is never rude to fans.

I was thrilled when he looked at my face outside and didn't seem to know who I am. It was a stroke of good luck that made me feel as if maybe this adventure wasn't a completely terrible idea. Now I'm back to doom, gloom, and terror. Don't get me wrong, I love fans, and I love getting to know them. I just prefer for our introductions to happen when I have a security team around and not when I'm alone in the middle of the night with this somewhere-over-six-foot man.

And now this is the point where fans either pretend they know very little about me, but I catch them staring at every turn, or they start flipping out and crying and having me sign random stuff. Sometimes I'm asked to call their mom or their best friend. Take a picture. Just something that lets them prove to their friends that they really met me. Maybe I could just go ahead and preemptively offer him a trade: one VIP ticket in exchange for not murdering me tonight? Seems like a good deal to me.

I step back into my Rae Rose skin. It's softer, gentler—more regal than mine. Rae Rose is everyone's best friend. She's pliable and easy to love. "Well, since the cat is out of the bag, I'd like to offer you a VIP backstage ticket to an upcoming concert in exchange for letting me stay here, as well as financial compensation, of course."

I look into Noah's eyes. They're bright green. Startling, sharp, and almost unnatural in their intensity. They're nearly the exact color as the stripes on a wintergreen peppermint candy. Pair those eyes with the strong set of his scruffy jaw and the stern pinch of his eyebrows—and the effect is . . . unnerving. But oddly, not in a frightening way.

With his arms still crossed, he raises and lowers a shoulder. "Why would I want a VIP ticket?"

That's not a question I was expecting. I flounder, and when I speak, it's a bumpy delivery. "Umm . . . because . . . you're a fan?"

"Also never said I was a fan."

Right. *Wow.* Okay.

Silence drops between us like a grenade. He doesn't feel compelled to say anything else and I'm uncertain of what to say, so we just stare. Propriety tells me I should feel upset right now. Offended even. Curiously, I'm not. In fact, there's a giddy sort of sensation building in my stomach. It makes me want to laugh.

We watch each other closely for a long moment, chests inflating and deflating in a perfectly mirrored rhythm. I know why I'm cautiously taking him in, but what I can't figure out is why he looks so concerned. As if I'm about to snatch his throw pillows and lamps and run away with them in the night. The Pillow Bandit on the run.

Okay, so he doesn't want to come to my concert, but surely he knows I can afford my own throw pillows?

The longer I stand here and watch his flexing jawline, I get the distinct feeling that he's not only Not A Fan, he's the opposite. The normal glowing adoration I see in people's eyes is replaced with annoyance in his. Just look at that deep crease between his brows. It's surly. Grumpy. Agitated.

I don't suspect he's going to hurt me, but he seems to have a low opinion of me. Maybe it's because I parked on his grass. Maybe it's something else. Either way, it's absolutely and wonderfully new for me, and because it's late and I'm slightly hysterical, I decide to press his buttons.

I mimic his pose. "I see what it is. A ticket's not good enough?" I give him a smile like we're in on his secret together. "You want me to throw in a signed poster, too, don't you?" I wiggle my eyebrows. There's no part of me that believes he wants a poster.

He blinks.

"*Two* VIP tickets *and* a signed poster? Wow. You drive a hard bargain, but I'll comply for my biggest fan."

His face doesn't change a bit, but something in his fierce eyes sparkles. I think he wants to smile but won't let himself. Sometimes people decide not to like me for the most arbitrary reasons. Sometimes it's just because I'm famous, and successful people make them uncomfortable. Sometimes it's because I voted differently than them. And sometimes it's because I frowned outside their favorite yogurt shop and now they want to cancel me forever because they think I'm against yogurt. I can't help but wonder if I've found one of those very people. Usually my very elaborate security detail is around to protect me, but there's no one standing between me and Noah right now, and I can't say I hate it. A thrill zaps its way through my veins.

Noah shakes his head lightly and looks down to pick up my bag again. He's done with this conversation.

"Follow me," he says.

Two words. A command. No one commands me anymore—oh, they still tell me what to do, but they phrase it so that it sounds like it's my idea. *Rae, you must be exhausted. The guest room is right down that hallway, perhaps it would be nice to go on to bed now and get some rest?*

Noah Walker is too confident for manipulation. *Follow me.*

He takes my bag with him down a hallway off the foyer and disappears into a bedroom. I want to wander around a little, but most of the house is dark, and it seems like invading someone's home and flipping on lights, opening some cupboards and digging around might be a weird thing to do. So I settle for walking down the hallway after Noah just as he instructed. *Follow me.*

I stop when I get to two rooms opposite each other in the hallway. One door is shut, and one is not. In the open room, I find my bag sitting on the floor, and Noah parachuting a fresh white sheet onto a queen-size bed.

I watch him in the doorway for a minute feeling very dreamlike. I ran away from my life of fame today, and now I'm standing in a strange man's house watching him make up a bed for me even though he dislikes me. His actions are as much a paradox as that butter soft sheet is to his scruffy jawline. Susan would undoubtedly at this moment tell me to get out of this house immediately and go somewhere safer.

"Noah," I say, leaning my shoulder against the doorframe. "How do you feel about yogurt?"

He pauses and sends a look over his shoulder at me. "Yogurt?"

"Mm-hmm. Do you like it?"

He turns his attention back to the sheets. "Why? Are you going to offer to throw in a tub of yogurt with the tickets and poster and money if I say yes?"

Aha! There is humor under that annoyance. I thought so.

"Maybe." I smile even though he's not looking at me.

"Well, don't. I don't want yogurt or the other stuff."

I take a big fat Sharpie and mark off *Angry because of yogurt shop picture*.

Noah spreads a well-loved patchwork quilt onto the bed. It looks like it's been passed down through several generations of loving family members. My heart tugs and twists to get away from the feelings the sight of that quilt evokes in me. I wonder if my mom even read my text message earlier.

"Can I help?" I ask, taking a daring step into the same cage as the bear.

He glances over his shoulder again and when his eyes land on me, his frown deepens. He turns back toward the bed and begins tucking the top sheet under the mattress. I don't tell him I'll immediately untuck it before I get in. "Nope."

I was reaching for a corner of the quilt, but when his single-syllable answer barks at me, I raise my hands and take a step away. "Okay."

Noah's eyes bounce to my lifted hands and for a fraction of a second, I see him soften. "Thank you. But no." And then we fall into silence again.

I've done hundreds of press events over the past ten years, interacted with thousands and thousands of fans during meet and greets. Was live on Jimmy Fallon just last month where I sang an ad-libbed song in front of a studio audience without a moment's hesitation. And yet, standing in front of Noah Walker, I'm not at all sure what to say. But I don't feel like being polite. Or gracious. That thrill pulses harder.

I hover somewhere between the door and the bed so I don't get in his way, watching as he silently retrieves a pillow and slides a pillowcase onto it. This is all so normal, and domestic, and it feels wildly out of place to be sharing it with a stranger who doesn't like me.

I glance around the room and then over my shoulder and register the closed door across the hall. Suddenly, a thought strikes me. Is Noah married? Maybe that's why he's being so prickly and standoffish? He doesn't want me to get any funny ideas. He's seen a movie, or the covers of tabloids, and assumes all of us famous types are amorous home-wreckers.

I clear my throat, trying to find the right segue to let him know I won't be trying to jump his bones tonight. "So, uh—Noah. Do you have a . . . special someone?"

His eyes dart in my direction and now he looks *considerably* agitated. "Is that your way of asking me out?"

I do a hypothetical spit take. "What? No! I just . . ." I have zero amounts of Normal left inside me to give tonight. I was trying to put him at ease, and somehow, I've managed to make it worse as well as apparent that I don't know what to do with my hands. I wave them back and forth like a T. rex trying to land a plane. "*No*. I just wanted to make sure before I spend the night here that I'm not . . . stepping on anyone's toes." I grimace. It's getting worse. "Gahhh, I don't mean stepping on their toes because I'm spending the night with *you*. I know I'm going to be sleeping in here alone. I'm not really into one-night stands anyways because they're always so awkward . . ."

Oh nooooo. I'm saying too much. I officially entered sex into a conversation for the second time tonight with a stranger who doesn't like me. I'm absolutely floundering, and I *never* flounder.

Noah sets the freshly cased pillow onto the bed and finally turns to face me. Wordlessly, he walks closer. I have to tip my chin up, up, up to see him. He's not smiling, but he's not frowning, either. He's the Unreadable Man. "I am single, but I'm also not on the market."

He continues to stand there as my face turns hot as lava and melts right off my cheekbones. That was the softest, most polite letdown I've ever received in my entire life, and I wasn't even asking him out.

Thank goodness none of this matters. I'll leave tomorrow morning, find the B and B, and Wilderness Ken will never have to be annoyed with me again.

But then why is he still standing in front of me like this? Why do I feel an instant connection to him? There's something inside me, tugging me closer to him, begging me to raise my hand to his chest and run my hand over his soft cotton tee. He's not moving. I'm not moving.

Noah's expression suddenly turns awkward and he gestures toward the doorway that I didn't realize I had sunk back into. "I can't get through with you standing there."

Oh.

OH!

Polite, polite, polite. "Yes! So sorry! I'll just . . . move." His solemn expression does not crack as I step aside and gesture dramatically toward his exit.

"Drinking glasses are in the cupboard beside the sink in the kitchen if you need water. Bathroom is at the end of the hall. I'm headed to bed. Feel free to lock your door, I know I will."

"Smart move. Wouldn't want to let the Pillow Bandit strike," I say, feeling that thrill surge once again after saying exactly what I want—untethered and without filter.

Maybe . . . just maybe this adventure wasn't a mistake after all.

Chapter 4

Noah

throw on my sunglasses and baseball hat and hold my coffee like a shield. I'm going to need the added protection for my walk from the communal town parking lot to the shop. It's only about a five-minute walk down Main Street, but that's plenty of time to run into every single one of those damn townsfolk. Doesn't matter that Rae Rose has only been in my house for nine hours. That's eight more hours than necessary for Mabel to have called every person she knows and started the most incredible game of telephone anyone has ever seen. At least this means business will be booming today. Everyone is going to want a pie with a heavy side of gossip.

That's the problem with living in the hometown you grew up in. They remember the time you sang "Mary, Did You Know?" in the church choir wearing an ugly-ass sweater vest at age seven, and when the sheriff got called on you and your high school girlfriend for fogging up the windows of your truck by the lake. And they sure as hell never forget when your fiancée broke your heart. So when a woman is rumored to have slept in your house—a pretty one no less—there's no way they're going to let me have any peace. These people forget absolutely nothing and they couldn't be more invested in my romantic life if it were a daytime TV show.

I'd probably close up the shop for the day and go fishing instead of sending myself right into the belly of the beast (aka the town square) if this wasn't a delivery morning. But James, a friend of mine who owns a local farm and provides all my fresh ingredients, will be dropping off several crates full of produce, eggs, and milk, and I need to be there to receive it.

If you would've told me I'd be living in this town at the age of thirty-two and running a pie shop (creatively named The Pie Shop) that my grandma left to me, I'd have thought you were out of your damn mind. Especially after moving everything I owned to New York with Merritt, planning out our life together there and trying to drop roots into a place where I only felt like a piece of driftwood in the ocean for an entire year. But here I am—back home and living a life I never saw coming, and loving the hell out of it.

Well, for the most part. I could do without all these nosy people kicking up dust around my life all day.

And here we go. Pass obstacle number one: Phil's Hardware. As I approach, I can see that Phil and his business partner, Todd, are standing outside pretending to sweep and clean the front glass even though they hire Phil's grandson to do exactly those two jobs after school.

They pause when I get close, frantically murmuring something under their breath I can't hear, and then act as if they're surprised to see me even though I walk by here at this exact time each day.

"Whew! It's a hot one we're having today, isn't it, Noah?"

"Same temperature as yesterday, Phil," I say, before taking a sip of my coffee. I don't stop walking.

Phil blinks a hundred times and looks around for some conversational genius to strike him that will snag my attention. He can't come up with anything so Todd tries his hand. "Maybe the heat will bring in some new customers for you? Some out-of-towners, perhaps?"

"Heat usually make you crave pie, Todd? Might want to see the doc about that. Seems odd to me." I keep walking and raise a hand over my shoulder after I've passed them in lieu of a parting greeting. They're lucky I didn't throw up the bird instead.

Now, obstacle number two: Harriet's Market. I pull my hat a little lower over my eyes because if there's anyone I really don't want to see today, it's Harriet. That woman is ruthless. I pass under her blue-and-white-striped awning and think I'm in the clear until her shop door chimes. I wince and consider speed walking away, but it's too late. I'm caught.

She cuts right to the chase. "Noah Walker, don't think I didn't hear you had a woman staying over last night." I have no choice but to take a fortifying breath and turn around to face Harriet. Her hands are perched on her slender hips, a severe glare on her face, adding new frown lines to the ones already present. The cheery yellow sundress she's wearing doesn't match her personality. Harriet keeps her salt-and-pepper hair tied back into a tight bun. It's not that Harriet is grumpy because she doesn't like people—it's that she's nearly 100 percent certain she's better than most people. Who knows, maybe she is.

"In my day, young men and women weren't so intimate before they were married. It left a little something to the imagination. Something to be desired." She tilts her head down so she can purse her lips and raise her brows. "Now who is this woman you spent the night with and do you plan on marrying her?"

That escalated quickly.

"Uh—no, ma'am. And I didn't spend the night *with* her. Her car broke down in my yard, so I offered up my guest bedroom to her." *Not that it's any of your business* is what I'd tell her if I wasn't chicken-shit and scared to death of this woman. I like to spar with Mabel, but I hide from Harriet.

She wags her finger in my direction. "Then you keep your hands to yourself. If you don't intend to walk her down the aisle, then don't go dipping your toes in her pond."

I grimace. Not entirely sure if that's supposed to be an innuendo or not but grossed-out all the same.

"Don't worry. I'm not interested in her . . . pond."

Yep. That felt as disgusting to say as I thought it would. Wonderful. Now I need to find a way to boil my brain today. This is also why I have to go outside the city limits if I want to spend any time with a woman. Which, let's be honest, I haven't done in a long time. I'm not really the one-night-stand sort of guy, because, like Rae Rose pointed out last night, one-nighters are always sort of awkward. I find the whole situation around them uncomfortable. I like to have an emotional connection with a woman before I sleep with her and it's damn inconvenient.

All that to say, I don't take any women back to my place because someone's always out with binoculars prowling for gossip in this town. Harriet will find out and send the Nazarene preacher over to knock on my door and remind me that lust is one of the seven deadly sins. Except Pastor Barton loves pie and will eat no less than three pieces while sermonizing. It'll take a whole afternoon.

Harriet nods, her scowl still deeply marring the space between her brows. "Well, good. Keep it that way."

Great, glad that's over.

"I'll have your peach pie ready at closing for you." It's Wednesday so I know she'll be by to pick it up on her way to her knitting group. I lift my coffee in silent cheers and then keep walking.

I pick up my pace and miraculously do not encounter anyone else as I pass the diner, and then the flower shop (which is run by my youngest sister, who I'm sure would be bursting out and demanding answers if she wasn't out of town currently with my other two sisters), and finally make it to the front door of The Pie Shop. I shove my key in the lock even though I could probably leave the thing wide open at night and no one would even consider vandalizing or stealing anything. In fact, Phil would probably come in and fix the wobbly barstool and then lock the place up for me on his way out.

Stepping inside the shop feels like a hug. It might not look like much to anyone else, but to me, it's home. This pie shop has been in my family for decades. Very little about it has changed over the years, which I'm grateful for. The same blue-and-white-checkered curtains hang above the double windows. The same scratched-up wooden countertop sits beside the pie case. I had to replace the high-top table that sits in front of the large storefront window because it was definitely the worse for wear, but I managed to find one that was nearly an exact replica.

I take ten steps into the shop, lift the folding countertop, walk through, and then latch it closed behind me. It, as well as the domed-glass pie case, separates the front half of the store from the back half. And back there behind me is a tiny kitchen where my mom, and my grandma, and her mom before her, and her mom before her baked our Walker family pies with their secret recipes. But that's basically it. It's small, or quaint, or whatever you want to call it, but it's all I need.

I spend the next few minutes getting the shop ready to open—turning on the giant oven, brewing a fresh pot of coffee for customers, wiping down surfaces. I'm just popping a tray of pies from the freezer into the oven when the back door opens and James steps in with a crate full of apples. Like me, he grew up in this town and took over his family's farm. We went to school together from preschool all the way through community college where we both majored in business.

"How's it going, Noah?"

"Good. How are—"

"So who's the woman?" he says, setting down the crate and crossing his arms.

I pour myself a fresh cup of coffee because I get the feeling today could be a several-cupper. "Damn. How do *you* know about her? It's only eight in the morning."

He shrugs a shoulder. "Mabel called asking if I could see anything from my porch."

James is technically my neighbor. Except our houses are separated by several acres.

I raise my coffee to my lips and take a sip. "Could you?"

"Nah—too far off."

"Couldn't find your binoculars?"

"I think I lent them to someone." James helps himself to a Styrofoam to-go cup and fills it with coffee before leaning back against the counter like he doesn't have a damn thing to do all day. He crosses one booted foot over the other.

"You comfy?" I ask in an annoyed tone. "Anything else I can get you? A magazine? A blanket? A chair?"

"I'm good, thank you." He smiles indulgently. Women often call James charming. I call him a pain in the ass. "So . . . what's her name?"

I actually don't know what the protocol is here. Are you supposed to tell people if you have someone famous in your house? "Rae," I say with a discreet clear of my throat.

"Last name?" He blows on his coffee and peers at me over the rim of his cup.

I turn my eyes up like I'm racking my brain for the answer. Like it's not been buzzing through my head all morning. Sitting on the tip of my tongue. Racing through my dreams last night. "Umm . . . I think it was Mind-Your-Own-Damn-Business. Don't you have more crates to unload? I know I ordered more than this."

I pick up the apples and carry them over to my walk-in pantry and start unloading them into bins. My annoying shadow follows. "Why are you being so secretive?"

"I'm not. I'm just tired of talking to you."

"Hmm, extraprickly today. This woman must have gotten under your skin. How long is she staying?"

I turn around and bump his shoulder on my way out of the pantry. "*You're* the one getting under my skin."

If he's not going to unload the crates, I will. This town is making way too much out of nothing. So there's a woman at my house? Big deal. She's not staying. In fact, I'm hoping she'll be out of there by the time I get home. The last thing I need is some privileged pop star running up my electricity bill.

I go out into the back alley and pull a crate of eggs off the bed of James's truck. I consider skimming one or two off the top and throwing them at his front windshield. When I turn back toward the shop, James is blocking the back entrance looking just as mischievous as when we were kids and he talked me into sneaking out at night so we could go swimming with the Fremont girls. It was a good night, though.

"Just give me the details and I'll leave."

I let out a deep breath and it escapes more like a growl than an exhale. "Fine. Her name is Rae Rose and her car broke down in my front yard. I let her sleep in my guest room and that's it. End of story."

His brows pull together and I can see that he's trying to place her name. He's heard of her—everyone has—so it's only a matter of time before he realizes just who is at my house. Annnnnd there it is. His eyes go wide and his mouth drops open. "You don't mean to tell me that . . ."

I nod, finishing his sentence for him. "The princess of soulful pop is in my house right now breathing up all my bought air."

"No shit!" A new dawning look that I don't quite like hits him.

Like he's imagining her face. Like he's imagining his new prospects. And then his eyes shift to me and his look changes. "Ohhhh, now I see what's up with the surly attitude."

"I'm always surly."

He's smirking now like he understands everything about me. He probably does. I hate it. "She's gorgeous and talented and you like her. But she's an out-of-towner, and you're too jaded to let yourself even talk to her."

"I talked to her just fine. Now move," I say, breezing past him and setting down the eggs. I run my hand over some pots and pans, making a ton of noise just for the hell of it. I don't like that he picked me apart so easily.

Unfortunately, James isn't scared of my moods like the rest of the town. "Man, you're being an idiot. Rae Rose is . . ." He trails off with another look that makes me feel like punching something. Or him. "Anyway, it's gotta be like a one in a million chance that she would break down in your front yard. Where's she headed any-way?"

I wish she'd dropped into his front yard instead of mine. Clearly he appreciates the situation more than I do. "Why should I care?"

"Because . . . I don't know. Maybe you'd have a shot with her."

"I don't want a shot with her."

He scoffs and rolls his eyes. "Man, come on. Are you just never gonna date again? Merritt messed you up that bad?"

I clench my jaw. "Don't talk to me about her."

He ignores my threat. "You're gonna have to try again eventu-ally. Why not go all out and try with a gorgeous celebrity?"

What makes him think I would have a shot with a woman like her, anyway? This town is nuts. Rae Rose is so far out of my league she wouldn't even give me a second thought.

It's clear that James is not going to stop pushing if I don't give him what he wants. So after filling my lungs as full as possible, I push through the uncomfortable feeling that comes along with sharing any emotional part of myself and look straight at him. "I'll date again when I'm good and ready. But I sure as hell won't be trying with another woman whose life exists outside of this town—because you know I can't go with her. And let's say the world has flipped upside down and she was interested in a pie shop owner from Kentucky; I don't care to date a celebrity and find out through a tabloid that she cheated on me."

James gives me a pitying look. "Just because—"

"No, we're done now." I open the back door to the kitchen, not so subtly telling James to get out. He doesn't budge. I'm going to have to rent a forklift for the day and physically scoop him out of here. "Will you quit making this out to be something it's not? She'll be leaving just as soon as Tommy tows her car to his shop and throws some oil in it." If I'm lucky, I'll never even have to see her again. It's what I should have done when Merritt passed through town all those years ago—ignored her. I left Rae a note on the kitchen counter this morning with the phone number to Tommy's Automotive shop, hoping that she'd get everything taken care of before I get home.

"What's she doing right now?" he asks, and I sigh, slamming the door shut again and going into the fridge and unloading the carton of eggs into it.

"I don't know, James. Scrolling through all the local cable channels? Like I said, I don't care."

He steps up beside me so he can look at my profile. "You're an asshole, you know that, right?"

"I had a hunch."

He shakes his head and rubs the back of his neck. "Your grandma would be ashamed of your manners."

Okay, well, that's a low blow and he knows it. My grandma is still my favorite person that ever lived. Even the slightest thought of her being upset at me makes my skin feel itchy.

I narrow my eyes on him. "How do you figure? I gave the woman a safe place to sleep last night and left her with the number of the local automotive shop. Just how does that make me shameful?"

"You left her alone in a random town to fend for herself in the midst of strangers."

I turn sharply to him. "I'm a stranger!"

He waves that off like it's not a valid point. "You know you should've done better. Imagine how she's feeling right now? That woman is ridiculously famous. I bet she's terrified to have to go anywhere by herself if she doesn't have a bodyguard."

Seems like something she should have thought about before leaving her house without any security. She's not my problem. She's not. Couldn't be less of my problem, in fact.

James's face shifts into an expression of complete and utter smugness. It tells me whatever he's about to say will land the final match-ending blow. "How would your grandma have treated her if she were around?"

What a little shit. Of course my grandma would say I should do everything in my power to help Rae. She would also probably smack me upside the back of my head for not making her breakfast this morning and giving her a ride to the mechanic's so she doesn't have to ride in Tommy's gross tow truck with his nasty dip in the center console. And oh man . . . the war stories. He'll for sure tell her every gory detail.

I groan and snatch my keys off the counter. "Get the pies out when the timer goes off and then shut off the oven. Lock up on your way out."

"Uh . . . I have a job, you know?" he says to my retreating back.

"Funny. Didn't seem like it five minutes ago when you were helping yourself to coffee and a chat."

I hear him chuckle. "Fine. But I'm taking a pie with me when I leave!"

Chapter 5

Amelia

Turns out, impulsive decisions really do look different in the light of day. Correction: not different—bad. They look *very, very* bad.

I am in a strange house, in the middle of nowhere, with a broken-down car, zero cell service, and my only somewhat-kind-of-friendish person left me with a note explaining who to call to get my car fixed, but no other guidance. I guess that's better than nothing. This is a completely new experience for me, though. Usually I have strange men climbing my gate to get into my house with me, not clearing out before I'm even awake so they don't have to see me.

"Okay, Amelia, you can do this," I say out loud, because it seems talking to myself is my new MO. It is completely ridiculous that I would be nervous to call an automotive shop, but it's been a while since I've done . . . well, anything for myself. I usually leave all scheduling up to Susan or Claire. I haven't made a single appointment for myself in ten years, and if that's not bad enough, I don't even drive myself to them.

Fame came swiftly for me. One day I was normal—a high school student posting a video on YouTube of me singing one of my original songs at my piano. The next, I was an internet sensation. I posted daily videos of my original songs as well as popular covers and people went nuts over them. Back then, when the term "going viral" was still new, I felt like an anomaly. Even before I ever released a professionally recorded album, people knew who I was from my YouTube channel. I was praised for my mature sound—a soulful voice that belonged to a thirty-year-old even though I was only sixteen.

I remember getting booked for weddings and special events for two hundred dollars and thinking I was filthy rich. But I didn't care about the money. It was worth it just to finally play my music in front of others. And then when I was seventeen years old, a manager (Susan) reached out telling me she thought I had something special and wanted to help take my career to big places. And she was right. It all happened so fast after that. Susan helped me land a record deal that made me internationally famous, and nothing could have ever prepared me for how completely it would change my life. How it would ruin my relationship with my mom.

Those first few years were pretty thrilling, and my mom and I were still close. Fame was deliciously satisfying . . . until it wasn't. I gained all these celebrity friends, who I quickly realized would never be anything more than surface level. You know, the kind that asks *how are you?* and you say *great!* even if your life is falling apart. Definitely not the sort of friends you can text an SOS from the bathroom at a party, admitting you accidentally clogged the toilet and need a getaway car.

From the outside, people would think I have it all. Rae Rose is strong, talented, poised, and oh-so-successful. She owns any room she walks into and her confidence behind a microphone will make your knees buckle. The problem is, even I am not Rae Rose. I don't run my social media, I don't choose my outfits for events or interviews, I want to call my mom more than anything but our relationship is crap so I don't, and most of the stories I tell on talk shows have been finely tuned and vetted by my PR team first. Rae is nothing but a character I hide behind, because I learned from a young age that faking confidence is the only way to make it through this business.

But the more times I have to put on that facade each day, the more I feel myself slipping away. I miss Amelia. I miss the days when playing music and singing was what it was all about. These days, I'm nothing but a maxed-out credit card that everyone keeps swiping.

And at this moment, I would trade my celebrity confidence for basic social skills in a heartbeat. Because I have to make a simple phone call and my hand is shaking. What do I even say when I call? I lift the ancient dinosaur phone from the receiver, and it's so heavy I'm going to count it as my upper body workout for the day. In my other hand, I clutch Noah's note like a lifeline. His handwriting is beautiful. I trace my thumb across the bubbly swoops and slashes of each letter, realizing how rare it is for someone to write in cursive these days. Somehow, these letters perfectly match the man. Intriguing. Commanding. Precise. And yet . . . there's a softness to them.

When I bring myself to stop fondling Noah's note, I steel myself and punch in the phone number. And, wow, that's the most satisfying thing I've ever done. Do people know these old phones are the equivalent of a fidget popper? My smartphone is going to be a horrific letdown after using this thing. I'm momentarily calmed by these satisfying buttons, but when the line starts ringing, my anxiety jumps up again.

Would it have killed Noah to give me a tad more direction? This note—however beautiful and frameworthy—is severely lacking. I'm told to *Ask for Tommy. He'll tow your car and fix it for a good price.* Well, I hate to sound like a snob, but I'm not exactly worried about the price. In fact, I'd love to pay this Tommy a million dollars if he'll assure me I won't be abducted by him or anyone else in his automotive shop.

The phone rings one more time before a man answers. "Ello? Automuphinandsons."

Huh? What did that man say? I didn't understand a single word. Was that even English? Honestly, it sounded like a pile of jumbled-up words being eaten by a garbage disposal. And *this* is a prime example of why I don't do phone calls. You never know what you're going to get on the other end, and it's almost never a pleasant experience.

"Uh . . . hi . . . is . . . Tommy there?" I ask, glancing down at the paper to make sure I got the name right, even though I've read it roughly twenty times now and might be pregnant with its babies due to all the caressing.

I wince when there's suddenly loud banging noises on the other end of the line, making it even harder to understand the man when he grumbles out his response, which honestly sounds like, "Uh-huh, you're a honking table."

That can't be right.

A cold sweat breaks out over my skin, and I'm about two seconds away from losing it in the form of epic waterfall tears. I feel like a toddler lost in an amusement park. I can't find my way and nothing looks familiar. I *hate* that I'm regretting leaving Nashville. I *hate* that I can't stand on my own two feet. And I really *hate* that I don't belong anywhere anymore.

And now I'm shaking. Maybe I'm not cut out for this. Maybe it's time to end this call and dial Susan instead. I'll beg her to send me a car, or a jet, or she can even send me a freaking unicycle for all I care. I could be home by dinnertime like nothing ever happened. But as I picture my life back there, a vise clamps down on my chest and screws tight. I can't go back yet. I can't give up on whatever I'm looking for in this town just yet.

"Ello?" the man says again, sounding more impatient than before.

"Yes, I'm here. Umm . . . I'm not actually sure what you said but—"

I gasp when a male hand reaches around my shoulder to take the phone from my hand. I whirl around and find myself staring right at Noah's mountain of a chest. I never heard him come into the house, and now my heart is not just racing, it's shouting and stomping indignantly on my ribs just to make sure I'm paying attention. Or maybe it's trying to flee my body and get to safer ground.

My eyes tiptoe up his neck, and jaw, stagger slightly over his full, moody mouth until I safely land on his green eyes. He holds my stare as he lifts the phone to his ear. "Tommy? Yeah, it's Noah. I got a woman here who needs you to pick up her car and tow it to the shop." He pauses and listens, eyes never leaving mine. The intense, unwavering way he looks at me makes me want to squirm. What an excellent Buckingham palace guard he'd be.

Noah nods. "Mm-hmm. That'll work. Thanks, Tommy."

He leans around me and his chest brushes delicate fire across my shoulder. The click of the phone landing on the receiver is so startling against the dead silence that I jump a little. I feel reactive to Noah in a way I've never experienced before.

"Thanks," I say, having to push my voice out from under a thick cloud of sudden attraction. "I can't believe you understood him."

The corner of his mouth twitches like he wants to smile, but won't. "Tommy dips. That combined with his thick accent makes him hard to understand."

"But you didn't have any trouble."

"'Cause I grew up here. I speak dip. It's a language in and of itself."

"Bilingual," I state with a light chuckle and let my eyes fall down the same path I traversed a moment ago. Nose, mouth, scruffy jaw, neck. When his Adam's apple bobs, I realize I'm staring. Drooling. I don't mean to, it's just that there's something different about him that turns me into a magnet. It's more than the fact that he's ridiculously attractive (and, hello, he is!), but there's this soft grit, this delicious paradox of rugged masculinity that mixes with a comfy normalcy that makes me want to wrap myself up in the gray cotton T-shirt he's wearing and live in it forever. I don't even know him and I feel safe. Noah is the blanket fort you used to make and hide in as a kid. So warm and reassuring.

I think it's that he's so different from the men I'm around in my day-to-day life. The artist types that are at all times worried about the swoop of their hair—or in my last boyfriend's case, only paying attention to me when we were in public where everyone could see.

The relationship wasn't necessarily fake—but it was suggested by our managers as "a good fit for both of us." I hoped it could end up being something great, but like the handful of other nonserious relationships I've had, it was ultimately flat. A two-liter bottle of soda that's been lidless for a week.

He wanted to publicly date Rae Rose, venture out to parties all the time, spend enormous amounts of money at restaurants, and milk our stardom to its fullest—always making sure the press was around to capture our "completely candid moments of affection" so we would be on the front page of magazines as often as possible. (And by the way, he was a terrible kisser. Two out of ten, would not recommend.)

I might have been into the sort of lifestyle he lived when I was twenty-one and not burned out by the limelight yet, but now, I just want someone to play Scrabble with me and get snuggly in a blanket. I never could get him to do that, so I ended it pretty quickly, just like all the others who were even less notable than him. (But at least better kissers.)

None of those men felt genuine. Unlike the man standing in front of me right now.

Noah clears his throat and steps back. "Tommy will be here at nine to get your car. He'll take it to his shop and diagnose it."

I swallow and nod, welcoming the cool air that replaces Noah's body heat. Etiquette nudges me. "Great. And thanks again. I'm so sorry to be putting you out like this. I'd love to repay you." *Polite, polite, polite.* At all costs, I am always faithfully polite.

"Don't worry about it" is all he says before the room drops into silence again, and I feel jealous of his ability to just *say things*. He says only the things he wants and not a single word more.

It's so quiet I can hear my own breathing. My thoughts knock around my head like a fly in a jar. I can't help but wonder where he was this morning and why he came back? His note implied he wouldn't be around today. But here he is.

As discreetly as possible, I size him up and speculate on what sort of job a man like him would have. He's wearing a baseball hat and a T-shirt that hangs appropriately loose over his torso, but still snug enough around his shoulders and chest that it's not sloppy or baggy. His jeans are simple yet still stylish. Well-worn and slightly whitewashed in areas that make me think they're his favorite pair. On his feet are brown work boots. But here's the catch, they're not real work boots. They're the kind that trendy guys wear to coffee shops in the city. *Interesting.*

"You're squinting at me," he states, making me blink out of my Sherlock Holmes investigation.

I feel compelled to a moment of rare honesty. "I'm trying to figure out what a man like you does for a living."

He lifts a brow and crosses his arms. It's a surly pose. "A man like me?"

"Yeah, you know . . ." I say, daring to give him a teasing smile. "All the muscles and scruff and commanding attitude."

"And?" His tone is clipped. He doesn't find me charming. I'm the most uncharming person in the world to him, and I think I love it.

"And what?"

He drops his arms (no more Surly Pose) and turns away to go open a cupboard and pull down a mixing bowl, leaving me lingering near the phone because I'm not sure where I should stand in his house. "What's your guess?" he prompts gently.

I'm taken aback for a second because I didn't think he'd play along. He doesn't seem like the play-along type. Okay, then. Let's do this.

"Hmm." I give him one more thorough and blatant perusal. *Damn.* His body is good. Like really good. He's got to be a little over six foot (I'd say three inches over if I had to bet), with veins extending out from under his short sleeves and wrapping down his long, lean biceps and sturdy forearms. I'd say he does something with his hands based on his upper body strength alone. And since he's wearing a hat, maybe his job requires him to be in the sun a lot? The golden hair lightly flipping out from under his hat lends weight to my suspicion.

"A rancher?" I ask, leaving my phone friend behind to take one of the stools on the opposite side of the little island where Noah's begun assembling ingredients for something.

"Nope." He pulls a carton of buttermilk and a few eggs out of the fridge.

"A farmer?"

Next comes butter. "Wrong."

"Okayyyyy. Then you own a lawn care service?"

Containers of flour, sugar, baking powder, and baking soda are the last to find their way to the counter. Noah's eyes glance briefly at me and then away. "Should I be offended you haven't mentioned a lawyer or doctor yet?" he says in a dry tone that somehow still conveys humor.

That tiny hint of teasing in his voice is enough incentive for me to try to win him over. He's a little grumpy, there's an edge to him that says *careful, I might bite,* but then his eyes whisper *but I'll be gentle.* What a mystery he is. Then again, everything is a mystery to me lately. I feel like I've woken up from a cryogenic sleep, and suddenly, I'm having to relearn this new and evolved world around me.

"I don't know many lawyers who would go to work in jeans." I lean my elbow on the counter and rest my chin on my palm.

"That's just because you haven't met Larry yet."

Yet. Why does that word make my stomach flip?

"Come on, tell me. I'm out of guesses."

He shrugs, and after adding ingredients to a bowl without ever using a measuring tool, mixes it all together. His forearm flexes and draws my eye to the soft sprinkle of blond hair across his skin. "Guess you'll never know."

Noah turns around, fires up his gas stove, and melts some butter in a skillet. Not to stereotype but he moves with way more ease around the kitchen than I would expect from someone that looks as . . . well . . . male as he does. I keep quiet, enjoying this puzzle of a man more than I should. He scoops out a dollop of batter and drops it into a pan, and now I realize he's making pancakes. Pancakes from scratch and without a recipe.

It hits me.

I gasp and point at him. "Baker! You're a baker, aren't you?" He earned those delicious forearms from kneading dough!

I can only see a sliver of Noah's face as he tilts his head, but it's enough to catch the hint of a grin. I feel that grin in the tops of my ears. In the tips of my toes. In the depths of my belly. "You guessed it, Nancy Drew. I own a pie shop."

My mouth falls open. "You do not."

"I do. Something wrong with that?"

So defensive, this one.

Shaking my head, I slide off the stool so I can go lean back against the countertop beside the stove. Noah doesn't look at me, but he cuts his eyes to where my palm is planted on the surface beside me. Thinking maybe it's in his way, I cross my arms in front of me.

"It's great. I just didn't expect it. Not with all your . . . well . . . you know." I gesture toward his masculine form again because my awkward ship has sailed and there's no pulling her back into port. "So what's your favorite pie?"

"I don't like pie." He says it so definitively.

I blink at him. "But you own a pie shop."

"Probably why I don't like pie."

I shake my head feeling dumbfounded. More paradox. How would he feel if I told him I don't like singing? I love to sing, though, so that thought's irrelevant. Or—at least, I used to love singing and I'm hopeful I will again.

"So if you don't eat it, how do you know if it's good or not?"

"I inherited the pie shop from my grandma. It's been in our family for generations. I use the same foolproof recipes they used." He glances down at me and takes in my curious frown. "Have you never loved something just for what it means to you?"

First, I'm stunned because Noah doesn't strike me as the sentimental type. But he owns his grandma's pie shop so clearly I'm wrong. Two, yes, I absolutely have. And her name is Audrey Hepburn. Immediately I'm transported back to that night when I was thirteen and couldn't sleep. I had a bad dream and woke up in a cold sweat, going out to the living room to find my mom. She was a night owl (probably because as a single mom, those few hours after I'd go to bed were the only ones she had for herself), and I found her curled up on the couch watching a movie.

"Hi, sweetie pie, can't sleep?" she'd asked, lifting the edge of her blanket so I could crawl under and snuggle with her.

"I had a bad dream," I'd said.

She tucked me up close to her and we both turned our attention to the black-and-white movie playing on the TV. "Well, I have the perfect cure for bad dreams. *Breakfast at Tiffany's*. Audrey Hepburn always makes me feel better when I'm upset."

Together, we'd stayed up late watching that classic movie, and my mom was right. For those few hours, I didn't feel scared or sad. It became a tradition for us to watch Audrey Hepburn movies together when either of us was having a bad day. Except now, I watch them by myself because our relationship fractured a long time ago and I don't think it'll ever heal.

But I can't tell Noah any of that because it's too personal. So I take a page from his book and simply say, "Yeah. I have."

He accepts my answer for what it is and flips a pancake. I have a thousand questions I want to ask—but just like last night, being this close to him ties my tongue. Right now, he smells like clean laundry, masculine bodywash, and sweet, buttery pancakes. It's the perfect scent.

The quiet stretches and I'm not eager to interrupt it. Instead, I watch the batter sizzle and bubble in the pan, wondering when the last time anyone felt comfortable enough around me to just be quiet. It's been years.

"You don't like pancakes?" Noah says, pulling me from my thoughts. When I give him a curious look, he adds, "You were frowning at the skillet."

I have zero desire to tell him I was frowning at the thought of my mom, so I sidestep. "Uh . . . no. It's only that I can't eat them."

"Gluten?"

"Carbs. I have a very strict diet I have to adhere to. Especially leading up to my tour in a few weeks. My manager will murder me if I come home with an extra inch on my waist." I have several costumes I need to be able to fit into—and believe me, Susan will tell me if she thinks I look too lumpy in them. Or she'll talk to the chef who makes all my meals for the week, and not so subtly adjust the menu to consist of smaller portions and nothing delicious.

"Okay," he says, scooping the most fluffy, golden-brown pancake I've ever seen out of the skillet and onto a plate. He drops another dollop into the pan and it hisses. "Eggs then?"

I narrow my eyes at him. "You're not going to try to convince me to eat the pancakes?"

This time he looks at me, confused and intrigued all at once. "No. Should I?"

"I was sort of hoping for it. Because then I could tell my manager you accused me of being rude by rejecting your hospitable offer, and she'd see I was left with no choice but to eat them or else you'd go slander me to the press."

He raises a brow, flips a pancake. "You need your manager's approval to eat?" I hear the challenge in his voice.

But more than that, I hear the simplicity of his question and how easy it should be to say *No, ha ha, of course not. That would be ridiculous!* But holy shit, I do. I think of how many times Susan's name has crossed my mind since I left last night and I begin to wonder if she's part of whatever problem I'm having. Have I let myself completely defer all decisions regarding my life to her?

My eyes follow the spatula as Noah lifts a golden pancake onto the beautiful stack he's already made. It looks like a piece of art. That pancake should have its own social media account devoted to nothing other than adoring it from all angles. "So . . ." says Noah. "Scrambled eggs for you?"

When I don't answer right away, Noah finally looks into my eyes. When our gazes connect, I feel that same thrill run through me from last night. It's terror and joy. Hope and dread. All I know is, it gives me the push I need to trust myself.

"No. I'll have pancakes today."

Chapter 6

Noah

"Come again?" I ask Tommy over the phone, hoping I didn't hear him correctly the first time.

"Ain't gonna be done for at least two weeks," he says, in his usual jumbled way. But this time, I'm uncomfortably sure that I hear him correctly. He'd just picked up the car a short time ago, and already he's ruining my day?

I look over at Rae, who's on her second stack of pancakes and chowing down like she hasn't eaten in years. Today she's wearing a light gray top, tucked smoothly into a pair of fancy, dark blue skinny jeans that end high on her bare ankle. It's tight—that shirt. It's made of a soft, stretchy material that begins around her collarbone, then hugs, licks, and bends over her chest and torso, revealing a slender figure that is fantastically *woman*. The sleeves cling down her long arms and stop just past the bend in her elbow. The only thing modern about the way she looks is her brown—nearly black if it weren't for the lighter pieces that stand out when the sun catches it—hair. It's still in a messy heap on her head, and she has one foot (with red toenails) propped up in the chair with her.

She's leaning over the stack of pancakes, thick lashes fanned down toward her cheekbones as she forks another bite into her mouth. I like her eyeliner (a makeup term I know from my sisters). It's a precise black line painted at the base of those pretty eyelashes, extending out slightly and making her look straight out of a black-and-white film. She looks . . . wonderful.

I grimace.

"That won't do, Tommy. We're gonna need it done sooner than that. My friend has a life she needs to get back to."

When I say the words *my friend,* Rae's big blue eyes lift to me, so full of gratitude as she swallows a giant bite of pancake that I have to look away. I shouldn't have said friend. I don't mean it. I just didn't want to say her name and alert the whole town to the fact that a pop star is in my house. Because believe me, I don't want to be Rae's friend or anything else to her. All I want is to ensure this woman gets on her way as soon as possible and out of my life so everything will go back to normal.

"Ain't up to you, Noah. Got a shortage on radiator hoses and the soonest they'll be back in stock is two weeks from today. I'll tell ya when they're in." And then he hangs up and my hope deflates pathetically to the ground.

Two weeks. Surely she won't stay in town for two weeks? Of course not. Who am I kidding? *You've already dealt with a woman like her before, remember, Noah?* Merritt was also a city girl, and she couldn't wait to leave after her business here was finished. I'm sure Rae Rose is itching to get back to her fancy life. No need for me to worry.

"Everything okay?" she asks, and I hear the clink of her fork as she sets it carefully on her plate.

"Uh . . . yeah." I face her, rubbing the back of my neck. "Well, no. Depending on how you want to see it, I guess. Looks like your car won't be fixed for about two weeks until they get a part you need. But the good news is, you can just call whoever it is that usually drives you around and get them to take you to . . . wherever it is you're going. Was it the beach?"

"What? No," she says in a daze.

"The mountains then?" I ask, taking the seat across from her in my small breakfast nook. I don't like the way the light spills around her shoulders making her practically glow. I need to shut the blinds.

She shakes her head, looking visibly distraught. "No, I mean I can't call anyone to get me." Okay, now red flags are going up. Is she in some kind of trouble? Am I harboring a pop star fugitive? "I don't mean to make it sound so dramatic. I'm just sort of . . . hiding for a while."

"Hiding?" I echo in a grunt.

"Yeah." She scratches the side of her neck and looks down at her now empty plate. "I'm not hiding from the law or a crazy ex-boyfriend or anything, if that's what you're thinking."

"I was. Thinking both of those actually."

She cracks the saddest smile, lowering her eyes to her plate. "My life quickly became too much. I needed a break from—"

I stand suddenly, making the chair legs scrape against the floor. That feels a tad too dramatic, but I don't have time to sit here and listen to all the ways the pop star has a hard life. She can't eat carbs? Big whoop. She asked for this life and I'm fresh out of pity parties. For a second there, I was nearly sucked into caring about her, wondering why her doe eyes look full of hurt and sadness. But I can't go down that road with Rae Rose. She can go cry to her entourage about it—I have enough people to worry about as it is.

"I gotta go to work. I've already been gone too long. But I'll take you into town so you can get a room at Mabel's bed-and-breakfast, because you can't stay here." That was blunt even for me. I can't help it, though. Something about her makes me feel like I'm batting a hand away from touching a raw wound on my skin.

"Oh." She blinks several times and then stands. Her movements are too gentle to ever make chair legs screech. "Of course. Yes. I'm sorry, I didn't mean to suggest I'd stay here. That was never my plan." She picks up her plate and scurries with it to the sink, two pink splotches now sitting on her cheeks. "I'll just put this in the dishwasher and then grab my stuff."

She hikes up her sleeves and frantically scrubs at the syrup on her plate, making me feel like the asshole James said I was. Great. Please explain to me why in the hell I feel guilty right now when she's the one who interrupted my life?

I watch her hips shimmy back and forth from the force she's using to remove that caked-on syrup with her hand and a drop of soap. Her shoulders are bunched up to her ears and I'm pretty sure if I looked at her eyes, they'd be clouded with tears. Did I mention I have three sisters? Yeah, I'm well acquainted with this frantic cleaning coping mechanism.

Except, clearly, Rae is a little out of touch with the world of cleaning.

I refrain from growling as I take two steps over to her, remove the plate from her hands, and use the green bristle pad I keep under the sink to easily wipe the plate clean. I can feel her watching me, but I refuse to return her gaze. It's not because I don't trust myself to look in her eyes this closely again (I learned my lesson with the telephone this morning), but because I don't want her to get comfy around here and think we're actually friends. This is what I call drawing a clear line.

"Thank you," she says quietly. "And . . . by the way . . . my name is . . ." A soft pause. "Amelia. Amelia Rose." She starts backing away. "Rae is just a stage name."

After she leaves the kitchen, I stand stock-still as her name rolls itself around my head. *Amelia*. Dammit, that's something I wish I didn't know.

The sooner I can get Amelia Rose out of my house, the better.

Chapter 7

Amelia

"We're full up."

I watch in dismay as Noah's jaw clenches. He leans his wide shoulders slightly over the inn's reception desk toward the sweet little old lady who dashed his dreams to the ground. I immediately feel sympathy for Mabel having to stare Noah down. Or up, since that's the direction she has to tilt her chin to see him. She is a Black woman who looks to be in her seventies, has silver, extra-curly hair, cropped short, is wearing deep mauve lipstick, and has just the sort of soft grandmotherly form you'd love to get a big hug from. Watching these two in a stare-off feels like a live action scene between the Big Bad Wolf and Little Red Riding Hood's grandma.

"That can't be, Mabel. Hardly anyone ever visits this town."

Her wise eyes flick briefly to me and then back to Noah. The sudden glint of mischief I see tells me I have this story all wrong. She's the one in charge here—not Noah. "Well, that just plumb ain't true, now is it? Besides, if it were true, I'd be bankrupt. And I've got piles of money."

Noah's nostrils flare as he takes in a deep breath. That man wants to get rid of me more than he's ever wanted anything in his life. I can feel his irritation leaking from his bones like fumes. "Can I see the scheduling book?"

Mabel abruptly shuts the book that was open in front of her and levels a frightening scowl at Noah. "No, you may not. And don't you try to manhandle me like that again. I changed your diapers and don't you forget it." She wags her finger in his face. He doesn't look chastised in the least. *Weary* is the word I'd assign to him.

"Mrs. Mabel," says Noah, slowly and gently this time. He has dipped his voice in thick, decadent honey. "She has nowhere to stay. Surely you can find a room for her in your wonderful bed-and-breakfast."

Mabel squints. "Sounds like you're trying to plagiarize a bible story." And then she grins. "Besides, Noah, it seems to me she does have somewhere to stay. Your guest room is still wide open and free as a bird if I'm remembering correctly."

The look Noah gives Mabel has me wanting to shrivel up and sink into a hole in the ground. What is this woman thinking? Clearly, she's lying and doing some sort of meddling to have me stay at Noah's house. And clearly, Noah doesn't want me anywhere near his house. I just can't decide if it's that he likes his space, or just doesn't like me. A thick combination of both, I assume.

I could solve all this easily by calling Susan and having her send a car. Two and a half hours and I'd be buckled up in the back of a blacked-out, armored SUV and this town would be nothing but a dot in the rearview mirror. But I don't want that. The longer I'm here, the more I feel my limbs tingling back to life. It seems important to stay, no matter how awkward it feels.

I step up to the counter, thinking that maybe if I finally do the talking, it will help. "Hi, Mrs. Mabel, I'm—"

"Rae Rose, yes, baby, I know. I have a TV and radio. Loved your performance on *Good Morning America* last month."

"Oh." I laugh lightly, not quite expecting that answer because she had scarcely looked at me before now. "Well, thank you." *Polite, polite, polite.* "I would be immensely grateful if you could possibly squeeze me into a room here. I'd be happy to pay triple whatever the usual rate is."

She smiles sweetly and raises her weathered hand over the counter to pat mine. I look down, a little shocked. No one touches me. Well, that's not completely true. If I find myself in the middle of a fan mob, everyone tugs, snatches, and gropes at me . . . but strangers never affectionately touch my hand like a grandmother would. The gesture is so kind and sweet it feels like bubble wrap around my heart. Again, I miss my mom.

"I don't need your money. I'm filthy rich. My sweet husband—may he rest in peace—had a *fantastic* life insurance policy. You'll stay at Noah's and I don't want to hear another word about it." She turns her sharp brown eyes to Noah and lifts her eyebrows as if she's daring him to talk back.

Something like a growl sounds from his throat and he rolls his eyes before his large form storms out the door. *Well, then.* I look at Mabel and smile awkwardly. She winks, and whispers, "Hold your own, darlin'." I get one more affectionate, fortifying pat on my hand before she releases it and gestures for me to go out after him.

Outside, I find Noah barreling toward his burnt orange pickup truck looking as stern and grumpy as a bull. I should be scared to approach him, but I feel like I understand him enough now to see that he's all bark and no bite. *Hold your own, darlin'.* To be honest, I feel oddly safe with him. Safer than wandering around by myself, at least.

He gets in his classic Chevy truck and slams the door behind him. I approach the passenger side slowly and peer through the window. Noah drapes his hand over the steering wheel and keeps his eyes facing forward, refusing to look at me. But then, in contrast to his grumpy, hostile exterior, he unlocks the door so I can slide in beside him. Minus the sweet scent of pancakes, his truck smells overwhelmingly like him. I run my fingers gently back and forth over the smooth leather bench, while I get up the nerve to say something to him.

"Hi," I venture, in an apologetic tone. "How's your day going?"

His mouth twitches and he cuts his woodsy eyes to me. "I'm being an ass and I know it."

"Okay, well, they say the first step is admitting." This earns me a genuine grin from his full lips to the soft crinkles beside his eyes. Oh, it looks so good on him. And I see why he doesn't do it often—it's disorienting. I want to poke his cheek right where that grin dimples, and only just manage to refrain. I've never felt this light with anyone before. There's not a single star in his eyes when he looks at me, and it almost makes me feel normal. If I'm not careful, I could become addicted to this.

"Why don't you like me?" I ask, not out of hurt, but genuine curiosity.

His eyes drop to the steering wheel. At first, I think he's not going to answer me. The silence stretches on so long before he finally speaks. "It's not you." His eyes slide up to mine, and now I'm submerged in a dense green forest.

I wait a minute for him to expound, but I'm learning that expounding is not Noah's specialty. I throw him a bone. "Listen, I know you didn't sign up for this. You definitely didn't ask for a spoiled pop star to crash your life and stay in your guest room. So . . ." I don't want to say it, but I have to. It's the right thing to do. "Just say the word and I'll call my manager and have her send someone. I can be out of your hair by the afternoon," I say, trying not to look too disappointed as I offer up my least favorite option.

"But you don't want to do that?"

I choose my words carefully. "I . . . was just hoping for some time away." I try to keep it short because I haven't forgotten how he reacted this morning when I started to tell him about my life.

His eyes stay focused on me. He's reading me, looking for

something and then finding an answer. He drags in a deep breath and stares out his front windshield. Three beats go by before he lets that breath out in one big gust. "All right. Tell you what, you can stay at my place through the weekend. But Monday morning you have to find somewhere else to go."

"Really?" My voice belongs to a three-year-old who was just offered a brownie before bedtime. Never in my life have I felt so desperate for something. So happy at a prospect. I clear my throat. "I mean . . . are you sure?"

He fights a grin. "Yeah. Just . . . I can't be your tour guide while you're here. I work a full-time job, so you'll have to fend for yourself. Got it?"

"Got it," I say with a firm nod. "I'll make myself scarce. Seriously, I'll be quiet as a mouse. You won't even know I'm around."

He starts the truck and puts it in reverse, mumbling, "I highly doubt that," over his shoulder as he backs his truck out of the space.

Chapter 8

Amelia

Now to do the thing that sounds less appealing than poking my eye out. I stare down at my cell phone and open Susan's contact info. I don't have any missed calls or texts from her because I still don't have service (a small mercy). Even though I want to drop off the grid more than anything, I know that I can't be that irresponsible. At this moment, I'm officially ten minutes late for my *Vogue* interview and I'm sure that Susan is wearing a hole through the floor wherever she is and seconds away from calling in the SWAT team.

I didn't mean to go this long without checking in with her, but I got caught up in the pancakes and the trip into town, and for once, I forgot about Susan or my responsibilities. They've caught up to me now, though, and my hand is trembling.

I walk out of the bedroom Noah is letting me stay in for the next four days and into the living room. Noah said he has to work, but he didn't leave immediately after we came home. Instead, he looked at the time and then sighed like he'd made a decision of some sort and set about doing random tasks in his house. He put a load of laundry in his washing machine. He started the dishwasher.

He slipped in and out of his room again, cracking it open just enough to walk through. My curiosity piqued to epic proportions. What the hell is in there, and why doesn't he want me to see it?

My imagination has been running wild. It's a kinky sex den. He's a Trekkie and the room is full of Star Trek memorabilia. Oh no, maybe he's a Beanie Baby hoarder. The horrifying options are endless, and I will never know what's on the other side of that door (probably for the best) because come Monday, I'll be finding somewhere else to stay. Maybe by then Mabel will have changed her tune and will have pity on me.

Noah's back stiffens ever so slightly when he hears me approach, but he doesn't turn right away. He lingers for a moment, wiping down his kitchen counter, and then he and his broad shoulders turn to face me.

"Hellloooo," I say with a bright smile.

"Hi," he replies, skeptically. His eyes radiate concern like he's waiting for me to do something terrible at any moment.

"Look, I'm not going to steal your pillows, okay?"

He frowns and shakes his head. "Didn't think you were."

I scoff lightly and roll my eyes. "Well, you sure seem like it from the way you're walking around here like a caveman guarding all his precious rocks." I stomp around and mime what I imagine a prehistoric male would look like when he's pissy and possessive. It's not a cute look on me.

Noah's brows go up. Arms cross. Surly Pose. "Is that supposed to be me?"

"Obviously."

"Huh." A pause. "I need better posture."

I feel my lips curl. "Is that . . . a joke, Noah Walker?"

"No." He says no, but the word slides across my skin as if he were whispering *yes* against the back of my neck. Confusing, confusing man. Also confusing is the temperature of my body right now as he and I have a stare-off that feels like our clothes might spontaneously burst into flames. Ridiculously, the procedure I learned in kindergarten but haven't yet found a need to use pops in my head: *Stop, drop, and roll.*

"Did you need something?" asks Noah, his eyes shuttering against any hints of finding me desirable a moment ago. All traces of it are gone, making me wonder if I imagined it.

"Uh . . . yeah. Do you have Wi-Fi?" I hold up my phone.

"Nope." With his arms folded he leans back against the countertop and crosses a boot over the other. The pose is a spin-off of his critically acclaimed Surly Pose (trademark pending) and it's so incredibly masculine the hairs on my arms stand. *Stop, drop, and roll.*

"You don't . . . you don't have internet?" Surely he's just not understanding the question.

He gives his sandy-blond head one good shake. "No internet."

Noah is like a piggy bank full of money. His words are coins and I have him physically flipped upside down, shaking him just to get a few cents to fall out. I almost wonder if he's withholding words just to annoy me. Just to get under my skin. And why do I like it so much?

I have two responses warring inside me. The first is my usual fine-tuned, never-failing *polite, polite, polite.* The second, and the one I decide to pursue, is a new instinct full of selfish primitive desires. *Play, play, play.*

"And you wondered where I got the caveman comparison." But no, he's not a caveman, he's . . . classic. Like his truck. Like his phone. Like his handwriting. Like the plaid shirt rolled up over his sturdy forearms.

"Is this your version of quiet as a mouse?" He holds his frown so well even though I can feel the amusement vibrating between us.

"Is that the longest sentence you've ever strung together?"

He tips one of his eyebrows. A hit. "She commandeers my guest room. Eats my food. Calls me a caveman. And insults my intelligence," he says while shaking his head in a mock reprimand.

"And next I'll ask if I can borrow some pj's." I wish I could train my face to be as frowny and stoic as his—deliver my jokes with wit so dry the single strike of a match would send it all up in flames, but I can't. I'm a cheeseball, smiling the entire time I say it.

"Why do you need my pajamas?" Ah—He's a starchy *pa-ja-mas* kind of guy instead of the cute and short *pj's* I like to say. This tiny distinction sums us both up so perfectly.

I smile faintly. "Because I assume you don't want me to walk around naked?" *Play, play, play.* I notice the tips of his ears turn pink, so I have mercy on him. "I forgot to pack something comfy for lounging."

He swallows, dips his eyes once over my body—very quickly—and then nods. "I'll be right back."

Noah escapes toward his room like the Pillow Bandit is hot on his heels, and I use the moment of privacy to call Susan. After reading her number from her contact information and punching it into the cathartic dinosaur phone, it rings.

"Susan Malley," she answers in her matter-of-fact tone.

"Susan! Hey, it's—"

"Rae! Oh thank GOD!" I have to hold the phone a little away from my ear so she doesn't permanently damage my hearing. For a moment, her obvious relief fills me with bursts of warm fuzzy light. She noticed I was gone and was worried about me! For a brief moment, it feels like I'm talking to the old Susan who first reached out and cared so much about me in the early years of my career. But then she continues and all that light fades. "Where are you?! It's really shitty of you to be late like this. And where has your phone been? I've been calling you all morning! You better be vomiting with a stomach bug is all I'm saying."

She wasn't worried about me. She's worried about Rae Rose missing an interview.

"I'm not sick. I just . . . don't have service."

Susan laughs, but it's clear she doesn't find anything funny.

"What are you talking about? You get great service in your house. Do you need me to order you a new phone? I'll pick one up this morning because we can't have this happening when—"

"Susan," I say, cutting her off. "I'm not at home."

A pause. "Okaaay," she says slowly, finally clueing in on the change in my voice. "Where are you?"

"I'm . . ." I press my lips together and look over my shoulder toward the hallway that leads to Noah's and my rooms. Do I tell Susan where I am? Do I trust that she won't come bang down the door immediately or send a whole team of security personnel to trail me? For once, I feel a taste of freedom and I'm terrified to lose it. "I'm taking a vacation before the tour."

"You're . . . taking . . . a . . . *vacation*." She says it all painfully slow, like a parent giving their child a chance to rectify the thing the child previously said.

I shut my eyes and steel myself. "Yes."

This time she lets out one frightening laugh. "You're kidding me?"

"No, I'm not. I'm taking some time away for myself because . . ." Noah's question from this morning pops into my head. *You need permission to eat?* Suddenly, I don't feel like explaining. I feel like being a piggy bank. "Because I need it."

Susan is not happy. The silence is so tense I feel myself beginning to waver. If she pushes this, I don't know if I'll be able to hold out. "You have obligations. Lots and lots of them, Rae. What do you want me to do? Just call and cancel them? It's promo for your tour! This is all to help you achieve *your* dreams and people have put aside precious time to accommodate you."

Ugh, I hate the way she makes me sound. Suddenly, I feel like a spoiled brat who needs a time-out to learn her lesson. Like all I ever do is think about myself. I'm starting to think if that were true, though, I wouldn't feel like the numb pile of garbage that I have lately. And the thing is, I never put up a fight. I never miss interviews, and I try to always be gracious with other people's time. This is the one instance where I've backed out of something. That has to count, right?

Noah turns the corner and when he sees me on the phone, does a half turn, pivoting into the living room and dropping himself onto the couch in a surprisingly boyish way. It's unnerving having him there, listening even though he's pretending not to.

I turn away from Noah and twist the rubber phone cord around my finger. "I'm really sorry, Susan. I'm just really tired and need some space to breathe and feel like myself again."

Early on, Susan and I were very close and talked about everything. I remember not long after my career took off, she took my mom and me on a radio tour. Susan booked us in the nicest hotels, and then after each interview, we went to all the best touristy sightseeing places and fun restaurants for dinner. Or we'd just order room service and watch movies in our plush hotel robes—laughing like friends. It was the best, I had my mom and a friend in my manager. Life was still exciting and new, and fame hadn't burned me yet.

During those days and nights, we talked extensively about my dreams and what I wanted out of this career. Susan was so invested and loving. Patient and understanding. I'm not sure when she stopped being those things, but it's clear to me now that the Susan I used to know is long gone.

I miss her, as well as the bright-eyed girl who played music and sang because if she didn't, the world felt wrong. Who woke up early in the morning because a song lyric was buzzing in her head that she *had* to write down. The girl whose fingers and back ached wonderfully at the end of the day from getting lost at the piano for too long.

But part of me wonders if Susan even noticed she's gone.

"We're all tired, Rae, but you don't see us just quitting and put-ting people out like you did this morning. Now, look. I'll give you through the weekend and then you have to come back. Also I need to know where you are so I can send Will to stay with you." Will—my bodyguard. He will follow me everywhere. And while I normally appreciate and need him with me, I think of Mabel and the soft pat of her hand this morning, and I don't feel like Will's presence here is necessary.

I realize I've turned back to Noah when he looks over his shoul-der and our eyes meet. "I don't need Will. I'm safe and staying under the radar."

"No. Unacceptable. I've got a pen, now tell me your address. Also, you're still going to need to do some over-the-phone press interviews while you're there. It's important we keep momentum up before the tour. You'll have time to rest on the tour bus in be-tween venues." Geez, has Susan always been this much of a steam-roller? I feel flattened to the ground.

Noah stands and walks over to me. Instead of giving me a re-peat of this morning, he stops a few feet away. Butterflies swarm in my stomach and I'm sure that if he knew, he'd force me to drink hot sauce or something equally brutal to kill them all. Having his eyes on me reminds me that I need to be here—that the slow tingling-back-to-life sensation is essential and that Audrey Hepburn is never wrong. I need to lean into whatever this is, and Susan will have to deal without me being available 24-7 for once.

"Actually, Susan, I'll call you Sunday night and tell you where to send a car to pick me up Monday morning. I'll be out of pocket until then."

"No, Rae, wa—"

I hang up.

And then I stare with wide eyes at the receiver. Did I really just do that? I feel free and powerful and INCREDIBLE . . . until the phone starts ringing again. I wince at the sound and look frantically over my shoulder at Noah. I have no idea why I'm looking at him. It's not like he can do anyth—

Just like this morning, he's behind me again. His arm reaches around my shoulder and he disconnects the landline, dropping the little curly cord to the floor. The ringing stops and I feel helpless to do anything but look up at him.

He's not quite smiling but he's not frowning, either, as he says, "Cavemen don't need phones anyway." He places a pair of pj's into my hands.

I unfold the bundled fabric, and why am I not at all surprised to find that he's handed me a matching, button-up, top-and-bottoms sleep set. Flannel fabric—slate blue with white vertical pinstripes. They look exactly like the sort of pj's Gregory Peck would have worn in *Roman Holiday*. Sophisticated, wholesome, *classic* pa-ja-mas. Of course Noah would own these.

He sees me smiling at the pj's and automatically knows why. "I have sisters," he admits, and it's truly a joy to witness his embarrassment. "They bought them for me as a gag gift at Christmas, because they say I'm like an old man."

"Careful. That was a lot of words. I might think you like talking to me if you keep that up." I smile faintly and raise the fabric to my face, running it lightly across my cheek, reveling in the softness. It's a weird thing to do—and I don't know why I feel comfortable enough to do it right in front of him.

He studies me closely for a moment and then looks over his shoulder, trying to keep me from seeing his smile. But I see it. "I have someone I have to meet for lunch before I go back to the shop." *Oh.* Is that why he was lingering instead of going right back to work this morning? He has a lunch date? He said he was single, but I guess that doesn't mean he's not casually dating. And WHY does that make me clench my jaw?

He picks up his keys from the counter. "So um . . . there's stuff in the fridge if you get hungry, and you know where the town is now, so there's a bike out back if you need to go in for anything. Call 911 if there's a fire."

"Stop, drop, and roll," I say with a grin.

He nods a few times. "Right. Well. I guess I'll see ya later."

"I guess you will."

Chapter 9

Noah

B eady eyes follow me everywhere I walk. Like annoying little gremlins that won't leave me alone.

Amelia has been at my house for almost three full days now, but other than Mabel, no one has been able to confirm her existence because she hasn't ventured out from under my roof, and I've kept a firm *no-comment* stance. I don't know what in the hell she's been doing there over the last two days because I've avoided her like I avoid Harriet at the . . . well, everywhere. But clearly speculation about Amelia—or Rae as they know her—has spread rapidly through the locals because my pie shop has had more foot traffic over the last two days than it's had all month.

No one around here really listens to mainstream music, because they prefer songs with a country twang and lyrics about a man and his beloved dog driving over dusty roads. So no one's been fanatic about seeing her or anything. No, they're only in it for the juicy taste of gossip on their tongues. They hope to stir their coffee in Sunday school while coyly distributing details of the famous star like they're graciously handing out hundred-dollar bills to the poor and needy.

Plus, they remember how it all went down with Merritt, and they want front-row seats to the potential sequel of my terrible love life. I've got news for them, they're going to be sorely disappointed because I'm not going anywhere near Amelia.

Those are the only reasons they're lurking around here. Everyone knows what pies I offer. They each have a favorite and I can name every town citizen's usual order while flat-out drunk. And yet, they have all lingered and stared at the pie case like these little round pastries are a fresh invention.

"And this blackberry pie is filled with . . . ?"

"Blackberries," I say, crossing my arms.

"Well, I know that, but it doesn't have any secondary berries in it?" asks Gemma, who owns the quilting shop across the way.

"Nope. Same ingredients it's had for the last fifty years." Gemma is around fifty years old herself, and also a town native, so she knows this as well as anyone.

She wrinkles her nose, admitting her stalling techniques have come to an end. I stare at her without a smile, willing her to just pick a damn pie and leave.

Phil and Todd are sitting at the high-top table, nursing the coffees they ordered an hour ago and eating bites the size of crumbs. I've seen mice tackle a larger mouthful. Thank goodness I can close up in about thirty minutes, and . . . wait, no, I can't go home. *She'll* be at home. What am I even supposed to say to her? How will I avoid her with so many hours left until I can justify going to sleep? I've been going to James's house every day after work until I'm ready to go to bed just so I don't have to spend any time with Amelia. But he told me—not very politely—to quit being a coward and that I wasn't welcome this evening at his house.

I've been kicking myself for agreeing to let her stay the weekend. Should have turned her away immediately. It's not like she's homeless or penniless. And when I stop and ask myself why I did let her stay, I'm not comfortable enough to answer. Because I'm pretty sure it would have something to do with the way I lingered in the bathroom over her bottle of body lotion like a freak. I told myself to leave it alone. Just leave it ALONE. But it was sitting there next to her hairbrush and makeup bag and it was too tempting not to pop the top to sniff it like the pathetic piece of shit that I am. Even worse, I felt disappointed when I smelled it because I knew—from standing too close to her on too many occasions—that the scent was all wrong. It changes when it's on her skin. Turns deeper, softer, and warmer.

I'm annoyed.

I'm angry.

I'm frustrated.

And I lean into those emotions like old friends because those are the ones that keep me from making a careless mistake like growing attached to a beautiful, talented woman with a great personality and a life far *far* away from Rome, Kentucky.

Gemma finally leaves the shop with her apple bourbon vanilla pie (the same one she always gets, by the way), and most everyone else, except Phil and Todd, clears out. I'm wiping down the counter when I spot a woman rolling up in front of the shop window on a bicycle . . .

No. What is she doing here? And why is she wearing my hat? *The little thief.*

The door chimes as Amelia steps in, sunlight spilling all around her form like she's a damn angel sent to earth to prove that heaven really exists. I wish I could say my eyes don't track the length of her tan, toned legs in her white shorts—the same ones she was wearing the night I met her—but they do. Her long dark hair is now braided over her shoulder and drapes all the way down to the middle of her abdomen. It's tied at the end with a navy silk ribbon that matches the blue in the striped tank top she's wearing. White canvas sneakers cover her feet, but I know there's red toenails hiding underneath. Needless to say, this classic and sophisticated style of hers is a complete contradiction to my old, faded Atlanta Braves baseball cap. Does she think it's helping her hide? She sticks out like a beautiful, radiant thumb.

She ducks her head a little and then approaches the counter hesitantly. "I know I said I wouldn't bug you, but your fridge was sort of empty, so I thought I'd come into town and get a few things to make dinner tonight. Earn my keep and all. But then I saw the name of this shop and remembered you saying you owned a pie shop, and *ohshootyou'remad*." She sizes up the frown on my face and starts backing away. "I'll just go. Sorry. This was a bad idea and—" She cuts herself off and turns around, heading for the door, braid whipping her back like it's spurring her to move faster.

Phil and Todd duck their heads together, whispering and casting me disappointed looks. Like James, they don't think I'm treating Amelia well enough. This town is too damn polite for its own good, and I wish I wasn't raised to think the same way. I wish I could successfully push her away like I've been trying to do instead of immediately tugging her back.

"Amel—Rae." Her shoulders bunch when I call her name, and she freezes, lightly spinning on the balls of her feet to face me again. I hitch my head toward the pie case. "Have a look around."

Maybe if I let her see everything now, she'll get her fill of the "normal life" and hit the road sooner. Because I'm sure that's all this is for her. The rich and famous star is stooping down from her stage to *ooh* and *ahh* over our quaint little lives and then she'll take some stories of our Mayberry-type town on the road with her to tell her friends. This town is just a layover for her type. Believe me.

I don't know if Amelia is smiling or frowning as she looks over every nook and cranny of my pie shop because I go into the back kitchen and clean up for the day. When I hear the front door chime, I audibly sigh with relief knowing that the bell means she's gone.

"Shouldn't have let her stay," I grumble under my breath as I scrub a mixing bowl in the sink. "Not worth it." Scrub, scrub, scrub. "Such an idiot."

"You talk to your dishes more than people."

I jump a mile out of my skin at the sound of Amelia's voice behind me. I startle so much that I accidentally fling a big glob of soap bubbles right into my eye. "Shit. Dammit!" Now my eyes are burning like they were just doused with bear spray. I'm trying to use my elbow to wipe them out, but it's not working and my hands are still too soapy to use them.

"I'm so sorry! Let me help." Amelia tugs my shoulder turning me toward her, and through my burning, squinting eyes, I can see that she has wet a dish towel. If she thinks I'm going to let her doctor me up, she's got another thing coming. I don't want her anywhere near me.

"I'm fine." I wipe my eyes with my forearm again, but it's getting worse. Involuntary tears are starting to stream from my eyes. I'm not crying! Let the record show my eyes are doing this on their own!

I shove my soap-covered hands under the stream of water and frantically try to rinse them so I can wipe what I now think might be straight-up battery acid out of my eyes. Amelia tries to tug my shoulder again, but I don't budge.

"Oh, for pity's sake," she says like she's lived in this town for more than two days. She then slides herself up under my arm, right between me and the sink. My arms are wrapped around her now and our chests are touching. Hot electricity surges through my veins and I'm left stunned. It's been too long since I've had a woman in my arms and that's the only reason my body is reacting so intensely right now.

"Just let me get the bubbles out and then you can go back to ignoring me," she says, lifting up on her tiptoes to push the dish towel into each of my eyes, wiping the suds out. It helps. Or maybe I just don't feel the pain anymore because my brain is zeroing in on all the places our bodies are touching. It takes me all of two seconds to note that her eyes have flecks of green. That when her vanilla lotion mixes with her skin it smells like brown sugar. A light dusting of freckles sits on the bridge of her nose. Other than that subtle black line that extends over her lid and flicks out beside her thick eyelashes, I don't think she wears much makeup. If I had to wager, I'd say those raspberry-pink lips are all natural.

I swallow when her hand lowers and my eyes are no longer burning. She doesn't move. I don't move. There's this magnetic sort of pull between us that I'm not happy to realize exists. More than anything I'd love to be repulsed by her—but I'm not. And I sure as hell don't hate staring at those full lips, wondering if they taste just as tart and sweet as they look.

I should step back. Drop my arms. Take a deep breath and cool off. But I can't—my feet won't move and my eyes won't budge from her mouth.

And then, I don't know who moves first, but our lips collide. My hand shoots up to cradle the back of her neck, and her arms wind around my waist, pulling my body flush with hers. *Tender curves. Warm scent. Greedy hands.* Her delicious mouth chases away my logical thoughts until all that's left is desire. I step forward, pressing her back against the sink. We should stop. This goes against everything I've told her—but she makes a soft sound of encouragement that spikes a sharper need in me than I can contain.

Usually, I kiss like I have all day. A gentle build of sensuality that's meant for savoring. Amelia unlocks something in me, though. *Impatient. Needy.* Her tongue glides over mine and she's so damn sweet I feel like I'm burning alive.

I glide my hands to her waist and wrap my fingers around her hips, one second away from hoisting her up on the counter when the shop door chimes. The sound douses us in reality and all my rational thoughts return.

I drop my hands and step wayyy back, feeling strongly that

whatever that was—it was a mistake. Amelia shuffles to the farthest corner of the counter. We're not making eye contact anymore, and the atmosphere turns awkward.

"Amelia, I'm sorry. That was—"

"Not supposed to happen," she finishes my statement in a rush. "I know. And I'm sorry, too. Let's just move on and agree not to do it again."

We're prevented from talking anymore about this—which is probably for the best—when a familiar voice calls out to me from the front of the shop.

"Noah?"

Oh no. Not now. Not yet. I thought they'd get back in town tomorrow!

"He must be in the back."

"Hiding probably."

I look at Amelia and grimace. "I apologize in advance."

Amelia only has a second to look confused before all three of my younger sisters barge through the kitchen door, eyes frantic and on the hunt.

"There you are!" says Emily, the oldest of my sisters, who I can best describe as a bottle of hot sauce. "You have so much explaining to do!" She just turned twenty-nine last year and has my mom's green eyes. The same ones I have.

Next comes Madison, second to youngest, pushing through the swinging door and peering over Emily's shoulder. "We just got back into town and had to hear from Harriet that you had a random woman stay over at your house last night!" Madison looks the most like my dad. She has dark hair and dark eyes. She pretends to be as assertive and unflappable as Emily, but she doesn't fool me—she feels deeply.

And then next comes Annabell (aka Annie), the baby of the family at age twenty-six, the soft, quiet, wholesome one, and also the only one with naturally bright, nearly white, blond hair. We used to joke that she got it from the mailman since neither my mom or dad had blond hair. Even Emily and I have more of a golden, sandy color than true blond. "But then, we heard from Phil, who heard it from Gemma, who heard it from Mabel that it's not a random woman but Rae Rose! As in *the* Rae Rose!"

Madison comes up and pokes me in the chest. "What were you thinking, keeping something like this from us? Do you not love us?"

I grin lightly. "How was the flower show?"

"Don't try to distract us! Go ahead, Noah, tell us you hate us!" says Emily.

Annie puts her hands on her hips. "It's the only reason we can imagine you wouldn't call us immediately and tell us that pop royalty is staying in your house." She pauses a moment and her face turns slightly abashed. "And the flower show was nice. Thank you for asking."

Like I said, energy of the sun. These ladies talk at a clip that only the most seasoned of listeners can keep up with. I happen to be one of them.

I clear my throat and then glance over each of their heads toward the poor woman with wide eyes in the back corner of the room, looking like a trapped bunny. This is good, actually. Maybe it'll scare her out of town. I should have sicced my sisters on her sooner.

My sisters follow my gaze until their heads are swiveled toward Amelia.

"Ladies, this is Rae Rose." *Amelia,* my mind corrects. "Her car unfortunately broke down in my front yard a few nights ago and she's stranded in town until Tommy can fix it . . . or . . ." I let that *or* hang. *Or until she gets sick of us and calls a driver. Or until my agitation drives her out. Or until I wake up from this dream/nightmare.*

My sisters' mouths are wide open, catching flies, and they are speechless for probably the first time in their lives. Amelia smiles, and I'm unable to stop myself from noticing how it's completely

different from the one she gives me. With what can only be de-
scribed as grace, Amelia raises a hand in their direction and waves
good-naturedly. "Hi. So nice to meet you guys."

There's about two seconds of complete silence before my sisters' shock wears off and they pounce. It's a swirl of peppy southern
voices bombarding Amelia with question after question. Fortu-
nately for Amelia, there's only three people in this town who are
genuine fans of hers. Unfortunately for Amelia, they're all currently in the kitchen with her.

The conversation goes like this but pretty much all at once.

EMILY: You're stuck at Noah's house? He doesn't even have Wi-
    Fi, you know?
MADISON: Noah is boring. Come out with us tonight!
ANNIE: We're going to Hank's if you want to come?
EMILY: Hank's is a local bar where we all go and drink on Friday
    nights.
MADISON: We can pick you up!
ANNIE: We'll make sure no one annoys you while you're there.
EMILY: You'll love it, I promise.

I fully expect Amelia to shove them out of the way and take off
running for the hills. There's no way she even comprehended all
those words pelted at her at once. But of course, I'm wrong again
and Amelia is apparently the one woman in the entire world who
can speak Excited Walker Women.

Her bright smile stretches across her mouth, and honestly, I've
never seen someone look happier. *Or prettier,* my mind adds again
because it's a little jackass. "Umm—Hank's, I'd love to go with you
guys. That is if . . ." Her eyes slip to me and her smile falters a fraction. "If Noah's okay with it."

I'm not given a chance to respond before Emily steps between
us and says, "Why the hell do you need his permission? Last I

checked he doesn't own the place. Well, he does own *this* place, but he doesn't own Hank's. So will you come with us?"

How has this woman infiltrated my life so quickly? I think tornadoes have blown through this town slower. And probably with less damage than she's likely to inflict.

Chapter 10

Amelia

t should feel weird staying at Noah's house. Why doesn't it feel weird? I haven't even felt this comfortable in lavish hotel rooms with my favorite snacks overflowing from the minibar and a security guard parked outside my door. Something about Noah's place feels homey. I glance around the room I'm staying in and realize it's because everything in his house seems to have a purpose—a history—or a sentiment behind it. Where he has a patchwork quilt that was probably made by a grandmother or an aunt, I have an expensive duvet cover, selected by my interior designer. And *this* is what my house in Nashville is missing. It's filled with stuff, not memories.

When did that happen? Sometimes I feel like the day I accepted the new title of Rae Rose, a big eraser zipped off behind me and wiped out my life before it. My heart aches thinking of those quiet evenings with my mom, huddled around the kitchen table painting our nails and eating popcorn. I never knew my dad, because when my parents got pregnant with me in their last year of college, he didn't want anything to do with a family. He made it clear she'd be on her own if she wanted to keep me. My mom said she'd always liked the idea of being a young mom and starting a family at an early age. She didn't see why we had to be any less of a family without my dad—so the decision was easy for her.

And she was right, I never felt like our household was lacking. I mean, things were lean, and she had to work a lot as a single mom, but we were happy. And our once-a-year epic road trips to the beach where we rented a soggy hotel room with sand in the carpet because we couldn't afford anything else are still some of my greatest memories. My mom was all the family I needed. My *best* friend. And then my first single went number one in the charts and that's when everything changed.

When things took off and all that money started rolling in, it slowly ripped us apart. We hopped in a moving truck and headed from Arizona to a big house in L.A. the first chance we got. It felt cavernous at first. The new furniture didn't have my butt's imprint and I couldn't get comfy anywhere. My mom loved it, though, and seeing her happy made me happy. She's always been the life of the party, and she didn't have any trouble making new friends in the celebrity circles I was inducted into. At first, we stayed close—and then after the first few years, she wasn't around as much. She stood me up for dinner dates, claiming it must have totally slipped her mind because she never remembered scheduling anything when I'd call her after sitting alone at a table for an hour. But I know we did because I had Susan confirm them—and Susan is the most thorough person I know.

There were so many instances that began to pile up like that, not to mention her constantly begging Susan to transfer more money into her account. She is always trying to go behind my back to get what she wants, but Susan has always looped me in and I end up okaying whatever the request is. But see, I would love to give my mom anything and everything she wants—I just wish she still wanted me, too, and not just my money.

The last straw for me was on her forty-fifth birthday. I planned a surprise getaway for just the two of us. I had it set up for weeks. Susan helped me book the plane and a villa in Cabo for five days. But when Susan sent the car to pick her up and meet me at the airport for the big surprise just like we planned, my mom said she wouldn't be coming. She already had plans with friends and didn't want to cancel.

And that was the day I stopped trying to have a relationship.

Despite feeling used, I continue to float her financially because it's the only connection we still have. And as it turns out, it's really hard to tell a parent no when they keep asking for more. Or maybe it's that I'm addicted to that hit of self-worth I get when she finally needs me. Now we mainly interact through Susan, which has been helpful for me to get some space from my mom, but every now and then I'll still get a text directly from her asking for something. It hurts, and usually I try to keep my responses pretty short.

Anyway, I like that Noah's house is small. The decor is pretty minimal, but it's clear that he lives in it and he isn't a neat freak. Other than my trip to The Pie Shop, I haven't left this house over the last few days, so I've become well acquainted with it. I feel like I've gotten to know Noah a little bit just through the purposeful items he has around it. A simple bouquet of gorgeous flowers sits in a milk-glass vase on the breakfast table. I've never known a man to keep flowers in his home before and that feels important to note. He has green mouthwash the same color as his eyes. It sits on the bathroom counter beside his toothbrush (nonelectric) and toothpaste (Crest original). I haven't gotten a peek at his bedroom yet because he still keeps that door shut as if he's afraid I'll rush in like an un-potty-trained puppy and pee all over his bedding.

I love it.

I love that he doesn't lay a red carpet down for me to walk over. He hasn't tried to entertain me once since I've been here—in fact, he's stayed away for the most part. I think it's because of the accidental kiss (ugh, that incredible kiss!) today, but I don't mind because he just lets me live like I'm normal. I can't explain how wonderful that is. Even the way his sisters treated me was different from most of the public. Yeah, they were intense, but the good kind. And I'll tell you how I could trust them right away. They invited me to go out with them tonight instead of asking a single thing of me. No selfies. No autographs. They just wanted me to come out with them tonight because they thought it would be fun. And after three days of hibernating inside this house and worrying myself sick with what I'm going to do about my life, *fun* sounds incredible.

Speaking of incredible, Noah's kiss pings back into my consciousness as it has about every twenty seconds over the last few hours. How could one kiss with a virtual stranger have hooked me this much? I have to block it out of my mind, though, because it absolutely cannot happen again.

But now the question is, what does one wear to a place called Hank's? Or was it Honk's? Tonk's? I think it was Hank's.

"Noah," I yell through my bedroom door. "What do I wear to Honk's?" I purposely use the wrong name because it has become one of my greatest pleasures to annoy Noah. I've made it a game. How long does it take to make the grumpy pie shop owner's head pop off? I should keep a log in my phone. Download a sophisticated app to track the differences in his facial expressions.

I know he's out there because I heard him go into the bathroom and turn on the shower when he got home from work. He was in there for twenty minutes. Twenty torturous minutes of me pacing this room like a caged tiger trying not to imagine what that man would look like in the nude. Oh geez. He would be a sight to behold, I just know it. A sight I will *never* behold because that's not what this trip is about for me. And frankly, it's really creepy that I'm imagining it anyway. *I'm ashamed of you, inner sexual goddess. Control yourself.*

A grunt sounds from somewhere outside my door. "Hank's. It's called Hank's. If you're gonna go, get it right."

"Okay, well, what do I wear to Hank's then?"

"Whatever the hell you want."

Not sure how it's possible, but Noah's gotten more grumpy since earlier today (probably having something to do with the incident we shall not mention). And each time he's looked at me after the bubble fiasco, a stern line is etched between his brows. I get it, we mixed personal spaces and he's upset about it. It won't happen again.

But here's the thing, I've dated three guys in my adult years: an actor, a model, and then my last boyfriend was a singer, too. They were all men that magazines and tabloids drooled over, saying they were some of the sexiest and most successful men out there. And yet, I never once experienced as strong of an attraction to any of them like I have to Noah Walker.

I can't let myself be attracted to him, though. I'll be leaving on Monday and Susan has forbidden me from dating a normal guy when I've considered it in the past. She says our worlds are too far apart. Unfortunately, I'm also forbidden from cupcakes, any sort of exhilarating activity, or blinking without Susan's consent.

Ugh. Thoughts of my normal life are bringing me down. Time to annoy Noah for sport.

"A cocktail dress it is, then! I have one that's covered in sequins and has a slit up the thigh . . . I mean, I already wore it to Harry Styles's birthday party, but I'm sure no one around here will mind if I'm seen in it twice. Plus, Harry loved it, so . . ."

I bite my bottom lip and wait.

Sure enough, I hear the heavy footfalls of Noah treading closer toward my door. "Don't wear that. You'll look ridiculous all dressed up." No one can accuse this man of not being honest. He's all blunt and zero sugar. *He's fantastic.*

PS. I didn't even pack a cocktail dress because I'm not an idiot despite what he seems to think about me.

"Just . . . wear jeans and a T-shirt," says Noah, sounding like he's being slowly tortured by having to act as my fashion consultant. Or maybe it's just having to talk to me in general? I don't know. But *boy oh boy* am I loving not having to act like a professional little ball of sunshine at all times. He thinks he's scaring me off with his snippy attitude. Little does he know, I'm thriving off his surliness.

I open the door, revealing the outfit I was already wearing: jeans and a T-shirt and a kiss-my-ass grin. "Like this?"

He eyes me head to toe, scowls, and turns to walk to his door. He only opens it a crack and practically wiggles inside before closing it quickly behind him.

"Careful!" I yell at his closed door. "You almost left enough room for me to dart in under your feet that time!"

He growls and I smile. Two points for Amelia. Zero for Grumpy Pie Shop Owner.

Chapter 11

Amelia

Noah's sisters are unlike anyone I've ever known before. They pulled up outside his house and then honked their horn for me to come out. Literally. They honked. When I stepped outside, they catcalled and yelled, "Woo hoo, princess of pop coming out to Hank's! Hop in the back with Annie!"

And by the back, they meant the back of their truck bed. If Susan could see me now, bobbing around on this pitch-black back road in the bed of a truck with no seat belt, looking like a popcorn kernel in a pan, she'd die. She'd just keel over on the spot. It's going to be a rowdy night, I can feel it in my bones. My jostling, jerking bones.

Unfortunately, all this bumping around is starting to trigger a headache. It might be nothing, or it might turn into one of those whopping migraines I've started getting more frequently. My doctor says they are stress induced and that I should take more breaks. But I haven't had time for breaks, so that's why I have prescription-strength ibuprofen in my purse, which I fish around for right now.

Finding the little orange container, I discreetly unscrew the lid and take out a pill, using my spit to swallow it before Annie sees. I don't know why I feel silly about this. It's only a strong ibuprofen, but people tend to get weird ideas in their heads when they see celebrities popping random pills, and I don't feel like launching into my whole medical history with the ladies right now. I toss the container back in my purse just as we pull up to the bar and Madison sticks her head out the passenger-side window, shouting, "Look out, y'all! Teachers gone wild!"

"You guys are teachers?" I ask Annie, gripping the side of the truck as Emily turns sharply into the gravel parking lot.

Annie smiles. "They are, but they're on summer break right now. I own a flower shop right next door to Noah's pie shop."

Flower shop. Suddenly, the bouquet on his table makes more sense. "So you must be the one putting fresh flowers in Noah's house?"

Annie laughs and shakes her head. "Sort of. Noah comes by the shop almost every day and buys a bouquet from me to take home. I think he's secretly worried I'll go out of business if he doesn't."

Uh-uh. Don't you do it, heart. I feel you trying to squeeze, but I won't allow it. So what? He's a good brother.

Big. Freaking. Deal.

Emily and Madison unload from the truck and come around to let the gate down for me and Annie to hop out. When I look at Hank's, my stomach jumps into my throat. It's a smallish bar, in basically the middle of nowhere, surrounded by a gravel lot and stuffed to the brim. A neon sign flickers above the bar confirming that we're indeed at *Hank's Bar,* and there are so many trucks here that the parking lot is packed in like Tetris. Those who got here first won't be able to leave anytime soon. Through the window, I can see that the bar is dimly lit, but there's so many people in there I know it's got to be breaking a fire code.

"Everything okay?" Annie says, stopping beside me and reading my nervous expression.

I swallow and gesture weakly toward the bar. "It just looks . . . busy."

Emily comes up on the other side of me. "'Cause it is. Everyone . . . and I do mean everyone, comes to Hank's on Friday nights. It's the only fun thing to do in the whole town so no one misses it."

Oh super. Everyone stuffed into one building and me without any sort of real protection. What are the odds anyone in there is obsessed with pop music? Suddenly, I wish Noah were here, which is such a ridiculous thought in and of itself. I've only known him for a few days, but somehow I know he'd make sure I was safe.

"There's not like a . . . back entrance we could go in, is there? And do you have a hat in your truck? I didn't realize this was going to be so crowded or I would have—"

Madison starts pushing me from behind. My body is being propelled toward the front door, and I look like a cat approaching water. She laughs. "This town is harmless. Trust us. We'll take care of you. And Emily runs the roost around here, so they'll listen to her."

Mm-hmm. Then why do I feel like I'm being offered up as a sacrifice to the neon beast?

Annie opens the door for all of us and gives me an empathetic smile when the country music spills out. It's loud and rowdy in there. Thrilling and terrifying. "Let Emily go first."

I hang back as instructed and practice a few breathing techniques I use before going on stage when my nerves get the best of me. I don't get through my second breath before Madison grabs my hand and yanks me inside with her.

I swear the next thirty seconds happen like this:

We walk through the door.

All heads swivel in our direction.

The group of people line-dancing in the middle of the room come to a swift halt.

The music cuts off.

Everything goes so silent we can hear the click of the door shutting behind us.

And everyone stares at me.

As it turns out . . . these people are familiar with pop music. Or at least just celebrities. Because they are definitely looking at me like I am one. The heavy scent of beer and sweat, mixed with the way my heart is ramming against my chest, makes me feel like I'm going to be sick. This was a bad idea. Leaving Nashville was a bad idea. Why in the hell did I think I could just slip into a town undetected and spend time here in blissful solitude? Now they all know I'm here and my peace has run out. Forget Monday, I'll have to leave tonight because any second now they'll lift their phones, snap photos, and upload them to all the social media platforms. Paparazzi will be here within the hour. It's how it always goes.

I turn to rush out the door, but Madison catches my forearm. "Hang on. It's okay."

She nods at Emily and I watch in amazement as the woman hops up on the top of the bar and cups her hands around her mouth. "All right, listen up, all you fellow hillbillies! I've got my friend Rae Rose here and she's looking for a good time and zero bother. So act like your mama taught you some manners and let's treat her with respect! Also, she's flying under the radar in our town for the next little bit, so do her a favor and pretend you never saw her. Everybody got it?"

There's a hearty roar from the crowd and affirming nods, beers raised, and wide smiles.

"Good! Now someone get me a drink!"

Emily is a goddess. That's all I can say, because everyone does exactly as she says. The music cranks up, laughter starts again, everyone turns back to what they were doing before we walked in, the man behind the bar helps Emily down and then puts a beer in her hand.

And that's that.

No one treats me differently. No one stares. No one asks for an autograph. For the next half hour, the Walker sisters and I laugh and drink and talk. I honestly forget that I'm considered important everywhere else in the world. Yeah, they want to know what it was like dating my ex, Tyler Newport (I imagine a lot like dating that vain Disney queen who constantly looked in the mirror and asked who was the fairest of them all). They also want to know my favorite thing about being a singer (an issue I sidestep because my career crisis has spiked to epic heights and I completely blank on any good aspects of it), but those questions end pretty quickly, and then our conversation moves along.

"I have to admit," I tell the ladies after finishing my first beer and feel a little more loose. "I was worried everyone was going to freak out when they saw me walk in. I've been in the middle of fan mobs before and I was terrified it was about to happen again."

Madison laughs, because to any outsider, a "fan mob" sounds like a whimsical scene in a Disney movie. In reality, it's painful, scary, and such an invasion of emotional and physical security that it's difficult to bounce back. But most people have no idea about any of that so I forgive her the chuckle.

"If they looked interested, it's only because this town's been looking for something to talk about ever since Kacey got knocked up and everyone was sure it was Zac's but the baby ended up just being her husband, Rhett's, after all. They've been bored ever since."

Emily leans over the table a little farther. "But seriously . . . I was sure it was Zac's. Especially after the way he—"

"Looked at her at church that Sunday! Yes!" Madison slaps the table making their beers slosh. Annie only contributes to the conversation with a quiet smile and chuckle. "But anyway, we're all good people around here. We just needed to set them straight from the start. They won't bother you now, and you don't have to worry about anyone leaking your visit on social media, because in case you haven't noticed, there's no cell service around here. Our brother doesn't even own a cell phone."

I'm not surprised that he doesn't own a cell phone. I am, however, curious at the way my skin prickles from only that tiny mention of Noah. How my mind flashes a montage of his hands on my body, his moody mouth eagerly exploring mine. The zing of rightness that flew through me when our skin touched.

"So," says Emily, leaning onto her forearms. "Where were you headed before you broke down in Noah's front yard?"

I take a sip of my second beer and then lick my lips. "Uh . . . here actually."

All three ladies frown.

"Here?" asks Madison. "As in Rome, Kentucky? You came *here* on purpose? Why the hell would you do that? I've been trying to get out of this town for years now, but Annie and Em won't let me."

"You're damn straight," says Emily before Annie gives them both a frustrated look and whips out a little pocket notebook, adding a tally to some sort of chart. "Sorry, Annie. I mean, you're *darn* straight," Emily amends, adding a jaunty little arm gesture to the word *darn*.

Annie sees my confused look as I peer at the notebook. The names Emily, Madison, Annie, and Noah are all written and have marks beside them. Actually, Annie doesn't have any marks, and Noah has at least twice as many as the sisters do. This makes me smile for inexplicable reasons.

"I'm trying to break them of swearing so much. When anyone reaches twenty tallies, they have to pay twenty bucks to the cussing jar," says Annie, closing the notebook and setting it aside.

I laugh lightly. "And why's that?"

"Because she's a wholesome, sweet, little baby angel," says Emily with a taunting smile.

Annie sticks her tongue out at Emily. "At least one of us should make it through the pearly gates and represent for the Walkers."

Madison grins sardonically. "Pearly gates? I'm just trying to make it past the city limits of the fu—orking town."

Annie smiles. "Nice catch."

Madison tips her beer. "Only because I love you and also because if I get one more tally I have to pay up. Now, will you return the love and ever let me leave Rome?"

In unison, Emily and Annie both say, "Nope."

Emily, who I get the feeling is the mother hen of the sisters, adds with a final note to her voice, "Noah's back, and we're family. This is where our roots are, and where we belong."

Noah's back? I really want to ask Emily where Noah came back from, but I don't get the chance.

Madison sighs and so much is conveyed in that one expelled breath. Longing, defeat, resolve. A whole slew of emotions I'll probably never learn the origin of because I'll be gone by Monday. She turns her eyes back to me. "Sorry, we get sidetracked easily. We were talking about why you came to visit."

Now that I've spent a few days in the town, I can understand her astonishment. It's not exactly a regular tourist destination. I take another drink of my beer to buy me some time to formulate an answer. But then the room wobbles a little, and my tongue feels heavy, but loose at the same time. Momentarily distracted by this sudden sensation, I blurt the truth. "I searched Google Maps for the nearest city called Rome, because that's where Audrey goes in *Roman Holiday*."

I'm met with blank stares, and I wonder what part of that statement is shocking them more. I decide to start with the least odd part of it. "You know . . . the classic movie?" More blank stares. "Oh, I'm sure you know it. It stars Audrey Hepburn and Gregory Peck. Audrey plays Princess Ann who runs away from her life of royalty one night, and . . . you have no idea what I'm talking about?"

All three women shake their heads. Emily speaks first. "I actually don't think we've ever seen an Audrey Hepburn film. Are they good?"

My mouth gapes open. I am epically distraught. How can they not know who Audrey Hepburn is? "What?! How have you gone through your whole lives without experiencing Audrey? She is all things grace, and precociousness. Beauty yet oddity." I shake my head, bemused. "She's . . . wonderful." *And my best friend,* I don't say because I have no desire for them to learn just how freakish I really am. Or lonely. Because only a friendless person would claim a dead movie star as their BFF.

Madison smiles. "Sounds like Annie." She pauses dramatically, cutting her eyes mischievously to her sister. "The beauty yet oddity part at least." It's clear this is affectionate banter by the singsongy way she says it.

But still, Emily nudges Madison's shoulder playfully. "Okay, enough picking on the baby for tonight. You know she's too sweet to fight back."

"Hey, you don't have to defend me. I can hold my own," Annie says, pulling herself up two more inches in height. Both her sisters eye her patiently and then wait with hands primly folded below their chins. "Maddie is so . . . well, she's just . . ." Annie grunts an annoyed sound, rolls her eyes, and settles back against her seat when she can't think of anything mean to say. "Clearly Madison is the grace and precociousness part, and you also look really pretty in that shirt tonight, Maddie."

The sisters erupt in laughter and Emily affectionately kisses Annie's cheek, who looks absolutely annoyed by her lack of zingers. "Don't ever change, Annie."

Sitting here watching these sisters banter, fuss, and love one another so well, I feel the lack of it in my own life so keenly. I'm desperate for this. To know and be known. I want to burrow my way into their little family and beg for them to make fun of me like they do each other. I want them to skewer me with the obvious truths about myself that I don't see. I want to laugh and roll my eyes and be one of them. Have what they have. But to do that, I have to be honest and open about myself. I would have to let them in, let them see that I'm a little weird and dysfunctional, and I'm not sure it would even be worth it since I'm leaving Monday.

Instead, I smile softly and sip my beer. *Polite, polite, polite.*

A few minutes later and after we've all ordered another round of beers, Madison looks over my shoulder and her smile grows even wider. "Oh, look, Noah's here with James!"

An avalanche of butterflies tumbles into my stomach and the sensation is so overwhelming I nearly fall out of my chair. Somehow, I can feel Noah's eyes on the back of my neck. My skin is warm. The hairs on my arms rise. My fingers are fidgety. I bounce my knee, but none of this works to erase the way I can sense him approaching. I raise my beer to my lips and chug half of it. I have no choice. I'm at the mercy of my frazzled nerves now.

Unfortunately, the room that only wobbled a little bit ago now feels like a spinning teacup ride. How am I drunk already? That doesn't seem right for finishing only one and a half beers. Tipsy, sure. But this sensation is different. Alarming.

Noah and the guy they said is named James make their way over. Noah stays on the opposite side of the table, because as usual, he's afraid I'll bite if he gets too close. His friend, however, introduces himself with a welcoming, open smile.

He extends his tan, calloused hand. I would be lying if I said I didn't immediately notice how attractive he and his dark brown hair and pearly white teeth are. "Hi, I'm James. And I'll save both of us any awkwardness by admitting right away that I know exactly who you are." He tacks on a good-natured smile that puts me at ease. "It's such an honor to meet you, Rae." Well, I would be at ease if I didn't feel so damn drunk.

I glance suspiciously at the remaining beer in my glass as nausea and exhaustion jump on top of me. I need to prop my eyelids up just to keep them open.

"It's nice to meet you, too, Rae," I say, feeling like my words are thick molasses coming out of my mouth.

James's face crinkles with a quizzical smile. *Oh, wait.* Did I accidentally call him by my name? I gently shake my head and laugh. "Sorry. I mean *James.* Nice to meet you, *James.*" I hold up my beer feeling like it weighs a hundred pounds. "Too much of this, I guess."

Annie frowns. "You only had one and a half beers and were fine a second ago."

Right.

It's weird I'm acting this way.

I look up and lock eyes with Noah. He looks stormier than a hurricane. His thick golden brows are heavily pulled together and his jaw is set. He's not happy. Well, is he ever happy when I'm around? His gaze feels so intense I have to look away, but from the corner of my eye, I can see that he's still watching me closely. Chill bumps fly down my arms and I need for him to stop staring at me like that before he burns a hole through my face.

Also, whew buddy, I feel like I've been hit by a truck all of a sudden and I need sleep more than anything. I'd like to lay my head down right on this table and—

Oh shit.

That's when I realize what I've done.

"Oh! This is my favorite song!" yells Madison. She sounds so far away even though she's right in front of me at the table. "Come on, let's go dance!"

The sisters pop up and head toward the dance floor with James, but Emily hangs back. "You okay, Rae?"

I try to give her a normal smile. I'm not even sure my lips move. "Sh'yeah! Be there in a second!"

She chuckles, but I still hear the worry in her tone. Mother hen is on to me. "Okay. Noah, keep an eye on her, will you? I think she's a lightweight."

Now I'm alone at the table and I feel an equal amount of relief in knowing someone hasn't slipped something in my drink, and dread for what I've done. The world is swirling around me, nausea churning in my stomach, and the desire to close my eyes is so overwhelming I can hardly fight it. But even worse, I'm completely vulnerable right now.

Trying to keep my eyes from crossing, I swivel toward my purse hanging on the back of the chair. I dip my hand inside and pull out my prescription migraine medication. It takes some serious effort to get my eyes to focus, but I'm finally able to determine that it's not the same circle-shaped pill I took earlier. Which means . . . *oh, no, no, no.*

I take out the other prescription bottle in my bag. It's a heavy-duty, knock-you-out-until-next-summer kind of sleeping pill that I only use when I'm traveling on tour and have serious jet lag in other countries. And yep, it's the pill I took earlier. I don't normally keep them in my purse, but I forgot that before I left town, I swiped everything from my bathroom counter into the bag I'm carrying now. I only take this medication when it's a dire situation and I absolutely can't sleep, because it knocks me out with the same power as a horse tranquilizer. Oh, and one more alarming realization, it's a major no-no to mix sleeping pills with alcohol.

"Did you take one of those?" Noah's voice rumbles right above me. I forgot he was here. Even my name is difficult to remember. Now he's squatting down beside me and gently taking the pill container from my hand. His fingers brush against mine and I shiver. He's so warm. And even his hand looks strong. Making pies really does it for this man.

I swallow. "Yeah. Accccccidentally." My words slur together as if I've had five drinks already. I feel absolutely intoxicated. And scared. And alone. "I thhhought I was taking my other mmmedication. Guess not."

"How many did you take?" His voice feels like a microfiber blanket draped over my body.

"Only one." I can't physically stay awake any longer. I feel the claws of sleep sinking into me and pulling me under.

Laying my head on the table, I crack my eyes open one more time to look at Noah. He's fuzzy and swimming in my vision but he doesn't look stormy anymore. He's got that wrinkle between his eyes. Worried Noah is cute. Worried Noah looks nice. Cozy.

And that's the last thought I have before everything goes black.

Chapter 12

Noah

Well, that escalated quickly.

Guess who's in my truck, loopy out of her mind and fresh from a checkup at our local doctor's office where I begged Dr. Macky to come in after hours? I'll give you two hints: (1) She promised I'd not even notice her around; and (2) She's been nothing but noticeably *around* since I met her.

This woman has only been in my life for a few days and she's going to be the end of me. The moment I saw her tonight I could tell something wasn't right. Her eyes were glassy and her normal sparkle was absent. She looked horrified and out of it all at once. For a split second, I thought someone slipped something in her drink and I was about to flip every table in that bar until I figured out who did it.

But then I saw her pull those pills out of her purse and stare at them and it all clicked. The relief I felt that she wasn't maliciously drugged was immediately replaced with terror. I checked the pill container only to find that she accidentally took a sleeping pill. I'm not a doctor, but even I know that mixing sleeping pills and alcohol is not a good thing.

Annie came back over to the table when she realized something was up, and I had her help me discreetly get Amelia to the truck. Luckily, everyone in the bar was so rowdy and dancing that no one seemed to notice us. I got her into the front seat of my truck and told Annie what was going on.

I sat with Amelia in the truck while Annie went inside and used the bar's phone to call Dr. Macky. I've never driven so fast in my life, and I've never been more thankful to show up late to the bar before. If I had been there an hour earlier, I would have been blocked in just like my sister's truck.

Anyway, we made it to the clinic and Dr. Macky did a quick evaluation of Amelia. Her blood pressure was fine, her oxygen levels were fine, and although she's loopy as shit, the doctor said she'll be okay and just needs to sleep it off.

Right now, she's passed out across the bench seat of my truck, and I'm standing outside the door with my sister trying to find a way out of this responsibility I didn't want in the first place. But even as I think it, I know there's no way I'm leaving her like this tonight. I want to, but I just can't.

Annie looks toward the open door of my truck where we can see Amelia with her dark hair fanned out around her and her cheek squished against the leather, mouth breathing to her fullest. "She kinda reminds me of a puppy. All lost and sad. Please will you keep her, Noah? Pleeeeease," says Annie, putting her hands under her chin and blinking a hundred times.

See, the thing about Annie is, she's quiet until she's alone with me. And then she has no problem speaking her mind.

I roll my eyes, not allowing myself to ask why my sister thinks Amelia is sad. I've gotten that feeling, too, but . . . it doesn't matter. I don't need to know. In fact, the less I get to know that woman, the better.

"No. And all I'm saying is you and the other girls shouldn't get attached. You can't trust a woman like her." I give her a stern look to drive the point home. I can already tell each of my sisters are falling in love with Amelia and there's absolutely no good that will come from it. We're no one to her. She won't even look over her shoulder when she leaves town on Monday, and they'd do well to remember it.

"Oooh, stern look. You must really mean business," she says with a deadpan delivery. "You know what? I bet she's not actually a pop star but an undercover agent, sent to this small town to scout out a base for her new assassin agency." She's nodding thoughtfully. "You're right, we better keep our distance."

I narrow my eyes at her and try not to smile. "Smart-ass. I'm just trying to keep y'all from getting your hearts broken when your new friend leaves you high and dry."

"Keep us from getting our hearts broken, or keep you from getting your heart broken? *Again.*"

It's annoying having siblings who know me so well. I refuse to play right into her hand, though. "Knock it off, and hop in the back."

"Fine. Are we going back to your place?"

"Nope," I say, closing the tailgate behind Annie after she's settled. "She's gonna take your bed tonight."

Annie gives me a horrified look. "Why? You're the one with the spare bed!"

"I may not like her, but that doesn't mean I don't want her to feel safe when she wakes up in the morning feeling like crap. She's sleeping it off at your place tonight where she'll be surrounded by women and not in a house alone with a man she hardly knows."

I can tell she wants to grumble but has too much of a soft heart to decline. "All right, I see your point. She can have my bed. I forget other people don't know you're a saintly old man like we do."

"Not so saintly according to your cussing chart."

She points a finger at me. "Which, by the way, you owe the jar forty dollars."

I groan. I've paid more money into that damn jar than my retirement fund. If Annie didn't donate it all to charity at the end of the year, I'd have stopped indulging her a long time ago. But for whatever reason, us not cussing is important to her, and so . . . I guess it's important to me, too. At least when she's around.

Just as I'm about to slide into the driver's seat, Annie's head pops around the truck. "And Noah? Grandma would've liked Rae, you know? No matter what you think, she's got a kind heart. I can tell." She smiles like she's reliving a memory. "Grandma always wanted someone like her for you."

I stare at Annie, trying to mentally bounce her words back to her instead of soaking them in. And then point to the bed of the truck. "Sit back. We're leaving now." She gives me a quietly stern look until I tack on, *"Please."*

Does everyone in this town know my weak spot? It's like I have a red-painted target on my chest. They know exactly the person to mention to rip my heart in two.

pull up the gravel drive to the house and cut the engine. Amelia's head is only a few inches from my lap and some of her hair is draped across my thigh. She whimpers when I poke her shoulder. "Hey, drunky. Wake up."

"Imnotdrunk," she says, cracking her blue eyes open to peer up at me. Shoot, Annie was right. She looks just like a lost puppy right now. I don't love the protective instincts it's triggering in me.

"You might as well be," I say, but she's already asleep again. That pill and alcohol combo steamrolled her.

I get out and walk around my truck to open her door. Annie hops out of the bed of the truck and stands beside me. "Should we just tug one of her arms until she's sitting up?"

"Seems like our best bet."

Annie and I work together to get Amelia sitting upright. Her head lolls back against the glass and her mouth falls open—eyes closed. If we stuck a pair of sunglasses on her, people might think we're reenacting *Weekend at Bernie's*.

"All right, upsy daisy," I tell Amelia, draping one of her arms around my neck and hauling her out. She gives zero effort—limply hanging off my side and forcing me to hold on so tight I'm afraid I'm going to bruise her. Annie goes to Amelia's other side, but my sister is only five feet tall (literally, not an inch more) and isn't much help.

"Screw it," I say, turning so I can scoop Amelia up in my arms and carry her inside. This is much easier somehow, especially after Annie resituates Amelia's face so her head is on my shoulder and she's no longer hanging off me like a dead person. Geez, what a weird couple of days.

Annie runs ahead of me to unlock the door and turn on the lights as I carry Amelia up the front steps, remaining mentally detached from how she feels in my arms and how sweet her hair smells or how her breath feels against my neck. I get her inside and set her down on Annie's bed, and no sooner than her body hits the mattress does she whimper and clutch her stomach, curling into a little ball with her eyes closed. Is she nauseated? Dr. Macky said it could be a side effect. Again that instinct to protect and soothe startles me.

I look down at Amelia with Annie at my side. We're both a little unsure of what to do now. Actually, I know what I should do. It's time to hand this situation over to my sister. She can take care of Amelia since she's the one who invited her out in the first place. The pop star is her problem now, not mine. I did my duty by getting her seen by a doctor, and taking her somewhere safe—now I can go home and sleep easy.

I should go.

She'll be fine.

Turns out, I'm not going anywhere except to the corner of the room to push Annie's reading chair closer to the bed. Next, I go to the bathroom and wet a washrag with cool water so I can dab it across Amelia's forehead to help with her nausea. Annie watches all this with an overly indulgent smirk.

"What?" I ask her, even though the clip in my voice is clear and I don't want to hear her thoughts.

She presses her lips together and shakes her head, amusement sparkling in her eyes. "Nothing. Nothing at all. I'm going to go get a shower really quick and try to wash off the smell of Hank's. Can you dab my head with cool water, too, when I get out? Looks really nice."

"Shut up," I say, pretending to try to kick her as she skirts out of the room chuckling. I like when Annie shows fire, though. I wish she'd do it more around other people.

I continue to run the washcloth across Amelia's forehead, not sure if this is even doing much, but I remember seeing someone do it in a movie once. Come to think of it, it might have been one of those old-timey movies one of my sisters made me watch. And I can't remember if the heroine was actually sick or just had a fever. Whatever, at least this makes me feel like I'm doing something.

Not even sure why I want to be doing something to help Amelia.

And then she groans again and her eyes crack open. She squints at me almost like she's trying to decide if I'm real or a dream.

"Feeling okay?" I ask quietly.

"Noah?"

"Yeah, it's me."

Amelia breathes in deeply and tries to keep her eyes open, but can't. "Am . . . I safe?" she asks in a sleepy slur that twists my heart.

"Yes. You're at my sisters' house. They're going to keep an eye on you tonight."

She lets out a sound between misery and embarrassment, never opening her eyes. "Noooo. They were gonna be my friends. Now they won't want to be."

I frown and use my knuckles to wipe away the tear that has just streaked down the side of her cheek. "Why do you think that?"

"High maintenance." She pauses and I think maybe she fell back to sleep before she speaks again. "People only like me when I'm easy." With her eyes closed, her brows squeeze together and another tear drops down the side of her face. "Must always be polite."

I shouldn't, but I use my hand to smooth away another one of her tears, because I can't stand seeing them streaking down her face. Amelia catches my hand with hers and squeezes it. I know she's loopy out of her mind—evidence that her eyes are still shut and her words are practically one long slur. But there's a raw honesty that cuts painfully through the triple-reinforced walls of my heart.

"But not with you." She nuzzles her cheek against the back of my hand. "I don't have to be polite with you because you don't like me anyways."

"That's not true," I say, more to myself than her.

She hums. "My mom used to be my best friend—but she only likes me for my money now. Susan only cares about my success. And the world only wants me for Rae Rose." There's a long pause as she sighs deeply. "I'm drowning and no one sees me."

I'm speechless as Amelia continues pressing my hand against her soft face like it's the most precious thing she's ever held. It's agony and heaven to have her confide in me. To feel her holding me like she needs me. I shut my eyes against her words, because, *dammit,* I don't want to feel anything toward her, but I do. She's hurting and lonely and for some reason, I care deeply that she not feel either of those things. I've worked very hard ever since Merritt to not let another woman have so much power over my heart again, and of course, this woman—the most unavailable one—is who squeezed her way through the bars and is making me *feel* things.

It's not infatuation. Not even lust. It's the worst of all the feelings . . . care.

Care is reckless because it doesn't come with the seat belt that selfishness offers. Care has so much to lose, and almost always ends in heartbreak. Unfortunately, I'm powerless against keeping my heart in check around her anymore. There's a very short list of people in my life that I allow myself to truly care for, and it looks like I just added another name to it.

I push Amelia's hair back from her ear so I know she can hear me. "I see you."

Chapter 13

Amelia

'm in a different house—one that is definitely not Noah's. The last thing I remember, I was at Hank's Bar. And now I'm waking up in a strange bed. Panic is hovering on the seams of my consciousness until I realize this room is incredibly feminine. A pretty floral comforter is lying on top of me, the color palette olive, dusty pink, and cream. There are succulents on the windowsill and a giant bouquet of flowers beside the bed. And I'm still in my clothes.

The sound of whispering female voices (that are doing a very poor job of actually keeping their voices down) floats through the closed door, and now with a sigh of relief, I know where I am.

"Should we wake her up?"

"No. The doc said to let her sleep."

The doc?

It all suddenly comes back to me in broken fragments. Feeling weird and woozy at the bar. Realizing I took a sleeping pill and then drank alcohol. And then lots of memories featuring Noah's green eyes: beside me at the bar, looking down at me in his truck, in an exam room as a doctor pried my eyelids open and shined a light

into them. And then one more view of his startling green eyes staring at me in the dark—not worried, but something else . . .

I cringe, shutting my blurry eyes and groaning. I bet I made a
real ass out of myself last night. If he didn't hate me already, he
really does now. Maybe that's why I'm here instead of at his house.
He packed my bags and kicked me out. I wouldn't blame him if he
did.

"It's almost ten o'clock. Shouldn't we at least make sure she's
still alive in there?" That voice most definitely belongs to Madison.

"Fine, but just peek in to see if she's still among the living and
then we leave her be. Noah will murder us if he finds out we woke
her up." And that's Emily.

"I still can't believe he sat beside her bed all night and monitored her. Did you take a picture? I'm so mad I didn't—*Ow!*" says
Madison, with a loud yelp on the end.

"No, she didn't take a picture. How are you so rude, Maddie?"

"Me? Annie's the one who's always pinching me! Will you
quit it?"

"I prefer pinching to arguing," says Annie in a better whisper
than either of the other two sisters.

And, *wait wait wait.* Did they say Noah sat by my bed all night
and monitored me? My gaze slides beside the bed to an innocently
empty accent chair that is now pulsing with importance. It's angled
toward the bed. Noah sat in that chair all night and made sure I was
taken care of. *I'm here. You're safe,* I remember him saying.

The bedroom door opens a crack and I don't even bother pretending to be asleep. Three pairs of eyes blink at me, and I raise a
hand in a weak wave. "Hi. I'm alive and I heard all that."

They push the door open all the way and groan. "Sorry. We were
trying to be quiet," says Annie. She's wearing a pj set covered in
cartoon bananas.

Madison hops onto the bottom of the bed wearing a bright tie-
dyed hoodie, turquoise joggers, and glasses with bubblegum-pink

frames. She props herself up on her elbow and rests her head against her knuckles. "So . . . sleeping pills, huh?"

"Madison! Don't pry into her life, that's rude," Emily reprimands, flashing me an apologetic smile.

"No, it's okay. I thought I was taking my other prescription for a headache but I totally forgot that I had also stuffed my sleep aid in my purse earlier this week. I usually only take it when I'm visiting another country and have horrible jet lag." I shake my head. "I feel so bad that I caused so much trouble last night. I'm really sorry, guys."

Saying I feel like an idiot would be an understatement. My eyes drift to the angled chair again.

Emily perches on the side of the bed, wearing a sophisticated, satiny lounge set in burgundy. She tucks the covers around my feet like I'm a burrito. "If it makes you feel better, you were only trouble for Noah and Anna-banana."

And now the banana pj's make more sense.

I look up at Annie. "I'm really sorry. And also, I thought your name was Annie?" She shrugs with a soft smile. "Annie. Annabanana. Either one. They're both short for Annabell." I don't think anyone's name has ever fit someone as perfectly as her name fits her. Soft. Southern. Kind and welcoming. It's not fair that they are being so hospitable and I'm doing nothing but taking from them.

I decide to give a little of the thing that's hardest to give— myself. "Well, my name is actually Amelia. Rae is only a stage name."

All three of them exchange guilty looks. "We already know," says Madison. She raises and lowers a shoulder. "Wikipedia is such a little snitch. You can find every celebrity's name and home address on that thing."

I laugh because here I thought I had this great secret about myself—and turns out, it's been public all this time. That's what I get for never googling myself. Suddenly, I wonder what other deeply personal information is available out there. If only Noah had a Wikipedia . . .

My eyes drift to the chair again. "Umm . . . so . . . Noah? Is he mad? I imagine he is since he kicked me out."

"Noah didn't kick you out," Annie says in a soothing tone. "He wanted you to stay here last night because he was afraid you wouldn't feel safe knowing you'd slept all night in his house when you were pretty much unconscious."

His woodsy eyes flash in my mind again. *You're safe.*

The teeny tiny crush I've been harboring for Noah flares into something a little terrifying and consuming. Why can't he be like the others? It would be easier to disregard his actions if he had made sure he was here when I woke up so he could gain all the credit. But no. Just like the first morning I woke up in Rome, Kentucky, Noah is nowhere to be found.

The odd thing is, if I had woken up in his house this morning, I wouldn't have felt unsafe. There's just something about Noah that feels honorable. Grumpy as hell, but honorable no less.

"Where is he now?" I ask, looking around like maybe he'll pop out from behind the door or something.

"Oh, he didn't want you to know he'd been here all—OW! Would you quit?!"

I look over just in time to see Annie's fingers reeling back from the underside of Madison's arm. "He had to go to work," she says like a soft little springtime butterfly. "But he said for you to stop by the shop when you're feeling up to it. Has something he wants to talk to you about. I can drive you in on my way to the flower shop if you want. I don't open until eleven on the weekends."

My stomach flips inside out. And whether it's out of excitement or dread, I'm not sure yet. There's still a good chance Noah's going to tell me to pack my bags and hit the road two days early.

After scarfing a bowl of cereal, finger-brushing my teeth, and running a brush through my hair, I turn on my cell phone for the first time. I'm told by Madison that if I stand on her bed and wave my cell phone around the ceiling for a minute, I'll be able to gain a bar. And she's right—it works. I finally get a bar of service, and along with it, sixty-seven text messages, and thirty-two emails. Most of the texts are from Susan, a few are from my mom.

I hate the hope I feel that maybe her texts will be about something mundane or simple like:

Saw this random flip-flop on the street and it reminded me of the time you got your foot stuck in a public toilet and had to leave the mall without a shoe! Miss you! Call me soon to catch up!

Nope.

Mom, 7:02 A.M.: Hi sweetie! Are you at your Malibu house this weekend? I was hoping to go stay there for a bit. LA is feeling cramped. Bleh.

Mom, 7:07 A.M.: You're probably busy with friends this weekend. I'll email Susan instead. Hugs!

I shouldn't, because I've learned from history that my mom doesn't care anymore—but for some reason, I find myself typing out a response to her.

Amelia: Actually, I'm in a small town in Kentucky called Rome this weekend. I needed to get away from everything.

I hit send and stare at my phone for her response—hoping she'll comment on the fact that I'm in *Rome*. Show some spark of a memory that tells me she still thinks of our Audrey movie nights and what we used to have. My heart is begging her to show any sort of concern to my subtle call for help.

Three dots appear for a while followed by her response.

Mom: Okay. Sorry for bugging you while you're away! I'll go through Susan for any other questions.

Right. That's my fault for expecting anything different.

I don't even bother reading all of Susan's messages. I glance through the first twenty, and at first, they are kind and placating. She gently asks me to reconsider and come back. They then quickly jump into reprimanding authority figure: *Remember your duty.* You would think by the guilt trips she throws at me in these texts that it was a war I didn't show up to rather than an interview.

But one thing is clear as her texts progress: Susan is not comfortable with me being outside of her reach. A little light turns on in the corner of my mind, but I don't have time to explore it right now. I shut off my phone without responding to anything else, making a mental note to call my housekeeping service later. I told Susan I would be in contact Sunday night, and I'm sticking to it.

The ride into town with Annie feels like a decompression chamber after a loud, exhilarating brunch with her sisters. How those women can all talk at once and still manage to follow each other's conversations is sheer talent. I felt like I was witnessing a sitcom and had to physically sit on my hands to keep from clapping when one of them would say something funny.

Now I'm in Annie's truck (apparently you have to own one if you live around here) and we're pulling into town. Most small towns I've traveled through are shaped like a square. Rome is shaped like a lowercase "t" with both roads extending out to farm-land and locals' houses. Most of the shops are made of brick, with colorful awnings above the storefronts. It's a tiny minuscule dot on a map, and if you blink while driving, you'll miss it. But somehow they manage to have everything you need right here. Just on Main Street they have an ice cream shop, hardware store, market, coffee shop, diner, flower shop, and of course The Pie Shop. No one parks on the street; instead, Annie drives us over to the communal lot beside Phil's Hardware. Morbidly, I wonder if when someone dies around here, the new store owner changes the shop name, or if they change their given name to fit the store? Maybe there's a whole cemetery somewhere full of Phils and Hanks.

Two steps out of the truck and I spot Noah's burnt orange Chevy. I knew he'd be here. He's the whole reason I'm in town right now, and still, I'm frozen as my eyes glue themselves to the side of his truck. An inanimate object shouldn't evoke the warm, fluttery feelings sweeping through my body right now, but it does. It really does. I blame it on the man's overall mystery and the added bonus of a time crunch. It reminds me of summer camp as a teenager. You know you'll only be there for a few days, so immediately you set out to find the hottest person available, zero in on them, and initiate instant-crush. That's all this is. It's a crush. Attraction. Forbidden. Temporary. My body likes his body and that's all there is to it.

When Annie clears her throat, I realize I'm staring at Noah's truck as if I'd like to make love to it. She graciously doesn't comment and I catch up to where she's been standing watching me drool. I feel like a supercool person right now, let me tell you.

Annie's flower shop is neighbors with The Pie Shop and she asks if I want to come inside with her first. Since I'm apparently the world's biggest coward, I jump at the chance to put off my meeting with Noah. Her shop is the Disney World of flower shops. It's bursting with color and natural light and the innate feeling that everything will turn out okay in life. Tubs of flowers line the walls and in the back of the shop is a giant old farmhouse table, painted white.

"What made you want to start a flower shop?" I ask her as I pick out a few different single-stemmed flowers and piece them together into a bouquet. A sunflower, a few daisies, a big, pink, puffy, cone-shaped one, and a few stems of greenery. I'm not sure I'm cut out for assembling bouquets after I see them all grouped together in my hand.

"My mom. She loved flowers." We make eye contact over my shoulder when she says *loved*. Past tense. Annie doesn't make me ask. "Or so I was so told. She died when I was little so I don't remember a lot about her," she says, all while taking the small bouquet from my hand, removing the cone-shaped flower and replacing it with a soft pink rose and then adding in a few orange carnations. *Much better.* She then places it on her worktable where she wraps the bundle in brown paper, fastens a little twine bow around it, and adds a sticker with her logo.

"I'm sorry to hear that. But it's a lovely idea to run a flower shop in her memory."

Annie's smile is like a ray of sunshine. "It is. And I think she'd be thrilled to know I named the store after her." She points to the hand-painted calligraphy sign behind her worktable. *Charlotte's Flowers.* A million questions float through my mind about when she passed away, and how; but none of them are any of my business, so I keep quiet and pull my wallet from my purse to pay for the bouquet.

Annie chuckles, shaking her head. "It's on me today."

"No, really, I want to pay," I say, immediately feeling guilty. I can't not pay for this. It would look tacky—especially since I'm the one sitting on millions of dollars over here, and she's running a niche business in a tiny town. Even Noah buys flowers from her often so her business doesn't go under.

But then Annie just hands the bouquet over the table to me with a soft, dimpled smile. "A token of friendship." Her gesture rams into me. She's not asking anything of me. Doesn't want my money. Just friendship.

Her smile dims into sympathy when she sees my face. "Are you . . . crying?"

"*No!* Absolutely not." I sniffle. "That's—no. I would be—it's the flowers. I think I'm . . . allergic. Or maybe just the sleeping pill still making its way out of my system."

She laughs. "Mm-hmm. Sure. I think you got hit with the feelings allergy."

I sigh and clutch the flowers desperately to my chest. "Yeah . . . maybe. Something about this town is really making them act up."

"Imagine living here," she says with an amused twinkle in her eye.

But no. I absolutely will not imagine that, because I know I would like it far too much. In fact, it's time for me to go and see the man that I know will wipe away any of these illusions. He'll be grumpy and stern and make me feel like my company is the last thing on earth he wants, and it will be lovely.

Before I leave the flower shop, I have Annie help me put together a bouquet of Noah's favorite flowers (which I convince her to let me pay for).

"You stand there much longer and your feet will grow roots, making those flowers sprout out the top of your head."

I expel a breath and look over my shoulder. Mabel is walking toward me on the sidewalk, floral print cotton dress swaying in the breeze, leather loafers lightly squeaking under her feet. Her wise eyes slip from me to The Pie Shop I'm standing just to the side of, and then back to me. She stops beside me, her ample hips nearly brushing against mine. I'm holding the flower bouquets against my chest like they're newborn babies and I'll protect them with my life.

"I'm too nervous to go in," I admit openly, because instinctively I know Mabel would accept nothing less. She'd see right through any lie of mine.

We stand quietly shoulder to shoulder like two soldiers on the outskirts of battle. She breaks the reverent silence without looking at me. "Why are you here, young lady?"

"Because Noah asked me to—"

"No." Her raspy voice barks, making me jump a little. A quick reminder that she may be nurturing but she's not soft. "In this town. Why are you here?"

I look down at the cheerful blooms. "I don't really know. I'm not supposed to be."

"What do you mean?" She will settle for nothing but exact precise answers. Mabel doesn't beat around the bush.

The desire to hightail it away from her in a full sprint is nearly unbearable. I think if I did, though, the powers of her stern mind would capture me by the collar of my shirt and yank me back. "I'm not supposed to be here outside of Noah's shop. In this town. Away from my life. On vacation." I say it as many ways as I can so there's no way she'll misinterpret.

"Heavens why, child?" *Child.* When was the last time someone thought of me as a child? The endearment is so nice and cozy. Like holding cold hands up to a crackling fire.

"I'm not supposed to take vacations if they're not planned a year out and okayed by five different people. My manager has reminded me repeatedly over the last few days that I'm neglecting my responsibilities and being selfish by leaving suddenly like I did."

"And let me ask you something? When the hell did it become such a crime to be selfish now and again?" Mabel turns to face me, propping her hands on her hips. "I tell you what makes me madder than a hornet. When people tell other people how they should feel. Everyone's getting too damn people-ly lately and I've had enough of it. Sometimes a woman is just worn out and needs a break, you know?" The lines on her forehead deepen. "That doesn't prove that you're weak or neglectful, it proves to all the women standing by and watching you pave the road to success that it's okay to say no. It's okay to shut your door every now and then and put up a sign that says *Busy taking care of me today. Piss off.*"

Tears choke my eyes. I look over at the woman who seems ready to do battle on my behalf and my truth spills out before I can stop it. "Mabel, I don't love my career anymore. I haven't even loved singing lately. That's why I'm here."

She smiles softly. "Well, of course you don't, darlin'. No one loves anything they're miserably chained to." Her eyes narrow thoughtfully. "But you own the key to your own lock and don't you forget it. Set yourself free for a while and that love will come back, just you watch."

I can't help but laugh lightly because with those words, I feel like she's rolled a boulder off my shoulders. The feelings I've kept strung up and gagged inside me for so long because I *knew* no one would understand are free and floating on the wind. Mabel understands.

She steps a little closer and takes my hand like she did that morning in her inn. She grins and her wrinkles multiply. "Go have your break, darlin'. And even better, have it with a good man who'll treat you right." She nods over my shoulder to The Pie Shop.

"Mabel, I can't stay. Noah said I have to leave his place on Monday."

"Oh, you're staying all right."

The confidence on this woman.

I give her a hopeful smile. "Does this mean you'll let me rent a room at your inn? I can even help out with chores to make it worthwhile for you."

"Nope. We're full up, told ya that already." I've never seen a woman enjoy telling a lie more. "But you'll stay in town. Mark my words."

"I can't help but feel like your hope is misplaced. Noah doesn't even want me around him."

She grunts a laugh. "Bullshit. I've known that boy since he was a baby. I can read him like a book, and I'd bet my entire living he's grumpy because he wants you around *too much*." I don't disagree, but I do turn my eyes to the shop window. "And I saw him staring at your backside when you weren't looking."

I whip my head back to Mabel. "He did not."

Her smile widens. "No, he didn't. But now I know by the rosy hue in your cheeks that you wish he did." She raises and lowers her eyebrows and begins trundling away, passing The Pie Shop entirely. "Oh, this is gonna be good," she says softly to herself. And when I glance down at my flowers and back, she's gone, just like a mischievous ghost sent to taunt the town. In all likelihood she just dipped into the market, but I like the ghost theory better.

Chapter 14

Amelia

Just as predicted, I walk through the door of The Pie Shop and the little bell ringing over my head alerts Noah to my presence. The sudden force of his gaze threatens to level me when he looks up from the counter where he's writing in a little notepad. A classic little notepad for the classic man. His eyes lock with mine and BOOM, grumpy face. It's good he doesn't smile. I wouldn't be able to stay standing if he did. But this . . . *this* I can make do with.

I approach the counter slowly. He's a lion I've just encountered in the wild. "Hiiii," I say, stepping closer, one little scooting step at a time. He doesn't say anything, just lifts a brow. I try not to tremble.

When I get close enough, I lay both bouquets on the counter like an offering right next to where his muscular forearms are resting. My eyes get tangled up with the light dusting of masculine hair on them. The hairs are so blond, fine, and unobtrusive you have to be close enough to see them. My mind reminds me unhelpfully that I am close enough to see them, along with the shadow his baseball cap casts over his eyes, nose, and cheekbones. The scruff of his jaw is a little more prominent than it was yesterday, telling me he might not have gone home after sitting by my bedside all night. I don't want to acknowledge why the thought of Noah worrying about me through the night sends a shiver through my body.

His eyes drop to the bouquets and then back up to my face. "Flowers?"

"For you," I say, scooting the bouquet I made for him closer before clasping my hands behind my back and rocking lightly on my heels. "An apology-slash-thank-you for taking care of me last night." I tip my shoulder. "And I know you like flowers. Annie told me you buy a bouquet from her several times a week."

He doesn't shift even an inch. "Just to be clear, I do it to help her. Not because I'm obsessed with flowers or anything."

I widen my eyes at that incredible word. "*Obsessed*," I say, letting it dissolve pleasantly on my tongue. "Sure you're not," I say, nodding and squinting my eyes. *Play, play, play.*

His eyes narrow. "Are you taunting me?"

"I'm just not sure why you're ashamed to admit you're obsessed with flowers." I press my lips together against a smile.

"I'm not—" He starts to say in an impassioned tone, rising up to his full height and taking the bait before realizing I'm just goading him. He grunts and crosses his arms. *Hello, Surly Pose. It's lovely to see you today.* "I like them. I'm not obsessed."

I mirror his stance, and it's too much fun. "It's okay to admit your deep infatuation. I won't force you to give up your man card."

The hint of a smirk touches his mouth now. He's on to me. "I own a pie shop. You think I give a shit about man cards?" He looks over his right shoulder, "*Please*," and then back to me.

"If that's true . . . then why so hesitant to fess up to your flower obsession? Annie claims you think she's at risk of bankruptcy, but do you want to know what I think?"

"Pretty sure you're going to tell me no matter what."

"I *think*," I begin in a fervent courtroom tone, "you very well know just how many people love and support her shop, and that her flower business is doing just fine. I think, good sir, that you use your brotherly care as a disguise for your . . ." I let the word hang as we stare at each other. "Obsession."

He leans his palms on the counter, angling himself closer. Something sweet and warm crackles in the air between us. "I think . . . my obsessions are none of your business."

"Aha!" I hold up a finger toward his face. "So you admit it?! Ladies and gentlemen of the jury, you heard it from his own mouth!"

To my complete shock, Noah hooks his finger around mine, lowering them both slowly down onto the counter. Too many sensations mingle in that small touch, and when he doesn't immediately remove his finger from mine after they're finally resting on the counter, my heart gives out. I flatline. Someone get the stretcher.

A grin hovers on the side of his mouth—a lovely addition to the dark shadow his hat casts over his eyes. "I like the way they make my house smell."

I can't say anything. I'm frozen in this moment with Noah softly gazing at me, the skin of his hand against mine, and memories of his hungry kiss swimming in my mind. I never want it to end. "And your mom loved flowers, right?"

Nothing, and I do mean nothing, could have been worse to say in this moment. A silence so menacing drops between us that it practically takes on a physical form. It would be a man gnarled with scars and slapping a baseball bat against his enormous calloused hand. I should run screaming in the opposite direction. Instead, I watch, holding my breath as Noah's brows pinch together and he rises to his full height again, removing his hand from mine. He doesn't acknowledge what I said, and maybe that's for the best since I didn't mean for it to come out. He turns away and disappears into the kitchen without another word.

I mentally punch myself for acting like I was close enough to him to bring up his painful past like that. Like I had any right to call attention to it, let alone *know* that his mom loved flowers and isn't around anymore. How vulnerable he must feel now.

Great job, Big Mouth. Real cool. Can't you just be normal for like a second and not ruin it?

I should leave. In fact, I will.

But after picking up the bouquet of flowers Annie gave me, I decide that now I have two things to apologize for and set the flowers back down next to the other bouquet. After I cross the shop and open the front door, Noah calls out to me while reemerging from the back. "You're leaving?"

I freeze and look back at him. He's holding two plates with a slice of pie on each one. "I thought . . . I thought you were mad and it was better if I left."

He rolls his eyes with a little hint of a smile before gesturing toward the slices of pie. "I was just getting you a slice of pie. If you're interested, that is?" He moves around the counter and out into the main portion of the shop, setting the plates down on the two-seater table near the window. One plate is uncovered and the other has plastic wrap over it.

"Something you need to know about me," he begins in a softer tone than I've heard him use yet. "I'm not talkative." I give a mock gasp of surprise, which makes him grin. "And I don't like talking about personal stuff when I'm not prepared for it. Sometimes I need a minute to process when I'm caught off guard. But if I'm actually mad, I'll tell you. I don't believe in the silent treatment when it comes to stuff like that."

I'm still standing halfway out the door because I can't move. I'm overloaded with how incredible and heartfelt that speech was. I don't think I've ever had a man articulate his emotions so well to me before. I didn't even realize that was something I should expect or hope for. It's clear that there's so much more to Noah than his Surly Pose and burnt orange truck. He's obsessed with flowers. Is protective. Feels deeply, but prefers to keep it to himself.

And damn if I don't find all that sexy as hell.

He lifts his eyebrows when I don't respond. "So. You in or out, pop star? If you're in, turn that Open sign around and lock the door on your way back in. It's my lunch break."

I laugh and step away from the door, letting it fall shut behind me before flipping the sign and the lock. "With your accent, it sort of makes it sound like you just called me a Pop-Tart."

"No, definitely not." He takes his seat and then flashes me a grin. "I actually like Pop-Tarts."

I laugh and throw a pepper packet from the table at his head. It bounces off his cheek and hits the floor. Noah *tsk*s while leaning over to retrieve it. "Bringing up my family history *and* littering in my pie shop. And to think this is how I'm rewarded for keeping your ass safe last night."

"I already bought you flowers for that. My debt is paid in full." I sit down opposite him, realizing belatedly that this tiny table makes it so our legs are pressing up against each other. I would move mine, but he's not moving his. So there they stay.

I clear my throat. "So is this my farewell pie?" Looking up, I see his confused expression. "I assumed you asked me to come here today because I've been a pain in your ass and you want me out of your house tonight instead of Monday morning." It physically hurts to think of leaving this town the day after tomorrow. It's too soon.

Noah chuckles. Actually chuckles. It's so deep and rumbly I imagine pressing my palm to his chest and feeling the laugh while hearing it. The complete experience. "You're definitely a pain in my ass. But I'm not kicking you out. In fact, just the opposite." Noah nervously licks his lips. "Do you remember anything you said last night?"

I didn't until he asked. But at his questioning, my memories hit me in bursts.

My mom only likes me for my money.

I'm drowning and no one sees me.

You don't like me anyway.

Ohhhhhh I hate all those words. They're so raw and vulnerable they make my skin itch. And that's why I lie right through my pearly white teeth. "No. I don't remember."

He studies me closely, and I must have a better poker face than I realize because he seems to believe me. "Well, you—" Before he can finish, there's a knock on the door. Noah looks out the window at the same time I do, finding two middle-aged men peering through the door. Noah ignores them so I do, too. Especially because I have got to know what he was going to say. The way he left it lingering has me terrified that I'm not remembering everything there is to remember from last night, and maybe I pulled my pants down and mooned him or something. Or worse . . . did I hit on him?!

"You're killing me. What did I say last night?" I ask as blunt as the knife edge piercing my gut. Dramatic? No. Not when there's a potential memory of mooning hanging in the balance.

He scratches his neck, the exact appendage I want to strangle at this moment until he tells me what I said and did.

"You told me you were . . ." He looks up, seeing my horrified expression, and then smiles softly. "Tired."

Noah has a poker face, too. We might as well be wearing neon visors and clutching cards to our chests. We stare at each other, wondering who will fold first. If I admit to knowing I never once said the word *tired* to him last night, then he'll know I remember my blubbering vomit of emotions and we'll have to discuss it. I'd rather not. And I think he'd rather not as well.

"Ah—tired, yes," I say, pushing my poker chips into the middle of the table. *I call.*

He grins. "So I was thinking . . . in light of you being so . . . *tired*—"

Our conversation is interrupted again by more knocks on the

door and I want to groan. A small crowd of townspeople are start-ing to gather out there. "Should we let them in?"

"No," he says with a shake of his head and then frowns at the window where at least ten people have gathered, gesturing for Noah to open the door. "No!" he says sternly. "I'm closed for lunch. Go away!" He swats at the air but they don't flee.

It's hard to focus but I'm determined to hear where this conver-sation is going. Noah has the same thought so he adjusts his chair, positioning himself so his back is to the window. I do the same. Now we're nearly shoulder to shoulder. This is excruciating.

"Anyway . . . I, uh . . . I thought about it, and I'm okay with you staying with me until your car is fixed."

"You are?" I ask, turning my face to look at him. We're so close I can see the tips of his eyelashes.

He nods—poker face still in place. "The guest room is yours if you want it. And . . ." He gives his throat a big uncomfortable clear-ing. "If . . . you want a tour guide, I moved some things around and have some free time now."

Now I'm blinking as if someone has just flashed a camera in front of my eyes. "All because I'm . . . *tired*?"

My mind autocorrects that word *tired* to *lonely*, and I think it's doing that in Noah's head, too, but he's too kindhearted to say it out loud. He's playing along in a way that makes me feel safe and I just want to know why. Anyone might have heard my sloppy speech last night and chosen to look the other way. What I said to him is messy and complicated. Instead, he's choosing to extend a hand to me in the water. *I see you*.

Still, past experience has me wary to believe his good inten-tions. "Are you planning to sell the story of my visit to a tabloid? Did someone offer you an exclusive?"

He looks deeply offended. Maybe even angry. *"No."*

"The pill I meant to take last night was a migraine medication. I've been getting them from all the stress and my doctor says I should take more breaks and get more rest, but I chose medication instead. That's a pretty juicy story, are you sure you don't want to sell it?"

"Why would I do that?" His voice is stern again. Irritated that I won't believe his kindness.

I laugh sharply. "Because anyone else in the world would. My own mom has sold personal stories about me to tabloids on multiple occasions." I didn't mean to say that last part, and I wince lightly at my slip. My poker face falters a hair and I think he can see my cards.

Noah's eyes are soft when I look at him. He shakes his head the tiniest amount. "Not me. I would never do that to you."

Oh no. Those are good words. Too good. I feel my heart trying to suck them all up at a frantic pace. It's dangerous to let myself believe him, and yet, I do.

I'm not sure what he sees in my face, but it causes his expression to soften. He lays his cards faceup and he has a winning hand. "You can trust me, Amelia. I won't exploit your *tiredness*."

And now, I'm beginning to think he's not wrong about that choice of word. I am tired. Tired of loneliness. Tired of distrust. Tired of being taken advantage of. And tired of hiding myself from everyone all the time.

"Okay," I say, while looking down at my pie and scooping a bite onto my fork. If I say more than that, I'll cry. And I've had enough vulnerability for the last twenty-four hours without needing to add tears to it as well.

"Okay? So you're staying."

"I'm staying." My stomach does a little flip.

Noah lets out a breath almost like he's relieved. And then pulls that classic little notebook he was writing in from his back pocket and sets it on the table between us. "You should write down a few things you want to do while you're here. So we have a plan." It's adorable how awkward he is right now. He won't make eye contact with me and it's painfully obvious that talking with me this much has him wanting to crawl out of his skin. I should let him off the hook and tell him he doesn't have to spend time with me. But I'll die before I do that, because even though it's the worst idea in the world, I want to spend as much time with him as I can while I'm here.

"Because you're my tour guide," I say, taking the notebook.

He fights a smile. "Because I'm your tour guide."

I'm already busy trying to think of everything I want to do while I'm here. Do I want to be restful or adventurous? Do I want to hide or see more of the town? I think some combination of all of it.

"Oh, but just one thing."

Annnnnd here it is. The catch. The hammer. The thing he wants in return. I knew it was too good to be true.

Noah leans slightly toward me and lowers his voice like maybe all the Peeping Toms outside the window will hear us or read his lips. "The other night. When I told you I wasn't on the market." My cheeks flush a little at the memory. "I meant that. And I think it's best if right out of the gate we get things straight. This isn't going to turn into anything romantic between us. It's just . . . friendship."

I should be disappointed that my summer camp crush isn't interested in me. But I'm not. Because little does he know, friendship is exactly what I want. What I *need*.

"Perfect," I tell him, feeling lighter than I've felt in years.

And then there's a firm knock on the window, making us both jump and look over our shoulders. Mabel has her nose pressed into the glass, and her brows pulled together sternly. "Noah Daniel Walker," she says, sounding slightly muffled from the glass. "You better open up. You know I get low blood sugar."

He sighs at her nose print on the glass. "Batshit crazy town." He smiles, and it's clear that he means that as nothing but affectionate.

That's when I notice the slice of pie sitting in front of him covered in plastic wrap. "Were you planning to eat that?"

"No," he says, standing from the table. "It's for someone else I'm meeting just as soon as I take care of these loons."

"You know? I can't help but feel it's completely unfair that you're allowed to have so many secrets when I continue to spill mine."

"Sounds like a you problem," he says with zero smile but amusement running through his voice, straight into the pit of my fluttery stomach.

Noah lets me borrow his truck to drive back to his place, and with the windows down and a smile on my face, the strangest thing happens to me. I catch myself singing along to the radio. Something I haven't felt like doing in a while.

Chapter 15

Noah

I haven't seen Amelia since this afternoon at The Pie Shop. Our meeting was cut short (which I was glad of) because this town can't hold their horses. Geez. Having to wait five minutes nearly killed them. After Mabel shoved her nose onto my glass window, she pretended to faint. Miraculously, when I opened the door, the smell of pie revived her.

I let Amelia take my truck home and I borrowed Annie's for my lunch date. I know Amelia was eaten up with curiosity about who I was meeting, but I'm not ready to tell her yet. Maybe never. We'll see. She also looked shocked that I'd lend her my truck. She assumed I was doing something special for her, but the fact is, that's just how we are around here. I let Phil drive it the other day when he needed to go into the larger town an hour away to pick up some things for the hardware store, and then Mabel took it last Friday when she walked into town and then got too tired to walk home. So she took my truck and then I borrowed Annie's to go home and she ended up swapping with . . . I can't remember. It was a shit show the next day, too, when none of us could remember who had the other one's truck and all had to meet in town to sort it out.

Anyway, Annie gave me a ride home from work a little while ago and casually mentioned that Amelia had spent her afternoon at Mabel's bed-and-breakfast, helping her repaint the lobby. If I know Mabel, she didn't lift a finger, but propped her feet up on the reception desk and stuffed a little umbrella in her drink while she watched Amelia push a roller across the walls all day. The mental image makes me smile. Is helping old ladies paint their small-town inn customary behavior for celebrities? I don't think so.

Unfortunately, it didn't help that my head was already full of charitable thoughts of Amelia when I got home and realized she was in the shower. My shower. The one right down the hall, so close to me that I could see the steam coming out from under the crack in the door. She sings in the shower, and let me tell you, I'm not one to spout poetry, but the sound of her voice sliding through the door had me writing sonnets in my head. People pay hundreds of dollars to hear her perform and I got a free front-row seat of listening to her sing "Tearin' Up My Heart" by NSYNC. Seems unfair.

I needed a distraction from her voice and the thought of her body and the smell of her shampoo filling my home, so I turned on the TV, and now here I am watching an old black-and-white western where men are being shot off horses to a playful *pew pew pew* sound.

It's the perfect distraction until . . . *holy shit,* I shouldn't have come home from work at all. I'm going to have to move out and let Amelia have this house, because the sight of her turning the corner in my blue pajama bottoms but with only her black camisole covering her top half is too much. The bottoms swallow her whole so she has them rolled down at the waist a few times and that camisole doesn't *quite* meet the top of the pants. There's this enticing little band of skin showing all the way around her body. This woman looks like a fantasy come to life. Plucked straight out of my best dreams and placed right in my living room. The audacity of her.

I keep very still as Amelia pads her bare feet across my living room; her damp hair is draped over her shoulder, so long it nearly touches her waist. It hangs in this loose, easygoing way that's somewhere between wavy and straight. A drop of water clings to the end of a lock of hair, and I watch closely as it lets go, dripping down the side of her bare arm. She belongs on a beach in Hawaii with a flower in her hair and sand clinging to her legs while a photographer snaps photos for a glamour magazine. She shouldn't be in my tiny, unimportant living room smiling at me in a way I definitely don't deserve. And yet, I find myself wanting to trace a line around her smiling lips so I can always remember the shape of them. I want to wind her long thick hair around my hand and wrist. I want to brush my fingers across her accentuated collarbones. *Shit, none of that is good.*

She opens her mouth but I bark first. "Where's the top of those pajamas?"

Amelia's eyebrows raise. Her face is clean of makeup right now, and unfortunately, she's somehow prettier this way. "In my room. Don't worry, I haven't lost your precious Christmas gift pj's." *That's* what she thinks I'm worried about?

Amelia sits down beside me and I stand up. We look like we're on a seesaw. "Wait, where are you going? I wanted to show you this."

I don't know what *this* is because my back is to her. I slip around the corner where I find the thermostat and turn it down to 60 degrees. My old AC unit turns on with a roar and only then do I feel comfortable enough to take my seat again on the couch. Far away. Nearly sitting on the armrest.

If she realizes I'm acting weird, fighting with every fiber of my being to keep my eyes from dropping to her chest, she doesn't let on. She smiles brightly at me and then tosses the notepad I gave her this morning onto my lap. She turns to face me, pulling her legs up under her. A little too comfy there if you ask me. I want to put my finger on her knee and slowly slide her to the opposite end of the couch.

"I finished it! The list," she says, nodding toward the notepad in a hopeful tone.

I drag my eyes away from her beautiful face. (Shoot, not beautiful. Just . . . fine, it's beautiful.) *Look at the damn list.* Just as I'm about to start reading, I notice a shiver race through her. "Cold?" I ask, a little too eagerly.

"Yeah. Does it feel like it just got supercold in here all of a sudden?"

I shrug with a light frown and then shoot from the couch to grab a plush blanket that was draped over the armchair. I bring it back with me, hug it around her shoulders, and then start wrapping it around her like plastic wrap, all the way up to her neck. She's a human burrito. I give the overlapping corner one good yank to make sure she's nice and snug and then I tuck it into the top (which is sitting just below her earlobes). Her eyes flare wide with disbelief because she can't tell if I'm playing or not. I'm not playing. I made a homemade chastity blanket.

"Umm . . . thank you?" she says, close to laughing.

Feeling pretty secure now, I sit back down beside her, pick up the notebook. "Just trying to be hospitable."

"Right. Mr. Hospitality. That's definitely the title that comes to mind when I think of Noah Walker." I cut my eyes to her head poking out the top of the plush burrito and it's impossible to keep the smile from my face. She still looks too damn cute so I turn my eyes down and read her list.

1. Explore the town
2. Go fishing
3. Do something exciting
4. Play Scrabble
5. Teach me how to make Noah's pancakes

"Play Scrabble?" I ask, lowering the list to look at her. She's somehow managed to loosen the burrito and now has it loosely draped around her shoulders and open in the front like a normal person would wear a blanket. It doesn't work for me at all.

"Yep." She runs her fingers through her hair like a brush.

"You don't need me to play Scrabble."

"It would be boring to play by myself. I'd win for sure."

I give her a derisive look. "What I mean is, you can play Scrabble anywhere. That's not unique to our town."

She pulls her feet out from under her and wraps her arms around her knees, hugging them to her chest, and thank God, wraps that blanket all the way around her again. "Actually . . . I haven't been able to find anyone back home who wants to play."

I stare at Amelia's soft face and downturned eyes as she pretends to pick at the red nail polish on her toenails, but I know she's only avoiding eye contact because she's embarrassed. A surge of protectiveness rams through my body and suddenly I want to hunt down anyone who has ever turned her down for a game of Scrabble and force them to play all night with her. *And you're going to smile and like it!* What kind of asshole wouldn't want to be friends with her? She's sweet. Funny. Easygoing. Gorgeous. It's unfathomable that she's single.

"We'll see," I say, attempting to sound harsh and noncommittal even though we both know I'm going to do it. I read the list again. "Exciting, huh? What's your definition of exciting?"

"Susan would say anything that could potentially break a bone, make me smile, or generally get my heart rate up at all."

"Well, that takes sex with me off the table." I wince the moment it's out of my mouth. Her jaw drops. "I'm sorry . . . I meant it as a joke but my delivery is always too dry and—"

"Don't be sorry!" Her face lights up with joy. "You joked! Mr. Classic Man just made a dirty joke and now I have to write it in my journal as the best day of my life."

"I thought I was Mr. Hospitality?"

She pokes my cheek. "What other jokes do you have in there?"

I throw my body dramatically to the side like her strength knocked me over. "Geez, don't be so rough."

She's shaking her head now, a wide smile on her mouth, eyes brimming with delight. "I don't even know who you are anymore."

I right myself and clear my throat. It's time to get serious and quit playing around. Playing around leads to flirting. And flirting leads to trouble. "Back to your Susan. Did you tell her you're staying in town longer?"

"Yes. And it did not go well."

"Did she give you crap about it?"

She fills her chest with air and her lips flap animatedly when she lets it out. I love this side of her. The messy, not-so-put-together woman. It suits her. "She was livid. Tried to convince me that I was being reckless and selfish by not telling her where I am and bailing on business engagements that I didn't even agree to!" Her voice rises on the last part, and I sort of love seeing this fire in her.

"And then she pried it out of me that I was staying with a single man . . . and in an attempt to make you sound harmless, I told her you're a pie shop owner, and then I might have accidentally talked you up quite a bit and now she's convinced I'm about to throw away my entire career for a guy."

I lift a brow. "You talked me up? What'd you say?"

Her cheeks flush and she dodges the question with a roll of her eyes. "Doesn't matter. I still can't believe I'm here and going head-to-head with Susan like this. I haven't . . . I haven't done anything for myself in years." She pauses and I don't rush to fill the silence. "Susan wasn't completely wrong, though. Leaving town without a bodyguard or having anyone from my team make sure I had safe accommodations waiting for me was reckless." A soft smile tugs at her lips. Like she wants to feel proud but isn't sure whether she's supposed to or not.

I look down at the notepad in my hand and then pick up the pen. "What are you doing?" she asks as I mark off *Do Something Exciting* from her list.

"Congrats. You already accomplished one thing from your list all on your own."

Amelia stares at that crossed-off item and looks as if she wants to clutch it to her cheek like she did my hand last night. Her eyes are filled with emotion, and I can tell she's breathing deeper to keep from tearing up. *Nope.* No tears, please. I'm not good at those.

In an attempt to lighten the mood, I lightly tap my knuckle against her knee and regret the contact instantly. "Not that you need my approval, but I think getting away was the right choice. Your Susan sounds like a real killjoy."

Amelia laughs and lays her head to the side on the couch cushion. My eyes trace the long exposed line of her throat and when I make it to her face again, Amelia is staring right at me. "Oh, she is. That woman doesn't let me do anything. But . . . she's good at her job. And is the one to thank for my career reaching the height it's at now. Plus, in her weird way, she's been there for me more than my own mom has lately."

"But you're not happy," I say as half question, half statement. Everything in me screams that I don't care if she's happy or not. I don't even want her in my house or taking up space on my couch or forcing me to be kind to her with her big puppy dog eyes and sunshine personality. But damn it, if I don't care, then why am I asking? Why am I already brainstorming ideas of other places I can take her while she's here? Who she should meet. What would make her smile. What could potentially make her look at me with warmth in her eyes. I'm so mad at myself right now I could kick the wall.

"Sometimes I'm happy." She keeps her eyes down to where she's resumed picking her nail polish off and placing the chips in a neat little pile. "Or at least I used to be. I think."

She turns her face away, and I can tell she's ready for this conversation to be over. I understand that feeling perfectly well, so I won't push it. She can talk to me when she's ready. Or never if she doesn't want to. Doesn't matter to me. I'm just here to be a safe place for her to hide away for a little while, because it's what my grandma would have me do.

Her eye snags on something in my kitchen and I watch as a soft smile curls on her full lips. "The flowers I gave you. You put them in a vase."

I'm pudding in her hands. Spineless, melted, wobbly, pointless pudding.

"One of my mom's old vases, actually. My dad gave it to her." I'm not able to look away from her soft smile, and I'm so angry that I can't keep the facts of my life hidden from her like I want. I usually don't like talking about my parents. Or anything that makes me *feel* in general. I'm not big on sharing my emotions with people. But for some reason, when Amelia's blue eyes slip to me, I feel stripped. I want to tell her everything.

"They both died when I was ten." I swallow. "They were big outdoorsy people and loved to go on extreme hikes for vacations. There was a freak accident while they were camping for their anniversary in Colorado. Storm came out of nowhere . . . and . . . there was a lot of lightning, and well, they didn't make it off the mountain. My grandma took over guardianship and raised me and my sisters after that."

Amelia's hand drops to mine and she squeezes. "I'm so sorry." Her voice is nothing but gentleness. And the way she's looking at me, it's been a long time since anyone has looked at me like that. Like she wishes she could take care of me. The skin of her hand is soft, and the smell of her bodywash is something warm and comforting, and because I suddenly find myself wanting to lean into her and kiss a line up her exposed throat, I stand up. Pulling my hand out from hers, I head into the kitchen just behind the sofa. There. A much-needed barrier.

"It was a long time ago. No need to be sorry for anything." Where's my metal trash can? I'll happily climb inside and pull down the lid right now, because I like being Oscar the Grouch. That trash can is comfy, and I've really made it homey in there. Keeps strangers out, and even better, keeps beautiful singers who will only treat my heart like an all-you-can-eat buffet at a distance.

She hesitates a moment. "Okay. Are you sure you don't want to—"

"Nope," I interrupt while slapping my baseball hat back on my head, knowing she was going to offer to talk more about it. Believe me, the last thing I want to do is talk. About anything. Ever. Words make me uncomfortable. And why would I share anything with her when she'll be gone before I know it?

She laughs lightly—but not with amusement. It's more like bewilderment. "I don't know what to think about you, Noah."

I pick up my keys. "Just don't think about me at all and you'll be fine." I want to look back at her, which is why I don't. "I'll be back late. There's leftover vegetable stew in the fridge. Don't take any more sleeping pills. Oh, and by the way." I pause and give into temptation, looking back at her wide puppy dog eyes one last time tonight. "You can't have my pancake recipe. It's a secret."

Chapter 16

Noah

After parking my truck, I walk to The Pie Shop, and see that my sisters have already beaten me here. It's dark outside so I'm able to see a straight shot into the lit-up shop, card table in the center of the usually open area, junk food on the countertop, and my sisters all gathered around the table drinking and laughing. It's Saturday night, aka our night to get together and play hearts. We've been doing it since I came back to town three years ago. And since none of us ever have anything to do on the weekend (singletons party of four) we rarely miss a Saturday night. Despite the fact that we're pretty much on display, it's after business hours, and the town knows not to disturb us. Because if there's anything citizens of Rome, Kentucky, love, it's familial traditions. No way in hell they'd stand in the way of that.

I open the door and step inside to the cheers and whistles of my overzealous baby sisters. "There he is! Casanova!" yells Emily, with her hands cupped around her mouth.

"No! Not Casanova . . . something more tragic and brooding. Romeo, for sure," says Madison.

I flip them all off and go over to the counter, where I set down the case of beer I picked up on the way in. It looks like each of my sisters brought a case, too, so I take this one into the back to stick in the fridge for next week. When I return to the shop front, my sisters are still debating my nickname. They think they are absolutely hilarious.

Emily is kicked back with her tube-socked feet up on the card table, catching jelly beans in her mouth in between debates. Annie is sitting cross-legged at the table, reading a book and minding her own business as usual. And Madison is sitting on the card table, painting her toenails. She always keeps nail polish in her purse for moments like this.

"Gross," I say, coming over and taking the brush from her hand, returning it to the bottle, and screwing on the lid. "Now the shop is going to smell like this shit tomorrow."

She sticks her tongue out at me acting more like the children she teaches than an adult. Then again, teaching has always seemed like an odd career choice for her. She's always loved to cook—even teaches a cooking class one night a week during the winter—and I always thought she'd end up going to culinary school. Instead, she surprised us all by staying in Rome and following in Emily's footsteps, becoming an elementary-school teacher. Sometimes I worry that Madison adheres too much to what Emily wants—even down to both teaching at the same school—when actually she's more fit to something freer. More explorative.

"You're just annoyed because we gave you a nickname, Lover Boy," says Madison.

"Don't call me Lover Boy." Well, shoot. That was a mistake. I know better than to tell these ladies not to do anything, it just makes them want to do it that much harder and with greedy smiles on their faces. Look at them. Their eyes are glowing now. Annoying me is their calling.

Even quiet Annie shuts her book and plays along. "Why not, Lover Boy?"

I groan and grab a beer from behind me on the counter. I'd leave if I didn't love them so much.

My sisters laugh, and Emily moves her feet to the floor to give her more teasing leverage. "Aw, Lover Boy, do you not like the nickname?"

Madison practically croons, "Come on, Lover Boy, be a good sport and grab me that bag of potato chips before you sit down."

These women.

Luckily, I have so much dirt on them I could make a whole new continent. I look at Emily. "Should I tell them about May twenty-third?" Her smile drops. "Mm-hmm. Thought so." I turn to Madison next. "How about the name of the guy I saw leaving your house the morning after Emily and Annie went to pick up that farmhouse table in Alabama?" Madison zips her lips.

I'm just about to unleash my blackmail on Annie when she holds up her hand. "Save it. Point made. We'll shut up."

"Thank you," I say, taking my seat at the table and stealing one of Emily's jelly beans. "Now, can we get the game going, please?"

Emily starts dealing. "Fine. But you're being a killjoy."

Her words immediately snap me back to that moment on the couch with Amelia. I can't stop thinking about her and what she said. *Sometimes I'm happy. At least, I used to be. I think.* But I don't want to think about Amelia tonight, so I force myself to focus on cards with my sisters.

We play a few rounds of hearts and shoot the breeze until they can't stay quiet about it any longer. They are all three practically vibrating with unasked questions. Their bodies can't take it anymore or they'll just pass out.

"Soooo," Emily starts. I raise my second beer to my lips and take a long sip, watching her with narrowed eyes. "How are you feeling about Amelia leaving on Monday because you won't let her stay at your place?"

"Amelia, is it?" I ask, trying to sound nonchalant.

"Yeah, she told us everything, including her name. We offered to let her stay with us since you're being rude. Told her she could have my bed and I'd sleep on the couch, but she's too nice and said she wouldn't put us out like that."

Yep. Amelia's got them under her spell just as I suspected she would.

I set my beer down carefully and try not to act too eager to discuss her. "Thoughtful of you guys."

"Mm-hmm," Madison says, laying down a five of clubs. Her eyes pop up to mine with an amused glint. I can tell she's trying to outsmart me in more than just this card game. "Does it annoy you that you're not the only one she confided in?"

I hold her gaze. "Not a bit. She can tell the whole damn town and I wouldn't care."

I would care. *I do,* in fact.

They all grumble and grunt and roll their eyes because the only thing these girls hate more than not making fun of me is being left out of the loop. I throw them a bone because they'll forever be five, six, and eight years old in my eyes, begging me to take them along on my adventures with James. "I told her earlier today that she could stay with me until her car was fixed, though."

They all squeal. My eardrums burst. I regret all my choices.

"All right, all right," I say, rubbing my ear and then standing to go grab another beer. Because I'm going to need it.

Emily points an accusing finger. "You do like her! I knew it! Lover Boy strikes again!"

"I do not." I pop the top off my beer. "I just feel pity for her and looking out for her is the right thing to do."

Madison wags her eyebrows. "Look out for her or check her out?"

"I'm serious. Nothing's gonna happen between us. She's just passing through town and needs a place to crash while she's here. Besides"—I sit back down at the table and look at my hand of cards again like I'm actually paying attention to this game—"I already told her I'm not interested."

"You didn't," Madison says. She's never been more disappointed in me.

"I did. It's only right to set expectations up front. I'll be her friend, nothing more."

Emily lifts her eyebrows while staring at her cards. "Well. Probably smart. It's fun to tease you, but I agree with not pursuing her. You're not really the fling type of guy and she'll have to leave eventually . . . and you can't go with her." We all feel the warning in Emily's voice in that last statement. She still hasn't fully forgiven me for moving away with Merritt to New York. I think Emily was the only one who wasn't upset when everything blew up between me and my ex-fiancée because she knew it meant I would stay in town for good.

Madison is appalled. "No! Not smart! You're an idiot, Noah, and I want to push your chair over."

"So violent. Play your hand, Annie." We all look up to see what's holding Annie up. She's smiling at me. A soft, knowing smile that prickles at me. Annie has always seemed to understand me better than my other sisters, and it grates on me that she knows something now that I'm desperately trying to pretend doesn't exist.

I chug the rest of my beer and decide to have another . . . and then another . . . and another.

Chapter 17

Amelia

t's midnight and Noah isn't back yet. Not sure why I'm fretting around like a wife whose husband didn't come home tonight, but I am. Does he normally stay out this late? What is there to even do in this town after ten P.M.? I'm only worried because I think I upset him earlier trying to talk about his parents. What I need to do is quit trying to pursue this odd sense of friendship between Noah and me, and let it go. He's essentially my Airbnb/tour guide. When I leave town, he won't think of me again. He made it perfectly clear that he wasn't interested in me. *Just let it go, Amelia.* And great . . . now I'm singing the song from *Frozen* because it's literally impossible to say that phrase anymore without singing it.

Wait, I hear something. It sounds like a . . .

AH—a truck!

I let the blinds I was freakishly peeking through snap back into place and dive away from the window. What should I do?! Where do I hide? He can't know I was just standing in here like a psycho waiting for him to get back.

I hear the door to the truck slam shut and I yelp. He's coming and I have the house still lit up like the Fourth of July. There's no way he won't know I'm waiting up. Or wait. He doesn't have to know I'm waiting up. For all he knows I'm a night owl and this is how life works for me. Yes, I'm a celebrity with a thriving nightlife. That's what I'm going to let him believe at least.

I race into the living room and slide in my socks across the floor, reenacting *Risky Business* in my oversized button-down pj shirt of his. Also, hello, Amelia, where's your pants? YOU NEED PANTS. Years of skimpy stage costumes and magazine covers have desensitized me to modesty, and I forget other people don't walk around half nude like I do.

Now I'm a cartoon trying to gain traction while running in place as I slip and slide my way to my room, jerk my legs into the pajama bottoms, and race back to the living room and dive onto the couch. There's a blanket nearby so I snatch it and cocoon myself inside it similar to how Noah wrapped me earlier today. Does this look staged? Does it look like I haven't moved since he left? That seems creepier somehow. At the last second, I decide to ditch the blanket, shut off the TV, and run into the bathroom. That's a more normal thing to do and doesn't scream I HAVE A CRUSH ON YOU AND HAVE BEEN WAITING UP TO SEE YOU.

The second I shut the bathroom door, I hear the front door open. I sag against the door and catch my breath. I flip on the water to make it sound like I'm washing my hands—buys me an extra thirty seconds of recovery. Except it's cut to fifteen seconds when I hear a crash in the living room.

Oh shit. Is that not Noah out there? Maybe it's an intruder. A stalker who found out where I'm staying. What should I do? I could call out his name but then it would also alert my presence to the creep in the living room. I look around the bathroom and find a mirror. Thanks to the movie that ruined my childhood, I know what to do with this thing. (The movie was *Signs* in case you were wondering and it was horrifying.)

I slip the mirror under the door and angle it so I can see into the living room. It's tougher to maneuver than it looked in the movie, but I finally get it to work. That's when I see Noah crouched down scooping something up from the floor.

Whew.

Not going to die tonight. What a relief.

Giving myself a quick once-over in the mirror, and not choosing to wonder why I care so much what he thinks of how I look, I put the mirror back and go out into the living room.

Noah is hunched over a pile of broken glass from a lamp that he must have knocked off the end table and is scooping it up . . . with his hands. He hisses and his muscles bunch underneath his T-shirt when a shard of glass pricks his hand.

"Noah!" I move quickly to his side so I can tug on his arm, getting him to leave the glass alone and stand. "Drop those! What are you doing picking up glass with your bare hands?"

When I get the man standing, he immediately sways as if we're on a ship and it was just pummeled by a massive wave. I have to wrap my arms around his torso just to keep him from stumbling backward. "I'm s'fine," he says in a long slur, but not fighting my help.

"Noah, are you . . . drunk?" I ask once I have him safely standing and can release him. I won't lie, I don't really want to let go. This man is sturdy as an oak tree. Holding on to him like this, I can confirm that everything below this thin cotton shirt is solid muscle. Tempting, well-formed muscle. How does a baker get a body like that? Not fair.

When I step back, I look up into his grinning face. He looks almost boyish right now. I can't help but chuckle because his hat is off and his hair is all askew and sticking up like he's been running his hands all through it. Or I assume it's Noah who's been running his hands through it. But maybe it was a woman. Maybe it's the mysterious woman he keeps meeting for lunch. Why does that inspire a jealous little troll to jump on my back and taunt me to start a war?

"Yeah. The girls can drink me under the table. *Butdon'tworry*, I didn't drive mysmelf home," he says, swaying heavily again. This time I take his arm and wrap it around my neck, steering him away from the pile of glass on the floor so I can plop him down onto the couch. He falls onto the cushions like a tree falling in the forest—on his stomach with the side of his face smashed onto the cushion, arm dangling off onto the floor.

I would take a minute to admire the way his body takes up this entire couch, but my mind is too busy obsessing over the word *girls*. Plural. Is Noah a playboy? How would that even be possible in a town this size? Although it's always the small towns you have to watch out for. They are the ones you see surface in Netflix documentaries about how they had a whole underground meth lab.

"Girls, huh?" I ask, propping my hands on my hips and staring down at him like I have any right to be annoyed.

He smiles. SMILES. It's blinding. My heart stops and then starts again, galloping right out of my chest. Good Gouda, that man has gorgeous teeth. And crinkles beside his eyes. When he smiles like that, he looks so approachable and comfy that I want to drape myself over him and just squeeze him in a giant hug. He's huggable. The Grumpy Pie Shop owner is absolutely *huggable*.

He wags his eyebrows. "You jealous?"

And he's *flirting*.

Noah is smiling, and flirting, and rumpled, and *wow*. I like drunk Noah a lot. Actually, I like every version of Noah and that's a real problem.

"No." I kneel down beside him and pick up his arm. He doesn't resist. Just stares at me with a smile hitching the side of his mouth as I raise his palm for inspection. Just as I suspected: he's bleeding.

"I'm just wondering why these mysterious girls got you drunk but then left you to take care of yourself tonight. But I'm thankful you didn't drive yourself home at least."

I gingerly set down his hand and leave his side to go rummage through his kitchen drawers and cabinets. "Anna-Banana dropped me off. Oopssss. I gave away the mystery. I was with my sisters."

I pause my rummaging mid-drawer to smile. Tension slides off my shoulders and the burning in my chest dissipates. Jealous Little Troll hops off my back and returns to his bed for the night. I won't let myself consider why I felt such a strong reaction to Noah being with other women. It doesn't matter. It can't matter. *He's a friend, Amelia, get it through your head!*

"Why didn't she come inside?" I ask, striking out with another drawer. I go to the back of the couch and peek over the top. Noah's eyes are shut but he's still grinning like a drunken fool. I love it.

"I 'spect she's trying to make sure you take care of me."

"Me?"

He cracks open an eye. "Yeah, you. She's scheming. She's a schemer."

"Why would she do that?" I shouldn't be baiting him for answers like this while he's out of his wits but I can't help it. His tongue is loose and I feel like this is the only time I'll get a straight answer out of him.

Or apparently not.

He smiles wider and raises a finger in the air. "Nice try. I'm not *that* drunk."

"Hmm. Can't blame a girl for trying." I nudge his shoulder. "Where is your first aid kit?"

He chuckles deep and low in his chest. "Who do you think I am? A mom? I don't have a *firstaidkit*." Those words were particularly difficult for him to get out. "Box of Band-Aids is in the bathroom, though."

I hurry to the bathroom to find a Band-Aid. I have to push aside his deodorant and toothpaste, razor, and bottle of cologne before I find the box of Band-Aids smooshed into the back of the drawer. What I really want to do is open that deodorant stick and sniff it until I pass out, but I don't because I'm forcing myself to act like a civilized woman. *Polite, polite, polite.*

. . . One sniff of cologne won't hurt anyone, though. I do it, and I'm immediately addicted. I spray a tiny—nearly microscopic—spritz onto my PJs. *Reckless, reckless, reckless.*

When I go back into the living room with a damp hand towel and a Band-Aid, Noah looks like he's almost asleep. His smile has faded and he's a sleepy bear. So cuddly and approachable. If he were awake, he'd snarl and bare his teeth as I approach him, but right now, he's pliable and warm. I sit down on the floor beside the couch and lift his hand again. There's a little stream of blood dripping down his palm, but I don't think it looks bad enough to need stitches. I also don't see any shards of glass, so that's good.

It's ironic that last night he took care of me when I was unconscious, and now I'm taking care of him. I'm not upset about the opportunity to level the field a bit.

Carefully, I pat the damp paper towel across his cut to clean him up. His hands are like big, hot bricks. He has those large man knuckles, too. Calluses line the top of his palms, and if I had to guess, I'd say he's never touched lotion a day in his life. I can't help but stare, tracing a line with my gaze from the tips of his fingers all the way up his palm and wrist, turning my head to slide my eyes up his masculine forearm and bicep to his shoulder. There I find his startling green eyes blinking at me.

I clear my throat and whip my head back around to plaster the Band-Aid on his palm. I need to quit this futile pining. *He's. Not. Into. You. Amelia.*

I work quickly with Noah's arm draped over my shoulder, palm nearly in my lap. He doesn't move or fight me. Which is good because I need to finish this up, clean the glass shards off the floor, and get my butt back into my bedroom before I fall in love with him.

"There ya go," I say, giving the back of his hand a gentle pat and then sliding out from under his arm. "All doctored up. That will be a thousand dollars for my service." I twist around to look at him, and when I do, he raises his hand and runs the back of his knuckles against my jaw. So tenderly, like he's afraid if his big bear paw comes in contact with my skin it will bruise me. I shiver.

"You're so pretty," he says, without a slur but words heavy with sleep. "And you sing like an angel, too."

"Thank you." A soft joyous emotion bubbles from the pit of my stomach. I know he's drunk. I know he doesn't mean this. But I still want to catch his words in a net like butterflies. "And you're sweet. Like powdered sugar." His eyes drop to my mouth and I feel my stomach lurch into my throat. "So damn sweet."

I smile and Noah hooks his finger under my chin and gently tugs me toward him. "Can I kiss you? Just one more time?"

My breath freezes in my lungs. I want to let him kiss me more than anything. His lips on my lips would be incredible—I know from experience. But I can't let him, because, you know . . . alcohol and all that. It wouldn't be fair to kiss a man who's not fully present in his senses.

So instead, I tip forward and I kiss his forehead. It's a soft little peck—there's no reason this nonlip contact should feel like a lightning strike in the rain. But it does. The feel of my lips against his skin, the closeness of our faces and bodies—it all pulses through me. And when Noah breathes in deep and lightly hums a sound of delight in the back of his throat, I'm permanently changed.

I break contact and look at him.

"Thanks," he says and his thumb lightly strokes my jawline. It's an indulgent gesture. So sweet my bones ache. So warm I'll never need a blanket again. Even drunk Noah knows how to be tender and safe.

His eyes don't open again, but he does smile. I can't help but sit here and stare at him as his breathing turns heavy and his hand falls away. I want to figure him out—but I'm afraid I never will. He's gruff and curt, and also poetic and kind. He doesn't want me in his house but he goes out of his way to make sure I'm comfortable and taken care of. He's strong and calloused, but tender and affectionate. He's not interested but he asks for another kiss.

I finally clean up the glass and cover Noah with a blanket, and when I'm buried under the soft patchwork quilt on my bed, I fall asleep to the smell of Noah's cologne and the misplaced hope that one day we'll kiss again.

Chapter 18

Noah

Morning hits like a brick to the head.

Apparently at some point in the night I stumbled my way to my bed. It's weird how drunk versions of ourselves can feel like totally different people. For instance, now that I'm sober, I'm able to cringe that I was so drunk I only managed to pull my shirt off over my head and out of one arm. It hangs limply off one shoulder until I rip it all the way off and throw it across the room to my laundry hamper. Just that slight movement makes me wonder if someone replaced my brain with a spike ball. Hangovers hit different after the age of thirty, which is why I never get drunk anymore. And definitely not at game night with my sisters. It was the only way I could get through it, though. They continued to pelt me with questions about Amelia and it was all I could do to stop thinking about her. Alcohol was my only shield, which actually turned out to be the knife I stabbed myself in the back with.

I groan, rolling over in bed and wiping my face with my hand. I feel a soft scratch of something across my face and squint at my palm. A Band-Aid. Annnnnnd there it is. Fuzzy memories of last night come back to me. I remember getting home and breaking a lamp when I bumped into the table. I tried to clean it up and then I cut my hand. And then . . . Amelia.

Oh shit. I woke her up and she took care of my bleeding cut and then I told her how pretty she was and asked to kiss her again. This is unbelievable. All the work I've been doing to keep her at arm's length, and after a few too many beers, I try to pull her *into* my arms. I'm such an idiot. Is it cowardly to climb out the window and hide until she leaves town? Even more unfortunate, it's my day off today. I have someone who runs the shop for me on Sundays and Mondays, but today, I need my employee to go home so I can have my hiding place back.

Also, is that . . . I sit up, sniffing the air, and yep, that's definitely smoke. I'm already throwing the covers off my body and launching out of bed when the fire alarm starts blaring. I fly out of my bedroom and into the kitchen where I find Amelia in her oversized pajamas, swearing like a teenager who just learned about cuss words for the first time. She's surrounded by a cloud of smoke at the stove and fanning it with her hand.

"AH! Noah! Help!" She's still swatting at the smoking pan.

I push by her and pick up the pan. She's already turned off the burner, and nothing is on fire yet, so I carry the pan over to the sink and douse it with water. It hisses and pops loudly when the cold water streams over it. I leave the faucet running while I open the front door and a few windows for ventilation. Amelia is now standing under the smoke detector, swatting at it with a dish towel like it cheated on her with her best friend. She's hopping to reach it over and over again. *Hop, swat. Hop, swat. Hop, swat.* The sight is too much. Before I realize it, my hands are braced on my hips and I have to angle my face down to keep from cracking up. It doesn't work. I feel the desire building in my stomach until laughter is rolling out of my mouth.

When the smoke clears and the alarm stops blaring, all that's left is the sound of my voice. Amelia gasps and walks over to me.

Her bare feet enter my line of sight. "You are *not* laughing at me right now."

"I am."

"Well . . ." she says, sounding righteously indignant. "Don't! I'm so embarrassed!"

I raise my gaze and look right into her big beautiful blue eyes. They're blinking and nervous—eyebrows crinkled together. I want to pull her into my arms and hug her, but I resist because that kiss request is still whispering between us. I can't touch her again. I won't. "What were you trying to do in here besides set my house on fire?"

Her shoulders sag adorably. "I was trying to make your pancakes."

"With what? Gasoline?"

"Stop it." She swats my chest with the back of her knuckles. At the same time, we both realize she's just made contact with my bare chest. Her eyes drop and her voice softens, making me feel like she just doused me in lighter fluid and struck a match. "It was . . ." She swallows. "The butter in the pan. I must have left it in there too long."

I feel exposed. I would not have come out here without my shirt on if I didn't think my house was about to burn down to the ground. But here I am, standing in the kitchen with Amelia in my jeans and no shirt. Her eyes are eating up every inch of my bare skin. They linger heavily over my left rib cage where my only tattoo lives. It's a pie nestled in a bouquet of flowers. Most people would think it's a ridiculous tattoo to have, but Amelia sees it and her smile says, *I knew you were obsessed with flowers.* And now I feel doubly exposed because not only is she seeing my skin, she's seeing my . . . damn, there's no less sappy way to put it, she's seeing my heart.

I step away and turn off the sink faucet so I can give myself a mental shake. Next, I survey the mess on my counter. It looks like a flour bomb activated in here. "So was this all an act to get me to feel sorry for you and teach you my pancake recipe?"

Amelia is near me in the kitchen again, and I swear I can't get away from her even though I'm trying my damnedest to. "First of all, rude. I tried really hard to make these, but I couldn't remember any of your measurements, and you don't have internet so I couldn't research a recipe. But! Before I added the second bit of butter to the pan, I made this whole batch!" Her voice is so proud and full of excitement that I have to clamp down on a smile.

"You've never made pancakes before?"

"Nope," she says happily.

"Never?"

"Never."

"Not even before you got into music?" I ask in a skeptical tone.

Amelia taps her finger to her lips giving the question a second thought. "Oh wait, yes."

"So you have?"

She rolls her eyes lightly. "No, Noah! I haven't. Ask me a hundred different ways. The answer will still be no. My mom was a terrible cook, so we usually just ate cereal or threw a bagel in the toaster for breakfast. I only ate pancakes when we'd go out on Saturday mornings to a restaurant. And before you ask, I have no idea if my dad is a good cook or not because he abandoned us when my mom got pregnant. So, would you like to keep asking me questions that remind me of my fractured relationship with my parents or try my pancakes?"

Hello, foot, meet mouth. I am such an ass. But also, I can't help but love the way she bites back at me. Every day she seems to be coming out of her shell more and more, and I enjoy it that much more, too. It's really becoming a problem.

"Point me to the pancakes."

Amelia comes up beside me, arm brushing my abdomen as she reaches in front of me to lift a sheet of aluminum foil off a stack of pancakes. My stomach clenches and I press myself back against the counter to evade her touch. It's like the game I used to play as a kid, the Floor Is Lava, except this time the game is called the Woman Is Lava. I can't touch her or I'll burn.

Amelia's hair is down and long again today, looking wavy and wild around her. She's still wearing my pajama set, but thankfully this time she's wearing the baggy button-up shirt, too. For some reason, I love that her eyes are a little puffy from sleeping, and her cheeks are pink. I've never met a prettier woman.

Her pancakes on the other hand . . .

I squint down at them. "Did you add cocoa powder to these?"

"No." She presses her lips together while poking the top pancake with a fork. "I think they might have gotten a little too done."

"Just a little," I say dryly, and this earns me a light elbow to the ribs.

And based on the fact that they have the texture of a wall, I'd say she used too much flour.

There's nothing in me that wants to try one of these pancakes, but she looks so proud of herself for making something from scratch that I can't help but take the fork from her hand, move a pancake from the plate, and cut off a sliver. Cut is maybe too generous of a word. More like I *break off* a chunk of the pancake. Amelia watches me closely as I raise the bite to my mouth. The second it hits my tongue, my body revolts and begs me to spit it out. But her eyes are lighting up and an excited smile is tugging her raspberry lips, so I keep chewing slowly and trying to think of anything nice I can say about her nasty creation.

"So? How are they?" She clasps her hands together under her chin. She's a kid on her birthday waiting for her present.

I swallow the bite. "Oh, they're shit." Yeah, I couldn't think of anything nice. "Like really, they're bad. What the hell did you put in these?" I say, with a chuckle running through my voice as I try to bounce away from the dish towel she's attempting to pop me with.

"Would it kill you to be nice?" She's laughing, too, and chasing after me with that damn towel. The edge of it licks me on the back once and it's for sure going to leave a mark.

I grab a pot and hold it in front of me as a shield. "You didn't let me finish! I was going to say . . . but they're *your* shitty pancakes that you made yourself, and for that, you should be so proud!"

"Oh yes, I'm just beaming with pride." Her voice is all sarcasm, as she gives up her chase and sinks down onto a barstool. She puts her hand in her hair and tosses it over her head, making it look even more alluring somehow. "Are they really that bad?"

"Like sand at the beach that a dog has peed on."

"Wow," she says with an incredulous look. "Fine. I guess you'll just have to teach me then." She perks up like maybe I won't remember I already told her no. Thing is, I could teach her the recipe. It's not actually some great secret I want to take to my grave like I let her believe the other day. But I sort of like the playfulness added to the air by me keeping it from her. I have something she wants but can't have. Seems only fair since she's quickly becoming the someone I want but also can't have.

"Nope. I already told you it's a secret." I pull down a mug and pour a cup of the coffee she made, hoping to all the coffee gods that it doesn't taste anything like her pancakes.

"I'll figure it out. How hard can pancakes be to perfect?"

I eye her charred stack. "For the average person, or for you?"

She scrunches her nose and then lobs the kitchen towel at my head. The towel lands elegantly on my shoulder.

"I'm wounded," I say dryly as I lift the mug to my lips and take a hesitant sip. It's good. Really good, actually. "Huh." I raise the mug in silent cheers. "You make shit pancakes but your coffee is great. So that's something."

Her eyes twinkle with amusement. If she had anything else near her, I know it would get chucked at my head, too. Instead, she has to settle for words, and somehow I know I'm not going to like whatever she's about to say. Amelia tilts her head, unconsciously showing off the graceful curve of her exposed neck. "Well, according to you, I'm also *soooo* pretty."

I groan and roll my eyes away from her. "C'mon, don't bring that up. I was drunk." I was hoping she wouldn't mention it—would just let us both go through the day pretending it never happened. Guess my hope was misplaced.

"You expect me to not bring up what happened last night?" She laughs like that's the most ridiculous thing she's ever heard, and she then glances over her shoulder. "You begged to kiss me."

I hold her taunting gaze and *hmm* lightly. Another leisurely sip, and I lean back against the countertop. "Begged? Interesting. That's not quite how I remember it."

Her smile falters and I could swear she holds her breath. *You want to play, Amelia, let's play.*

"Well, you were the drunk one so I'm not sure how reliable your memory can be."

"You came out of the bathroom. Wearing those pj's. Wrapped your arms around me when I stumbled, guided me to the couch where I lay down on my stomach. You left me to go find bandages and when you asked where my first aid kit was I told you I'm not a mom but Band-Aids are in the bathroom." I take a step forward, set my coffee mug on the kitchen island where she's sitting. I lean on my forearms. "And then . . . when you came back from the bathroom, and before you doctored up my hand, I remember privately thinking how much you smelled exactly like *my* cologne."

I know my speculation is completely accurate because Amelia's eyes are wide as saucers and she's almost holding her breath. Her cheeks are strawberries. I want to run my thumb across them. Instead, I throw my last memory on the table like a gauntlet. "And after I asked if I could kiss you, *just one more time* . . ." I let the words dangle, waiting to see if she's brave enough to make the last leap or if I'll have to push her.

The Amelia I first met would have made an excuse right now and probably slipped out of the room to avoid an uncomfortable situation. Or she would have laughed it off and blamed the tender forehead kiss on how tired she was or something. The new Amelia is dangerous. She sits forward—so close our mouths could touch if I tipped forward—and she controls that embarrassed strawberry blush into a seductive sweep of color as delicious looking as her full raspberry lips.

And then she grins. ". . . I kissed your forehead." She pauses to stare at my mouth, a memory sparking in her eyes. She looks sharply up at me. "Because I wanted to kiss your mouth but knew you were too drunk."

Mouth. Eyes. Mouth. Eyes. Mouth. Eyes. That's the pattern of my gaze. The urge of my body is chanting, *Do it! Kiss her.* I already know it would be so good. And now it's my turn to squirm. I lightly clear my throat and scratch the side of my neck, standing back up and hearing alarm bells sound in my head. I shouldn't be tempting whatever this is. There's no future for us—and I'm not into casual. Nothing has changed. I still have to stay in this town, and she still has to go eventually. *So just knock it off, Noah.*

"I'm sorry I asked last night. Shouldn't have because I'm still not looking for anything romantic." *Lies.*

For a fraction of a second, Amelia really does look wounded. Her eyebrows twitch into the beginnings of a frown. But she wipes it away quickly and recovers. "Who said anything about romance? It was just a forehead kiss, Noah. Plain and simple. Innocent at best. And you would have never asked me if you were sober—so it's fine."

My instinct is to bat that placative shit out of the park, but I can tell she's saying it as a mercy to me, so I let it land between us and become the barrier it was intended to be. I wish it didn't make me like her more. Respect her more.

"Well, thank you for this." I hold up my palm showing her the bandage. "I'm sorry you had to deal with me last night and all the glass, too."

She smiles softly. "It's no problem. Besides, romance or not, it's nice to know that you think I'm pretty and sweet." She blinks playfully. "Like powdered sugar."

And that's my cue to leave. With another groan, I take my mug with me toward the bathroom. She follows, like a puppy nipping at my heels. "Is it really true, Noah? Does the Grumpy Pie Shop Owner really think I'm sweet like powdered sugar?"

I try to shut the bathroom door, but she sticks her foot in the way so I can't close it. I set the mug on the counter and look down at her. "Right now you're just a pain in my ass," I say, not realizing until I glance in the mirror that I said it with an overly indulgent smile.

She angles her chin up to me. "But you think I'm a *pretty* pain in the ass?" She says it softer this time, still playful but her tone conveys what she's really asking. She wants to know if I meant what I said. I guess I'll be walking a tightrope for the remainder of the time Amelia is under my roof. I like her. She likes me. And we have intense chemistry between us that I can't indulge.

I hold her gaze and take a deep breath. "Everyone thinks you're pretty. You know this."

She doesn't let me off the hook. "But do *you?*"

My eyes drop for a fraction of a second to her mouth, and I remember all too well how much I wanted that kiss last night, and still feel the desire today. "I always mean what I say." I teeter a little on the tightrope. "Now, can we let it go and act like adults about all this?"

She laughs lightly. "That's way too much to ask." She turns away, grabbing hold of the bathroom door and pulling it closed behind her. But just before she shuts it, she peeks her head back in, eyes falling unashamedly over my chest and torso before looking in my eyes again. "But just so you know, I think you're pretty, too."

She shuts the door, and I don't want to, but I smile again.

Chapter 19

Amelia

Noah and I hitchhiked into town. Hitchhiked! He left his truck near the shop last night, so after he finished his shower and came out of the bathroom smelling like a divine being from the depths of a woodland forest, he asked if I'd like to check the first item off my list. We walked down to the road to hitch a ride into town.

It wasn't as thrilling as I had hoped, though. Despite using the words *hitch a ride* he had already called his friend James and asked him to pick us up at the end of the driveway. So now I'm sandwiched between two beautiful men and bobbing my way into town, fully intending on telling Susan that I hitchhiked during my time away and allowing her to conjure up fantasies of me in an 18-wheeler beside a big burly man with tattoos and a lecherous smile.

James is nice, though. He has a sunny disposition and wants to know how I'm enjoying my time away from the big-city life. He's full of ideas of places I should explore and things I should do while I'm here. Most of his sentences start like this: "Oh, Noah! You know what she should do? . . ." And "Noah! You oughtta take her to . . ." I'm realizing that he seems to think Noah and I are a package deal, and for some reason, I'm not mad about it.

Noah, however, is back to his grunty self—pressing himself against the truck door so our arms don't brush. Yesterday I would have thought it was because he found me annoying. Now, after the Kiss Request, there's a new piece of this puzzle falling into place and it looks like Noah telling me I'm pretty and sweet. *I'm powdered sugar.* I don't think he hates me after all. I think he likes me a little and that scares him.

James drops us off at the front of the town square with a little wave, saying he's headed out of town to take an order of produce to a local market. When his truck drives off, it's just me and Noah, standing here like two phone poles.

I bite the corner of my mouth and look for something to say, because I've realized I can't wait for Noah to speak first or we'll become silent monks. "So . . . what store should we—"

"The flirty stuff between us has to stop," he blurts.

I laugh incredulously. "I'm sorry, what did you say?"

If someone was watching us from a distance, they would think Noah is standing on a tack. "You and me. Flirting. Or whatever that was this morning . . . it has to stop. We're not—we're friends. That's all."

"Noah." I turn to fully face him and make some serious eye contact. "You have to stop worrying. I'm not looking for a relationship either. We are allowed to be two adults who talked about kissing that don't plan on doing it again, and to admit that the other is attractive without jumping into a romantic relationship."

Some of the tension in his face melts away. He nods thoughtfully. "Okay. I just didn't want to lead you on."

I sort of want to burst out laughing. I love that he treats me like this . . . as if I'm just a normal woman he met when her car broke down in his front yard. Most men wouldn't have the guts to say something like that to me. Wouldn't have the guts to turn me down in the first place. There's no pressure with Noah, and although I could totally see myself falling for him if I lived in this town, I know that my life will come calling shortly and I'll have to go. Friendship works better.

"Thank you. And for that, I think you're as sweet as maple syrup." He groans and rolls his eyes when he realizes I'm teasing him again, and he begins walking away from me, one booted foot at a time. I continue, "Not quite powdered sugar, of course, but don't worry! If you try hard enough, you'll achieve my highest level of sweetness!"

He stops walking abruptly and then falls in step behind me, softly poking my back. I frown over my shoulder. "What are you doing?"

"Trying to find the off switch." Now I stop walking and he passes right by me, an easy grin plastered on his mouth like he didn't just *play* again, continuing to shatter all my preconceived notions about Grumpy Pie Shop Owner. "Come on, chatterbox." He signals with his arm for me to catch up. "We're starting at the diner, where we don't have to eat sand-pancakes."

"What should I get?" I ask Noah, looking over the top of the laminated, and slightly sticky, diner menu.

"Whatever the hell you want."

I get it. He needs more coffee. I've been around him enough now to know that he requires a steady stream of the stuff to maintain a less-than-murderous attitude. And he takes it black, no sugar, no cream. Just like his personality. Noah is a no-frills guy.

"I think I'll get the—" I'm interrupted by my phone buzzing on the table. It must have just grabbed a random bar of service because it is buzzing its heart out with incoming text messages. I shouldn't have brought it with me, but it felt wrong leaving it behind when I'm so used to having it on me at all times. Now I regret it. Noah stares at the poor little thing with lifted eyebrows.

"Whoa. Someone really wants to get ahold of you."

And just like that, the happy feelings I've had floating around me all day vanish. Reality always finds me. I pick up my phone and swipe it open even though I already know what I'll see.

> Susan: Please tell me you are still maintaining your nutritional plan while you're gone? Just because you're away doesn't mean it's a true vacation. Your stage costumes are already finalized.

> Susan: Pie is not on the nutritional plan btw.

> Susan: And speaking of, neither are pie shop owners. Keep your head on straight while you're away. You're too good for a man like that.

> Susan: Surprise, surprise, your mom emailed me this morning from your Malibu house asking where the key to your Land Rover is. Also, I extended your offer to have her join you for the first few dates of the tour but she said she has too much going on.

I set down my phone and look up. Noah is studying me. I muster up a smile and resume my menu-reading. "Okay . . . what was I saying? Oh yeah. I think I'm going to get an order of the French toast, too. Is it good?"

When he doesn't answer, I glance up again. A frown is etched between his eyes. Strong jaw working. He shakes his head lightly. "You don't have to do that."

"Do what?"

"Fake it." He gestures toward where I just put my phone. "Do you want to talk about it? Whatever it is you just read?"

Ugh. Here he goes again! Why is it the one person who can only be temporary in my life is the one who wants to understand me? Be there for me without me having to ask for it?

"I think I'll respond to that question with the same answer you gave me before you left last night. Nope." I overly pronounce each letter, reveling in my ability to squash the voice chanting *polite, polite, polite* in my head. Not with Noah. Never with Noah.

His mouth tilts in a grin. "Fair enough."

A moment later, a young waitress comes to the table. "Hi y'all. What can I get for you?" Other than smiling extrawide at me, she doesn't treat me any different than Noah. I'm not sure I'll ever get used to the freedom the people in this town give me. I want to package it up and take it back to the real world with me.

"I'll have an order of pancakes and French toast," I say, "and he needs more coffee ASAP. Gets really grumpy if I don't keep a steady supply dripping through his veins."

Noah scowls at me but the waitress tilts back her head full of pretty red hair with a delighted laugh. "She's right on the money! Glad you finally found yourself a woman who knows how to handle you, Noah."

Noah hurries to say, "She's not my woman."

I give her a polite smile. "I'm making a sign to carry around the rest of the day with those exact words just so he'll quit getting his panties in a wad about it." This earns me another frown from Noah. But here's the thing, the frown is laced with a smile. I don't know how he does it, but the man can smile and frown at the same time.

"Well, I'll admit," says the waitress, turning to me while taking her pencil and settling it behind her ear. "I was surprised when I heard the rumor that you two were an item given his history and general dislike for women since then."

I raise a brow. "His history?"

"I'll have eggs and a biscuit, Jeanine," Noah barks across the table. Jeanine pays him no attention.

"Girl, yes. He was head over heels for that fancy New Yorker for years, you know?"

My eyes widen. "No. I had no idea." I look at Noah, trying to picture this old-fashioned man who hates Wi-Fi and doesn't own a cell phone and drives a burnt orange pickup truck with a pants-suited New York elitist on his arm. Another paradox.

"Yes!" Jeanine says with wide, excited eyes. Gossip seems to be her lifeblood. "Had the man so bewitched after her summer in town cleaning up her deceased uncle's house and selling it that when it was time for her to leave, Noah up and moved to New York with her! It was a real Hallmark movie. But then when he had to come back for his grandma she didn't come with him and—"

Noah lifts his hands from the table. "I'm right here, you know? Can hear everything you're saying."

Jeanine whips her head toward Noah. "Why haven't you told her?"

"Because it's none of her business. We practically just met." Poor Noah. He's exasperated.

Suddenly, a man who is on the other side of the booth behind me leans around, draping his arm over the back so he can address me and Jeanine better. "Don't feel bad. He doesn't like to discuss it with anyone. That woman broke his heart and he's not been the same since."

"Oh good Lord," says Noah, propping his elbows on the table and pressing his face into his hands.

"You know what, Phil? I agree. I don't think he used to be this surly until he came back from New York." Jeanine helps herself to the seat beside me so I have to slide over in the booth to make room. "Now, darling, I'm rooting for you. But I think the fact that you're a famous singer is going to hinder things a bit, because of the long-distance hurdle. Don't give up. Noah's worth it and you won't find a better man than him." It's sweet the way this town adores him.

"Yep, okay. I'm going to go pour that coffee since you're clearly not going to do your job today."

"So we can keep talking about you?" Jeanine asks him with pleading eyes.

"Wouldn't dare stop you." Noah slides out of the booth and I watch all six foot three of him unfold from the table. I would put a stop to all this, but . . . I don't want to. It's sort of fun watching him squirm while also getting to learn all his deep dark secrets. Plus, he just gave us permission. There's no backing out now.

"Oh, honey, will you pour me a cup while you're at it!" the waitress says over her shoulder while still looking at Phil.

"Yep," Noah grumbles. "Cream and sugar?"

"Just a tad."

Noah goes behind the diner's counter and starts pouring coffees. A few people at the bar seem to need a top-off, too, so he does it. I stare at him, unable to take my eyes off his handsome face as Jeanine and Phil keep prattling on beside me. His forearms flex with every tilt of the coffeepot. Occasionally his mouth slants into a single-dimpled grin at something someone says to him. I feel my heart tumble off a ledge it shouldn't have been on in the first place.

"I wish I could wring that woman's neck for treating him like she did. Heaven help me if she ever sets foot in this town again," says Jeanine.

"But you're not going to do that to him, are you?" Phil asks me. "You're going to treat our Noah right?"

"Uh—" But now I'm lost. They seem to think Noah and I are more than we are. "Really. We're just friends. A step above strangers, really."

They both make *pish posh* gestures like the fact that I met Noah only a few days ago is just semantics. "I know a good couple when I see one," says Jeanine, cinching up her ponytail to make it perkier.

"Mark my words, you two have something between you. Just don't go cheating on him like his ex-fiancée did and that alone will make you miles better than her."

I blink in Noah's direction, who's just finished serving up a plate of pancakes to someone at the bar. He was engaged? Lived in New York? Was cheated on? There's so much I don't know about him, and I feel that lack of knowledge keenly now. I want to know him. Every nook and cranny of him. I want to study him like I'm cramming for an end-of-the-year exam. But there's a very real chance he'll never let me know him.

We make eye contact and he doesn't smile at first, but the longer he looks at me, his lips start to rise in the corners like he just can't help himself. And all at once, I think maybe my chances aren't hopeless after all.

Chapter 20

Noah

"So I guess you're going to want to hear the whole sob story now?" I ask Amelia after we leave the diner and are alone again.

She looks up at me with a smirk. "You sound like you're resigning yourself to a root canal."

"About the same pain level." It's supposed to be a joke, but it falls a little flat. Or maybe a little too on the nose. Because thinking back to Merritt hurts every time. In hindsight, I see myself eagerly following that woman off to New York, truly believing that our little summertime fling was real, and I cringe.

As Jeanine pointed out in the diner, Merritt came to town to take care of her uncle's property after he died. It was her first time in town, and being the only lawyer in her family, her parents thought it would be best to send her to sell off his property and tie up all the other loose ends that come along with a family member dying. Well, that and because her mom and uncle had a bad falling-out before Merritt was born and never spoke again. I thought Merritt seemed pretty lonely in town while handling all that business on her own, so I offered her company. I spent my afternoons helping her box up his house and then that turned into her spending nights at my place.

I spontaneously proposed on her last day in town, because it felt romantic and exciting. She agreed for those same reasons, but only if I'd move to New York with her. My sisters and grandma were shocked that I left with only giving them a day's notice. Now, I want to go back in time and punch myself right in the stomach for being so naive and thoughtless.

We made it work for the first few months, but when that physical chemistry started to wear off (which was probably because Merritt was getting it with her co-worker instead), we had nothing. She was all about work, which was fine, except for the fact that she wanted me to be as well. In New York I used my business degree and got a job in a low-level position at a bank, and, boy, did I dream of clawing my eyes out each day at that boring, lifeless job.

I was never enough for Merritt and she became obsessed with wiping all the "country" from my personality. She made sure I worked my ass off so I could climb the corporate ladder and claim a position that she could be proud of when she introduced me to her friends. So I worked a crap ton up there, was incredibly lonely, had very little joy, and because I'm loyal to an absolute fault, it took me a whole year to end it. Fine . . . loyal *and prideful*. I didn't want to drag myself back home and explain to everyone that I had made a huge mistake.

I can't say I'm necessarily happy she cheated on me, but it did give me the push I needed to end things, or else I might have wasted a lot more time being miserable with a woman who was all wrong for me. And after it officially crumbled, I vowed I would never force a relationship with someone whose life doesn't automatically fit with mine from the start. Because that's what Merritt and I boiled down to—two people who needed different things and couldn't find any common ground.

Amelia hesitates a minute and must see something honest in my expression that I don't mean to be showing, because she smiles and shakes her head. "Then no. I don't want to hear it. Sounds like a real buzzkill to our morning." Her blue eyes dart up to mine and they're glinting. I shove my hands in my pockets and lightly bump my shoulder against hers. In quiet, introverted, hates-discussing-feelings language, I just said *thank you.*

Her shoulder bumps mine back.

"So what part of the town do you want to explore first?"

Amelia pauses and looks thoughtfully around. With her eyes distracted, I'm able to really take her in for the first time today. She's wearing a simple cream-colored summer dress, with thin straps. I like the way the dress hugs her chest and torso, but sort of flares out a little at the waist. The bottom half of it sways back and forth when she walks. She looks so pretty it hurts.

"What's that place?" she says, squinting at the building across the street. Her lips are extrapink today and I wonder if she's wearing lipstick or tinted ChapStick. I know the difference because I used my sister's tinted ChapStick once thinking it was the regular kind and had ripe, red lips for the rest of the night because my sisters thought it was hilarious not to tell me. I don't think Amelia's wearing lipstick, the color looks too natural. Kissable.

Right. Enough about her lips. I know exactly where to take her. I turn in the direction she's pointing. "That's the hair salon."

"Wait," says Amelia, hitting the brakes on the sidewalk. "It's too scary. I can't go in there."

"It's just a beauty shop."

Amelia's eyes slide to the front window and she peers inside like a woman eyeing a diamond necklace in the shop display of Tiffany's. A few minutes ago, she told me she's wanted to cut her hair for so long but could never get up the nerve to do it. She's contemplating doing it now, so I go stand beside her, shoulder to shoulder as we stare into the salon like creeps.

Heather, Tanya, and Virginia are all in there working to loud music and laughing with clients. The scene is cheery, if not a little over-the-top.

I look down at Amelia. "I'm failing to see the threat here."

"I can't do it," she says in a daze. "I realllyyyy want to, but I can't."

"Why not?"

"Because Susan will be mad. Like really mad. My hair is a *thing*. It's part of what I'm known for."

With this new insight, my eyes trace the long waves of her hair cascading down her back. It is beautiful—the kind of hair that makes me want to tangle my fingers in it. Part of me is sad I'll never get to do that, but I'm also getting real sick of hearing Susan's name, so I will encourage Amelia to chop it off to her ears right now if that's what's going to bring her freedom. "Oh, sorry. I didn't realize it was Susan's hair. That makes sense then." I'm being a smart-ass but she likes it.

She laughs with sad amusement and then looks up at me—shoulders sagging in premature defeat. "I can't, Noah. I just can't. I know it's silly but it's how things work for someone in my position. I don't own my image anymore."

"Okay." I shrug. "But I'm just saying, if you want to be rebellious and break the Law of Susan, I'll whip the truck up to the curb and you can slide in *Dukes of Hazzard* style when your haircut is finished, and we'll make sure Susan can never catch us."

She grins. "*Us?*"

"Well, yeah. I've seen you drive my truck. Snails were passing you—flipping you the bird and everything. It was embarrassing." Amelia laughs and shakes her head, turning her eyes back to the window. And I realize in this moment, I'd do just about anything to make her laugh. *What's happening to me?*

Looking through the window, Amelia takes one full breath and then nods once—firmly. She looks up at me again, and this time, she's determined. There's fire in those crystal-blue eyes. Determination looks so damn sexy on her. It's making that fierce desire to kiss her boil up inside me again.

"Okay, I'm doing it. I'm going in there and I'm getting my hair cut. Better get the truck ready, Bo Duke," she says, bouncing from foot to foot like a prizefighter about to step into the ring. If she had a mouthguard, she'd slip it over her teeth. I need to tape her knuckles. "I'm a woman who eats pancakes and gets her hair cut when she wants to. I'm my own damn boss, and I'm taking my life back!" She heads toward the door, puts her hand on the doorknob, and then quickly lets go and paces back to me. Nope, she passes right by me. She's zooming toward the truck, and then abruptly freezes again. Slowly, she turns back around and treks her way to the door once again. We repeat that whole process two more times.

So on her fourth trip to the door, and when I can tell she's about to lose steam again, I go up behind Amelia, open the door, and push my hand against her low back, nudging her over the threshold. "It's been entertaining as hell to watch, but I'm starting to get dizzy from all the back and forth."

She looks at me over her shoulder with a thankful smile. "I was going to go in that time anyway."

"Sure you were."

"Are you going stay with me?"

I'd be lying if I said I didn't want to. Hell, I'd hold her hand in there if she asked me to. But I know I can't let myself do that. If I'm going to keep myself from falling for her, I've got to keep some boundaries. Get some space and clear my head.

I hitch my thumb over my shoulder as I step backward. "I'm supposed to meet someone for lunch. I'll be back in a little bit."

I hurry out before Tanya's heavily eye-shadowed eyes can sweep to the front desk and catch sight of me and Amelia. She'd sink her teeth in me and then I'd end up with a haircut I never asked for. Just before the door closes behind me, I hear, "Darlin', yes! I've been hoping you'd stop in here since I heard you popped into town. Sit down and make yourself comfy. Wanna Coke? I know you're probably used to wine but I'd have to drive home and grab the box from my fridge and that might take about twenty minutes."

I just hope she doesn't come out with a perm.

Chapter 21

Amelia

'm faced away from the mirror, like the way hairstylists always do (which I'm convinced is so if they mess up, they can fix it before you notice), and haven't been given a peek at my hair this entire time. Heather is the twenty-one-year-old daughter of Tanya, and the one who has been working on my hair. It's been—as Tanya would say—*a hoot* listening to these ladies volley conversations back and forth. I don't think I'd even notice or mind if she accidentally shaved my head. Worth it to hear them spill the town tea. I just wish I knew all the people they've been southern-politely slaughtering. I'm invested no less.

"Now, give us the scoop about you and Noah," Heather asks me a touch too loud. Even over the sound of the hair dryer, everyone seems to have heard. All heads swivel in my direction. It's my turn to spill the tea, I guess.

Tanya and Virginia (the other two stylists) are each working on elderly clients, rolling pink perm rods. Virginia has bright yellow-blond hair that is teased up to the ceiling. She's smacking her gum while aiming a mischievous smile at me. "I tried to date him, ya know? Hell, I didn't even need to date him! I offered to climb right into that man's bed."

Thankfully they can't see my hands clenching into jealous little fists under my cape. I try to laugh lightly but there's a quaver in my voice.

Virginia winks at me. "Don't worry, baby. He's too much of a gentleman. Turned me down and sent me home with an apple pie." She rolls her eyes up to heaven like she's reliving the taste of it—or maybe trying to see if she can spot the top of her hair. She'll never find it. "And if that man's hands can make a pie that good, imagine how delicious the sex would be."

"Virginia!" Tanya scolds. If I had to guess, I'd say Tanya is about fifty years old with chestnut brown hair, heavy eyeliner, big hoop earrings, and six-inch-tall high heels that she walks in with the same ease as if they were slippers. *Jealous.* "Don't be talking like that around Heather."

Virginia throws her head back laughing and I can see her gum in the side of her mouth. "Oh come on, Tanya. The girl's getting married soon. Surely she's allowed to talk about sex now?"

Heather takes this moment to lean down and whisper quietly as Virginia and Tanya argue about appropriate salon conversation. "Mama, God bless her, still thinks I'm a virgin." She looks at me with a laugh and wide eyes. "She somehow got it in her head that Charlie and I are waiting until our honeymoon to sleep together even though that already happened the day I got my license back in high school."

"I heard that, young lady!" says Tanya with a speaking glance at her daughter while pointing a pink rod in her direction.

Heather rolls her eyes and continues tugging a round brush through my hair. "You heard nothing!" She lowers her voice just for me again. "Something I've learned about southern mamas: They pretend they know everything even when they don't just to get you to confess. Never confess. It's always a bluff on their end."

I laugh and adjust in my seat so my butt will regain some feeling. "Good to know."

"What about you?" Heather asks, peeking over my shoulder. "Is your mama a Nosy Nelly, too?"

A sharp—nearly offensive—laugh jumps from my throat before I can stop it. "All my mom cares about is my career in a how-can-it-benefit-her sort of way. And I've never known my dad."

I can't believe I said all that to a stranger. What is the air made of in this town? Truth serum? I imagine these scheming southern mamas all huddled around an air vent each morning with a vial labeled Liquid Truth so they'll never be left out of the loop.

Other than blurting it to Noah when I was loopy on a sleeping pill, I've kept that secret about my parents locked inside me for years. Even through countless interviews where everyone wants to know about my perfect life and perfect family, I just smile and nod and, even though our relationship is nothing but a rotting apple core lately, I say how thankful I am for my mom.

Heather cuts off the hair dryer and stares down at me with her bright red lips parted. Her perfectly shaped eyebrows are pulled so tightly together they're making a unibrow and I'm afraid she's going to burst out in tears. And then suddenly, her arms are around my neck and she's hugging me. HUGGING ME. I don't hate it.

"Oh," I say, slightly startled, but definitely not turning my nose up at it, and I awkwardly pat her back. "A hug. Wow. Thank you."

She pulls away. "That is the saddest thing I've ever heard. You should definitely come to my wedding."

I blink, trying to figure out how those two points connect when the door to the salon opens. I see who it is and my stomach flips. *Noah.* Why does the sight of him do this to me? Someone tell me why the air shifts and my breath feels heavy in my lungs? A strange electricity pulses through my fingertips and I'm afraid the only way it will resolve is if they run over his skin.

"Well, if it isn't Noah Walker in the flesh," Heather says, alerting the whole salon to his presence. "Will you bring Amelia as your date to my wedding?"

Noah stands in the doorway, unmoving. He hasn't looked at me yet. I inspect him from head to toe—so thoroughly I could describe him to a sketch artist and come away with a perfect likeness. I would describe the scruff on his jaw first. It's important to get it right—because it's not long and beardy—but it's not trimmed or edged to slicing angles either. It's just sort of a natural dusting that wouldn't burn you if he kissed your skin, but might tickle a little. Next, comes his hair. Oh—that sandy-blond hair. It's tousled lightly with styling cream. A matte pomade—flex fiber. I know because we share a bathroom and I'm a dirty little snoop.

And I also know that under that white T-shirt clinging to his broad shoulders is a tattoo. The most adorable, perfectly fitting tattoo I've ever seen on a man in my life. My mind jumps back to this morning, seeing him run into the kitchen shirtless. It's the image of that man's taut body that will play on a loop through my mind until the day I die. Golden-tanned skin. Light freckles across his impressive shoulders. Cut biceps and abs that track their way down to his tapered waist.

He is in a word: gorgeous.

I smile as a primal satisfaction, knowing that I've seen Noah in a state that Virginia only wishes she could, pumps me up. *Oh crap.* Am I pathetic? I think I am, since I'm developing very real feelings for a man who has made it abundantly clear that I should under no circumstances develop feelings for him.

Noah's eyes finally slide over to me and I see him hold his breath. Is that good or bad? His expression is so intense that now I wish I had seen my hair before he did. Maybe I have jagged edges. Or there's a big gap missing somewhere. Oh well, even if he doesn't like it, it doesn't matter. This haircut was for me, and I'm glad I did it.

But I can't take him staring at me any longer. I blink and look down.

"Heather," Noah starts and I hate that I love the sound of his voice so much. I need to start making a list of things I *don't* like about Noah just to keep myself from truly falling into the feelings pit. "Don't make the woman come to your wedding. She's a celebrity for crying out loud. People don't even want to go to weddings for people they know, let alone strangers. No offense."

"Hey!" I say, raising my eyes and glaring at Noah. "How about you let the *her* in question decide for herself what she likes and doesn't like, thank you very much, Mr. Grump." The corner of Noah's mouth twitches. I know why, too. He's mentally adding yet another nickname to his ever-growing list. "I would love to come to your wedding, Heather. Thank you very much for the invitation." I toss Noah a saucy look. "I will be there, even if Noah already has a date. When is it?"

"A month from today."

I resist looking in Noah's direction. His face will be smug. "Oh . . . Actually, I will not be there." I give her a sheepish smile. "I'll be on tour. Sorry."

"Should've listened to me."

"Oh hush, you," I say and the whole salon laughs. It earns me a genuine smile from Noah's scruffy, moody mouth.

But then, just behind Noah's shoulder, someone catches my eye. It's a man, and the way he's dressed immediately has me on edge—all in black with a long-lens camera slung across his back. He's a paparazzo, there's no doubt.

"*Shit,*" I say in a frantic whisper, ripping the cape off my neck and looking around for somewhere to hide. "They found me!"

"Who found you?" Noah asks, sounding stern and protective. That voice chases a shiver through my whole body.

"Paparazzi." I gesture with my hand out the front window toward the man who has his back to us, assessing the town square. If he finds me and confirms that I'm here, it's all over for me. This whole adventure will go *poof.*

Unfortunately, I don't even have to think twice to know who sent him. My mom is the only person who knows where I am and, unfortunately, has been known to sell stories to tabloids in the past. I should have known better than to tell her where I was. I can't wait to find out what she'll spend her money on. Designer bag? Shoes? Of course, she'll deny it until the day she dies because she's terrified I'll cut her off if I learn the truth, but Susan always finds out through anonymous magazine sources that it was my mom who tipped them off. I've never had the guts to call my mom out on it, though. Because the sad thing is, I like the attention from her even if it's fake. It's nice to pretend she's genuinely interested when she asks about my life. That she doesn't have ulterior motives when she talks to me or spends time at my house. But it's past time to start reevaluating our relationship. I can't keep going through this.

Noah is at my side in an instant, his long legs eating up the salon floor with determined strides.

"Honey, don't you worry," says Heather, pushing me from the chair. "We'll hide ya."

"Thank you! I'll come by and pay later. I promise."

"Don't you worry a minute about that." Tanya frantically points toward the back of the salon. "Take her out the alleyway, Noah."

But there's no time. We only make it to the far end of the salon when the door chimes. Noah whirls around in front of me, so my body is pressed against his. We are one right now and my heart can't take it. The *feel* of him. The *smell* of him. The *warmth* of him. *Oof,* it's all so good. And then he has to go and make it worse by reaching behind him and taking my hips in his hands, adjusting me an inch to the left so that I'm more squarely lined up with him. "Hold still," he says as if I would want to go anywhere but here right now.

Good luck ever peeling me off you, buddy. I live here now.

"Afternoon, sir!" says Tanya in a chipper tone. "You here for an appointment?"

I can hear my heart beating in my ears. Noah and I are in the far corner of the salon, partially hidden by the nail tech tables and hooded dryers, but still, I can't imagine this little bodyguard trick is going to work.

"Uh . . . no. I'm actually looking for someone."

Virginia laughs and I hear the click of her high heels moving across the floor. "Like a sweetheart? I'll date you, honey."

"Flattered, but no thanks. I work for *OK* magazine and I've received a tip that Rae Rose might be staying in your town. I was wondering if any of you have seen her? I'm willing to compensate for your help."

I swallow, all too ready for one of these women to point an acrylic fingernail in my direction. I rest my forehead on Noah's back, needing support. It's not until my face is resting against his sturdy back that I realize he might not like me leaning on him like this. I'm wrong. Suddenly, I feel Noah's fingers discreetly brush against mine. He wraps his hand around my fingers and squeezes. I feel that touch like he's brushing his fingers across my very soul.

"Rae Rose?" Heather exclaims loudly. I hear her rushing across the floor toward the man. "Are you kidding me? She's here? In this town?" Her voice is so high it's going to crack a window. "Mama, can you believe it?"

"I know, baby. That's what he says but I don't believe it. If she were here, we'd know about it. This town is only as big as a whisper."

I smile, and relief drenches me. They really are going to protect me. These women who owe me nothing are hiding me. Noah squeezes again as if he can read my thoughts.

"So . . . you haven't seen her then?" the man asks again. He sounds skeptical. Or maybe he's just trying to find the top of Virginia's hair, too.

"Heavens no! Oh, but look! Is that her across the street?"

"Where?" he asks frantically right as Noah spins toward me and starts tugging me by the hand to follow him to the back door. I look over my shoulder and the whole salon is gathered by the window, making a wall between me and the paparazzo. I make eye contact with Heather, mouth *thank you,* and she winks before turning back to the man. She shoves her finger over his shoulder and points. "Over there! See that woman?"

"Ma'am. That's an elderly woman walking with a cane."

"Oh . . . ha! I guess I do need glasses after all."

And that's the last I hear before Noah and I escape into the alley. His fingers are still intertwined with mine, and I'm having to take three steps to his one. We quietly zigzag around dumpsters and trash cans toward the parking lot. When we run out of alleyway, Noah gestures for me to wait as he walks out into the parking lot and surveys the area. Something about his face right now looks lethal. Like he's Jason Bourne and navigates situations like this on the regular. When he makes it to his truck, his green eyes lock with mine and he gives me a subtle nod telling me the coast is clear. I stay low, running hunched over so the row of cars and trucks protects me, until I'm at Noah's truck. We both jump in at the same time and when our doors shut, I let out a breath and sink down against the bench seat. He does the same.

It's quiet in here and safe. Just like Noah.

"Thanks for getting me out of there," I say, rotating my head toward him.

He's staring at me. Not smiling. Not frowning.

Noah doesn't respond, but he lifts his hand to gently brush his fingers across the edge of my new fringe bangs. I had forgotten about my haircut. I still haven't even seen it, but I'm really hoping it looks like the picture of Zoey Deschanel I showed to Heather as inspiration, and not like one of the photos that magazine articles use to convince readers to never cut their own bangs.

"I chickened out on a full haircut," I say, feeling a little self-conscious. "But I've wanted bangs for a long time and Susan always talked me out of them saying they wouldn't look right with my face shape." I want to close my eyes against the feel of his calloused fingers touching my skin. My voice shakes as I continue to babble. "I really hope she was wrong. But I guess it's too late now. They'll grow back, though. And if they look bad, I can pin them back."

His hand falls away, and I look up into his evergreen eyes. His jaw flexes and he turns forward, gripping his steering wheel with one hand and turning the key with the other. "Dammit," he whispers and then looks at me one more time. "You look very pretty."

I feel a smile in my soul before it reaches my lips. "You say that like it's a bad thing."

"It is for me."

And that's all he says before backing up and driving us both home in stunned silence.

Chapter 22

Noah

'm putting myself on a diet. It's going to be tough, but I'm cutting out all Amelias. Today got out of hand. I think I touched that woman at least a million different times, and each time I told myself to walk away and go do something different, I ended up closer to her somehow. We even made dinner together tonight. DINNER. Well, I guess I made dinner and Amelia helped by sprinkling salt and pepper into the soup when I asked her to. We had chicken soup. Like a little old couple who's been married for thirty years, we sat on the couch side by side and watched *Jeopardy!* because that was all that was on my basic channels at the time, slurping our soup in tandem.

Amelia is an interactive viewer. She yelled her answers at the TV, and I tried not to stare at her the whole evening. So I guess you could say we were both busy tonight. And then when her arm brushed mine while dropping our empty bowls into the sink, I almost rolled my eyes at how my body reacted. Like an electric shock took hold of me. An arm brush should *never* do that sort of thing to me.

I realized tonight that I'm in real danger here of developing feelings for her. That's a problem, because admittedly, I'm that loyal guy who develops feelings and then falls way too hard way too fast. I don't know how to keep things casual. I hate casual. It's pointless to me. Like city girls wearing Carhartt beanies.

So yeah, I'm keeping myself cooped up in my bedroom for the rest of the night where I can't do any more damage to myself. I'm in bed with a book in my lap. Except, I read the same paragraph four times. I'm distracted by my own addiction to Amelia. Every time I hear her bare feet padding down the hallway, I twitch. I cannot let myself touch that doorknob. *You can last one freaking night without seeing her, Noah. You survived every night without her before you met her.*

But I hear her walking again so I lower my book. My heart rate picks up when I notice her shadow under the crack in my door. Also, I notice that I forgot to fully close the damn thing. It's resting against the doorjamb so she can't see inside, but still. One little press of her finger to the door and it would glide right open.

She's standing there and I know she's contemplating opening it. I don't think I want her to. I've kept my room purposely closed off from her because I didn't want her getting to know me at all. This room feels too personal. Too much of *me* in here. I like controlling the part of me that Amelia gets to know, and if she came in here, it would be a slippery slope to telling her everything.

Her shadow disappears and I breathe again. She wouldn't just barge in here. I raise my book again and tell myself to focus on reading.

Chapter 23

Amelia

Don't go in there, you loon! Ugh. I'm acting ridiculous. Noah went to his room to get some space from me, I know it. So why in the world would I go in search of him? Except, his door is not latched. And that door might as well have developed cartoon eyes and a mouth because it's smirking at me. Jiggling its eyebrows up and down. Hitching its head a little trying to tempt me inside. *Seducer.*

I walk away from the door and in an attempt to clear my head of Noah and how much I want to be hanging out with him right now, I slip into the kitchen to call Susan. I realllyyy don't want to, but I can't completely step away from my responsibilities. The least I can do is check in with her from time to time to let her know I haven't been kidnapped. Then, maybe her relentless emails will let up a little, too.

I dial Susan's number and wait for her to answer. It's been ringing so long that I think I'm going to get lucky and be sent to her voicemail, where I can at least tell her I tried to reach her. Except the line connects.

"Having fun playing house?" is how she greets me. My heart

drops. I knew she wouldn't be gushing with excitement, but I didn't quite expect those harsh words right away, either.

"Uh . . . what are you talking about?"

"The guy you gushed about last time we talked," she says in a clipped tone. "I assume he's the reason you're still hiding wherever you are. Please at least tell me that you, a world-famous star, are not contemplating having a relationship with an average pie shop owner who will never be good enough for you?"

"Goodness, Susan. That's harsh, don't you think? He's a great guy."

"Oh my gosh, you are. You're considering it." She scoffs. "I honestly can't believe you're still wasting your time there. This whole thing makes me worried about your mental state."

"HA!" I bark out an unamused laugh. "*Now* you're worried about my mental state? I'm trying to tell you, Susan, that I feel better than I have in years. I needed a break." I'm done apologizing for needing a vacation.

"I would have scheduled you a spa day, you know? Anyway, I'm just going into a meeting. Since you're on the phone, I'm going to hand you to Claire so she can go over the scheduling I need answers for. When you're ready to be a professional again, call me and I'll send you a car."

My jaw is on the floor, almost unable to believe she would talk to me like this. But then I guess she's never had to talk to me like this because I've always nodded, smiled, and agreed to everything she's ever asked of me. *Polite, polite, polite.*

"Hi," Claire says tentatively after Susan hands her the phone.

"Hey, Claire."

"So, Susan wanted me to talk to you about the opening week of the tour and—" Claire pauses and I hear a door shut. She then lets out a full breath. "Okay, she's gone. Listen, I just have to tell you a few things because I can't keep it to myself any longer. First, I'm not sure how many more days I'll be working for Susan. She's a nightmare. So much of a nightmare, I see a therapist weekly where I do nothing but talk about Susan." She pauses, but not long enough for me to interject.

"The thing is, she's terrible and there's a lot going on behind your back that I just found out about. I don't have time to fill you in now, but I will when you come back to town. Which, I hope you don't do quickly, because I'm so happy you finally took a vacation. I could see you needed it, but I've been too cowardly to say anything until now." Another brief silence that I don't fill because I'm too stunned to speak.

"Listen, I don't want you to have to worry about work. So I'm going to tell Susan your call dropped and I couldn't get ahold of you again." Who is this person? I'm having trouble reconciling her with the quiet woman who usually stands in Susan's shadow. I want to jump through the phone and hug her.

"Claire," I say quickly because I can feel that she's getting ready to end the call. "Thank you. Just . . . thank you. Do what you need to do to take care of yourself, but I'll be sad to lose you from the team. Let's talk when I get back."

"Sure thing," she says and I can hear the smile in her voice. "Bye, Amelia."

When Claire hangs up, my head is spinning. I needed something to take my mind off Noah and, boy, did that do the trick. I have so much to consider now. So much to decide. And what is going on behind my back that I don't know about?

I march my way down the hallway, intending to disappear into my room and contemplate all my options for the future. For once, it doesn't feel set in stone. I feel like I can make some changes. Like I *should* make some changes. Except I never make it to my room, because while walking down the hallway, I trip on the bottom hem of these too-long pj bottoms and flail right into Noah's door where my body throws it open with the force of a 60 mph wind. I fall flat on my belly, sprawled out over his floor like a starfish.

I gasp and sit up, where I find Noah, wide eyed and gaping at me from his seated position on his bed. He blinks. I blink. And then we both talk at the same time.

Me: I'm sorry I fell into your room, it was an accident!
Him: Holy shit are you okay? That was a hard fall!

We both make no attempts to move.

He lets me talk first this time. "I'm fine. My ego is a little bruised, but I'm—" My eyes finally snag on Noah's chest and he's . . . he's wearing the exact same pj set as the one I'm wearing, but in the color gray. My smile blooms wide and wicked as I pop up to my feet with renewed vigor. He gives me a warning look after noticing the sparkle in my eyes.

I point anyway. "You have more of these pj sets! And you wear them!"

He wets his lips and rolls his eyes, snapping shut the book he was reading—*oh my gosh Noah is a reader*—and sets it aside. "Okay, get it all out of your system."

"These weren't just a gag gift. You own them because you love them. Noah, the Classic Man, is even more classic than I ever knew. Look at you wearing collars on your pj's. Oh my gosh, you have them all the way buttoned up!" And still looks fine as ever in them. It's unfair.

He should look ridiculous in a buttoned-up matching set of *pa-ja-mas,* as he would call them. But no. He looks sexy as hell. Comfy in cotton. Like a handsome businessman in the 1950s just before he puts on his suit, and fedora, and goes to his fancy job on Wall Street to do businessy stuff. And the way his broad chest and shoulders fill out that shirt is undeniably, knee-knockingly delicious. Mainly because I can imagine sitting across his lap and unbuttoning each and every one of those little buttons.

"The first pair was given to me as a gag gift." He pauses. "But then I wore them and liked how warm they were."

"How many, Noah? How many do you own?" I ask and I think it sounds a tad bit too seductive. But I can't help it. Apparently matching pajama sets on men get me hot.

He swallows. "Ten."

"TEN!" I practically chant this word. I'm so delighted by his answer I can't stand it. Noah owns ten pairs of adorable old-man pj's. "Do any of them have cute little prints on them?"

"No. They're all plain."

"Of course they are," I say happily. He'd never be caught dead in something festive or peppy.

This is bad news. Very bad news. Because now I officially, without doubt, feel something for Noah. I like him. I genuinely like him. And I'm attracted to him in a big way, and just the scent of him has my blood rocketing through my veins. My heart is inflating like it's attached to a bike pump. Now that I'm in here, I don't want to leave.

"Noah," I say softly, not taking my eyes from his face. "Can I look around your room? I won't intrude on your privacy if you don't want me to." I mean it, too. I'll shut my eyes right now and stumble out of here if me seeing his room makes him uncomfortable.

His emerald eyes hold mine, he fills his lungs with air, and then lets it out in a whoosh. "You can look around."

He just gave me the keys to Disney World.

I smile and turn to look at the room. And that's when I see the shelves and shelves of books. This man does not just read . . . he's a book nerd. I feel Noah's eyes on me as I step up to the wall-to-wall floating bookshelf. It's a beautiful design. It's made of exposed wood and black brushed steel. I don't know if he built it or had someone else install it, but clearly it's important to him, because it's very well crafted—which makes it achingly sweet.

Noah lightly clears his throat. "My dad was a big reader. A lot of these books were actually his."

Pies, flowers, and books. Little by little I'm able to string together these parts of Noah. It's sort of terrifying that he's turning out to be more wonderful than I expected.

I tuck my hands behind my back like I'm in a museum and everything around me is precious and fragile. "Why do you keep it hidden away in here?"

He chuckles lightly, and I love the rumble of it. "It's not hidden away."

I look at him over my shoulder. "You literally have it inside a room that you keep shut at all times and never let me peek into. It's hidden."

He's still sitting up against the headboard, and the sight of it is so intimate for some reason I have to look away. I think he would feel less vulnerable if he were standing in front of me completely naked. But seeing him lounging in bed in his favorite pj's in his favorite room around all his favorite books is intensely vulnerable.

"All right, I guess it's a little hidden. I like to keep my life private. I only let certain people know me on this level."

I touch a hardback—a biography of a World War II soldier. "But not me because I'm just a celebrity passing through." My voice is light and airy. I don't look at him, I just keep looking through his library of mostly nonfiction books. Apparently he enjoys learning about anything and everything. It doesn't surprise me.

"Right," he says quietly. "I guess you could say I'm a little jaded. I like to keep the number of people who know the emotional parts of me to a minimum."

I look at him. "I understand. I really do. I think you've already endured enough heartbreak for a lifetime, and if I were you, I'd protect myself, too." His brows pinch together like my words are a punch to his gut. I see his jaw clench and he blinks before turning his green eyes to the corner of the room.

"You can hang out if you want. Pick out a book." Noah gestures with his head toward the corner behind me.

I turn around and there's the most comfy, masculine-looking cracked leather armchair in the corner of the room. A cozy blanket is draped over the back with a standing lamp behind it. It calls to me. It would be a hug, that chair. The most comfortable place to sit in the entire world from years of being worn in by Noah's body. I can't sit there. I can't invade his space like that.

"That's okay. Thank you, but I'll let you have your night to yourself back here." I turn to flee, but Noah's voice stops me.

"Amelia, stay. Please."

I slowly slide my gaze to him, and I know my face is contorted into a wobbly expression. "Are you sure? I won't be a quiet companion. I'm incapable of it." Best to get this truth out in the open now.

He grins. "I know."

I start backing toward the chair. "And I don't sit still very well. I'll probably be noisy over here. I bounce my foot when I sit too long."

"That's okay."

"Will you read to me from your book?"

"Absolutely not."

"Please?"

"No."

"PRETTY PLEASE?"

He gives me a look over the top of his book like I'm annoying him to his core, and I smile and turn my attention to the shelf, making a big show of looking for the perfect book. "Do you at least have any romance books? Something steamy and emotional?"

He laughs. "No."

"And you call yourself a reader. You should be ashamed. Do you only have these boring nonfiction books?" I slide a book about ancient philosophers from the shelf, knowing this one will help put me to sleep.

"Put that one back. You'll hate it. Grab the thick one down there near the bottom."

"Bossy." I do as I'm told and slide out what looks to be a fantasy novel of some sort. At least it's fiction.

I take my treasure with me to the most perfect chair in the world and settle in. I groan loudly and purposely when I get comfy and Noah gives me side-eye from behind his book, but he doesn't say anything. I grin to myself and turn to page one.

I continue to flip pages over the next hour, but I'm not reading. I don't even look at the book. I'm soaking into my pores every detail of Noah's room. The way it smells just like his bodywash. The way the chair's butter-soft leather feels against my skin. The soft scratching sound of Noah turning the pages in his book. I etch his handsome, manly profile into my memory. I note the way his face softens when he reads. He smiles every now and then, and if it's because he can sense I'm staring at him or because his war book is funny, I'll never know.

Just beyond Noah, there's a picture on his dresser of a boy, three girls, and a mom and dad. My heart squeezes and twists and before I know it, I'm wiping a rogue tear from my cheek. He's so good—this man. I can't imagine how I'll be able to walk away.

How did you do it, Audrey?

Chapter 24

Amelia

The house smells like popcorn and Pop-Tarts. I don't know how to cook many things, so when Annie called earlier suggesting we have an Audrey Hepburn introductory movie night tonight, I turned to the only things in Noah's pantry that I could make without fear of setting the house on fire. Even the popcorn was touch-and-go there for a minute.

"You have everything you need?" Noah asks me, lingering by the front door with his keys in hand.

He and I have steered clear of each other today. Something happened yesterday that has set us on a trajectory that neither of us can afford to follow. First, there's this ridiculous sexual chemistry between us that, at times, feels like desire is going to set my skin on literal fire. Second, we have an emotional connection. Friendship. Those two combined feel absolutely lethal.

So without acknowledging it, we took a step back. I hung out at his house this afternoon and read more of the fantasy book he let me borrow, and even though he's supposed to have Mondays off, he went into the shop and worked for most of the afternoon. Now, he's going to James's house while the Walker sisters and I take over his house.

"Yep!" I say, mimicking a normal person who isn't nervous to spend an evening with other women having a girls' night. But I am. I don't want a repeat of Hank's. I'm determined to show them that I'm completely normal. N.O.R.M.A.L. Or at least, trick them into thinking I am.

Noah sees right through me. He can feel my nervous energy from a mile away. My foot is tapping. I'm blinking too much. I'm a bottle rocket about to take off.

He tilts his head slightly, those green eyes zero in on me, and when he lifts his brow invitingly, that's all it takes for me to spill my guts.

"Okayyyyy. No! I'm so nervous! I don't think I can do this. Do you know how long it's been since I've had a girls' movie night? High school, Noah! HIGH SCHOOL! We were still talking about Backstreet Boys and layering our Hollister polo shirts!"

His moody mouth grins, and he takes a step toward where I'm standing on the threshold of the entryway. "You'll be fine." He takes another step. *Closer, closer, closer.* This is why we've avoided each other. This keeps happening when we're in the same vicinity, and I think we're both incapable of stopping it. Our bodies are on a wavelength our minds are not privy to.

I have to tilt my chin higher and higher as he gets closer. I love that he's taller than me. "You don't have any better advice for me?"

"Nope."

"No tips for how to get your sisters to love me?"

He shrugs. "Don't get water rings on the coffee table."

"That will make them love me?"

He's so close now our chests are nearly touching. "You'll be fine."

"Noah?"

"Hmm?"

"What are you doing?" I ask quietly. Like someone else might overhear our secret.

"Hell if I know. I think I was going to hug you."

I bite my lips against a smile. "Was?"

"Well, now I'm here and I don't feel like it's a good idea anymore."

I nod, unable to keep the smile from my mouth. He doesn't have to explain. We both feel it like a change in pressure before a storm. There's no wondering if he likes me or not—I know he does. He wants me, and I want him, but we can't let that happen. Because for whatever reason, he's not interested in anything romantic with me. *Smart*. A relationship with me would complicate his life beyond what he even realizes.

"Might still do it anyway," he says, either hesitation or nerves touching his voice.

Honesty bleeds between us. "I want you to."

A soft smile touches his full lips. "Okay, I will. Here I go. I'm going to hug you now." I've never been preemptively warned about a hug. It's adding a whole new anticipation to the embrace.

His hand slowly rises and I stay very still as his fingers settle lightly against my bicep. His thumb rubs a quiet little streak of heat across a one-inch section of my skin, and I feel myself melting toward him. I shuffle a little. He tugs a little. The result is me entering his arms, and just before we're settled into what I know would be a life-changing hug, the front door flies open.

"Hiya! Oh *shiiiit*!" It's Madison, holding a pan covered in plastic wrap. She whistles while coming to a stop in the doorway. Noah and I jump apart looking as guilty as teenagers emerging from a dark room. The other sisters come up behind Madison.

"That's another dollar in the jar," says Annie, popping her head over Madison's shoulder.

Emily surfaces on the other side. "What? What did I miss?"

My face is on fire. Noah rubs his jaw.

"I think I just interrupted a little sensual rendezvous," says Madison with an indulgent eyebrow arch.

Noah grabs a hat from the coatrack on the wall and pushes his hand back through his hair before slapping it firmly on his sexy head. *Sexy? No . . . stop that, Amelia.*

"It was not . . . that," says Noah with pain in his voice. "Okay, I'm leaving." He won't make eye contact with me. I think he's too embarrassed.

The sisters part as Noah barrels through them out the door and into the night. I've never seen someone jump into a truck and back out of a driveway so quickly.

The moment he drives off, they all turn their eyes to me. I am one big prickle of embarrassment. Did we just get caught naked playing Twister rather than about to hug? Feels like it. But geez, that was going to be some hug. A hug so powerful it would've made Noah's baby.

I hold up my hands and lie. "It wasn't sensual."

Madison scoffs. "Yeah right, that was so sexy. I know because I was grossed-out seeing my brother in a sexy situation."

"A hug! That's all," I plead defensively for myself as much as them.

"An erotic hug," Madison adds with a wicked gleam in her eye as she closes the front door with her foot, closing us all in together.

We all sniff and wipe our eyes as THE END flashes across the TV screen.

"I love her," Annie says in a weepy voice.

"I told you she was incredible." I use a tissue to blot under my eyes. It doesn't matter that I've seen this movie twenty times, *Roman Holiday* never fails to make me cry at the end. Weep. Like a pitiful little baby.

"But . . ." Emily has to take a moment to collect herself before continuing. "But why did she have to leave in the end?"

Madison blows her nose. "She had to! She had a duty to her country. She couldn't just stay in Rome with him forever. She had to go, Em."

We're all spread out in various positions of sitting and lying down across Noah's living room. I'm on the couch with Annie, Emily is in an armchair, and Madison is lying on a pallet of blankets and pillows on the floor. We're all disheveled and dressed for nothing but comfort in sweats and messy buns. I've been having to blow my bangs out of my eyes every other second because I'm not used to them yet, but they're worth it. I love them. I love what they represent to me.

The girls all see me fidgeting with the bangs and look at me meaningfully. "What?" I ask, lowering my hand from my freshly chopped locks.

"You cut your hair," says Madison.

Emily's eyes bounce from me, to the TV, and back to me. "Just like Audrey did in the movie."

"And you're in Rome," Annie adds.

I gasp and my hands fly to my head. "You're right. But, you guys, I swear I'm not being creepy and trying to copy the movie. I just . . . well, I did intentionally copy it in the beginning by leaving in the night and coming to Rome and all that . . . but the copying stops there!"

Emily nudges my knee with her foot. "That's not why we're worried. We're worried, because . . . Audrey leaves in the end. There's no happily ever after."

Oh. That.

I swallow. "Well, that's not necessarily true." I'm grasping at straws. What felt liberating about this movie at the beginning of my adventure is now feeling like a death sentence. "I think Audrey did get her happily ever after. It just . . . wasn't with Gregory Peck. She had a happily ever after for herself. And that was enough for her. I think we can all learn a lesson there."

I have three puppies staring back at me that all look as if I've just mercilessly kicked them. Madison is the first to attempt to recover the happy mood, but her voice sounds too peppy. "True. And . . . it's not like we actually expected you—I mean Audrey—to stay in Rome for good. That's impractical for your—HER career."

"But now we know you—her—or . . . ugh. Forget it. We're all talking about you, and we know it," Annie says quietly, pulling that mood right back down. "And it's going to be hard to say goodbye."

"And Noah . . ." Emily adds, ensuring that the mood is now buried six feet under and completely unrecoverable. "He'll have to say goodbye to you . . . just like Gregory Peck did with Audrey." All our glittering eyes shift to the TV screen frozen on the downcast face of the man himself.

Oh, Gregory. How have I never realized before that this movie is a tragedy? It might as well be Shakespeare! GOD! How could Audrey just leave like that in the end?

I blink at the TV. "Maybe they stay in contact."

"Uh-uh," grunts Emily, clearly projecting when she says, "He has major trust issues. He'll never have a long-distance relationship."

"You know a lot about Gregory Peck's character's backstory?" I ask sarcastically.

Emily gives me a pointed look. "I know every bit of it. I know what he's been through. I know that he deserves a woman who's going to stick around and love him like he needs. And I know that erotic hallway hugs are not going to help the situation if Audrey knows she's leaving in the end."

Emily then takes a pillow to the face when Madison launches one from her pallet. "Mind your own biscuits, Em! Gregory wouldn't want you meddling. He can make his own choices."

"*Gregory* has been through a world of hurt, and I just don't want to see him go through it again, because the last time a woman passed through this town and stole his heart, he uprooted his life to follow her, and then when he had no choice but to come home, she stomped on it, making him lose faith in all women!" Her eyes snap to me—expression softer than the one she's giving her sister. "No offense to you, Amelia."

I shake my head. "None taken." And really, I don't take offense to what she said, because in no way would I want to hurt Noah. Or anyone. And I think she's right. There's no way I can give Noah what he needs or wants. I'm about to set out on a nine-month world tour for goodness' sake. Noah seems like a matching-rocking-chairs-and-multiple-children kind of guy.

Suddenly, my mind snags back on something Emily said. "Why did Noah have no choice but to come home?"

"Okayyyy!" Annie stands from the couch, grabs another one of the amazing spicy-chicken-calzone-things Madison made, and then settles back on the couch. "I think we're getting off topic here. *Gregory* would not like it if we were spilling all his beans during girls' night."

Madison barely contains a laugh. "You can't say *spills his beans* in reference to a man, Annie."

"Why not?"

"Because I've heard men refer to their balls as beans sometimes."

Annie gasps. "*No.* Why would they do that? That's gross."

Madison gives Emily a look. "This is why we need to take some trips and get out more. She needs to experience more of the world."

"So I can learn more words for male genitalia? No, thank you," says Annie, snuggling deeper into her blanket and munching on the calzone.

Emily raises a brow at Madison. "You haven't seen the world and you seem to be doing just fine with terms for male anatomy."

"But I could learn more! Just imagine. I could learn how to say balls in French! Italian! Spanish!"

Annie *tsk*s. "Audrey Hepburn would never say anything so crude."

"Actually," I interject, "Audrey was a call girl in another movie. That's what's so great about her. She's unpredictable. You'll see her in a ball gown in one movie, and a man's oversized shirt with no pants in another. And in her personal life, she had a baby deer for a pet."

"That's it. I want to be her." Madison holds her hand up and begins ticking items off her fingers. "She travels. Has an incredible fashion sense. And would definitely teach me the word for balls in French."

"Why do you think I'm always turning to Audrey when I feel lost?" I don't mention how watching Audrey movies also makes me feel close to my mom again when I miss her.

Madison points at me. "YES. I'm doing that from now on. I need a life coach and she seems like the closest thing."

Emily scoffs. "I thought I was your life coach?"

"*Self-appointed* life coach."

"But a life coach no less," Emily says grinning.

Madison does not return her sister's smile. "You turned me into a teacher."

"And?"

"I hate being a teacher."

"Oh, you'll grow to like it."

The three sisters continue to banter back and forth and it's enough to erase the tension that had filled the room after the movie. At least it is for them. They're laughing and my heart is sinking. It's sinking right down to the floor where my feet have been trying to sprout little baby roots. For a moment there, I forgot I'll be leaving. This town is like an antigravity chamber. I'm light and hopeful inside its city limits. But I know that when it's time to go, I'll leave. Just like Audrey.

Whatever has started to develop between me and Noah has to stop. Not only am I leaving soon, he made it clear in the beginning that anything romantic was off the table. I just wish his body language and eyes weren't saying something different. I need to be careful with him. As the one who will be leaving when her car is fixed, I need to be the one to reaffirm the boundaries he originally put in place to protect himself.

Annie—the ever emotionally perceptive sister—must read my thoughts. I'm starting to think it's her superpower. "You'll figure it out—and you'll do what's best for you in the end, and whatever that is, it's okay. We're your friends so we will support you. So will Noah."

Chapter 25

Noah

"You slept here?" asks James—his head leaning over the back of the couch to stare at me accusingly.

I grunt and throw my legs over the front of the couch, sitting up. Everything on me hurts as I press the heels of my hands into my eyes wishing I had gotten about seven more hours of sleep. Turns out sleeping on a couch in my thirties is not as easy as it was in my twenties. "Yeah. You need a new couch."

"That's it? That's all you're gonna say about it?" James laughs, coming around to settle into an armchair, steaming cup of coffee in hand.

I shrug. It's too early for conversation. Not too early for James, though. He starts his day on the farm around five A.M. I bet that's his second cup of coffee. Maybe even third.

"I left you in here with the TV on at nine o'clock assuming you'd go home when the girls left your house. And then I come out here to find you hiding on my couch, snoring away."

"I don't snore." I pick up my shirt from the floor and tug it down over my head. "And I'm not hiding."

James is smirking. "Oh yeah? What do you wanna call it then?"

I press my tongue into my cheek. "Avoidance."

He chuckles lightly. "Well, at least you'll own up to that much."

It's time for coffee. It's always time for coffee, actually. Standing up, I go into James's kitchen and find a full pot and a mug. James makes his coffee like a damn cowboy. I could throw a horseshoe in it and it would disintegrate. I take a sip and grimace. "How do you drink it like this?"

"Started when I was a kid. I think I burned up all my insides at an early age so I don't even notice anymore."

"Does Tommy drink it like this, too?" Tommy is James's younger brother. James inherited the farm when his mom and dad got older and didn't want to run it anymore, but Tommy has never been interested in being a farmer. He's a successful entrepreneur, always traveling and starting up new companies, restaurants, and hotels all around the world. He's good at it. But he's also a douchebag. Can't stand him if I'm being honest.

James laughs. "Hell no. Tommy won't touch coffee if it's not in some sort of latte form with a nasty syrup in it."

"Sounds about right." I take another drink, thankful that James seems to be distracted from any conversations of Amelia. I just need a few more milligrams of caffeine in me before I'm ready to discuss or even think about that woman. "Where is he now?"

"New York, I think. Working on a new gourmet noodle restaurant and sleeping with supermodels."

"What a life."

He groans. "Whatever. You know you'd choose this life over that one any day. In fact, you did."

"To be fair, though, supermodels weren't in the mix. Might have been different if that option had been available."

James shakes his head with a smile. "Bullshit. You're not into supermodels." His smile turns searching. "You're into dark-haired singers with a sweet smile and curves for days."

"Easy," I say, before I even realize that I'm getting territorial about the thought of James admiring Amelia's curves. What the hell is wrong with me? She's not mine to get territorial over. If James wanted to go for Amelia, that would be completely . . . unacceptable. Who am I kidding? I'd kill him. Limb by limb, I'd make it as painful as possible.

James's eyebrows go up. He's pleased to have successfully hit a nerve. "Knew it. Dammit, you're falling headfirst for that woman." He shakes his head. "You're in trouble."

I set down my mug of gasoline that James likes to think is coffee and raid his pantry. "You're so dramatic. I'm not falling for her. I'm attracted to her. There's a difference." I pull out a loaf of home-made bread that I know is from Jenna's Bread Basket and pop a slice into the toaster. Actually, I throw in two. "And that, if you must know, is why I spent the night here. Because I have enough sense to stay away from the woman I'm attracted to after the sun goes down."

He pulls a face. "Does that mean I'm always going to wake up to you on my couch?"

"Hell no. I think I strained my neck sleeping there." I rub the spot that feels like someone stuck a corkscrew in my neck and twisted. "I just needed a night away to get my head on straight again. I'm good now."

"Sure. Yeah." James gives a mocking nod. "A night away cured you."

The toast pops up and that's my cue to leave. I slap some butter on the slices of golden brown toast and then rip off two paper towels. One for each piece of toast. James notices because he's way too invested in my life at the moment. "Why do you have two paper towels?"

"Why does it matter? You the paper towel sheriff?"

"Just want to know why you're wasting all my good paper when you could just put your two slices of toast in one paper towel." His voice is thick with amusement. He doesn't care about his *good paper*. He cares about annoying me.

We're interrupted by a light knock on the door. James and I both frown before he goes to open it because no one in this town makes house calls this early. He opens the door and there stands the woman I'm avoiding. Her new bangs are framing her pretty face and the rest of her hair is tied up in a messy bun on her head . . . and she's wearing *my* sweatshirt. Does she ever wear her own clothes?

James's house is small like mine, so even in the kitchen, I'm able to make eye contact with Amelia standing right outside the front door. She sees me frown as my eyes drop. Her cheeks pink. She's a thief, caught red-handed in an alley. Those big blue eyes flash and she crosses her hands over her chest like I might steal it right back. "I was cold. It's cold in your house. And I didn't pack a sweatshirt." She pauses and when my eyes narrow even further she adds, "I found this on the coatrack!"

James chuckles lightly and glances over his shoulder at me before looking back at her. "Morning, Amelia, what can I do for you?"

She dimples at James and I find myself wanting to cup my hands over her cheeks so he can't see them. Like those dimples are an intimate part of her that only I should be entitled to see. *Shit, I'm in big trouble.*

"Actually, I was looking for Noah."

James steps aside and gestures for Amelia to come in. She does and that's when I notice she's still wearing shorts. Tiny ones. They just peek out from under the sweatshirt, and James notices as she walks by him. Because he's a good friend, though, he looks away quickly. Straight into my glaring eyes in fact.

Amelia crosses the room and stops in front of me in the kitchen. Memories of last night standing with her in my entryway assault me. I touched her. *Tenderly.* While sober. I haven't touched a woman that way in a long time. Yeah, it felt sexy, but it was also something different. The moment my skin connected with hers, it was all I could do not to savor it. The way I would with someone I care about. I keep trying to tell myself it's only attraction, but I'm not sure that even I can believe that anymore. Not when she smiles up at me and it feels like my insides burst with light. When I'm dying to know how her night with my sisters went. Wishing I could cancel my day and spend the whole of it just listening to her talk. I'm terrified.

When Amelia is within arm's length, I hand her one of the slices of toast. At first she hesitates. "I don't want to take your toast."

"I made it for you," I say with an easy shrug. "I was about to head home."

I accidentally make eye contact with James and he shakes his head, mouthing, *I knew it.* Then he makes a headfirst-dive gesture with his hands.

"Thank you!" There's an awkward pause as Amelia shuffles on her feet and then glances briefly over her shoulder at James. He just stands there smiling like an idiot, not taking the hint that she wants to talk with me alone.

"Do you want to ride back over with me in my truck?"

"No!" she says a little too firmly and then smiles. "Sorry. Uh— I was actually just coming over to tell you I'll be out of your hair today. Annie invited me to work with her at the flower shop and I said I would."

"I don't think I've ever heard anyone say *invite* in terms of work before. Don't feel like you have to say yes. You're here so you can get a break, not work for free at my sister's shop."

She fiddles with her bangs. "Oh, I know! I want to. It'll be fun. I haven't worked a job that wasn't on a stage in forever. I'm actually looking forward to it." She shoots a little airstream at her bangs to shift them. And before I can control my hand, I reach up and brush my fingers against her bangs, sweeping them out of her eyes. She smiles softly—curiously—at the gesture. I would give an excuse, but I don't have a good one anymore. So I just shrug with an it-is-what-it-is smile. And then I make it worse.

"You can work with me at The Pie Shop." The words are out before I can reel them back in. Why the hell did I say that? I had just decided to spend less time around Amelia and now I'm inviting her to spend the whole day with me?

"How come you've never invited me to work at The Pie Shop with you?" James asks, clearly trying to shorten his life span.

I look around Amelia toward my idiot friend. "Don't you have something better to do? Corn that needs shucking? Cows to milk?"

He shakes his head and settles back into the armchair facing us. "Nope. Not a damn thing."

Amelia looks at James. "Actually, I was hoping I could get a tour of your farm one of these days while I'm in town."

I'm not annoyed. I'm not annoyed in the least that she bypassed my offer to work at The Pie Shop and asked James for a tour of his farm instead. Not annoyed *at all*.

"Of course. You wanna come work with me for a while tomorrow?"

Amelia's face beams. "Yes! Can we go to lunch at the diner, too? I'm trying to soak up as much of the town as I can while I'm here."

"Sure," says James indulgently, and I fantasize about storming across the living room and tossing him through the window.

She looks back at me and lightly bumps my chest with the back of her hand. "Look! Now you don't have to worry about me being in your hair for two whole days. Aren't you happy?"

"So damn happy." I take one more swig of battery-acid coffee just because I want to feel the burn, and then grab my keys off the counter. "I'm gonna head—"

"WAIT!" Amelia says, pressing her hand firmly into my chest. Her eyes are wide, eyelashes practically touching her eyebrows, and when she sees my expression, she drops her hand. She slowly backs away toward the window with her hand outstretched toward

me like I'm a spooked horse about to bolt. "Just . . . wait a second."
When she reaches the window, she peeks through the blinds in the
direction of my house and then sighs. "Okay, you can go home
now!"

Her bright tone immediately has me suspicious. "What'd you
do to my house, Amelia?"

"Nothing."

"Amelia."

She crinkles her nose and starts heading for the door, moving
faster and faster with each step. "Really, it was nothing. Just . . . a
small fire on the stove! But-the-fire-department-put-it-out-and-
they're-gone-now-so-see-ya-later!" she yells in a frantic rush, before sprinting out the front door with her piece of toast clutched in
her hand.

The door slams behind her and after a moment of silence, I
look at James. "Don't say a w—"

"Amelia and Noah sitting in a tree . . ."

"Be sure and have a shitty day, James!" I say in a chipper tone,
throwing him the bird over my shoulder.

"Tell your girlfriend I can't wait for our lunch date. Love you!"

I then hop in my truck and drive exactly one minute over to my
house. Getting out, I slam the door with determination. I will *not*
care that Amelia will be spending the day with Annie instead of me.
I will *not* be jealous that she's spending tomorrow with James. I will
not think about her for the rest of the day, in fact. I'll enjoy my
solitude at the shop just like I always do.

Chapter 26

Amelia

've been in the flower shop with Annie for a few hours when the door flies open and Noah steps inside. The door bangs back against one of the displays, nearly knocking it over. Annie and I jump, and Mabel—who is gathering bouquets for her B and B—squeals.

Noah winces. "Sorry about that." A rare color of red sweeps over his cheekbones. "I didn't mean to make such a dramatic entrance."

Mabel shoves a finger in his direction. "Are you trying to give me a heart attack? Don't bother trying to make me kick the bucket early, because I love you but I'm not leaving you the inn in my will. It's going to my niece."

Noah gingerly closes the door behind him. "I don't want your inn, Mabel."

She scoffs. "Well, you would if you knew what's good for you! Honey, there's all kinds of money sitting in that inn. And I don't mean tied up in the equity, I mean hidden in the floors!"

Noah frowns. "That's not good. You shouldn't store money in the floorboards, Mabel. What happens if there's a fire?"

I don't particularly love the way he looks at me when he says that. It was a tiny fire, okay? Minuscule, really. I had already put it out when the fire department arrived. They just helped me get all the smoke out of the house. But anyway, lesson learned. Don't leave a pancake in the pan while you're mixing up another batch.

Mabel puts her hands on her ample hips. "And who's gonna do that? Are you planning to start a fire, Noah? If you need money, just tell me. I can work out some window-washing days with you so you don't have to go doing nefarious acts for attention."

Noah looks dumbfounded. And then distraught. And then back to dumbfounded. "No . . . Mabel . . . I don't need money. And how would starting a fire even . . ." He shakes his head and lifts his hands up. "You know what? Never mind."

Noah sends Annie a look, and in a split second, she is rushing over to the meddling old woman. "Mabel, let's get those bouquets finished up for you. I'll help." The two continue picking flowers around the store and Noah finally walks over to where I'm standing behind the counter, looking like a real workingwoman.

"Hi," he says, in his quiet, rumbly way. His voice isn't necessarily deep, but it has a grit to it that just *feels* good to hear. I need to plug my ears. I'm trying to distance myself from him, and not imagine him whispering in my ear while I'm soaking in a bubble bath with his fingers tracing a quiet line over my skin—even softer than the caress of his voice. *Shoot,* now I'm picturing that. And it doesn't help that he has his hat off today, giving me the full effect of his startling woodsy eyes. I'm drowning in a lush evergreen forest.

"Hello," I reply, pulling my mind out of that fantasy bubble bath. "Are you here to buy flowers?"

He darts his eyes away, heavy lashes blinking. "Nope."

I watch as he delicately runs his finger over a velvety petal from a long-stem flower beside the counter, and it makes me shiver given my last fantasy of him. "Did you need to talk to Annie?"

Again, I'm met with a no.

"Going to the market then?"

He shifts on his feet and shakes his head. "I'm good on groceries."

Goodness, Noah is always cryptic, but this is too much. And awkward. He's standing there practically vibrating with nervous energy and in return it's making *me* nervous. I'm starting to sweat. I'm one more anxious minute away from getting pit stains on my shirt.

Why is he just standing here? Why won't he say more?

I'm not the only one who notices. Mabel sighs deeply from across the room and practically yells, "*Bless it,* child! He's here for you! Now go ahead and ask the lady out, Noah, so we can all be finished with this barrel of awkwardness."

My face flames. I'm sure it looks like I've just dipped it into a vat of tomato juice. Noah smirks lightly, eyes crinkling in the corners. "I'm taking off early and going fishing. It was on your list so I thought I'd come by and see if you want to come with me?"

Spend the afternoon with Noah? I don't know. I was trying to spend the day away from him so this thing we've had humming between us would hopefully die down. It's why I'm planning to spend the day with James tomorrow, too. I thought Noah and I were on the same page—that he would want me to stay away from him given he spent the night at James's house last night. But looking into Noah's eyes, I go weak. I may be confused, but I couldn't say no to him even if I tried.

But of course I have to annoy him first.

I bend slightly to rest my elbows on the counter, propping my chin on the backs of my knuckles. "Why? You miss me?"

He rolls his eyes, the corner of his mouth twitching. "Absolutely not. Just trying to live up to the title of Mr. Hospitality."

"You did miss me. You were just sulking around the shop because you don't know what to do without me being all up in your life anymore."

"Are you coming or not?"

I move around the counter to stand by him, blinking up at him like a coy Disney princess. "Was it so lonely without me?"

He starts pushing me by my low back toward the door. Looks like I'm going with him then. "It was a hell of a lot more peaceful than it is now."

"Just admit you missed me!" I'm giving a half-hearted attempt to put on the brakes, but he keeps pushing me right along with him, touching my back like he's done this a thousand times. Like the warmth of his hand seeping through my shirt doesn't send a current across my skin. Like I wouldn't willingly go with him anywhere he wanted.

"Annie, I'm taking this spoiled pop star off your hands for the rest of the day."

"Annabell! Make him admit he missed me!" I say, over my shoulder. My quick glance shows me a smiling Annie and smirking Mabel before Noah closes the door behind us.

"Quiet, you," says Noah, pausing to look down at me when we make it out to the curb. I'm bubbling with laughter that I can't contain even if I wanted to. It's the kind of happy laughter that slows you down, makes you want to anchor your hands on your thighs just so you don't fall to the ground.

Noah's eyes drop to my mouth. They linger there for a full in and out breath, before his lashes rise back up to my eyes. "I missed you."

My laughter stops.

My heart skips.

My lips part.

But before I can respond, he adds, "But you're still a pain in my ass."

How does he manage to say that in a way that makes me feel like I'm back in that fantasy bubble bath?

When I was younger, there was an oak tree in my front yard. It was enormous. In the summer, my favorite thing to do was sit at its base, lean my back against it, and listen to music. Sometimes I'd take my guitar out and play, writing songs and soaking in every last drop of sunshine. Nothing bad could touch me under that oak tree with the sun brushing my skin. No place in this world has ever been able to recapture that feeling of absolute soul-cuddling peace.

Until now.

My arm is hanging out the window of Noah's truck, and my old friend Sunshine is rekindling our past love and kissing my exposed skin. The wind is twirling my hair all around my face, and at my side is Noah—hand draped casually over the steering wheel. A soft grin on his perfect chiseled face. And when I say perfect, I don't mean classically perfect. Noah isn't a pretty boy by any means. His face is tan and scruffy. Freckles down the bridge of his nose from too much sun and not enough sunscreen. He has a random little scar above his eyebrow and another above his lip. I imagine he got them in a fight as a boy. Someone called his best friend a mean name and he stepped in. But the unique concoction of rugged scars and long thick eyelashes framing bright green eyes—it should be illegal. Right up there with crystal meth.

Except for the wind, we've been driving in silence, me quickly sneaking peeks of Noah over my shoulder when I'm sure he's not looking. Normally I like the quiet between us. But right now, I feel fidgety—which seems like it would be at war with the peace I've been feeling, but it's not. They go hand in hand. It's the very feeling of calm and serenity that lets me know something is unmistakably *different*. Noah has struck a chord inside me and it's quivering. I need to bounce my knee. Gather my hair up in a ponytail. Check my phone, see that it still has zero bars of service, and turn it off again.

Noah notices, but his only reaction is a slight raise of his eyebrow. He knows that if I want to talk about it, I will. He's not a man who needs constant reassuring—what I used to think was grumpy is really just him being earnest.

And that's exactly why I'm dying in here with my body alone with his body. And my body wants to make him pull over so I can climb onto his body. Did I not just remind myself last night to stop pursuing my attraction to Noah? To not explore why I hang on his every intentionally spoken word. I decided to stay away from him. Far, far away. Put up a damn fortress between us. But now here I am, eyes tracing the lines of his face like a map I'm memorizing.

We need some music to fill this silence.

Reaching forward, I push the dial on his radio. It's static—making me wonder if he even listens to music—so I turn it to the nearest station. It's country. An old George Strait song fills the air and rides the breeze perfectly. I'm not really a fan of country music, but I have to admit that something about it pairs perfectly with golden sunshine and a warm day. I shut my eyes and let my head sink back against the headrest, enjoying the moment of stillness.

Over these last few days, I feel parts of me coming alive again. Like when you've been sitting on your foot too long and then finally walk around. It's tingly and uncomfortable at first, but then you shake it back to life and can move normally again.

Our comfy moment suddenly slices in half when a different song comes on and changes the whole vibe of this drive. It's a song by Faith Hill and Tim McGraw. One so sexy I want to die. *"Let's make love . . . all night long . . . until all our strength is gone . . ."* I snap my eyes open and look at Noah. His hand is tightened on the steering wheel but otherwise not betraying that he feels as prickly as I do all of a sudden. I wonder if he'll make a move to change the station, but he doesn't. Whether it's because he doesn't want to tip me off to discomfort, or because he wants to see if I'm affected by these lyrics or not, I have no idea. Or maybe he finds it hilarious.

Either way, I lurch forward and change the station. "Whew!" I say loudly, trying to cover the awkward moment and that I nearly just broke his radio dial from the force I used to turn it. "You don't mind if I surf the radio a bit, right? I'm not really in the mood to listen to country today."

The corner of his mouth hitches up. "Shame. That's one of my favorites."

I give him a side-eye look and keep scrolling, making him chuckle. "So sorry to disappoint you."

I finally settle on a commercial about a men's hair loss remedy. Perfect. Zero sexual tension here. And at each new point the radio announcer makes, I give mock encouraging eyes to Noah. "Well, see there, Noah!" I swat his bicep playfully, desperate to recover the levity from a few moments ago. "There's hope for your bald spot after all." He contains his amusement so I push harder. "I bet you didn't even know you had one. But you do. It's back there. A gaping shiny bald spot. And you know what? I'm a good friend, so if you want, I'll buy this cream and apply it for you. I won't even expect anything in return other than pancakes made for me daily with whipped cream and chocolate chips on top."

"I'll gladly make you pancakes every day if you'll quit trying to burn my house down."

I'm just about to respond with something sassy and delightful, when my own voice stops me in my tracks. It's my latest chart-topping single. When it plays through the speakers, I freeze. My joy dims, and a boulder settles back over my chest. It's a reminder of the real world that I don't want or need.

"You're about to tour for this album, right?"

I nod and swallow the lump in my throat.

Noah nods, too. After another pause, he asks, "How long will you . . . how long does the tour last?" His voice sounds suspiciously light. Like he's working extrahard to convince me that he could care less and is just making small talk. But I know.

I fidget with the hem of my shorts. "Nine months. I'll have a break between the U.S. leg and the international leg, but it'll be short."

Again Noah nods slowly. And this time, he's the one to abruptly end the song. "Okay, enough with the radio. Besides, I hear that singer is a real diva. And wants everyone to like yogurt for some reason," he says with a smile before clicking the CD button.

"You would have a CD in there. Who still listens to CDs?" *Says the woman who owns and continues to watch DVDs.*

He gives me a look. "Just be glad it's not a cassette."

I settle into the bench again, looking out the window, excited to learn what is in Noah's personal music library. I don't know what I'm expecting to hear, but I can promise you I never in a million years would have guessed Frank Sinatra. "Love Me Tender," Frank's version of Elvis's classic song, croons through the cab of his old truck and it's so lovely that even the sun swoons. Of course he would have this. Of course because he's the classic man. *My* classic man, my mind wants to tack on, but I swat that thought away like a pesky gnat.

I turn sharply to look at Noah. "This is *not* your CD?"

"Why?"

"Because you're a thirty-year-old man living in Rome, Kentucky."

"Thirty-two."

"Fine. Thirty-two. You should be listening to . . . I don't know, some weird rock music from your youth. Or since you like classic things, maybe Hank Williams. Johnny Cash! I don't know . . . anything but *this*!"

He glances at me and then back to the road. "Do you not like Frank?"

Frank. He would be so familiar with him that he feels inclined to be on a first-name basis with the man. Like I am with Audrey. It physically hurts now how smitten I am with Noah. I can't take much more.

"I *love* Frank Sinatra." I say this in a tone similar to a person trying to speak while their insides are being squeezed. "As well as the other greats of that time like Ella Fitzgerald, Bing Crosby, and—"

"They're on here, too," Noah states casually like this doesn't completely floor me. At my silence he looks at me with an amused smile. "It's a compilation CD. My grandma bought it for me a long time ago." He chuckles and turns his eyes back to the road. "She bought it for me because I was listening to too much of that weird rock you talked about. Said I needed to know the classics if I had any hopes of growing into a good man."

Mission accomplished, I want to whisper loud enough for him to hear, but instead I stay quiet, and together we let the song wrap around us. An already perfect moment feels like a dream now. When the song ends, I look at Noah. "I love your grandma. I wish I could have met her."

A real genuine smile splits across his face like the sun popping over the horizon at dawn, but he doesn't say anything.

Noah pulls into a small parking lot that overlooks a dock, stretching out to a small scenic lake. There are trees lining the bank, making it feel secluded and intimate. We both get out of the truck, and he pulls two fishing poles and a tackle box from the back of his truck. Together we walk down the long dock until we end at the small platform. I remove my white canvas sneakers and sit down, dangling my legs over the side. It's high enough up that my feet hover about a foot above the water. Noah sits beside me and our shoulders touch. My face flushes with an innocent pleasure I haven't experienced in years.

The tips of Noah's ears turn lightly pink—something that happens to him when he's embarrassed, I've learned—and he scoots away. If there were a window between us, I think we both would have rolled it up slowly and dramatically. We're acting as if we've never touched anyone of the opposite sex before. It's absolutely ridiculous. And wonderful. And confusing. And incredible.

"What was she like?" I'm desperate for any glimpse of a picture he'll paint for me, and also to break the tension between us.

"My grandma?" he asks as he pops open the tackle box and begins baiting his hook. I nod. "She was . . . tender and fiery at the same time. That woman loved to love on people. I swear no one made it out of her pie shop without a hug. Even strangers. It's just the way she was."

"What was her name?"

"Silvie Walker. Believe it or not, she and Mabel were best friends since their teenage years. Those two got into all kinds of trouble together. And since my grandad had already passed away by the time my grandma needed to take guardianship over me and my sisters, Mabel acted like our second parent in a lot of ways. I rarely went a day without seeing her."

"Ah—that's why Mabel loves you so much."

"That's why she *bugs* me so much." He smirks, but I hear the tenderness in his voice. "I may have lost my parents, but I've been really lucky to be loved by so many people who feel like family to me and my sisters. It's why I didn't hesitate to come back when they needed me here."

I open my mouth to ask why they needed him back here, but he continues talking before I can. "Speaking of names . . ." Once he gets his hook baited with a nasty-looking rubber worm, he sets his fishing pole down and turns his face to me. "I've been wondering how you chose your stage name."

"Rae is my middle name." I shrug lightly. "My mom used to call me Rae-Rae when I was little sometimes, and so it felt like a sweet choice for a stage name. And I thought having people refer to me as Rae instead of Amelia would help me have some separation between my private and professional life."

"Did it?" he asks, and this is something about Noah that is so different from other people. Most people would hmm, nod, and then move on. But he wants to know the answer. *Did it?*

"No. In fact, Rae Rose just absorbed me. I feel like I haven't been Amelia in so long. Except for you and your sisters, everyone just calls me Rae now. Even my mom. It's . . ." I falter for polite words to describe what it feels like, so I settle with a basic childish idea instead. "I *hate* it. I feel so jumbled and unsure of who I am."

"That must be hard," Noah says without accusation or shock. He doesn't even offer advice or throw a pile of *should*s on me. Doesn't even seem to expect me to come to any conclusion right now. I just get to say what I feel, and if that's not freedom, I don't know what is.

"Mainly it's the loneliness that makes it so hard. The second I became famous, everyone stopped seeing the real me. All they see is Rae Rose now and what she can do for them or give them. You know my mom used to be my best friend? Even she just sees me as a twenty-four-hour ATM now. It sucks. And the thing that's so weird is I'm rarely ever alone, and yet I can be standing in a room full of hundreds of people that supposedly love me and feel completely isolated."

"Do you feel lonely right now?"

Noah's question punches me in the heart. "No."

Everything would be so much easier if my answer were yes. Part of me wishes I could have come to this damn town and found my joy of music again without also finding something *more*.

"Good. I'm glad." He sounds genuine. He *is* genuine. "And maybe after this time away, you'll find your love for your career again."

"That's exactly what Mabel said."

"And she's never wrong. Or at least, that's what she'll lead you to believe." He grins and turns his eyes to the tackle box. He pulls out a nasty, squirmy, wet worm that is 100 percent a bucket of cold water to the intimate mood. *Good.* We need it. "So do you want to bait your own hook?"

"Am I a wimp if I say no?"

"Definitely."

I make a thinking face before answering. "I'm realizing I'm okay with that."

"Suit yourself, but you're missing out on all the fun."

I laugh and bump his shoulder. "That *would* be your idea of fun."

"What's that supposed to mean?" he asks, but it's clear by his tone that he's playing along.

"You just don't seem like the type of guy to pursue *fun.* So something sedate and peaceful like this would be considered fun to you."

"I'm very fun," he says deadpan. "Forget Mr. Hospitable. Everyone else calls me Mr. Fun. You just haven't been around long enough to hear it."

"Mm-hmm. Sure."

He raises an eyebrow, his full lips turning up at the corners. "Want me to prove it?"

"Yes," I say with a firm nod and then have to blow my bangs out of my eyes. "I would pay good money to see it, in fact."

"Well, you're in luck. It's free of charge today." Noah sets down the fishing poles and quickly hops to his feet. I frown up at him as he extends his hand to help me stand. I slide my palm into his and my heart flutters wildly. He tugs me up to my feet until we're nearly chest to chest. I stare up at him expectantly. "Okay, Mr. Fun. What's it gonna be?"

I watch in awe as his face opens into a full smile, eyes crinkling at the corners. He then puts his hand softly to my abdomen, and I gasp—which is perfect since the next thing I know, he's pushing me off the dock right into the water.

Chapter 27

Amelia

surface from the water in complete disbelief. Noah actually pushed me into the water. I drag in a breath and stare up at him standing proudly on the dock, eyes squinting and hands on his hips—smile marking his mouth.

I point at him as I tread water, pushing my wet hair back from my face. "What if I couldn't swim?"

"But you do."

"You didn't know that, though!"

He waves me off. "I would have saved you. I was a lifeguard in high school."

Of course he was. So dependable. And I bet he looked amazing in those red swim trunks.

"I hope you know you're in trouble now. You just wait until I—" I cut off my own threat as I watch him reach over the back of his head and tug his shirt right off. "Uh . . . what are you doing?" I ask, deeply in shock at the sight of his tan, sculpted torso so easily on display. I wish more than anything I was up there on that dock where I could run my fingers over his bronzed skin. First, I'd tenderly touch his tattoo on his ribs because there's something about it that makes me feel like it should be revered. And second, I'd touch every other centimeter available. (Because in this fantasy there are no barriers between us and I'm his girlfriend who he's deeply in love with.)

But apparently, Noah wants me to see more of him. He grins mischievously as he unbuckles his jeans and shucks them down over his hips, leaving him only in black boxer briefs. "I'm jumping in, what's it look like?"

It looks like this grown, toned, gorgeous man is stripping down to his underwear in broad daylight! My mouth is gaping open. My cheeks are turning into boiling flesh. It's a wonderful thing he was a lifeguard because I'm at real risk of drowning as I try to tread water while confronted with his fantastic, strong body. I don't care, I will sink to the bottom and die a happy woman because I have now seen perfection.

Noah is built of lean lines and cut muscles that aren't bulky or overdone. They're natural muscles. Not the kind that are meticulously crafted each day in the gym, but the unfair kind that come from a mixture of genetics and push-ups in the living room. His shoulders are bold and broad—stomach taut and a whisper of a V dipping down into the waistband of his boxers. He's not a hairy guy, either, just a few light patches of golden hair here and there. But I don't look to where *there* is leading or my pupils will dilate and blind me and Noah will know immediately what I'm thinking. And what I'm thinking is I'd like to climb right up that sturdy man. Even just his exposed wrists have been making my mouth water all week, let alone his powerful, rugged body.

I'm relieved from having to rely on my willpower to stop ogling him when he runs and jumps off the dock, cannonballing into the water. He comes up with a smile and shakes his head to throw the water off his face.

"I cannot believe you just took off your clothes and jumped in the water."

Noah—pie shop owner, stern face, and grumpy mumbler—just stripped and jumped into the water with a childlike grin on his face. This adds a new layer to him. Something exciting and lively to his comfortable-calm. Unfortunately, it's making his sexy meter ring off the charts.

Noah's shoulders and pronounced collarbones hover above the surface of the water, and now I'll have to find a way to forget how his hair darkens two shades when it's wet. The way droplets cling to his eyelashes and firm skin. "You challenged my ability to have fun. I had to prove myself."

"But how come you got to take your clothes off first and keep them nice and dry, but I didn't?"

His eyes darken when they fix on me. "I think you already know the answer to that question." *Because he wouldn't be able to keep his hands off me. Because this heat I've been feeling between us is not one-sided.*

But the way he's looking at me—I feel naked. I watch with appreciative eyes as Noah raises his hand and pushes it back through his hair, wicking water away and flashing me his bicep in the process. *Flash away, biceps. I'm at your mercy.*

"Noah!" I reprimand sternly while sloshing water at his face. "You can't say stuff like that!"

He chuckles, twisting away. "Why not?"

"Because you yourself said we have to stop flirting. And . . . you're flirting! While you're practically naked! In the water!"

I wish he wouldn't smile at me like that. I wish he wouldn't swim closer. I wish I could think clearly enough to swim away. But I can't. I continue to weakly slosh water at him until he's close enough to wrap his hand around my wrist. I want to whimper at the sight of him. Strong jaw, moody mouth, green eyes, wet hair. And the feel of him . . . it's unreal.

His smile is gone now. Neither of us are amused. I watch him swallow—eyebrows pulled together like he's in pain. "I'm trying so hard to stay away," he says in a low rasp. His eyes track over my face and now the pull between us feels crushing. Unbearable. "And I'm failing."

My heart rate is sky high, and it's not from treading water. It's because he tugs me closer and my soft curves press against his hard lines. He wraps an arm around my waist with nothing but complete intention. I suspected all Noah's muscles weren't just for show, and I was right. Taking my legs, he guides me to wrap them around him and hold on to his neck as he treads water for us both. *Lifeguard, indeed.* One of his hands lifts above the water to gently push my bangs to the side of my face. Those eyes, the same bright green as the trees lining the lake, drop to my mouth.

Slowly he swims us toward the sandy bank. I know why we're headed there and my entire body cries out for me to stay quiet. Keep my lips zipped and don't ruin this moment. But I can't do that to him.

"Noah," I whisper, struggling to make myself say it. "Nothing has changed. I'll still have to leave."

He doesn't stop swimming. "I know. I'm okay with it if you are?"

I nod quietly then and hold on until his feet make purchase with the sandy bank, giving him the support he needs to hold me without treading water. The sunshine combined with Noah's gaze sweeping over my skin is scorching. He pulls me tightly against his body and I hold on tighter around his neck. It's heaven and torture rolled into one. His mouth hovers over mine, his breath whispering promises against my lips. I adjust impatiently and press my fingers into the heavy slopes of his shoulders because he won't kiss me yet and I'm feeling greedy. His smile is soft and taunting as he clearly enjoys drawing this out—proving that he doesn't just show restraint with his words, he shows it with his body.

I, however, have no restraint because it's been too long since we kissed. I'm also not sure I've ever been kissed or held like this by a man I liked this much. I cinch my legs tightly around his torso, making him grunt a laugh. I angle my face for the optimal kiss. *If you're going to do it, do it.* His eyes turn absolutely black now. One of his hands splays out against my back and the other moves up to grasp the side of my jaw. His hold is as possessive as mine.

I hold my breath as his lips close the gap and press into mine. *Bliss. Wonder. Magic.* The soft scratch of his facial hair is a match strike against my senses. Tactile evidence that he's real and his skin is colliding with mine. My heart kicks frantically against my ribs, and my skin is set ablaze with pleasure and desire. As if it's possible, I hold him tighter. His hands press into my back, my hips, my thighs. Not frantic, but measured and intentional—just like *Noah.* Our mouths explore this new intimacy in unhurried caresses. His tongue teases my lips and I surrender willingly. I make a soft noise that lands somewhere between a moan and a whimper, and it spurs his hands into a more thorough exploration, sending a tingle through every part of me. We find that unique rhythm of kissing that feels like surrendering to a riptide. It's dangerous and there's nothing to do but let it build and carry you wherever it wants.

He tilts his head and I match his angle. I retreat and he follows. He retreats and I follow. His touch brands me, carves his name everywhere, and I hold on to him like letting go would mean certain death. Kissing Noah is more than I bargained for. It's more than I could have hoped—and it convinces me of something that it shouldn't: we're good together.

His wonderful calloused hands slide up the soft skin of my back as he lifts my shirt off my body and I raise my hands in the air to aid him. I'm wearing a simple, cotton, navy bralette, and although I've always felt insecure about the small size of my chest, Noah looks at me as if I hold the keys to the world. As if I am so precious and desirable that he is afraid to touch me.

"So beautiful," he mumbles, while kissing me softly down the line of my throat and over my collarbones. He trembles as he holds me and I don't think it's because he's getting tired. And suddenly, this all feels too much. I let go. One of us needs to be thinking straight, and now I'm angry it has to be me. But I won't let this get too carried away and turn into something that even remotely resembles heartache in the end. A kiss is one thing—but *more* is off the table.

When our mouths separate, I take in his rugged face and swollen lips. I trace the line of his strong jaw and neck and collarbones with my finger. He must see the pain in my face—the turmoil boiling below my skin—because the delicious bite of his fingers softens. His hold on me loosens and he pinches his eyes shut, breathing deeply before opening them. "This was not a good idea, was it?" His eyes linger over my mouth again like he's a fraction of a second away from continuing what we started. The look in his eyes says he would carry me up on that bank and make love to me here and now if I gave him the okay.

I swim backward to put some distance between us, dragging my shirt with me. "It was a very good idea—but now we have to forget it." *Again*.

He nods and watches as I wring my shirt out and wrangle it back over my head.

Scraping both his hands through his hair, he stands a little higher in the water to where I'm privileged with the sight of his chest, abs, and sinewy flesh all expanding and shifting with the motion. His ribs push against his skin and water beads over his taut body and I'm afraid my tongue is hanging out the side of my mouth. I'm the overheated emoji. Face red and panting.

We both take a few minutes to settle ourselves and then dry off in the sun while finally doing the thing we came here to do: fish. But guess what? Fishing is boring, and it turns out I'd much rather be making out with Noah. Which is why I need to get away from him for a bit. I look over my shoulder at Noah, opening my mouth to ask him if he could take me back home where I'll plan to lock myself in my room for the rest of the day, but he says something first.

"I have someone I need to go meet. But . . . I was hoping you'd come with me?"

That is the opposite of space. The opposite of forgetting. And definitely the opposite of locking myself in my room.

And yet . . .

"Yes!" I say immediately.

Chapter 28

Amelia

Noah pulls into the parking lot of an assisted-living home and cuts the engine. His face is full of worry, and if I had to guess, he might be regretting his choice to bring me here.

I look toward the long one-story building and back to Noah. "Who are we visiting?"

After our little lake adventure, Noah took me home so we could both quickly change and hop back in the truck. I took a little longer than anticipated, though, because while brushing out my tangled, wet hair, a new song lyric popped in my head. It's been months and months since I've felt musically inspired, so after running to my room and quickly typing out the verse in a note on my phone, I fell back on the bed and laughed like you do when joy is just too much to contain. I wanted to call my mom and tell her since she used to be the first person I'd share songs with, but we haven't had that kind of relationship in years. It would be too awkward and out of the blue to call and tell her I felt my first creative spark in a while, so I just kept it to myself instead.

Now, in the truck, Noah takes off the hat he's been wearing all day and sets it aside. "My grandma."

"Your—" I'm stunned. My head is reeling. I thought Noah's grandma had already passed away based on the way he talks about her. "The grandma who raised you?"

He nods, weary eyes darting to the assisted-living entrance and back to me. "I know you thought she had already died, and I let you believe that, because honestly, it's just easier than launching into everything. And I can't stand it when I tell people and then they start *aww*ing like I'm some saint or they give me these pity eyes for having to take care of my grandmother. So now when I meet someone new, I don't tell them. Or at least . . . not until I can fully trust them."

My mind grabs on to that last sentence like a support bar on a subway. "And you trust me now?"

He smiles and nods again. "I do. And if you're up for it, I want you to meet her. But . . . she's not the grandma that raised me anymore. She was diagnosed with Alzheimer's three years ago. That's when my sisters and I moved her into this assisted-living home. It was such a difficult decision, but she's so much safer here, and they have incredible care for Alzheimer's patients."

The last of the puzzle pieces snap together. "Your grandma is why you came home from New York?"

"Yeah. Her memory started getting really bad the year I was gone, and my sisters would call me almost daily saying how worried they were. Grandma would drive to the market and not remember how she got there or how to get home. Luckily, everyone in the town knows and loves her, so she was usually safe. But it was getting pretty scary. And after Emily took her to the doctor and had a confirmed diagnosis, I couldn't stay away any longer." He frowns, looking like his mind dipped back to a place that he tries to avoid. "Merritt—my ex-fiancée . . ." He clarifies as if I actually needed for him to remind me even though I already carved her name on my *hate, hate, hate* list. "She couldn't understand why I needed to move home. She thought I should let my sisters *handle* her and live my own life." He scoffs. "I still can't believe she used that word. So demeaning. Like the woman who sacrificed her life, to raise and love me after my parents died, deserved to be reduced to being *handled.*" His hands clench into fists.

At a loss for words, I put my hand on his and squeeze. Noah looks down at it, and his fist relaxes. I can see the moment he lets go of some of that pain. "Anyway, it was for the best. Merritt wasn't right for me in the end. Not even in the beginning if I'm being honest."

There's more to that story. I remember Jeanine at the diner saying Noah was cheated on, but I'm not going to bring that up now. Feels like a bit much. "Thanks for telling me," I say, genuinely meaning it. "So this is who you come to have lunch with so often?"

"Yeah. My sisters and I rotate so she has someone here almost every day. And Mabel comes most evenings. In the summer it's a pretty even schedule, but when school starts back, Emily and Madison can't get out here in the afternoons, so Annie and I come more often." He nods toward the facility. "The staff is incredible to my grandma. But . . . we still want to make sure she's okay. That she's not lonely."

There's so much I want to say right now. Actually, I want to dive over this bench seat to wrap my arms around him and squeeze. But I know that's not what Noah wants. He's not mushy. And I think lavishing him with how wonderful he is would only annoy him. "I'm glad. It's good she has you guys." I look in his eyes with a tender smile, making sure to keep any "pity eyes" far, *far* away.

"If you want, I'd like for you to come in and meet her. But you have to know that she doesn't always live in the present. And it's better for her if we don't correct her when she's wrong about something. I try to jump into whatever place or time she's at in that moment."

"I'll follow your lead," I say, hoping to put him at ease and prove that he can trust me with her.

His smile is tense and he looks like he wants to give more directions and caveats, but he ends up opening the truck door and hopping out instead. I do the same and we walk side by side through the sliding doors of the facility. I wish I could hold his hand, but I keep mine clasped behind my back instead.

We stop at the front desk and Noah offers a nice smile to the woman in scrubs behind the desk. "Hi, Mary," he says, picking up a pen from the counter and signing both our names on a visiting sheet. *Noah and Amelia.* Side by side. In his beautiful cursive. Briefly, I wonder if they'd notice if I stole this sheet on my way out to keep it as a memento for the rest of my life.

"Noah! I was wondering when you'd be by today." Her eyes slip to me and widen. I probably should have worn Noah's hat in here, but I completely forgot. "You have . . . a friend with you today," she says, turning into a dazed zombie. I know this look. It's the look of a fan, and I'm worried it's going to immediately make things hard for Noah. He'll regret bringing me, and the nice bubble of trust we've formed will pop. The end.

"I do," he says softly, leaning a little over the counter and dropping his voice even lower. "But we'd appreciate it if you not say anything about her being here to anyone else. It wouldn't be good for my grandma if there was a sudden mob of nursing staff in her room."

He twinkles at Mary, and . . . huh. Would you look at that? It does the trick.

Mary turns her eyes back to Noah and her fandom dies away as quickly as it appeared. "Of course. Y'all go on in and see her. She's in a great mood today and very alert."

"That's good to hear. Thank you, Mary."

As Noah and I walk through the facility, he stops and talks to no less than twenty people. All the old ladies adore him. He leans down often so they can pat his cheek. He gives out hugs like candy on Halloween. He's so soft here. Tender and loving to all these people who desperately need both those things. Noah is such a natural at caring for others. And it's that realization that has my heart leaping off a high dive straight into the deep end of the feelings pool.

Noah and I finally make it to his grandma's door, both steeped in the scents of at least twenty different perfumes. I laugh when I see that someone left a red lipstick stain on Noah's cheek, and I wipe it off. He rolls his eyes lightly with amusement like he'd forgive these ladies anything.

"One time I had an eighty-year-old lady pinch my ass when I leaned over."

I laugh and give an exaggerated look to the buns in question. "Can't say I blame her. You've got a good ass back there."

"Stop it." He groans before knocking lightly on the door and then opens it. He gives me one quick glance over his shoulder and I see the hesitation in his eyes. He's worried about showing me this part of his life. I smile and make little pinchers out of my fingers, angling them toward his butt to get him to keep moving. He grabs my wrist before my fingers can make contact with any cheekage, and then he slides his hand down to clasp with my fingers. I'm light-headed from the emotional connection. More intimate than that kiss in the lake somehow.

He pulls me with him inside the happy, sunlit room. We pass a wall of pictures, filled with Noah and his sisters at all stages of their lives. I want to linger and stare at each one, but Noah moves me toward the sweet little woman sitting in a chair, looking out a massive picture window toward the facility garden.

"Well, hi there, darlin'," Noah says and the buttery soft tone of his voice has each of my bones melting into goo.

His grandma—Silvie—looks up at him and it's clear she doesn't quite know what to think at first but is trying to understand. She has short, white hair, curled in that adorable way that many older ladies like to style their hair, and has porcelain skin so thin it's nearly translucent. But Silvie is not wearing a sweat suit. No way. It's clear that this woman is every inch the southern belle she's always been. A strand of beaded pearls lies around her slender neck, and she's wearing a bright pink cardigan with nice black linen capris.

"Well, yes, hi . . ." she says kindly with only a soft furrow to her brow. It's clear she has no idea who Noah is, and my heart squeezes for him.

He doesn't wait for her to ask any questions. He pulls me up beside him and wraps his arm around me like I belong here with him. "I'm sorry I'm late for our usual lunch date," he says with a sunshine smile. "I hope you don't mind, but I brought an addition today. Mrs. Walker, this is my friend Amelia. Amelia, this is Silvie Walker. This lovely lady graciously has lunch with me a few times a week to keep me company." I know he explains this for Silvie's benefit rather than mine.

"It's so wonderful to meet you, Mrs. Walker. Do you mind if I stick around and intrude on your lunch date?"

Silvie's eyes—green like Noah's but more cloudy in color than his—bounce between us a little nervously. "Of course . . . you two go on and have a seat. But I'll warn you, I can't visit for too long. My grandson and granddaughters will be home from school shortly and I need to finish baking some cookies for them." She winks at me. "Because all little ones need a cookie now and again when they get home from learning."

Noah's fingers squeeze my shoulder lightly and then he lets go of me, gesturing for me to take the chair beside him. "Lucky kids," he says with a chuckle. "I love cookies."

Her eyes brighten, and it's amazing to watch how well Noah knows her. How to disarm her immediately and smooth her worry away. "Well, do you now? I'm more of a pie woman myself. But I do like a good cookie from time to time. I only make 'em because my grandson doesn't like pie, the little rascal." She smiles and I can see through her memories how loved Noah was as a child. Still loved . . . just in a different way.

If he's hurt by her not realizing that he is her grandson, he doesn't show it a bit. He crosses a leg over the other and looks at me. "What about you, Amelia? Do you like cookies or pie?"

I give an exaggerated look of consideration before I grin. "You know? I'm more of a pancake gal, actually."

Silvie raises her eyebrows. "That so? Pancakes are good, too . . ." she says in a grandmotherly way that makes me feel validated and important.

The conversation continues like this for the next few minutes, and when it's clear that Silvie starts to feel tired by our visit and look more distant, Noah makes an excuse for us, saying he needs to get back to work. He asks if he can hug her before he leaves and she opens her arms wide to accept him. And then shocks us both by doing the same for me.

And it's in that moment, locked in Silvie's warm hug, that I look up and see Noah staring at me, and I could swear his eyes are misty. Gregory Peck's downcast face flashes in my mind and my heart sinks. I shouldn't have kissed him. I shouldn't have let him introduce me to this important part of his life.

It's going to make it that much more painful when I leave.

Chapter 29

Noah

"We need to talk," says Amelia, turning abruptly to corner me by the door as soon as we walk into the house. This isn't a good, sexy sort of cornering. There's a heaviness in her eyes and she's worrying her bottom lip. I extend my hands to rub the sides of her arms, but she shakes her head sharply.

"No, don't do that," she says, and the look in her eyes makes me drop my arms by my sides.

I start to panic. Did I do something wrong? Was that kiss in the lake too much? Maybe she wasn't ready for it and I misread all the signs.

Amelia breathes in deeply and lets it out in one slow exhale. "Noah . . ."

"I'm sorry," I blurt, unable to stomach the thought of having pushed her too far or upset her. "I was thoughtless at the lake and I should have explicitly asked what you were comfortable with, and—"

She laughs, cutting off my apology. Her eyes are sparkling with humor, and maybe a drop of sadness. "You think I'm upset about the kiss? Noah, I'm upset because . . . I like you." She smiles tentatively. "And I shouldn't have let you kiss me, because for me, it wasn't just physical. I have . . . well, I've developed very real feelings for you even though you told me not to."

Now it's my turn to expel a heavy breath. I run my hand through my hair and resist the urge to lean back against the door for support. *Damn.* This is bad. We definitely shouldn't have kissed. It was okay when it was just a physical urge, but knowing she has feelings for me changes everything.

It's a problem because I also have feelings for her. Big ones. Inconvenient ones, and I don't want to do anything about them. Two people can't live under the same roof for weeks knowing they both have the same feelings and not inadvertently propel their relationship forward. And that's why I don't admit to her that I'm crazy about her. That I can barely sleep at night because I lie awake tormented with the thought that she's sleeping across the hall from me. That I've never met anyone who makes me feel the way she does.

"Ameli—"

Her hand races up to press against my mouth. "No. Don't say anything! You were very clear in the beginning with your intentions, and I don't expect a single thing from you. Nothing will change. We're friends, and it's going to stay that way." She drops her hand when she feels content that I'm not going to try to interrupt her. "I'm only telling you now because I need for us to set up some rules from here on out so I'm not tempted for us to cross the line again."

"Rules," I say, not liking the way that word sounds coming out of my mouth. "Like what?" I ask while going into the kitchen for a beer, because something tells me I'm going to need it.

Amelia follows me and sits on the barstool under the island while I pull two beers from the fridge. She accepts hers and takes a long drink before setting it down firmly on the counter, wincing when she adds a little too much force to it and nearly cracks the bottle.

She gives me a cute, apologetic smile before making her face solemn again. "Well, for starters, no more kissing. But that one's obvious."

Obvious or not, I hate it. I want to kiss her all day every day until I eventually die from lack of oxygen.

"Okay, go on." I set my beer on the counter and cross my arms.

She watches my movements, wearing a private grin, and then lightly clears her throat. "I also think it would be better if we just didn't touch at all. Ever."

The extra addition of that *ever* feels like an unnecessary punch after a boxing match that's already over. Never touch Amelia again after knowing what it's like to have her in my arms? Knowing what it's like to feel her satisfied sigh against my lips? Torture. It'll be nothing short of it, but I know she's right. This has to happen.

"No touching, got it. Is there a minimal distance I should keep from you? I could stop by the hardware store and buy us both a tape measure to carry around."

Amelia's eyes narrow playfully. "Let's say four feet to be safe. And last, I think we should not hang out alone anymore."

I suck in a sharp breath with that one because it somehow hurts more than the others. I want to fight it, but it wouldn't be fair of me to push back against her rules when she's trying so hard to respect mine.

Raising my beer to my lips, I take a long pull of it to put off having to respond. Her blue eyes watch me intently like she's on the edge of her seat for my answer.

I finally set down my beer and brace myself. "I thought I could make it work with Merritt even though I could see our differences from the moment I met her." This was obviously not the sort of response she anticipated. Amelia's eyes widen a little in shock, and her brows lift. I feel that familiar thundering in my chest that always precedes spilling an emotional part of me, but I need her to know.

"Our worlds were completely opposite from the start, but I chose to ignore it, and that's what eventually led to the end of our relationship. She was a city dweller who thrived on stress and the hustle and bustle of New York; and I liked being here with my family, having quiet game nights on Saturdays and knowing the name of every person I pass on the sidewalk. When I proposed to Merritt after her visit here, she accepted, but made it clear that she could not live here, and I'd have to go with her to New York."

I think back to those months in the big city and how much I hated brushing shoulders with strangers in every corner of it. It was so populated. And busy. Everyone had a purpose at all times. I couldn't understand for the life of me how city life energized Merritt. How she loved the subway and hailing a ride everywhere we went. The longer I was there, the more I hated it. Also, the job at the bank didn't help. I missed the soft edges of my town—even if the people here do drive me nuts.

"You really don't have to explain anything to me, Noah."

"Thank you, but I want you to know why I'm so hesitant to start something between us . . . if you want to know?"

She nods. "I do."

So I continue. "I really thought our feelings could make up for all the differences between Merritt and me. But it wasn't enough. Turns out, we had both fallen in love with the idea of each other, rather than who we really were." I look down just to get a break from Amelia's focus and tap the counter with my knuckle. "I still spent a miserable year there, rarely seeing her because of her job, and then fighting most of the time when we were together. And then when I needed to come back here for my grandma . . . well, that's when it all imploded and I was able to really see that Merritt and I were never meant to be. Oil and water." I look at Amelia again and shake my head. "I gave so much of myself striving to make it work with her, and I just can't do that again. Not even sure I'm at a place in my life where I *could* do that if I wanted to."

Unfortunately, so much of what's happening between me and Amelia mirrors how it went with Merritt. A whirlwind romance with a woman passing through town who never plans to stay. Except on an even greater scale because Amelia has fame on top of a demanding career. She's going to need someone who's comfortable with a long-distance relationship, who can drop everything and fly to her when she needs me. And as much as I want to, I can't be that guy for her. I'd just weigh her down like I did Merritt.

We're both quiet for a minute, until Amelia stands and picks up her beer. "Thanks for telling me. It helps knowing why." And I can tell she means it. Her voice is soft and her smile is kind. She's so understanding it makes me ache. "These rules will work. Let's follow them, okay?"

I hold her gaze and nod slowly. She turns away, heading toward her room, but pauses before facing me one more time. "And Noah?"

"Hmm?"

"She didn't deserve you. I agree that sometimes opposites are terrible together—like pickles on brownies." She shivers in disgust, making me laugh. "But sometimes . . . I think they can make each other better. Like maple syrup and bacon."

She gives me one more of her heart-stopping smiles before she goes to her room for the rest of the night. I go to mine and try to read, but I can't focus because all I can think about is how much I damn well love maple syrup with bacon.

"Hi Noah, it's me. Amelia. Ha ha, you probably already knew that. I'm calling from James's house . . . which . . . you probably knew, too, since I'm not at your house and also leaving this message on your answering machine. Anyyyywhoooo. Just letting you know James thought it would be fun if we threw a little dinner party tonight with you and your sisters. So I'm going to hang out here for the day and help him make dinner. If you see smoke, send help. If you don't see smoke, come over around six. Your sisters are already confirmed to come, too. Sooo yeah, okay, I'll hang up n—" BEEP.

My white-knuckled fists are leaning on the counter, bracketing the answering machine I've never wanted to throw out the window as much as I do now. What the hell is wrong with me? I've never felt like a jealous asshole before, but hearing that Amelia and James have already spent the entire day together on his farm and are now throwing a dinner party like some sort of white-picket-fence couple has me contemplating murder for my best friend. It's not fair that James gets to spend endless time with her, and now she and I have these new rules.

Damn rules.

I sigh and scrape my hands over my face hoping to clear my head of this pounding jealousy. It doesn't subside even a bit.

Instead, my mind lingers back to that kiss yesterday that I felt all the way in my soul. She was so right in my arms—sweet and soft and holding on to me like she *needed* me. Of course, it was a mistake. A sexy, hot, unforgettable mistake. But really what else could it be?

Why did it have to be the best kiss of my whole damn life and all I could think about at work today? Three times I realized I had zoned out while rolling out the dough for a piecrust. By the time I came back to reality in the pie shop instead of treading water with Amelia back in the lake, the butter in my dough had melted and I had to start over. Everyone noticed, too. Harriet came in for a pie while Mabel was also in the shop and all hell broke loose. I'd mixed up who got which pie and the next thing I knew, Harriet was giving me the third degree.

"See? It's that woman that's making him all scrambled in the brain!" Harriet had said it like an accusation.

"Well, of course she is. The boy is smitten, anyone can tell. And what's wrong with that? He deserves happiness," said Mabel. Everyone is so used to talking around me. Rarely do they ever need me to participate, which is just fine by me.

Harriet had scowled. "At what cost? I'll tell you what! His soul. That woman is sleeping in his house and tempting him in all sorts of ways."

Mabel scoffed and rolled her eyes. "Leave his soul alone, Harriet, and mind your own beeswax. I think you could stand to be tempted a little . . . maybe it'd make you less bitter all the time."

But Harriet wasn't wrong—about the brain scrambling at least. My soul is still up for debate. And the problem is, I can't afford to have my brain scrambled right now. I need every lick of sense I can get to help me withstand falling in love with Amelia Rose. Except . . . no. I think I already have.

'm standing outside of James's front door at 5:58. That's a whole two minutes early. And because I can't have Amelia thinking I was so eager to see her after our first full day apart, and that I hustled through a shower and practically sprinted across the long front yards to make sure I got here at six, I stand out here quietly and wait until my watch says exactly six o'clock to knock.

But as soon as I raise my hand, the door flies open. I'm immediately greeted with Amelia's pretty smile. Well, first her face is surprised, and then she smiles, and then she wipes it off again like maybe she wasn't supposed to smile. She's a slot machine for possible emotions.

"Hi! Sorry. I didn't know you were out here. I was actually just about to run to your place to grab a sweatshirt." She means *my* sweatshirt. I wouldn't be surprised if that thing turns up missing after she leaves town.

"Oh. Okay . . . and I was just getting ready to knock. I haven't been standing out here or anything." I gesture toward the now-open door in case she might have been tempted to think I'd knock on the house's siding instead.

She smiles again and I'm lost in it. "Yeah. I figured."

We stare at each other for a minute and it feels hard to breathe. Hard to think. Hard to do anything but imagine wrapping my arms around her and pulling her into my chest. I'd kiss her hair. Her forehead. Work my way down her temple and her cheek to the corner of her mouth to . . .

"Did you have a good day?"

"No," I say quickly before I realize it. And then when she smile-frowns, I say, "I mean, yeah."

She's confused now. *Rightfully so.* We fall back into awkward silence. I've never been good at small talk anyway. My brain just won't do it. Instead I'm dying to say exactly what I'm thinking: *You look gorgeous. I like your jean shorts—I haven't seen these on you before. Your white tank top is cute. Has your manager bugged you today? I don't want you to go. I've been dreaming of kissing you again. I don't trust myself alone with you. And I want to hear every single detail of your day from start to finish, don't leave anything out.* I know she'd tell me. She'd spill her pretty guts and her eyes would sparkle and light up like they do when she's happy.

Instead, I don't say any of this because I'm an addict trying to cut myself off cold turkey.

"What about you? How was your day?"

"Good. It was good."

"Good."

We both nod. We're robots doing a poor imitation of humans. Next I'll bow and she will curtsy. This is so messed up. One amazing kiss and we don't know how to interact anymore.

"Okay, well, I'm going to go grab that sweatshirt," she says cheerily.

"Right." I step aside so she can pass, but she steps forward in the same direction. We almost collide and she hits the brakes. One quick awkward chuckle and I step aside. For a brief moment when she looks up at me, I see her shoulders relax slightly. Her smile turns self-deprecating but sweet. It's the moment in the movie when we both lift our human masks and reveal that we're the same ole robots we've always been, trapped inside the role we've been forced to play.

As she slides by me and out the door, I catch a hint of her sweet scent. A montage hits me of my hand tangled in her hair. Her mouth eagerly exploring mine. Her legs tied around my waist. The taste of her lips, and her neck, and . . .

"Well, that was weird to witness."

I look up and James is standing with a beer in his hand, on the edge of the kitchen obviously having watched that whole scene play out. I grunt and slam the door shut behind me with the heel of my boot.

He wants me to engage, but I won't do it. Instead, I go into the kitchen and see what they've got cooking. Surprise, surprise, it's breakfast food. Scrambled eggs are steaming on the stove, there's biscuits in the oven, cooked bacon on a plate, and gravy simmering in a skillet. I recognize it as one of my grandma's old ones. She gave it to James one night several years ago when he came over for dinner and confessed to her that he didn't own a cast-iron skillet.

I block out the intruding images of James teaching Amelia how to make country gravy with my grandma's iron skillet. I swear if he put his arms around her to teach her how to whisk the flour into the milk and bacon grease I will punch him in the throat. I've never been the violent type, but it's never too late to change.

"You gotta see these," James says, completely oblivious to my new hatred for him. He walks over to a plate covered in foil and even before he lifts it, I know what's under there. I can see the height and recognize the smell because it's the same smell that's been lingering around my house the past few days.

Pancakes.

Really shitty pancakes.

I can feel James watching me closely for some kind of response, so I keep my face neutral. I nod slowly with the corners of my mouth turned down. "Pancakes."

"That's all you're going to say?"

"What else were you hoping for?"

James sets his beer down and folds his arms. "I want you to explain to me, what sort of hold this particular breakfast item has over her? That woman obsessively worked on these pancakes for an hour and wouldn't let me give her a single instruction for them. Barely looked at me or responded to questions while she was making them—just kept tasting them and getting upset when they *didn't taste anything like his*." Still he searches my face for a hint of acknowledgment, but I don't give in because I'm practicing. See, this is just the minor leagues compared to when my nosy sisters get here. And if I don't want anyone finding out about what happened in the lake yesterday, I have to make sure I'm as stoic as ever.

I shrug and turn to open his fridge in search of a beer. I find it, pop the top, and then resist the urge to go over and inspect each and every one of her pancakes. See if she's getting any closer to figuring it out. They don't look as crispy as last time so I think she's at least learned she doesn't have to butter the pan each time she puts in a new dollop of batter.

"She likes pancakes. That's all there is to it." I don't tell James about Amelia's list, because, frankly, I don't want him to know. He's spent all day with her and might've figured out things about Amelia that I'll never get to. That thought makes me sick with jealousy, and now I want to withhold anything I can from him on principle.

"She like the farm?" I ask this question in the same tone someone might ask, *Did you ever get that suspicious mole removed?*

But this guy has been my best friend since I was born. Any

poker face I think I'm holding is clearly transparent to him. He chuckles. "Just ask me, you little shit."

"Ask you what?"

He raises his chin slightly. "Ask if I like her."

"No." I take another drink.

"Ask if she flirted with me today."

I clench my teeth and look down, swallowing the lump in my throat. "No."

He groans so loud and dramatically, tipping his head back to stare into heaven. "You're so obnoxious with your stoicism. You don't deserve it, but you know what? I'm gonna tell you anyway because I hope someday when I'm lovesick, another poor idiot will put me out of my misery."

I don't know what he's about to say, but my heart rate ratchets up. I think I accidentally tip forward just the slightest bit, too. Thankfully, he doesn't notice because he's stirring the gravy or else he *would* have commented.

"I don't like her, because number one, I'm a great friend and could see from day one that you have a thing for her. Number two, I'd have to be a fool to compete with you after the way she mentioned your name at least a thousand times today."

I have to press my tongue into the side of my cheek to keep from smiling. "She talked about me?"

He rolls his eyes. "Yes. Everything was a commentary about what she thinks you would have said at any given moment. Wondering if you've ever helped me on the farm. How long have I known you? Wouldn't Noah find this hilarious? Anything and everything Noah Walker related. So now what I want to know is how you feel about her, because I'm starting to think she's got real feelings for you."

I take a swig of my beer and prepare my lie. "I think she's been in town for a week and can't have feelings for me that fast."

"Bullshit."

"I think she's trouble."

"Double bullshit."

I sigh and look at the stack of pancakes. "I think I'm in trouble."

"Bingo. There it is. So do you think you two can—" Whatever James was going to ask gets cut off when Amelia flies back through the front door, slightly out of breath and whirling into the kitchen.

"I forgot to get the biscuits out!" She slams down the oven door, hair flying around her shoulders, and cheeks flushed from the full-tilt sprint she must have done from my house back over here. Her eyes light up when she sees them. "Come out of there, my little biscuit-angel-babies. You're too wholesome to burn like your evil pancake cousins over there." Amelia peeks over her shoulder with a mischievous grin in my direction. "And yes, I did ruin another batch of pancakes and I don't need any comments from the snooty peanut gallery about it, m'kay? I can perform on a stage in five-inch high heels for three solid hours, simultaneously dancing and singing in front of thousands of people, but I can't make a freaking batch of pancakes. Absurd. Inexcusable, really. But that's okay because now I can make BISCUITS AND GRAVY." She grins from ear to ear. "I'm so country now I don't hear my own voice in my head, it's just Reese Witherspoon and Dolly Parton talking in there."

She continues on babbling to herself like I've come to realize she often does, but I'm not totally listening. I'm focusing on how she's wearing my sweatshirt again. How the image of any other woman wearing that sweatshirt will never compare to the sight of it draped over Amelia. She definitely has to take it with her when she goes. Or I'll have to burn it. Give it a Viking's funeral and send it down the lake in flames.

When I finally glance up, James is staring at me with a smug smile. He runs his thumb across his neck in the universal symbol of *you're a dead man.*

Chapter 30

Amelia

"Oh stop, it's not that bad!" I rest my elbows on the table and point my empty fork at Madison across the table.

Madison wraps her hand around her throat and gags after taking a bite from one of the pancakes I made. She mouths the word *water* like she's been in the Sahara Desert for thirty-five years. I grab an uneaten biscuit and throw it at her head.

She grabs the biscuit from her lap and takes a big bite. "The biscuits are good. Your pancakes, however, are inedible." A big smile wraps around her mouthful.

"That's because the biscuits were from a can," James offers unhelpfully from down the table.

I gasp in mock outrage and look daggers at him. "You can't just out my biscuits like that!"

Emily laughs. "Hate to burst your bubble but we all took one bite of those biscuits and knew you didn't make them."

"So rude! Annie, tell them my pancakes weren't that bad."

My sweet Annie presses her lips together with an apologetic smile. She says nothing. I drop my head into my hands, laughing and feeling my own heated skin on my face. I've had two glasses of red wine, and red wine always makes my cheeks pink. Well, that and the table roasting. But I love it. We're all sitting on James's back porch, eating and drinking. I'm free and untethered here surrounded by these people. All day I've felt like singing—something I haven't felt like doing in a long time.

The sun set an hour ago after painting the sky in a dusky pink and orange sunset, and now the warm string lights around the edges of the screened-in porch cast a thematic glow on the evening. Beyond this porch are hundreds of acres of vegetable crops, barns, and greenhouses. I know because James gave me the full tour—and although I would have rather spent the day with Noah, I enjoyed every second of my new friendship with James.

I still can't believe I'm here with these people. These people who like me enough to poke fun at me. To acknowledge when I'm bad at something. To let me fail and enjoy the hell out of it over and over again.

And then the other reason my cheeks are pink is sitting down at the foot of the table to my right. *Noah.* I can hardly think of his name without breaking out in chill bumps. Just having him in the same vicinity as me after that kiss has my skin so hot I could fry bacon on it. I have been studiously avoiding glancing at him tonight because I don't trust myself to look in his evergreen eyes and not think of his hands on me. Of his smile. Of the feel of his laugh.

I'll blurt to everyone that I caught feelings, and then his sisters will be upset because we *just* talked about how it would be best if I didn't get romantically involved with him. But now I have and all I can see is that still frame of Gregory Peck's downcast face at the end of *Roman Holiday.* Is that what Noah will look like when I leave? Maybe I'm being presumptuous. Maybe his life will keep moving and he won't miss a beat. Maybe it was just a kiss for him and it won't leave him with a completely gutted, hollowed-out sort of feeling like it has me.

I feel his eyes on me now and it's agony not to look at him. I need a reason to get out from under his gaze, so I set down my now empty wineglass and stand. "James, is that piano in your living room in working condition?" My stomach flutters. Because the truth is, I've been dying to play piano all day, ever since I got here this morning and noticed it. I'm also a little nervous to play it because it feels like testing out a leg after removing a cast. When I put my weight on it, will I feel that old sharp pain or will it have healed?

"Of course," he says happily.

"Great! Who wants to play a game with me?"

Ten minutes later, we're all huddled in James's living room, laughing our butts off. They were skeptical when I first suggested we play a musical game, but once they learned the rules, everyone was up for it.

It goes like this: One person suggests a genre ('90s pop, grunge rock, R&B, etc.), another selects a children's nursery song, and then one of us has to sing it in the chosen style while I play the piano. I was actually introduced to the game when I was a guest on *The Tonight Show Starring Jimmy Fallon,* and then I enjoyed it so much that it's become my go-to game when I'm in the studio creating a new album and feeling blocked. It's been forever since I've played it, though.

Surprisingly, everyone participates. I started us off having to sing "Twinkle Twinkle Little Star" in the style of '80s funk songs. Don't tell anyone, but I played the chords for "She's a Bad Mama Jama" and then replaced the lyrics. It worked a little too well. James went next, completely shocking me with his phenomenal piano skills, and sang "Oh Where, Oh Where Has My Little Dog Gone?" in a blues style. He and I then took turns playing piano for everyone else when it was their turn to sing.

We're about an hour into the game, and the later it gets, the more fun it becomes. Even Noah sings, putting his whole heart into his '90s pop rendition of "Hickory Dickory Dock." It seems I was wrong about Noah in the beginning. He's a master of fun, and the more I get to experience these small moments with him where his eyes are crinkled in the corners and his mouth is spread wide in a smile, the harder I fall for him.

Everything about this night is wonderful. It feels too good to play and sing just for the hell of it again. It makes my fingers itch to create something new. To wear my voice out and really push myself with new riffs and runs. I feel that light inside me that had begun to dim burn a little brighter. My mind races to my upcoming tour and butterflies swarm my stomach—feeling an eagerness to get back into music and performing.

But then I think of leaving all the people I've grown to love in this town, and my heart feels heavy again. I want to find a way to make it all work out—but I don't know that there is a way. If I continue to visit—or let's say for the sake of an argument that I move here permanently after the tour—eventually, word would get out, and it would take away the town's privacy. Not only would paparazzi swarm here, but fans, too. This sweet quiet place could get turned upside down. I'm not sure I could do that to them.

Suddenly needing a break from the piano and attention of everyone in the room, I stand and start in the direction of the kitchen. Of course Noah does the same, and just like our episode at the front door earlier tonight, we pause facing each other.

"Sorry." Even just that single word from his mouth makes me feel tingly.

"No, I'm sorry." I stare in the general vicinity of his broad chest. "You go ahead."

"No, you go first. I got in your way."

We're being so polite it's ridiculous. If we can't interact in this small way, how are we going to manage living under the same roof for another week? We'll have to take shifts. A spreadsheet and a schedule will need to be made. I'll use different colors of tape to mark lanes on the floor so we make sure to never accidentally fall in the other's path again.

When I tell myself to stop being a coward, I look up. The heat in his eyes wraps around my heart and smothers it. *He will have a Gregory Peck face,* I think. *He likes me, too.* Those thick dark eyelashes will be cast down, hands in his pockets walking away, and I'm not sure I can take it.

"Whoa, whoa, whoa!" Madison rips our attention to her.

Noah and I both swivel our heads back to the group, chests still facing each other. Everyone is frowning and staring. Madison points in our direction, flicking her finger back and forth between us. "What's going on here?"

"What do you mean?" I was going for nonchalant and normal. I think it sounded scripted.

The siblings and James exchange looks around the table and come to a unanimous, silent conclusion.

"You guys slept together, didn't you?" Emily asks sharply.

Noah and I are immediately a clash of words.

"No!" I say, honestly, because we didn't. Haven't. Won't!

"Absolutely not." Noah has the audacity to sound commanding and not at all bumbling like me.

"We would *never.*" I give that last word a little too much force and Noah looks down at me with pinched brows. His eyes say, *Never?*

"What the hell, y'all?" says Madison, and then immediately turns toward Annie's reprimanding expression. "This is not the time for your delicate sensibilities, Cherub Annie."

James casually shakes his head while skewering Noah with a grin. "I knew it. It was only a matter of time."

"Stop." Noah is back to stern and grumpy. Just how I like him. "You know nothing. We have not slept together. Not that it's any of y'all's business."

I'm trying not to combust in flames of embarrassment. And it doesn't help matters that Noah seems to somehow discern my discomfort and moves even closer to me. Like he's going to use his body to shield me from their knowing eyes.

"Okay, that's it. Sit down and explain, because we can all tell that something has happened." Emily sounds frighteningly close to a mother right now. "You haven't looked at each other all night, barely spoken, and now whatever that uncomfortable little encounter was is the icing on the cake. Y'all did *something*."

"Fess up." Madison crosses her arms, like a mob boss. She needs a leather jacket.

Annie is the only one who doesn't look concerned.

Noah and I retake our seats, looking as guilty as kids with orange powder staining their fingers saying they never ate the Cheetos.

"We kissed," he states plainly.

It's a sea of pearly white molars as everyone's mouth—including mine—hangs open. I thought he'd deny it. We'd go on happily as if nothing ever happened for the rest of the week and I'd implement our color-coded lanes and that would be that. But no. He just dropped a conversational grenade and stepped back to watch it explode.

"You kissed?" Emily does not look happy. "That's worse!"

A line between Noah's brows deepens. "How is that worse?"

"I don't know, but it's not better."

"Why do you care so much?" Noah's gaze zeros in on Emily with an intensity that for once reveals their sibling dynamic. Emily is loud and in charge most of the time, but Noah is the oldest and they all look to him for guidance at the end of the day. He carries so much on his shoulders.

"She's *leaving*, Noah." That's the only explanation Emily offers and I feel her words like little jabs to my lungs. Emily looks at James, clearly hoping for backup. James shakes his head and looks down—not jumping in like she'd hoped. Madison lays her hand on

Emily's forearm, but Emily rips her arm away. The levity from our musical game has disappeared and the atmosphere turns thick.

I watch as Noah's entire demeanor shifts. His large shoulders tip forward, his eyes are pillows, his smile is calming. He puts his hand on Emily's knee. "Em, I'm not leaving again. And I promise that if I ever do, you'll get plenty of warning. Not like I did last time."

An entire conversation passes between these two in the quiet moments after his words. Emily relents, softening and nodding her head. I'm not sure what that was about, but the heaviness in the air tells me it was important. She looks like a woman slowly sobering. Embarrassment washes over her face.

She bows out of the argument gracefully by slipping from the living room and returning with a cold, rock-hard pancake on a plate. She sits down, balancing the plate on her lap, and shovels a bite onto her fork. I think this is her way of apologizing to me.

"You don't have to do that. Really, we're good," I say meaningfully, because I wouldn't force these pancakes on my worst enemy.

She raises the fork to her mouth anyway, and we all watch in silence as she takes a bite. She chews. And chews. And chews. And then finally shivers it down and nods before chugging her beer. She then nods firmly at me and I smile in return. That was more than an apology, that was a pledge of her life.

A chuckle runs through the room, and after a while the conversation hums back toward normalcy. The siblings talk through their schedules for the next week—determining which days they will each visit their grandma. We all joke and cuss too much while Annie keeps adding tallies beside all our names so we know how much money to pay out at the end of the night. She didn't ask me if she could add me to the list, she just did. I caught a glance at her little notebook earlier and there it was. *Amelia.* Right next to the rest of the group and my heart burst like confetti.

Now Emily stands, collects the empty beer bottles and plates around the room. The group begins to break up, murmuring about how tired they are and *blah blah blah*. I don't care how tired they are, they can't leave us.

"Wait!" I'm frantically grabbing hold of Annie's shirt to keep her from getting away. "You guys can't leave yet. It's early!"

"It's after ten." Madison is suddenly the timekeeper apparently.

"Like I said, early. Stay. Let's all play another game. Monopoly or something."

James laughs. "The hell we will. Monopoly would take all night. Some of us have to be up with the cows in the morning. Y'all better get out of my house now."

"Don't worry," Annie tells me in her sweet southern drawl. "We'll have another group dinner before you leave town." She's completely misconstruing my reasons for wanting them to stay.

I'm losing. They're all scattering across the room like marbles now, and just Noah and I are left seated. I make eye contact with him, which is a mistake. His grin twists—the same unease I'm feeling sweeping over his expression. We're both terrified to go home and be alone together. Both unconvinced the other has enough willpower to stay away.

Chapter 31

Amelia

t's well after midnight now but I'm still wide awake staring at the ceiling. Noah and I didn't say a word to each other when we got home. He unlocked the door, flipped on the lights, and I scurried off to my room like a mouse escaping with cheese. Noah made no attempts to stop me, so I feel like it was the right decision.

To keep my mind from racing down the path of *What if we just,* I hold the image of Gregory Peck in my mind. But after a while, I begin to resent that face and so I use an imaginary marker and draw a little mustache across his lip. Gregory's face then transforms into Noah's and he's smiling because Noah would most definitely find that fake mustache funny. He might only show it in that usual, quiet, inconspicuous way of his, but he would smile for sure. And then he'd roll his eyes and make me pancakes.

Sadness leaks into my heart because more than anything, I want to explore this relationship with Noah. I want to follow my impulses. My heart says, *This could be good. Very good.* But my mind replays all the valid reasons we can't. Why Noah doesn't want it.

I'm feeling about as cheery as a Snickers bar run over by a truck on 100-degree pavement. Normally, when I'm in this sad state of being, I would get up and turn on an Audrey film. She would wrap me up in her comfortable familiarity, and by the end, I'd be feeling more hopeful. But tonight, I don't, because the only movie I brought with me on this trip is *Roman Holiday*. For obvious reasons I don't feel like watching that one right now. Maybe never again. I'm mad at Audrey. And I'm mad at myself for following in her shoes and coming here in the first place, and meeting Noah and his surly eyes, and his overly wonderful town, and his kindhearted, quirky sisters.

I kick the covers in a minitantrum. And then I kick them more. And again. This time, I add a little body swirl where I completely disrupt all my covers at once. It feels so good to let myself be angry. I fist my hands and pound them into the mattress now because I'm really getting the hang of losing my control and I don't want to stop now. I add in a quiet little piggy squeal as I dig my heels into the mess of sheets and comforters, because I AM MAD.

Mad, mad, mad.

I'm mad that my car will be fixed and I'll be leaving here in a week. I'm mad that I don't want to give up my career. I'm mad that I'll go home to loneliness. I'm mad that my mom is not my friend anymore, and that my dad never wanted to know me. I'm mad that over the years, I've let myself turn into a people-pleasing robot who's afraid of upsetting anyone. And I'm mad that here, in this town, in this house, in this bed, is the first time in years I've been able to unleash my feelings and just be me without fear of repercussions.

But most of all, I'm mad that I've fallen in love with Noah, and I'll never get to have a life with him.

As if the earth is angry with me, a loud peal of thunder shakes the house. I want to cheer and fist pump the air because it feels so good to just be pissed for a minute. What sounds like a deluge starts dumping over the house and the wind picks up. I think I must be the next Marvel villain because clearly my attitude summoned this. I want to stand on the bed and hold my arms out and let the storm take me. Cackle loudly with my fingers flexed.

Instead, I sob.

It's the kind of cry you hold off as long as you can, pretending you don't see the need for it even though it's glaring you right in the face. And then one day, your emotions break, and anger dissolves into frustrated tears that won't quit until your pillow is soaked through. There's nothing for it—no magical answer or earth-shattering conclusion to be found. All I can do is wrap my arms around my abdomen and let my body rid itself of all this pain until it doesn't hurt so much.

I hear a knock on my door and I sit up with puffy eyes and tearstained cheeks. "Noah?"

My door opens and there he stands in the dark. My heart hammers wildly in my chest, and when a sudden bolt of lightning strikes, filling the room with bright light for only a split second, I see the agony on his face. This isn't a nighttime booty call. Something is wrong. I wipe under my eyes with the back of my hand.

Wordlessly, he walks over to the side of my bed and when he looks over the mess of sheets and comforter, I feel a twinge of embarrassment. "I was throwing a tantrum," I say honestly, because that's all I can be with Noah.

He nods, that painful scowl still etched between his brows. His eyes move to me, and instinctively, I reach out and take his hand. The hem of his long-sleeve pj shirt brushes against my knuckles. He's in my room, in the middle of the night, in his favorite pajamas. This is level ten vulnerable for him. He notices that I've been crying, but he doesn't ask me what's wrong. I think he already knows. Instead, he brushes his thumb across my cheekbone, catching another tear.

"Can I sleep with you tonight? Just . . . sleep." And the way he says it makes me know he means it.

There's not a single part of me that hesitates. "Yes."

Noah untangles my sheets and comforter, smooths them out over the bed before lifting a corner and sliding in. The mattress dips with his weight, and that small action shouldn't make me need to swallow, but I do.

Once he's under the covers, both of our heads lying on our pillows, we stare at the ceiling. Another flash of lightning illuminates the room and the wind beats the window. It sounds extreme. Noah rolls onto his side to face me, drapes an arm over my abdomen, and pulls me close to him so my back is pressed against his chest. It's a tight hold. Like one someone would use if they've been out floating in the ocean near death and miraculously find a flotation device.

A warm ache settles low in my stomach. His body is so strong and solid against me. He smells crisp and cool and clean. And I can feel his breath against the side of my neck, blowing the tiny hairs around and making me dizzy.

I feel him take in a deep breath. "I . . . don't like storms." He pauses and I wonder if he thinks I'll laugh. I will fight anyone who ever dares laugh at this man. "I'm terrified, actually." He sounds shaken, so I wrap my hand around his forearm that's holding me so snugly to him.

"We all . . . Well, after my parents died, I haven't been able to sleep through a storm again. I usually just stay up and pace until it's over. Sometimes I obsessively check the news. I call each of my sisters when it's over just to make sure they're okay. It's probably a ridiculous reaction since I wasn't even there when it happened to my parents."

Another pause, and I wait.

"My sisters don't seem to be as scared of storms as I am, but they each have their own things, too. Like earlier tonight, Emily's freak-out wasn't actually about you. It was because she's afraid of abandonment in a big way. And the last time I was in a relationship, I packed up and left for New York without giving anyone much notice, and I didn't come back for a year. She's afraid that will happen again, and I'm afraid with each and every storm that it'll take someone I love again."

Words feel inadequate. That was so personal it felt like blood spill. I want to find a way to convey how much I hurt with him. But I can't, so I just take his hand and raise it to my lips where I kiss his palm. I feel his chest move with a soft hum, and when my lips release from his hand, he pulls me in close again. I never want to not be surrounded by his body. We fit perfectly together and it's not just because our pajamas most likely came in a set.

Lightning strikes again, and loud thunder shakes the house.

"Distract me," Noah pleads, and I can feel how fast his heart is racing. "Say something."

He doesn't have to hold me as tightly as he is, I would cozy up to him even if he didn't. He might not realize it, but there's no getting rid of me now. I run my fingers up and down his arm, feeling the fine hairs tickle my fingertips. I'm not sure I've ever felt this comfortable with someone before.

"Your sisters already know, but I'm obsessed with Audrey Hepburn." I blurt my truth, not even sure why I'm nervous to tell him. But I am. My confession is a finger prick compared to his open heart surgery.

"The actress?" he asks, and I'm relieved he knows who she is, unlike his sisters.

"Yeah. The actress." Thunder rumbles around us and the walls tremble from it. Noah's hold doesn't loosen. "My mom and I used to watch her movies together. It was our thing. But then after I became famous, we drifted apart, and now I feel so distant from her that I don't know where to even begin to get that relationship back." I pause a moment when I realize that finding a way back to my mom is something I do want to pursue. I just don't know how. "Anyway, I continued to turn to Audrey Hepburn movies when I needed a hug or guidance. That's why I'm here in this town with you, actually." It sounds even more reckless than I thought when I say it out loud. "I played eenie-meenie-miney-mo with each of her movies, landed on *Roman Holiday,* and took it as a sign that I was supposed to escape to Rome just like Audrey's character did because I was feeling scared and desperate. But since Italy was too far to drive . . ."

"You came here."

"Right. Except I wasn't supposed to find you here . . . and now, you're Gregory Peck and don't even realize it."

Noah kisses my head like I didn't just speak gibberish to him. "I like Gregory Peck. He's a classy guy."

"You would care about that." I twist around and stare at the buttons on his shirt. I'm dangerously close to sobbing again, so I distract myself by counting his buttons.

He runs his palm over my cheekbone and his fingers splay into my hair. "I've been lying to you."

I pause my counting on button number five. "Are you Hillbilly-Joe-serial-killer after all?"

"You really do have a lot of nicknames for me, don't you?"

"More than I've even told you."

He runs his hand through the length of my hair, and then repeats. "I *do* want something romantic with you. I have since I first laid eyes on you. And you're not the only one who has developed feelings." My heart stops. "But I'm still not ready for a relationship. I don't see how it would work when I can't leave my family right now until my grandma . . . well, anyway, I can't leave. And you can't stay."

"What about—"

He knows what I'm about to say. Noah cuts me off gently, his hand cradling my jaw like he wants to soften the blow of his own words. "I can't do long distance, Amelia." I hate how final his voice sounds on the matter. Like he's already contemplated it a hundred times and could never find a suitable solution. "When I had to move home for my grandma and Merritt wouldn't come with me, I told her I'd come back to the city after I got everything situated at home. But after I was here about a month, I got a text from her that she obviously meant to send to the guy from her office she had apparently been cheating on me with for several months. It was an incriminating text to say the least, and I've had major trust issues since then. I don't think another long-distance relationship is the best way to get back into dating."

There is a part of me that wants to beg and plead. I will spend the entire night convincing him with a PowerPoint presentation that I would absolutely never cheat on him. But in the end, I stay quiet, because I don't want to force, persuade, or manipulate Noah into anything he's not comfortable with. He's been through enough hurt—and I don't blame him for wanting to avoid any possibility of it again.

Besides, I'm not completely convinced that he wouldn't be better off with a regular woman who could put down roots right here. She'd work at The Pie Shop with him. They'd plant a vegetable garden. She'd probably love fishing, too. And most of all, she wouldn't have to travel around the world for the next nine months. Noah deserves a secure happily ever after and I haven't known him long enough to be sure I could give that to him. It's a lot to have to gamble on right away when someone's heart is on the table.

"If things were different . . ." he begins. "If you weren't a celebrity, and I didn't have . . ."

"It's okay, Noah. I understand. I really do." I finish counting his buttons because tears are an imminent threat. "You have eight, by the way. Eight buttons."

His fingers continue to trail languidly over my face and hair and neck and arm and back up again. He touches me like I'm precious to him. It makes me ache all the more.

"Distract me." I'm the one to ask this time.

His fingers pause momentarily before they continue their repeating pattern. "I cheated on a biology test in high school. James let me see his paper." This one makes me laugh. He does, too, after blowing out a dramatic breath of air. "It's good to get that off my chest."

I curl up into a little ball at the front of his body. "I accidentally killed my goldfish," I say, making Noah chuckle, full and rumbly. I softly pinch his arm. "Don't laugh! I feel terrible about it. I left for my last tour and completely forgot to arrange for anyone to come feed it. When I came home, it was floating belly-up. Still haunts me."

"Remind me to never let you own a dog." Noah's hand slides down to settle against my low back. He holds me close and his face tips forward so he can whisper his next confession against my ear. "I love your voice."

Love. Oof. That word takes on a life of its own and beats between us. I know we haven't known each other long, and somehow it hurts that we'll never get the chance, because I think I've fallen in love with Noah.

"But not enough to own any of my albums apparently," I tease, desperately needing to lighten the air between us.

"It's better that way. Imagine how creeped out you'd be if you'd turned on the CD in my truck and it had been one of yours."

"I would have been flattered."

"Liar."

I nuzzle my face against his warm neck shamelessly. Because somehow I know that in this darkness, all bets are off. I can be as nuts as I want. I could snort his skin if I wanted and he would smile. "You're the only man I wouldn't mind being obsessed with me."

"Sorry," he says, and he lets that word dangle a moment. "I reserve my obsessions for flowers, Pop-Tart."

I actually like Pop-Tarts, he had said that day in The Pie Shop.

And there it goes. My heart grabs hold of a swarm of balloons and leaves the earth. Off to find heaven it goes. Thunder booms again, but this time, Noah doesn't seem to notice. He's enamored with my hair and the curve of my ear.

"Amelia . . ." he says in this raw way that lets me know his head is in exactly the same place as mine. It keeps diving back into *what if* and hunting around for options that don't exist. "I want to let it happen so badly—but I don't think I'm the kind of guy who will ever be okay with you being gone for nine months at a time."

I almost tell him it would be more like three months at a time, because I'll have small breaks here and there. I could use those breaks to come here, and I'd fly him out to visit me on tour in between. But I don't think it would matter. "Noah, you don't have to keep explaining it to me. I really do understand and see where you're coming from. It's difficult to date a celebrity, and that's honestly why relationships don't last long in my circles. I get it. And I wouldn't want to put you in that position."

He laughs but it sounds more self-deprecating than humorous. "This would be a lot easier if you were just a little selfish and annoying. Could you be more terrible from now on?"

"I'll try." A tear that's been clinging to my lashes slips down my cheek. This feels more painful than it should. It really sucks to be mature and decide all this on the precipice of something instead of the end. Why did I have to fall for someone whose world is on a completely different axis than mine?

"So what do we do now?" I ask, as his soft cotton shirt caresses my cheek and absorbs the tears I really wish I wasn't crying.

"I don't know," he says honestly, his fingers still idly playing with my hair. Twisting it around his fingers. Letting it drop and then twisting it all over again like he's finally getting to do the thing he's wanted for days. "What happens at the end of *Roman Holiday?*"

Gregory Peck's face surfaces once again in my mind. "Audrey—Princess Ann—leaves and goes back to her life. And Gregory Peck—Joe Bradley—stays in his."

His fingers press into my back. It's not a hopeful press. It's a desperate one. "What about before that?"

I laugh sadly, thinking of Audrey and Gregory eating ice cream, riding a moped, touring Rome. "They have fun together."

Noah presses his lips to my forehead, lingering there for a full in-and-out breath before pulling away. "What if we do, too? Is that too selfish? What if I suggested we just drop all our rules and . . ."

"Accept the time we have together? It could work if we manage expectations from the start." I finish his thought—hoping a little too hard that that's what he was going to suggest. Because if there's an option where I hang on to Noah for dear life while I can—selfishly soak up every memory with him that is available to me—I will. I have a feeling that a temporary fling with Noah would be better than an entire year with another man.

He sighs after a thoughtful pause. "Yeah. Is that a terrible idea?" But his fingers are already tracing my collarbone. His touch is dazzling.

"Most definitely." I'm struggling to breathe. "And very dramatic. But I'm up for it if you are."

He tilts forward, lips pressing into that tender spot on my neck, just under my ear. "Mm-hmm. I love drama. You can call me Mr. Drama from now on."

I laugh and nudge him back so his shoulders are flat on the mattress. And then I climb over him, placing my knees on either side of his hips, feeling (as do the Regency heroines in my favorite romance books that Noah doesn't own a single one of) very wanton. "Don't intrude on my nicknames. I'm in charge of those. And Mr. Classic fits you too well. Just look at you lying here all buttoned up in your cotton *pa-ja-mas*." My fingers bounce like a skipping rock over each button.

I can barely see him in the dark, but I can sense his smile. His hands lightly grip my outer thighs. "They come as a pair. You don't like the shirt?"

"I like what's under it better. Can I?" I ask, my hands hovering at the top of his collar. My fingers tremble, giving away that I'm feeling some serious nerves under this cool and collected facade.

"Go ahead."

Green light.

My heart beats painfully as I pop open the first button. I trace that warm sliver of skin at his chest and my finger comes away burned from his heat. With each button I undo, nerves twist my gut and pump into my heart. My pulse is a jackhammer. I fumble with the fourth button and I think it gets snagged on a thread because it won't release. I yank it a little. Inhale and exhale in a rush. Tug a little more and it's not budging. My movements are sharp and clunky.

Noah's hand covers mine with a chuckle. "You're shaking."

"Yes, and it's ungentlemanly of you to point it out." My voice sounds embarrassingly breathless.

"Is this too much? You want to stop?" He's cocooning my hands. Won't let them go—not that I'm trying to free them.

"No, I don't want to stop. It's that . . ." I let out a little whimper and slump over, resting my forehead against his broad chest. "There's been certain expectations for me in the past. Because I'm . . . a celebrity and all that, guys have thought I would be a certain way in bed and then seem disappointed when I'm not." I wince feeling major embarrassment slide around me. "I don't know. Sometimes I get in my own head about it."

Noah makes a hum of understanding so deep that I feel it reverberate from his chest through my skull. He nudges me upright again and then ruthlessly rips the thread that is snagging his button before finishing the rest for me. He sits up, so we're chest to chest with my legs wrapped around him, and he shrugs out of his shirt. *Ah—skin.* Noah's skin. It's perfect under my fingertips.

He cups my jaw and I can feel the intensity of his eyes. I think Noah can see right through to my bones. "To me, you're Amelia.

Maker of shitty pancakes and a smile that rivals the sun. All I want is *you*." And just like that, I feel safe.

I give his mouth one soft kiss before pulling back. I trace my hands over his wide shoulders and biceps, his taut chest and then his lips. I sweep my fingers up to feel the lines where he's now grinning. I will memorize him if it's the last thing I do. I will carry the feel of his smile in my pocket for the rest of my life.

In one fluid motion, Noah flips us over so he's pinning me in. The weight of him against me is earth-shattering. Euphoria. Delight. I'm finally anchored after drifting for too long, and in some corner of my mind I realize that his hands are the only ones I want against my body for the rest of my life.

Noah's lips caress mine slowly, giving me rich kisses, sparkling with pleasure. His broad palms smooth and knead over every inch of my body with quiet confidence until my pulse is languid again and my limbs are melted. He whispers things against my skin and I feel coddled and held and like I'm absolutely darling to him. *I want this forever,* I think.

Outside, the storm continues to rage, but neither of us notice. For the rest of the night, we're lost together as Noah proves that I am all he wants.

Chapter 32

Noah

"Are you ready?" I ask Amelia as we both round the truck and stand shoulder to shoulder, facing the town. She is wearing tight checkered capris today with a white tank top tucked in (which I was lucky enough to watch her slip into earlier this morning). Her long braid hangs over the front of her shoulder, and the fabric of her shirt fits her smooth curves like a second skin. I have to tuck my hands into my pockets to keep from sliding them all over her out here in broad daylight.

"Should I be worried or something?" The tone of her voice, paired with the skeptical look in her eyes, tells me she thinks this town is innocent and harmless. *So naive.*

I tilt her chin up to look away from the town and at me instead. She has faint charcoal-colored shadows under her eyes that make me smile, because I helped put them there. But I can't think about last night again. I already have too much residual desire I'm trying to stuff back down. This morning after a shower (together, nudge nudge wink wink) we both drank our coffees on the porch while reading our separate books until it was time to come in to work. Of course she tried to get me to read to her aloud from mine, but I refused because it's too much fun watching Amelia pout. Also I've wavered on all my other resolutions concerning her, and I want to keep at least one of them.

"Never underestimate this town's power to sense gossip."

Her eyes widen. "What does that mean?"

"It means, they are all going to be waiting for us. They'll feel that there is something new between us."

She stares at me with nothing but sheer amusement now. She's sure I'm blowing this out of proportion. "I think you need to get out of this town more." She taps the side brim of the baseball hat I'm wearing. "It's getting to your head."

I catch her finger with mine and lower it to my side, before shifting so I can lace my fingers with hers. I don't think it should feel as incredible as it does. I've *never* felt this with anyone before. I've never wanted to hold a woman's hand just for the hell of it. I didn't realize I was an affectionate kind of guy until I met Amelia and now all I want to do is hold her and snuggle her and kiss her and touch her. I almost don't recognize myself.

"Maybe you're right." This ridiculous town seems like a comfortable excuse to blame for a lot of things. "Now wipe that sunshine smile off your face and look a little less approachable," I say as we start walking toward the hardware store.

"Like this?" Her smile drops into a clown's frown. It's so over the top she looks terrifying.

"Perfect."

As we approach the hardware shop, Phil and Todd are outside just as expected. One is sweeping, and the other is writing on the chalk sign HAMMERS 50% OFF!

"Looks pretty harmless to me," Amelia says with a sassy lilt to her voice. I smirk and we continue walking.

Phil looks up from his task of sweeping and his eyes shift down to Amelia's and my intertwined hands. He practically sparkles with excitement. "Well, good morning, you two. Fine day we're having, isn't it?"

"Just dandy," I say sarcastically, picking up our pace.

"Easy," Amelia warns me in a whisper. "I didn't wear the right shoes to run a marathon today." I'll pick her up and carry her over my shoulder if I have to. She sees me contemplating it as my gaze sweeps over her head to toe and she adds, "Don't even think about it."

Phil is trying to form a barrier with his body so we can't get by. "Ah yes. Dandy is the word for it. The sun . . . it's . . ." The closer we get, the more frantic Phil's conversation becomes. And then, just before we pass him, the man takes his broom and holds it out like a gate. "Whoa, hold your horses there, youngins. Let's talk a little. Shoot the breeze! What's new?"

Amelia fills her naive lungs full of gossip-producing air that will make my life a living hell, so I speak before she can. "Thinking of adding a new pie to the menu."

It's clear by the look on Phil's face that this is not the information he was after, but he's not disinterested. He lifts a bushy brow. "Oh? What's it gonna be?"

"It'll have a honey base. I'll call it Mind Your Own Damn Beeswax." Amelia stifles a laugh in her throat after my stoic delivery. Phil's face drops into something reprimanding. I lift the broomstick handle like it's a carriage door and gesture for Amelia to walk under before me.

"But . . . but . . ." Behind us Phil is sputtering, trying to stall us. "Wait! Have you seen the big sale we're having? Tell him, Todd!"

Poor Todd. His voice shakes a little. "Right! There's a sale. A big one. On hammers!"

Amelia looks up at me, her round puppy eyes telling me she's wavering. "I have to go and buy a hammer. I *have to*, Noah. Just listen to them."

I tighten my hold on her hand. "Stay strong. This is the least of it."

She sets her chin forward and keeps walking, but she's not happy about it. Right before we make it to the next store, I take a sharp turn and steer us across the street.

"What are we doing now?" she asks, slightly out of breath. The urge to carry her surfaces again.

"Avoiding Harriet."

"Why?"

"Because she's scary, that's why, and she'll go on and on about your pond."

"My p—Never mind. I don't want to know."

"For the best," I say as we pass under another shop awning. The door behind us opens, the cheery bell chiming. "Shit," I mumble. "Walk faster."

"NOAH!" Oh man. That's Gemma.

Amelia's head tilts in preparation for looking behind her, but I step closer to her, meshing our shoulders together so she can't. "Don't look back. She'll trap you with her eyes."

Gemma raises her voice. "NOAH WALKER I KNOW YOU HEAR ME!"

"Who is that?" Amelia whispers.

"Gemma."

Amelia expels a breath. "There's so many busybodies in this town it's getting difficult to keep them all straight."

"She owns the quilting shop. She's in cahoots with Harriet, though, so you can't trust her."

"Noah, you can't just ignore her. That's rude."

"I'll send her a free pie later. She'll get over it."

Amelia tucks her arm in mine as we cross the street again to get to the shop. "Such a surly grump." She says it sweetly with a little nuzzle of her face against my outer arm.

I pull out the shop key and unlock the door, going about my

morning business as usual. I flick on the lights. Pull the barstools off the table. Head into the back to turn on the ovens. And then when I realize Amelia isn't with me anymore, I look to the front of the shop and find her standing in the middle of the room, looking completely shaken. Her eyes are a little dazed and I can feel the emotions swarming around her.

"Amelia?" I ask cautiously.

"I don't want to go back," she says, her eyes snapping to me. "I'm going to live here now. No more celebrity life for me. Cancel the tour. I'm done with music."

Chapter 33

Amelia

Noah approaches me until we're an arm's length apart. He stops and crosses his arms, shoulders stretching the fabric of his T-shirt and looking as stern as a rock. *Surly Pose.*

Truth is, I don't intend to quit and he knows it. I can't cancel the tour even if I wanted to. Contracts have me bound at the ankles. But I am *feeling.* Feeling so much and so strongly about everything that I can't quite handle it. I love being here with Noah. I love walking through this town and feeling the heartbeat of its personality. I can't believe I have to leave it. And because I can't fall into tears right now, and there's nothing I can do about my quickly approaching real life, I have to fight with Noah. Because I know he'll let me, and it'll help.

His eyes narrow lightly as he scans my soul. "Say it again," he says in a steely tone that has shivers running over my skin. "I need to watch your face as you say it."

I take a moment to summon my best lying skills so I can pass this test. I need him to think I'm serious. *Fight with me, Noah. Distract me from these feelings.* I tilt my chin up. "I said, I'm quitting music." Unfortunately, I think the last word ratted me out. My voice shook. Also, it probably doesn't help that this morning as I lay in bed with Noah, I sang to him the few verses I've been work-ing on the last few days and told him how excited I was about them.

Something sparks in Noah's green eyes. He knows I'm a little liar now because he's come to recognize my tells.

"You can't quit. I won't allow it," he says sharply—argumentatively—and he's onto my game but is putting a fresh spin on it. A hot spin, judging by the way the corner of his moody mouth twitches ever so slightly. *You want to play, I'll play,* says his grumpy-handsome face.

"I can if I want." I'm defiant as I take a step toward him. With anyone else I'm grace and poise—I'm Audrey. *Polite, polite, polite.* But with Noah, I speak my mind. I'm not afraid to look silly. To fight and argue and get messy. I cast an explorative glance around The Pie Shop. "In fact, I think I'll just work here . . . with you."

"I'm not hiring." He pauses. "Besides, I've seen your baking skills."

"That's only because you refuse to teach me. I can learn, though."

Noah steps forward, the gap between us slowly disappearing and searing heat crackling between us. "No. I won't let you work here."

"Ha!" I raise my chin. "I'm Rae Rose. I've built a musical empire and a cult following that would risk their lives if I asked them to. I'd like to see you try to stop me from doing anything." I wish I was actually this confident.

"If you quit, I won't talk to you again."

This makes me smile. "Really?"

"Yes."

"You think you can hold out?"

He grunts an affirmative response, but his actions are telling a different story. His hands are somehow on my waist and he's been slowly backing me up until I'm close enough for him to lift me up onto the counter. Memories of last night dash through my mind and my pulse sledgehammers against my ribs.

"Easy." He's cocky with that hat casting a dark shadow over his eyes. Brooding and commanding. I rip it off—splashing his face in light and then running my hand through his messy hair. It's tossed and perfect. On the brink of needing a haircut, but not quite there yet.

"So let's just say I quit and I'm living here. I'm at your sisters' house making pancakes while you're over there. You see me reach for the salt instead of the sugar and raise it over the mixing bowl. You still don't say anything to me?"

His mouth tilts sardonically. *Amateur hour,* his eyes say. "I don't eat your pancakes anyways so it doesn't affect me." First of all, rude. Second, I never want to stop playing with Noah.

"Fine. I'll up the stakes then." My hands glide up his chest and clasp at his neck, pulling him between my legs, lightly toy with the hair at the nape of his neck. His fingertips press firmly into my hips. "I'm crossing the street, and I don't see an oncoming car. You still don't say anything?"

His eyes hover down at my lips. "Not fair."

"I'm not trying to play fair."

"And I'm trying not to be the reason you give up your dreams." *Bam.* Truth falls between us and ruins the game.

There's a moment of silence, where only the tension in our bodies is speaking, where our fingertips say words that our mouths never will. My hold around his neck tightens. He slides his hands all the way around to hug my hips up close to his.

And then because he knows I need for him to lighten this moment, he grins lightly and tacks on, "Forfeiting so soon, Pop-Tart?"

I quickly press my mouth against his. It's so forceful he rocks backward slightly and I nearly fall. But he stabilizes us quickly and kisses me back, just as forcefully. We're still fighting, but it's on new terrain. It's bumpy and jarring and our mouths will be bruised. I nip at his lip and his hands grip my back. None of this is helping—it's making it worse. I whimper from a fresh stab of emotions and Noah pulls away quickly.

He cradles my face and studies my eyes. "Did I hurt you?"

I shake my head and try for a smile. It's weak and pitiful. "Noah. I won't ask you to come with me when I leave, but I need you to know that if you ever change your mind you're always welcome wherever I am. Always."

His stares at me, a crease etched between his brows, and takes a deep breath. He tilts forward and kisses me again. Softly this time. Our lips don't part. We don't explore. We soothe and settle.

The bell chimes above the door, and then a woman's scratchy voice echoes through the shop. "Unlock those puckers, kids!" It's Mabel.

And she's not alone.

"Oh, sweet bread and butter on Christmas morning."

"Now, Harriet, you just tuck those delicate sensibilities away for another day. This ain't the time."

Noah and I peel ourselves from each other and I look over my shoulder to find Mabel and Harriet catching their breath. I quickly fix my skewed shirt and would most definitely feel embarrassed by the scene they just found us in if there were enough time. But these two ladies are pink cheeked and panting from shuffling their way in here like they were trying to win a fast-walking competition. All that's missing are hot pink windbreakers.

"Don't try to boss me around, Mabel, I'm older than you."

"And stodgier, too. Haven't you ever seen a couple in love doing a little bit of kissing before?"

Harriet lifts her nose. "They should wait to show that sort of affection until marriage."

Mabel rolls her eyes. "Oh, like you and Tom did?" She says this with a sassy slur making Harriet gasp. "*Yes*, don't act so surprised, Your Supreme Holiness. Can't tell me your little last-minute wedding back then was because of love. It was because you'd been *making love* and a baby! You had yourself a good ol' fashioned shotgun wedding." Mabel grunts again. "*Honeymoon baby, my ass.*"

"Ladies," Noah says, somehow managing not to laugh at these two bickering grannies I hope to grow up and become exactly like one day. "Was there something urgent you came in here for?"

"*Shit!* Yes!" says Mabel.

Harriet jumps in before Mabel can finish, also taking a delicate but poignant step in front of her. "You need to hide!" she says, aiming her hawk eyes on me.

Mabel nearly pushes Harriet out of the way to step in front of her this time. And now it's clear they weren't here on a joint mission—they were each racing to get to us first. "That fellow who's been snooping around all week with his camera is in town again right now."

"The paparazzo?" Noah asks.

"No, the pizza man has a new photography hobby! Yes, Noah, the paparazzo! But even worse, there's more of them!" Poor Noah. He takes it like a champ, but Mabel is downright lethal today. Actually, I think Noah secretly adores it because the corner of his perfect mouth is doing that slight twitch again.

"Phil and Todd saw him coming and waylaid him with facts about hammers. But I don't know how long they'll hold him, and the others are all scattered around." Harriet says this while lifting the folding countertop and trying to push her way through it. I say *trying* because Mabel is also trying to push through and the two are only getting themselves wedged in that little space together.

"Mabel! Would you just—"

"I would, Harriet, if you would just . . ."

Now, Noah has stepped away from me to help pull these ladies through the counter. "Now look at what you two have done," he says gently. "Mabel, suck in and twist."

"How many of them are out there, Mabel?" I ask, feeling sick.

Noah tugs her arm lightly and they both pop through to our side of the counter. "Oh honey, there's gotta be at least twenty of them. A whole crowd. You need to get out of here quickly."

I look to Noah and our eyes both convey the same message: Game over. Our time together is up.

Chapter 34

Amelia

Noah and I race down the back alley just like the last time, except now, there's a heavy dread in the pit of my stomach. If there are as many as Mabel says, it means they've had some kind of confirmation that I'm here and they won't let up until they've gotten the pictures they want. Which reminds me.

"Noah," I say, tugging him to a stop. "You can't be seen with me. I need to take your truck by myself and you can get a ride with Annie."

His brows stitch together and his jaw tightens. "Why?"

I look down to where our hands are clasped together. "This is why. If you don't want your life to change, they can't find us together." My voice shakes. "They'll take photos from a hundred different angles, and tomorrow morning, you'll be all over social media and tabloids."

I expect him to drop my hand. I'm preparing for the loss of it. Instead, his grip tightens and he answers, "I'm going with you."

"Noah!"

This time he breaks our hold and crowds me, cupping my jaw in his hands and looking fire into my eyes. "I'm not leaving you. I thought I could keep this temporary but—" He breaks off, shaking his head and kissing me hastily. Nearly painfully. It's the most exquisite torture. "I don't want it to be over between us. I *can't* let it be over."

I'm breathless with hope. "What are you saying?"

"I'm saying fears be damned. I want a relationship if you do."

"I do!" I say so fast he was barely able to finish his sentence.

"But you'll have to be patient with me—"

"I will!"

"—because it's going to take some time for me to get used to the distance thing. And I still need to be around to take care of my grandma so I won't be able to visit you much."

I go up on my toes to wrap my arms around his neck. "We'll figure it out. And I'll give you so much patience, you'll be overwhelmed with how benevolent I am. But, Noah, are you sure? Just last night—"

This time he cuts me off. "Last night, I held you in my arms and realized I'd be an idiot to ever let you go. Not only an idiot, but I'd be miserable. I could never forgive myself for letting you get away."

I shake my head frantically, smiling and trying not to cry. "Mr. Romantic."

"Mr. Ridiculously Lucky."

"Shush. I told you not to encroach on my nicknames."

He grins and his eyes lower to my mouth. "So is that a yes? You'll officially date this lowly pie shop owner?"

"As long as you never refer to yourself as that again, yes. Absolutely times a million."

He kisses me once more and slides his hand up my arm before taking my hand and continuing our escape down the alley. "We'll figure out the details when we get home." *Home.* The sudden burst of joy I feel hearing that word nearly trips me.

But when Noah and I surface from the alley, we immediately realize our mistake. Somehow they knew this is where we'd end up, and all sorts of paparazzi and media are gathered in the parking lot—waiting for us. My heart lurches and I try to turn back before they notice us, but I'm not fast enough.

"There she is!"

"Rae Rose!"

"Rae, over here! Who's the guy?!"

"Is it true you've been having a love affair with a pie shop owner?"

They're all shouting and racing toward us. Noah grips my hand firmly and looks down at me. "What do you want me to do? Do we make a run for it?"

I swallow and allow myself one second of anger before I train my face into an impassive expression for the flashing cameras. I cover my mouth and angle my face up to him so they can't read my lips. "We need to get to your truck. Don't say a word to them other than asking them to move as we walk." I wish I could have had more time to prepare him for how to interact with the media, but there's no better way to learn than as you go, right?

Holding hands and keeping our gazes down, we walk toward his truck. But the paparazzi are hungry today and they form a barrier around us, taking advantage of my lack of security.

"Excuse me. Move. Let us through." Noah is doing a valiant job of trying to get me through the pressing maze of media, but they're not budging. I keep tugging on his hand because I can feel his rage building and I'm afraid he'll do something rash like shove the guy who's currently putting his camera about five inches from my face and yelling questions at me.

"Who are you with right now, Rae?" He's so close I smell what he had for lunch.

"Back off," Noah barks at him, but he doesn't relent.

"Is he your new boy-toy? Are you finally veering away from your rich and successful type?" He's trying to provoke us into an answer, and I can feel that Noah is close to snapping.

Noah angles his shoulder in front of me so he can make better eye contact with the paparazzi. "I said back off and let us through."

All the others are closing us in as well, shouting questions and begging for a comment, but they're not as *in-our-face* as this man. "Sure thing, big guy. Just answer my question and I'll back right off. What makes you think an average guy like you is good enough for a worldwide star like her? Care to comment?"

Panic seizes me at his question. I've been cornered like this before in my career, and it's terrifying each time, but I've never heard a paparazzi say something so cutting or intentionally insulting. Also, something about his question is niggling the back of my mind. Like I've heard it before.

Is this how it will always be for Noah? The media constantly reminding him of his place? This time it's me who is about to snap. I ball my fist—to what—punch him? I think so, because in the next moment, Noah is covering my fist with his hand and when I look up at him, he shakes his head the tiniest bit. *Don't do it.*

To make things worse, new voices enter the mix.

"Hey! Get away from them. Leave our girl alone!"

I look over my shoulder to the sound of Mabel and Harriet, along with Phil and Todd yelling angrily at the paparazzi. *No, no, no.* They need to go inside. There's no reason anyone else should get dragged into this breach of privacy, but they're relentless until their voices are heard and half of the flashing cameras turn in their direction. This story is getting juicier and juicier for them by the minute.

But then two familiar blacked-out SUVs whip into the parking lot and blare their horns. As soon as they come to a stop, I see my usual bodyguards jump out and race toward the paparazzi, followed by Susan until they're at my side.

"Are you okay? Let's get you out of here!" she says, and my guards provide coverage for me and Noah as we're guided through the crowd, pushing them back in the process.

I've never been so happy to see Susan and her jet-black bob in my entire life. I could kiss her matching pantsuit.

"Get back," Will, my head bodyguard, says forcefully and everyone complies because Will looks like a street fighter you'd never want to cross. He also makes the very best gingersnaps I've ever had and is a wizard with a travel sewing kit, but I'm thankful this zoo of paparazzi doesn't know that.

I jump in the SUV first, quickly followed by Noah. He settles close to me on the bench and puts his arms around me. I breathe in his comforting scent. "Are you okay?" he whispers close to my ear.

"Better question, are we okay?" I ask, because I'm terrified that Noah is rethinking everything after that run-in. That our relationship will go down in history as the shortest ever lived. I know he has all kinds of trust issues already, so I'm afraid what that man said today is going to change his mind about us.

To my shock, he lets out a soft laugh through his nose and grins, kissing my forehead. "It'll take more than that to get rid of me now. The only person's opinion I care about is yours. If you're still up for 'dating an average man,' I am still in."

I sag against him with relief just as Susan steps up into the SUV and takes the bench facing us. "Are you two all right? You're lucky we got here when we did." The door shuts and immediately the cries of the paparazzi are blessedly muffled.

But when my eyes lock with Susan's, realization knocks into me. I suddenly remember where I've heard that guy's question before.

"Susan, where's Claire? She's usually always with you."

"Oh." She pulls a face. "Sadly, I had to let her go. Just wasn't doing her job well anymore." She shrugs, and a boulder settles in the pit of my stomach. Something is not right.

The ride home is quiet as we all settle and process. The other SUV hung back and blocked the exit of the parking lot so we were able to make it to Noah's without being followed. Will drops us off close to the front door, and then backs down the driveway again, angling the vehicle so that no one can enter the driveway if they find us. I should feel safer with my team around me again, but I don't. At least not with *all* my team.

Noah and I are thinking in tandem. We both watch Susan closely as she pulls out her cell phone, registers the lack of service, and then tells us she needs to walk back down the driveway to give Will instructions. "Go ahead and pack your things, Rae. We're going to leave as soon as possible so we can get you safely back in Nashville before they find you here."

She doesn't wait for my answer because Susan is used to me complying without hesitation. When the door shuts behind her, I head into the kitchen where I pick up the phone and immediately dial my mom.

"Do you think Susan's timely appearance was fishy, too?" Noah asks.

"Yep. And her assistant told me the other day that things are going on behind my back that I don't know about. It's time to get some answers."

The phone rings several times and I bounce on my feet, anxious to talk to my mom before Susan returns. Noah tells me he's going to step outside to give me privacy and keep Susan away for a few minutes.

Finally, my mom answers. "Hello?"

"Mom, it's me."

Her voice is level ten cheery. "Amelia! Hi, sweetie! It's so good to hear from you. What's going on? I'm at the beach so you might not be able to hear me very well. Listen to this ocean today. It's roaring!"

"No, Mom. I—"

She removes the phone from her ear and is extending it toward the ocean. I know because it sounds like I'm practically inside a wave. "Mom!" I yell a few times. "I need to ask you a question! Put the phone back on your ear!"

"Doesn't that sound amazing? Wish you were here. Oh, the sun is incredible today. And Ted is here, too! Do you want to say—"

I cut her off before she hands the phone off. "Mom, this is important and I'm in a hurry. Did you tip off anyone from the media to where I am staying right now?"

I have never once confronted my mom after she's done this. In the past when Susan would tell me that she confirmed it was my mom leaking the stories, I've silently stewed and pulled further away from her. But now, I need to know.

The line goes silent. At first I think it's because she's guilty, but when she speaks again, I realize that she sounds hurt instead. "No. Of course not. Why would you think I'd do that?" I can't answer right away—too many responses are swirling around my head. But apparently my silence speaks volumes. "Amelia, I don't know where this is coming from, but I swear to you, I would never sell a story about you to a magazine. Never in a million years."

My gut twists. I shut my eyes trying to sort this out—and all I keep coming back to is the fact that the aggressive paparazzo said nearly word for word the same thing Susan said to me over the phone a few days ago. It is possible that someone from the town called a magazine and told them where I am. But . . . it's rare for the media to all gather like they did today. Like it was organized and planned. Someone would have had to go through a lot of trouble to orchestrate the ambush today—and I really don't think anyone in this town would have done that to me. There's only one person who has been upset by my time here in Rome and would want to smoke me out of hiding.

"Mom," I say, swallowing against a suddenly dry throat. "Why aren't we close anymore?"

I hear my mom release a sigh, and I think it's one of relief. "I wish I knew. I've wanted to bring it up for a while now, but didn't know how. Is it me? Did I do something? Because I want to know and make it right if I did."

I might have thought it was mostly her fault a few days ago, but now, I don't think she's the only one to blame. I should have spoken up long ago. Questioned my mom about the tabloid stuff instead of just blindly accepting everything Susan has ever told me. I wish I had fought for my relationship with my mom instead of quietly stepping back from it. I'm finding my voice now, though. "I think we have a lot to talk about and sort through, but I can't get into it all right now. I just need you to know, I miss you a lot. And . . ." My voice hitches. "I love you. I want to get back to the sort of relationship we used to have."

She breathes in deeply and then sniffles. "I want that, too. Yes, call me back when you can. Or we can FaceTime. Or I'll fly to wherever you are. You name it! I'm just . . ." She's crying—I can hear it in her voice. "I'm happy you brought it up. Things have been so weird between us, and sometimes, I've wanted to call you and catch up, but . . . I've chickened out because I've gotten the impression that you don't want to talk to me anymore."

"That's because I thought you were selling stories about me to tabloids." As well as the constant money requests and mooching, but I don't feel like now is the time to mention that. Not sure I'm even ready to admit my feelings about it to her yet.

"No—hon. Please believe me. I have never once contacted anyone from the media and tipped them off to anything about you. I love you too much to do something like that."

"I believe you," I tell my mom because I really do. I can hear the earnestness in her voice. Plus, too many other puzzle pieces are falling into place. "But, Mom . . . is there anyone—even a friend you might have told that I'm in Rome, Kentucky, right now? Your boyfriend, maybe?"

"No, I haven't even told him." She pauses a moment. "But . . . actually. I did tell someone."

"Who?"

"Susan," she says, and it makes my pulse jump. "When I called her to help me set up the flight, she told me how worried she was about you and afraid something terrible had happened since you hadn't checked in. She asked if I'd heard anything and so I told her what town you were in because she sounded really freaked out. Was that wrong? You normally tell Susan everything." She sounds so concerned. History suggests that she's only showing this worry because she's afraid I'm going to cut her off financially. But in light of everything I'm learning today, I wonder if that's not true. I wonder if some of the wedge between my mom and me only exists because of the woman I've given too much power over my life.

There's no time to answer her question. I have a few more that need answers first. "Mom, a few years ago, for your forty-fifth birthday, did Susan ever send a car to pick you up for the surprise weekend away I planned for you?"

"What?" She breathes out. "No. I had no idea you did that. In fact, I thought you forgot about my birthday that year."

I see red. Susan's fingerprints are all over my relationship with my mom—and although it's my fault for delegating so much to that woman, I thought she was a safe place. Turns out, she sabotaged my relationship with my mother. How could Susan do that to me?

"I actually had planned a fun getaway for us, and Susan told me when I sent a car for you that you declined, saying *you* already had plans with your friends."

"Oh, Amelia. You must have been so hurt."

I laugh but it's not in amusement. "You must have been, too."

"Well . . ." She lets it dangle.

My mom and I still have so much to talk through, and I need her to understand that only contacting me when she needs something has been hurtful. But first, I want to hear her side. Maybe I'm not seeing the whole picture after all. Maybe she has been reaching out and Susan has been getting in the way—making a point to tell me when my mom asks her for something so she'll look worse.

"Susan also told me you declined my invitation to join me for the first few U.S. dates of the tour. Was that true?"

"Absolutely not. I would love to come to those concerts—she never called me."

I feel like I could punch through a wall right now. A Susan-shaped wall.

"Mom, I'm so sorry. I think . . . ugh, I think this is my fault. I've let Susan have too much power in my life, and . . . I'm pretty sure she's been purposely getting between us."

Now I think back to all the times Susan encouraged me to not confront my mom, but to just cut off communication with her, and I want to scream. How could I not see it? How could I let so many years go by like this without my mom? I had completely gone to sleep on my own life. Not anymore.

"Oh, hon—it's not all your fault. I should have questioned things, too. Reached out to you even when it was hard. I'm so sorry, Amelia."

"It's okay, Mom. We'll figure it out. I've got to go, right now. But I'll call you tomorrow and we can talk through some more of this. Oh, and you're absolutely invited to those concerts, okay? I want you there—I love you."

"I love you, too, Rae-Rae." My heart cracks open—but this time with hope. Maybe my relationship with my mom isn't so far gone as I thought.

I hang up at the exact moment that Susan walks through the front door, Noah hot on her heels.

"What's going on here?" she says, looking over her shoulder at

Noah. The sharp edge of her bob whips her jawline. "Why was he trying to keep me out of here?"

"You're the one responsible for the paparazzi showing up today, aren't you?" I ask Susan as she walks in.

She's so stunned by my accusation that her purse falls off her shoulder and hits the floor. After blinking several times, she clears her throat and bends gracefully to retrieve her purse. "I'm going to pretend you didn't just throw that horrible accusation at me, and instead, help you get packed like we discussed."

"You discussed it, not me. And I'm not leaving." I say this calmly, while anger pulses through my veins. Noah steps past Susan and crosses the room to stand beside me, putting his hand on my low back. It's such a supportive gesture without trying to handle anything for me that it jostles the release mechanism on my tears. *Not now, emotions.*

Susan's eyes drop to where Noah is touching me and she sighs with annoyance. "Let me guess. He is the one who planted this idea in your head?" She scoffs. "So typical. Rae, open your eyes and see that he's not right for you. In fact, have you stopped to think that maybe he's the one who told the photographers where to find you? Or maybe that money-sucking mother of yours. We both know that she—"

"Enough." My voice is sharp as the crack of a whip. "I just got off the phone with my mom. It wasn't her. In fact, it's never been her, has it? You've been leaking stories about me to the tabloids for years and using my mom as your scapegoat. Also, how many of those *money-sucking requests* you tell me she makes actually come from her?"

"This is ridiculous. You're going to trust your mom—the one who's been using you for years—over me?"

"Yes." My reply comes instantly and Susan looks like I just impaled her. Noah presses lightly against my back. Quiet solidarity. "I know it was you, Susan, and now I know you're responsible for so much more than I ever realized, so you can cut the shit. And thanks to finally talking to my mom about all this, I know that you've been meddling in our relationship and purposely not relaying messages and making up lies instead." I shake my head at how obvious it seems to me now.

Susan crosses her arms and I have the strongest urge to push them back down by her sides, because that's Noah's Surly Pose and she has no right to it. "You're wrong. Your mom is the one who continues to lie and let you down. I've always been the one to take care of you."

"No, Susan. You're fired." The words glide right off my tongue, and suddenly, I feel lighter than I've ever felt before. Like my feet might lift off the ground.

Susan's mouth falls open. "You've got to be kidding me?" Her eyes bulge. "I have done nothing but bend over backward for you the last ten years! I have gotten you the best gigs. Major deals on your contracts. The best endorsements. I have single-handedly grown your career, and you wouldn't be anywhere right now if it wasn't for me!"

"If you had truly cared about me, you would have been looking after my well-being, too. Noticing that you were working me into the ground. That I was so lonely without my mom. But instead, you were so consumed with making more money that you just used me. You used me and you pushed the most important person in the world away from me."

She stares at me—no, glares at me—for two beats. Her eyelids are twitching from withheld rage. "It's him, isn't it? Is he pressuring you into this? He's brainwashing you into thinking I'm the problem." She's grasping at straws, but it's too late. I can see the truth perfectly now.

"Stop. You need to go."

Susan's lips tremble but not from tears. It's pure anger. "You're making a mistake."

I shrug. Even if I am (which I'm not), it's my mistake to make. It feels incredible to allow myself to follow my gut again. "This is your thirty-day notice since that's what is in our contract. But consider it a paid vacation because I don't want to see or hear from you over the next thirty days or thereafter."

She grips the strap of her purse so tightly, her knuckles go white. "I'll leave, but you need to know that you're wasting your life out here, and that man"—she spits those last two words while nodding in disgust toward Noah—"will only bring you down just like your mom was doing. Believe it or not, what I did today was for your own good."

"So you're admitting to being behind the paparazzi ambush today?"

Susan takes a second to think it over, and when she decides she has nothing left to lose, she nods. "Yeah. I did. And I'd do it again in a heartbeat because I could tell you had deluded yourself into thinking this place could be your new home. It never will, Rae, because your life and his life don't mix." I grit my teeth against her words. "So I brought what would have inevitably happened anyway to you a little sooner—was that really so wrong? Was it so terrible to force some space between you and your mom who were so obnoxiously inseparable? I mean for shit's sake, Rae, you were attached to that woman's hip when I found you. You always listened to her advice over mine, and she held you back. So yes, I meddled a little, but it was necessary to help you achieve *your* dreams."

I take one step toward her. "Get out." *Before I throw something at you.*

Her nostrils flare once, and then she turns around, chin held high as she leaves the kitchen.

"Actually, wait, Susan!" She turns around hesitantly. "Send me Claire's number the moment you're back in service. I'll be hiring her immediately as my own assistant." I have no doubts now that Claire was fired because of what she uncovered about Susan. And I could really use her help now as I begin the process of finding a new manager before the tour starts.

Susan rolls her eyes and then walks away, muttering, "Go to hell, Amelia," before the door shuts behind her.

Well, at least I know she *does* remember my name.

And then she's gone. Only when I see her disappear past the window do I spin around and sag right into Noah's chest. He wraps his sturdy arms around me and holds me close, pressing his lips to the top of my hair. "You were incredible."

I'm trembling now and my legs feel like they're going to give out. The adrenaline is wearing off and I'm left feeling raw.

"I've got you," Noah says, scooping me up and carrying me back to his bed where he lays me down gingerly.

"She's wrong, you know?" I say, looking up at him with wide eyes. "We're going to be great together."

He tucks a blanket around me and kisses my forehead, lips lingering in a soft, delicate press. "I know."

Noah climbs on the bed beside me. He sits upright against the headboard and retrieves a book from his side table, and then he does the most incredible thing: he reads aloud to me. All week I've asked him to and he said no. But now he is, and his voice is rumbly and comforting in the most perfect way.

My heart quivers and I press a kiss to the outside of his bicep. His eyes glide like a smooth caress over my face and my hair and my neck until he focuses his gaze on the book again and continues reading aloud from his boring, nonfiction biography. It's wonderful. I wouldn't change a thing.

We have so much to talk about, so many decisions to make, but instead, I let myself rest in this moment and lean my head back against the pillow, smiling as I run my fingers up and down his arm while he reads.

Maybe he won't have to have a Gregory Peck face after all?

Chapter 35

Amelia

I step out of the bathroom and go into Noah's room, where I find him lying on his side on the bed, a Scrabble board laid out in front of him. We've been playing a lot of it together over the last week, as well as having drinks at Hank's last Friday, where I managed to not accidentally take a sleeping pill and pass out, a hearts tournament with his sisters on Saturday night at The Pie Shop, reading his terrifically boring book together in bed every night, and then *not* reading together in bed at night.

After I fired Susan, Tommy called and said my car was fixed and ready to go. But I wasn't ready yet, and neither was Noah, so we decided I would stay until I needed to leave to get ready for the tour. Unfortunately, that day is tomorrow. But I was given one more incredible week with Noah, his sisters, and this kooky town, and the memories from it will get me through the next nine months. My mom and I have also talked on the phone more. She's going to meet me a few days before the start of the tour to help me pack and officially reconnect.

Things have been a little different with Will always hovering nearby when we go out, but it surprisingly hasn't been that strange. Paparazzi lingered in town the first few days after the big incident, snapping pictures every time I went anywhere in the town; but soon, when they realized this sort of life is way too slow and boring to most people, they vanished. I've had my privacy back.

What I thought would be a problem for the town ended up being the highlight of their year. The moment a paparazzo was sighted, everyone transformed into peacocks, flaunting random talents and trying their best to get their picture taken. Mysteriously, Phil's hardware sign has crept closer and closer to The Pie Shop each day, where photographers have been known to lurk outside, always advertising a new sale.

And no one seems to mind Will hanging around. Actually, everyone seems to love him. It's a little unconventional that he's become our third roommate and taken over the room I had been staying in, but he holes up in his SUV, surveying the driveway until late at night, and then comes in to sleep for a few hours before he's out with the sun again. Mabel keeps buying him pies because she thinks he needs more calories to support all his muscle. I think she has a crush on him. When I come back after the tour like Noah and I have discussed, we'll have to figure out a more permanent solution for security. But right now, Will is not in this house, and that's all that matters.

"Thief," Noah says when he notices what I'm wearing. I stole his hoodie again and I'll never give it back. Underneath, I'm wearing a delicate pair of sleep shorts. Noah notices—or rather notices the lack of clothing on my legs. He smiles to himself and aims his gaze back to the board, dumping out the tiles before sitting up and perching on the edge of the bed.

"More Scrabble?" I ask, stepping between his legs. He puts his hands on the backs of my thighs and looks up at me with a gaze so reverent I feel outrageously beautiful even in my wet hair and his oversized hoodie.

"I just thought since it's your last night in town, you might want to play one more time," he says, and I don't like the sudden sadness that statement has introduced to the conversation.

"Last night *for a while*," I correct.

He smiles a little but it's clear he's still keeping a barrier around his heart. I've noticed he's grown more quiet and pensive over the last two days.

Earlier tonight the town threw me a little goodbye party here at Noah's house, and through the whole evening, he stayed in the shadows. I think he's terrified that we won't last. That history will repeat itself and I won't be faithful to him. Poor thing doesn't realize he's never getting rid of me now.

His eyes snag on my lips. "Yeah, *for a while*."

"You don't believe I'll come back?"

He hesitates to answer. "I want to. It's just . . ."

"Hard for you to fully trust again. I know." I intertwine my fingers in the back of his hair and he closes his eyes with a look of pain. I lean down and kiss his cheek. "I promise I'll be back, Noah. And you know how you can believe me?"

"How?" he asks, with his eyes still closed.

I take this moment to study him. To memorize every centimeter of his face. Every wrinkle, eyelash, and curve of his mouth. "Because I found a home and a family with this town and I love them." I drag in a breath and cup his jaw, angling his face up toward me. "And I love you."

He opens his eyes, and his hands remain fixed on the backs of my legs. His face is tender astonishment, because we haven't exchanged those words yet. But I can't hold them in any longer.

And then Noah smiles. Full. Wide. Glorious smile. "I love you, too, Amelia."

"Oh, thank goodness," I say on an exhale while removing his hands from my legs, tugging his wrists up in the air, and then pulling his shirt off. "I was beginning to sweat there for a second." Not true. I've known he loves me even before he even knew it.

He laughs as I give his shirt one final yank over his head. Now he's shirtless, just the way I like him. My eyes greedily roam the expanse of his tan, summertime body. Muscled shoulders and biceps. Broad chest and masculine veins winding down his forearms. Beautiful tattoo bursting with color and flowers and pie against his rib cage—a direct contrast to his grumpy unapproachable maleness. His blond hair is waving in slight disarray and the slash of his moody mouth hitches up in the corner as I ogle him.

He then watches as I remove my sweatshirt and reveal the silk spaghetti strap camisole underneath. It's blush pink and matches my skin after my shower. I asked Claire (who is officially my new personal assistant) to bring me a few things from my house after I decided to stay here another week, and I want to kiss my past self for having the forethought to make sure this little number was among those items.

Noah's eyes fall all over me and I feel the hot press of his gaze. He watches me as I walk to the bedroom door and lock it. I don't suspect Will would come inside before midnight, but I'm making a point that what I have intended for tonight should not be interrupted.

When I come back to Noah, he's standing—arms crossed. *Surly Pose.* I mirror it. The feminine delicate version. *Surly in Silk.* This makes him laugh and then his eyes drop to my shoulder. He runs his finger along the wispy strap of my camisole. Along my skin. "So soft," he says, almost to himself. He loops his finger under the strap and glides it down off my shoulder. My knees nearly buckle. A man this strong and rugged shouldn't be able to be this tender. His other hand presses against my low back, pulling my hips firmly to his. His breath moves to my bare shoulder as he bends down to lay one melting kiss to my collarbone.

I feel strangled by my own need for him. But I stay still and let him press hot kisses all over my shoulder. My neck. My mouth. I feel wired—strung out with anticipation as I feel his tongue touch my skin.

"I don't want to let you go," he whispers in my ear during his traverse of the other side of my body.

"This isn't goodbye, Noah."

"Then why does it feel like it?" he says as his lips brush down the line of my throat. "Why do I feel like I might never see you again?"

I close my eyes and run my hands up his solid chest, feeling his heart beating against my palm—savoring the heat of his lips and the sweetness of his touch. Right now, in his room, surrounded by his body, I feel confident that we'll be able to make our relationship work. But I have to admit, when my thoughts tiptoe out to the future, I feel nervous. My life is about to become jam-packed with work, and I'm going to need Noah to trust me when I'm not able to check in frequently or when he reads something questionable (and untrue) in a tabloid at the grocery store. I'm terrified this isn't going to last, and at the same time, I know that Noah and I are so *right* together.

I wrap my arms around Noah's abdomen and hug him tight. He looks down into my eyes. "The future is full of unknowns. We can't try to figure them all out tonight. Let's just savor the moments we have together right now."

He bends to kiss me tenderly, and it skewers me through the heart. This better not be goodbye. *Don't give up on us so soon, Noah.*

Noah's hand moves up my arm where he slowly lowers the other strap from my shoulder. Warm breath fans my skin. I stand motionless—savoring and roasting alive as his hands slide and press. Tease and soothe. I have never trusted or wanted anyone more in my life. *I love him.*

As Noah leisurely unwraps me, I have the privilege of watching him unravel. His breath trembles when I'm all skin and his eyes flare. His fingers flex against my hips as he pulls me closer to him. I feel gloriously empowered by his gaze and tug every stitch of clothing from him.

Tonight, he tells me how much he loves me with his mouth. He tells me how he's going to miss me with his hands. He tells me we'll make this work with his body. And when there is nothing left between us besides skin and desire, our hearts tangle with our limbs until I don't know what's what anymore. We fall and twist together into this place between reality and dreams. There's no existence outside these four walls. All I feel is Noah's strong, warm body, cherishing me in this moment. His fingers leave trails of fire over every inch of my skin, leaving me consumed.

We spend the evening loving each other joyfully, recklessly, *tragically* until we're both dozing as his fingers languidly trail my spine. I try to keep from falling asleep as long as possible, because I know when I wake up, I'll have to leave.

The tour starts in a few days, and I have no choice but to go.

Chapter 36

Noah

The bell above The Pie Shop door chimes as I step through just like it has every day since Amelia left three days ago. The door shuts behind me and I stand in the silence feeling acute loneliness for the first time in my life. I used to revel in this quiet. Crave it. Now all I crave is her.

I miss her laugh. Her eyes. The curve of her smile, the feel of her skin, and even her shitty pancakes. What I wouldn't give for a whole stack of them today. She left a message on my machine yesterday saying she was going into a meeting for the tour and she asked me to call her when I got in to work today, but I can't bring myself to call her yet because I hate the distance I feel between us over the phone. I'm going to have to stay busy over the next nine months to get through them.

This morning, I plan to work myself to the bone here at the shop, and then I'll go check on my grandma for lunch. I'll come back to work this afternoon and stay open late, and then maybe Mabel has some chores I can do for her. The fence outside her inn could use a fresh coat of paint. Annie's truck probably needs an oil change. Maybe I'll run for town mayor.

"Wow, you look like shit," says Emily after coming into the shop behind me. I grunt. I'm so depressed, I don't even have any surly comebacks.

"Noah, I mean it, you look terrifying."

"Heard you the first time," I say, aggressively wiping down the countertops.

"Have you talked to Amelia today?"

I move to the high-top table and practically sand it down with how hard I clean it. "Nope."

"Are you going to call her later?" Why is she suddenly so interested in my phone schedule?

"Maybe."

Emily watches as I throw the rag onto the floor and use my shoe to scrub a stubborn stain. "Annie said when she was over at your house the other night, Amelia called and you let it go to your machine."

I shrug because I really don't feel like having this conversation with her right now.

Emily puts her hand on my arm and tugs me back when I try to pass her. "Hey, stop for a second. We need to talk."

"Fine. But I don't want to talk about Amelia." My eyes are fixed on the wall across the room. I won't look at my sister. I'm grumpy, and all my emotions are one tick away from boiling over and I don't want her to be the one to absorb them if they do.

"Tough, you're going to. Sit down." She points to the high-top table. I don't budge because I feel like being defiant. "Now," she barks and I snap into motion, because *damn,* that woman is scary when she's serious.

Emily doesn't wait for my ass to fully warm the barstool before she cuts right through my heart with a butcher knife. "Amelia is gone for the next nine months."

I swallow and glare at her. "Yes, thank you, Captain Obv—"

"She's gone . . ." Emily presses on. "Now what are you going to do about it?"

I snap my mouth shut because I wasn't expecting that question. What does she mean what am I going to do about it? What *is* there to do about it? Amelia's tour starts tomorrow and she'll call me when she gets settled on the bus. From then on out, we'll play phone tag for weeks on end until she finally gets sick of the hassle I cause her and breaks up with me. (We didn't plan that last one but I'm fairly certain that's what will happen.)

"Nothing. I'm staying here in Rome and taking care of everything and everyone while she's on tour. I should think you of all people would be happy to hear that." Emily grimaces like I punched her. And maybe I sort of did. This is why I didn't want to talk to her about this. My reflexes are set to *destroy*. "I'm sorry . . ." I sigh heavily and run my hands through my hair. "I shouldn't have said that."

"No, don't be sorry. You're right, and that's part of why I'm here." She pauses and inhales deeply, exhales, then says, "I haven't been fair to you—or to the girls. You and I are old enough to remember Mom and Dad and what they were like. We are old enough to remember exactly what it felt like that day when we got the call about them. And so we know exactly where our trauma comes from, whereas the girls feel it, but don't always know why."

My gut twists painfully. And when Emily's eyes start filling with tears, it's all I can do to not push this barstool out from under me and take off running. All I want is to escape pain, but it always finds me.

"I've realized recently that I accepted my trauma and decided to live within its bounds so I didn't get hurt more. It was easiest to know that I'm afraid of losing anyone and to not let them out of my sight because of it. But now I'm seeing that I've been more comfortable with the cost to everyone around me. Madison . . ." Emily pushes out a painful breath and shuts her eyes tightly. "Madison wanted so badly to go away to culinary school and I talked her out of it. She's in a teaching job she hates because of me and my fears. Annie is so devoted to me that she hasn't even considered the possibility of ever leaving this town, and I'm afraid she'll never dream big now. And you . . ." A tear leaks down her cheek. I cover her hand with mine.

"And you have carried your own hurt as well as all of ours ever since you had to grow up at ten years old, and it's not fair, Noah. And the one time you did let yourself really feel again, Merritt exploited it. And then, I did, too. When you came to help with Grandma, I should have been there for you and encouraged you to get back out there. To not give up on love. But instead, I used your hurt to my advantage to keep you close to us so that I could feel safer. But it's time for both of us to stop padding our lives so we don't feel bumps in the road anymore. I think we'll get hurt a lot in this life, but maybe it's worth it because sometimes we will experience really amazing things, too. Maybe not everything will end in hurt. But we'll never know if we don't try."

I laugh incredulously as I squeeze Emily's hand, threatening my own damn tears not to fall. "You came to this life-changing conclusion yourself?"

She smiles a little guiltily. "Did I mention that I also started going to a therapist the day after I blew up at you over dinner?"

"No. But I'm proud of you, Em."

"Don't be proud of me yet. I might never go back. That woman does open heart surgery in her office and it's painful as hell."

We both laugh before Emily's expression softens again. "You love Amelia, but I can tell you're already giving up because you're scared to death of her being the one to do it first. Don't push her away and become unreachable because you're afraid to lose her."

Damn. She's right. I am doing that.

"You love her, Noah. Give your relationship everything you've got. Really go for it, and make her a priority instead of keeping yourself unattached in case you get hurt."

"How? She's going to be all around the world for nine months."

Emily laughs. "They make these things called airplanes. And if you decide to use one, we'll be here to cover for you while you're away. We know how to take care of Grandma just as well as you do. And we'll make sure the shop runs smoothly, too. Go spend some time with her on tour. Don't let your breaks apart be so long."

"You'd really be okay with me leaving town more often?"

"I'll get used to it. Don't worry about me so much." Emily stands and leans over to kiss my forehead. "Also, stop being a grumpy ass and get a cell phone. And Wi-Fi while you're at it so you can text and send pictures. It'll help a lot."

I grumble even though I'm thankful for her input.

"I love you, Noah."

"Love you, too." And now, I need to say those words to Amelia again face-to-face.

Chapter 37

Amelia

There's a quick three-tap knock on my dressing room door, so I know it's time.

"Come in," I yell and the door opens.

Claire steps inside. "Ready?" she asks with a big smile and I return it because having Claire as my assistant has already been such a relief. I feel like I finally have an advocate and a friend in this business. A friend other than my mom, who is hovering around somewhere backstage, flirting with all the stagehands. Our relationship isn't perfect yet, but it's getting there. We're slowly untangling the lies that Susan wove around our relationship over the years. After a little digging, I realized that my mom hasn't even been accepting money from me the last few years. All those "requests" that came from her through Susan were actually going right into Susan's pocket. Needless to say, Susan is going to need a really good lawyer.

I also hired a new manager, Keysha, a powerhouse woman who's been in the business for thirty years managing some of the top artists of my time. But I've decided to do things a little different this go-around. I delegate most of my personal-life stuff to Claire (except for talking with my mom, which I do myself now) and leave the big-picture stuff up to Keysha. I really trust Claire. Also, she freaking loves my bangs, so take that, Susan!

The only thing that's missing from my life right now is Noah. I miss him so much already. I miss that town. I miss his sisters. I miss his hands and his chest and his pajamas and his moody face and his smile and his absolutely *everything*. We talk on the phone, but not nearly as much as I'd like, and the last few times I've tried to call him, I've only gotten his answering machine. It's possible he's busy, but more than likely, he's pulling away.

But tonight is the opening of the tour, and I have to focus. It starts in my very own Nashville, Tennessee, playing a sold-out show at Bridgestone Arena. After this one, we hop in the tour bus and go to Atlanta, and then Houston before hopping on an international flight to London. I'll spend a few months on the international leg of the tour, and then have a short break before finishing with the remainder of the U.S. portion. I know that by the end of all this, I'll be burned out and exhausted all over again and ready to escape back to Rome, Kentucky, to see my favorite people—but for now, I'm taking care of myself and enjoying the ride.

"You ready, Freddy?" says Claire because she's sort of dorky in the most supportive kind of way. And best of all, she never calls me Rae. Firing Susan was the smartest thing I've ever done, second only to driving my car into Noah's front yard.

"I'm ready." I stand and slip on my earpiece. My short, sparkly silver dress glints in the dressing room light, and I make sure my heels are secured to my ankles.

Claire and I leave the dressing room. Will drops in line behind us, staying glued to me like he will every day of this tour. The chanting of the crowd grows louder with every step I take down the back hallway of the arena. There are tons of crew members scattered around and wishing me luck as I pass by them. I pass my mom and she squeezes me in a tight hug, telling me I'm going to be great.

No matter how many times I do this, I never fail to feel a swarm of butterflies, adrenaline, and downright fear in this moment. But in about thirty seconds, I'll be standing dead center stage in front of fifty thousand people waiting to watch me perform, and absolute joy will take over.

Backstage my band is gathered and waiting for me. I step up into their circle and we all hold hands and say a quick prayer that no one face-plants on the stage and has to be rushed off with blood gushing out of their nose (it happened to me once and I'll never forget it).

A crew member takes my hand then and helps me step inside the riser that's going to lift me up where I'll appear in the center of the stage. The roar of the crowd is so intense I feel like it's going to lift the roof off the arena. I insert my second earbud and it quiets the noise. Shutting my eyes, I breathe in for five more seconds before the riser lifts. On an inhale, I picture myself staring straight into Noah's woodsy eyes and on an exhale, I imagine him pulling me into his arms.

And then the floor rises. Fire shoots all around the portion of the stage I'll be emerging from, and I know that while it's flaming, no one can see me. I take 1.2 seconds to get in position with the mic in my hand, and then just as they are supposed to, the flames dissolve and everyone can see me. The audience erupts and I raise my chin, smiling and looking around the arena, soaking up this moment. The band starts playing and I raise the mic to my mouth.

The only thing that could have made this night better is if I knew Noah was waiting backstage to kiss me when the show is over.

"Thank you, Nashville!" I yell into the mic after finishing the last song of my encore. I take a few minutes, waving and blowing kisses to all the fans, accepting a bouquet of flowers that gets tossed onto the stage and freezing when I realize they are sunflowers in brown paper wrapping tied with a string of twine. My heart races even though I know it shouldn't. But still, I think of Annie and her flower shop, and maybe . . . just maybe . . . I squint out at the crowd trying to see who they came from, but the lights are too bright. When three more bouquets make it onto the stage—all various types of flowers—I have convinced myself these sunflowers are not from Noah.

I give one final air kiss and bow to the crowd while clutching the bouquet to my chest and walk offstage. Immediately, a stage-hand is at my side, giving me a towel for my sweaty forehead and a bottle of water. Claire is there, too, telling me how great the show went and going on about the crowd, but I'm exhausted and a little disoriented after being shocked by this bouquet of flowers.

"Claire," I ask, stopping abruptly in the middle of the hallway, forcing her to stop and face me. "Did you happen to see who threw these flowers?"

She shakes her head. "No, sorry. There were tons of people throwing bouquets tonight. Do you want me to have them all brought onto your tour bus?"

I shake my head and hand her the sunflowers. "Just these. Thank you."

"Okay," she says sweetly. "Why don't you go rest for a few minutes in your dressing room?"

I'm already unfastening my heels and then carrying them with me as I walk toward the dressing room. Currently, I'm wearing my last costume of the night—a floor-length, gauzy dress in dark purple. It has lots of layers that fly all around me as a stage fan blows. It's my favorite costume of the entire concert, but right now, I'm sweating so hard all I want to do is drop it to the floor the second I step into my dressing room.

As we walk down the hallway, everyone I pass offers congratulations on an epic tour opener, and I feel grateful to be back here, doing this another year. When we arrive at my dressing room,

Claire opens it for me and then smiles wide. Too wide. Suspiciously wide.

"Why do you look like that? Did you booby-trap my dressing room or something? Is a bucket of water going to drop on me the second I walk in?"

Her smile only grows. "Find out for yourself."

I cringe as I step through the door, bracing for any and all kinds of impact. Water, slime, a burst of feathers—I'm ready for it. I never could have braced myself for the impact of Noah's presence, though. Well, Noah's and my mom's since she's currently releasing him from a big hug. She pats the side of his arm and walks to me, whispering, "He's cute! I like him," before leaving and shutting the door behind her.

We're alone now and my breath catches as my eyes collide with his. Greenest green as intense as an avalanche. He's here. In this room with me, and all I can think is *Dear Lord, please don't let me be severely dehydrated and seeing things that aren't really there. Namely, Noah Walker.*

"You're . . . here," I say, still having trouble formulating words.

A slow smile unfurls over his lips and he steps toward me. His eyes track the length of my body and then to my face again. "I am. And you are stunning. Your concert was incredib—*Oof!*" I slam my body into his before he can finish his sentence and crash my mouth into his. I wrap my arms tightly around his neck, so he gets the message that I'm never letting go. I hope he doesn't have stage fright because I'm going to have to perform like this from now on.

He laughs and encircles my waist, holding me tightly to him.

"You *were* out there!" I say once I finally stop kissing him. "Did you throw flowers from Annie's shop?"

He nods. "I'm sorry I've been distant this week."

"It's okay."

"No, it's not," he says as his face shifts into a frown. "Emily stopped by the shop yesterday and pointed out that I've had my head up my ass." I laugh because I can perfectly picture Emily giving Noah a dressing-down. "Turns out, I've been distancing myself from you because I worried this wouldn't work between us."

"I figured when my third call went to your answering machine."

He grimaces. "I'm so sorry. But you have my word that I'm all in from now on. No more playing it safe. I want to give this relationship everything I've got. And to prove it . . ." Noah's hand dives into his pocket and then pulls out an iPhone. He takes my hand, turning it over and placing the phone in my palm.

"You got a cell phone?" My voice is pure awe. Tears are clinging to my lashes. For most people this wouldn't mean much, but for Noah, adjusting to modern technology is on par with changing religions.

"And Wi-Fi is being installed in my house as we speak. If I have to be apart from you for months on end, I at least want to be able to see your pretty smile on FaceTime."

"You really are getting internet installed at your house?"

"Yep. And I'm going to need you to show me how to use this damn thing. Why are there so many little pictures on the screen?"

"Those are called apps."

He grunts. "I don't like them."

"We'll delete all of them except for the ones you need."

"I still don't love it."

I smile and toss his phone onto the dressing room couch so I can wrap my arms around him again. "I'm all in, too, just so you know."

"Good, because there's more." He runs his fingers across the fringe of my bangs and then down the back of my hair like he's savoring me. "If your offer still stands, I'd like to join you on tour more often. I don't want to spend these entire nine months without you."

A happy sigh escapes my ear-to-ear smile. "Really? What about your grandma and The Pie Shop?"

"I worked it out with my sisters. They were happy to adjust the schedule to where they take more days visiting Grandma. And I already have someone who works weekends for me who said she'd be happy to cover for me while I'm gone."

I give him a quick peck on his mouth again like I'm proving his frown doesn't exist now. "What about this week? Could you take off and come with me to the next two shows?"

He bends and kisses my cheek. And then my jaw. And then my neck. "I was really hoping you were going to offer that because Claire already had my bag taken to your tour bus."

A joyful laugh spills out of me. Along with an embarrassing amount of happy tears. "Are you kidding? We are going to play so much Scrabble now!"

His kisses turn hotter—blazing one after another up the line of my throat while his big hand cups my backside and squeezes play-fully. "I don't know . . . I was thinking of something else we could do that would be more fun."

I give a delighted hum, telling him just how much I approve of that idea.

He pulls away long enough to give me a slanted smile. "Finish the book we were reading together, obviously . . . what did you think I was meaning?"

I kiss him. Slowly and tenderly. "Oh, me, too. Reading for sure."

RAE ROSE CONFIRMS ENGAGEMENT IN CRYPTIC SOCIAL MEDIA POST

For months fans have speculated on the possible relationship between Rae Rose and the mystery man who was spotted with her in a small town in Kentucky before her world tour began. Things seemed to heat up on her tour, as they were photographed together holding hands while getting in and out of vehicles, and even sharing a lingering kiss in line at a coffee shop in France. Anyone who saw the photo can confirm that the kiss was most definitely French.

Since the end of her tour the princess of soulful pop has disappeared from the public eye, only tweeting the day after her final concert that she loves her fans dearly and is taking an extended step out of the spotlight to rest and recover. The singer has not been seen or heard from for three months, until yesterday, when she broke her social media hiatus and posted an Instagram photo of her hand clasped with a man's—a gorgeous princess cut engagement ring gracing her finger. The caption read: "When in Rome . . ." leaving fans buzzing with anticipation and hungry for more news.

Is Rae Rose officially off the market? And could it be that she's been hiding in Rome, Italy, all this time?

Acknowledgments

had high hopes of writing a beautiful, elegant acknowledgment section, but after finishing what ended up being a beast of a book for me, I'm nothing but a thankful, blubbering mess. This book was an emotional roller coaster for me—stretching me and growing my craft in ways that felt impossible to me at times. It wouldn't be in your hands today without the team of people who encouraged me to finish it, and then helped me transform it from a pile of nonsense into a book that I'm incredibly proud of.

First, I want to thank my brilliant, kind powerhouse of an editor, Shauna Summers. I will never stop being thankful that you wanted to be my editor. Thank you for your encouragement, handholding, and making Amelia and Noah's story as beautiful as it is! I'm convinced you're the best editor in the entire world, and I don't deserve you!

Next, to my incredible agent, Kim Lionetti, THANK YOU! Thank you for reading the few messy early chapters of this book and seeing the potential in it and for steering me in the right direction to finish the damn thing. I still can't believe you even answered that first email from me and continue to no matter how many ridiculous ones I send you. :) You're the best. Team Kim for life! And a huge thank-you to the entire Bookends team!

To my lovely, incredible UK editor, Kate Byrne, I'm so honored that you loved and wanted to publish my books! I'm still pinching myself and so grateful for your support.

To my entire team at Dell: Taylor Noel, Corina Diez, Jordan Pace, Mae Martinez, Laurie McGee, and so many others who I'm sure I'm missing; a huge bear hug to you all! I'm so thankful to be working with each of you.

Amber Reynolds, I think you've beta-read each of my rom-coms now. I'm convinced you're my lucky gem, and therefore, you're never allowed to stop. I'm sorry, but you have to continue reading my terrible drafts, because I love you and need you. Seriously, thank you!! You're the best. I'm so grateful for you.

To Ashley and Carina, my best ma'ams, whom I love like sisters, thank you for being yourselves and letting me cling to you guys like an annoying barnacle. To Chloe, Becs, Devin, Jody, Gigi, Martha, Summer, Aspen, Rachel, Sophie—you all make this career one hundred times better. I'm incredibly thankful for your friendship!

And to my readers and bookstagram community!!! How do I adequately say thank you for all the love, support, tweets, posts, reviews, emails, aesthetic boards, and encouraging DMs?! Grace, Katie, Morgan, Molly, Addie, Marisol, Alison, Madison, and so many others! The biggest, most heartfelt thank-you!

To my family: Your support means everything to me. Thank you for encouraging me to keep going, and I really hope you skipped all the steamy parts.

And last, but most important to me, my husband, Chris Adams. My best friend, my favorite work colleague, my partner, my eye-candy, my biggest cheerleader, my absolute favorite person in this entire world: I love you. (Is it cheating on our game if I say infinity and beyond in a book? Probably, so I'll refrain.)

XO,
Sarah

About the Author

SARAH ADAMS was born and raised in Nashville, Tennessee. She loves her family, warm days, and making people smile. Sarah has dreamed of being a writer since she was a girl, but she finally wrote her first novel when her daughters were napping and she no longer had any excuses to put it off. Sarah is a coffee addict, a British history nerd, a mom of two daughters, married to her best friend, and an indecisive introvert. Her hope is to always write stories that make readers laugh, maybe even cry—but always leave them happier than when they started reading.

authorsarahadams.com
Instagram: @authorsarahadams